The Lost Women

The Lost Women

TIM WEAVER

PENGUIN BOOKS

UK | USA | Canada | Ireland | Australia
India | New Zealand | South Africa

Penguin Books, Penguin Random House UK,
One Embassy Gardens, 8 Viaduct Gardens, London SW11 7BW

penguin.co.uk
global.penguinrandomhouse.com

First published 2026

001

Copyright © Tim Weaver, 2026

The moral right of the author has been asserted

Penguin Random House values and supports copyright.
Copyright fuels creativity, encourages diverse voices, promotes freedom
of expression and supports a vibrant culture. Thank you for purchasing
an authorized edition of this book and for respecting intellectual property
laws by not reproducing, scanning or distributing any part of it by any
means without permission. You are supporting authors and enabling
Penguin Random House to continue to publish books for everyone.
No part of this book may be used or reproduced in any manner for the
purpose of training artificial intelligence technologies or systems. In accordance
with Article 4(3) of the DSM Directive 2019/790, Penguin Random House
expressly reserves this work from the text and data mining exception

Set in 13.5/16pt Garamond MT
Typeset by Falcon Oast Graphic Art Ltd
Printed and bound in Great Britain by Clays Ltd, Elcograf S.p.A.

The authorized representative in the EEA is Penguin Random House Ireland,
Morrison Chambers, 32 Nassau Street, Dublin D02 YH68

A CIP catalogue record for this book is available from the British Library

HARDBACK ISBN: 978–0–241–71673–1
TRADE PAPERBACK ISBN: 978–0–241–71674–8

For Erin,
I'm so proud of you

One Year Ago

I pass through the gates of the cemetery.

It's quiet, the sweeping lawns empty except for headstones and beds of long-fallen leaves. As I walk, I spot the occasional lonely flower, lifted from its place at a grave somewhere and carried away by the wind, and if it's obvious where it belongs, I do my best to return it. Mostly, though, I just trace the paved path that winds towards the remembrance garden. I try to think how long it's been and feel a spear of guilt when I can't recall.

Pushing open the gate, I pass into an enclosed area called 'The Rest', tall fir trees on one side. Copses of five graves are gathered together in small, fenced areas, and Derryn's is towards the back. In the low winter sun, a shadow lies across her name, across the date of her birth and the day I lost her. Under those are two inscriptions. The first says, *Beloved wife of David*. But it's the second I stare at now: *In the end, all that matters is love.*

I drop to my haunches in front of the headstone.

'Hey, sweetheart,' I say quietly.

Wind passes through the cemetery, stirring the leaves. I brush some dirt from her name, from the base, and then take out the box I've brought with me. 'I thought you might like this,' I say, opening it. 'You always loved the warm weather, and let's be honest' – I look up at the turbulent sky – 'we don't get very much of that.'

I place the potted cactus down, smiling to myself as I look at it. There's a line printed on the side: *I'm a prick . . . ly cactus.* I imagine her face, her reaction, all of it still clear to me, even after so long. And as I look at her name again, I feel the emotion gather in my throat.

'Do you remember the diary that you left for me?'

I hear my words catch.

'I still read it often, even now. I just . . .' I stop, looking around me. 'This place, it's always made me feel close to you, but not like the diary does.' I stop for a second time, and it takes me longer to find my way back. 'You're just so *alive* in those pages. I can hear you. I can *feel* you. After all this time, you'd think your words wouldn't hit me so hard. But they do. They always do . . .'

My voice falters.

'I don't know . . . talking to a diary, it just felt weird.' A smile traces the corners of my lips, because I can almost hear her response on the wind. *What, weirder than talking to a grave?* 'You're right. Coming here is pretty weird too.'

Again, my eyes go to the inscription beneath her name.

In the end, all that matters is love.

'I need to tell you something,' I say.

I adjust the potted cactus on the base of the grave.

'The last few months,' I start to say, but then the words get lost. It's sixteen years since she died, and the pain is no longer the same as it was.

But it's still there.

It's still pain.

I start again: 'I keep finding myself coming back to something you wrote in that diary. *"You need to promise me that you won't become stuck."* I think maybe I did become stuck without you. I mean, you were my wife. You were everything. You were my entire world. I think, in a way, I've been stuck for most of the last sixteen years.' I touch the ends of my fingers to her name. 'And maybe you already know what I'm going to say, but . . .' I take a breath. 'I think, finally, I've become *un*stuck.'

I trace the *D* of *Derryn*, the *R* of *Raker*.

In the end, all that matters is love.

'I've met someone,' I say. 'Her name is Rebekah.'

*

Rebekah picks up her glass of wine and tucks her legs under herself.

'How was your day?' she asks.

'It was good.' I think of my visit to the cemetery earlier on. 'Yours?'

'Busy. Lots of paperwork to get signed off before I fly home.' The reminder that she will be leaving in a couple of days draws us back into silence for a while. 'Are you working a case at the moment?'

'No. Just dealing with some stuff from the last one.'

'It must be hard to let go of them sometimes.'

'The cases?' I nod. 'Yeah. It can be.'

'What about before you began finding missing people? Was there ever a story you had as a journalist that you've never stopped thinking about?'

I pause, pick up my own wine glass, looking at her. She probably thinks I'm trying to decide which of the thousands of stories I wrote is the one I can't let go of.

But, in reality, I already know.

Because it's always the same story.

It's always the Lost Women.

It's a bitterly cold day in the middle of April, eighteen years ago.

I'm not the man who visits the cemetery to talk to my wife. I'm not the man who shares a bottle of wine with Rebekah that same evening and longs for her not to go back home to the States. I'm not even a man who finds missing people. Not yet.

I'm a different man with a different life.

I've just driven seven hours from London to Cornwall.

The closest car park to where the disappearance happened is on the other side of the water from the island, and I don't have a problem finding a space today. The last time I was here, this place was swarming. Today, I'm alone.

It feels like the last stop at the end of the world.

I lock my car, zip up my coat and start to head down a slope towards the shore. There's a raised path of wooden slats at the bottom that will take me across the water that lies between the mainland and Porthtreno. As I walk, I take in this side of the island, its seas of beachgrass, their perpetual ballet of movement. But eventually, inevitably, my gaze keeps returning to the same place, to the rooftops of the buildings at its centre.

As I step on to the walkway, my phone starts ringing.

It's Derryn.

'Hey, sweetheart,' I say, answering the phone, a gust of wind ripping across me. When I don't hear my wife's reply, I realize the wind must have hidden her response. 'Sorry,' I say. 'In the middle of a tornado here. Say that again.'

'I just wanted to make sure you got there okay.'

'Yeah, I did. Just arrived. It took forever. Are you all right?'

'I'm good.'

'Are you sure?'

It's been ten days since her last session of chemotherapy. She seemed to cope with the first treatment pretty well, but the second round has hit her hard. As I listen to her voice, I start to regret leaving her.

'No,' she says.

'No what?'

'No, you're not coming home again just because I feel tired.'

'That wasn't what I was –'

'Raker.' She cuts me dead with one word, and I smile to myself. 'Do you know how much of a pain in the arse you are to live with when you're hung up on a story like this?' And then she quickly adds: 'That's a rhetorical question, by the way, before you give me some clever answer. The correct response is, of course, "I'm a huge pain in the arse, wife-of-mine." You drove five, six, whatever-it-was hours to do your thing, so go and do your thing. I really only had one reason for calling, and that was to remind you that if you fail to pick me up a lot – and I mean, a lot – of Devonshire clotted cream, our marriage is over.'

'I won't forget,' I say, as my heart swells for her. 'I promise.'

'I know you won't. I love you, D.'

'I love you too, sweetheart.'

I ring off, pocket my phone, and pick up my pace across the wooden-slatted walkway. Ahead of me, on this side of Porthtreno, thick knots of beach-grass shimmer in the wind on large, sloped banks of sand. The sandbanks have created a twelve-foot-high natural wall and the only way past them is over — or through.

I opt for through.

Moving off the walkway and on to the white sand, I pass along a thin path that snakes between two dunes, and then up a steep slope to the undulating spine of the island. From here, Porthtreno's highest point, I have an uninterrupted, 360-degree view of the island, of the car park I left behind, of the ragged frill of coastline it sits on, and of the vast, grey Atlantic beyond. But it doesn't take very long for my attention to shift away from all of that.

Because I didn't come here for the views.

I came here for the village.

It sits in a hollow just below me. As I get out my camera and take a couple of pictures, I wonder what it would have looked like five months ago when the three women came to make their documentary. There would have been half-walls and punctured roofs, open doorways and glassless windows, just like there are today.

But it wouldn't have looked the same.

That's what makes the tiny village of St Petroc, in the middle of the island of Porthtreno, so unique: every day — on the back of every surge of wind, after every storm that rolls in off the ocean, and every fractional movement of the island's sand — its appearance alters.

There's no human life here any more.

But the village is still alive.

It lives and it breathes and it changes.

'What do you mean, "it changes"?' Rebekah asks, pouring us some more wine.

I get up off the sofa and go to the sideboard in the living room. Somewhere in it are the photos I took that day.

The sleeve has yellowed over time, and the photos inside have faded a little, but as I take them out, I'm instantly transported back over a decade and a half.

I hand them over.

'St Petroc was the name of a village they built on Porthtreno about a hundred and fifty years ago. Five houses on a slope. They were in this hollow, to try to protect them from the winds that roll in off the Atlantic, especially in the winter, and to get the men closer to the sea to fish. But all the hollow did was create a place for the sand to fall into and gather.' I watch her leaf through the pictures. 'It started as a slow drip over the first few months, but then it became an avalanche – these immense walls of sand would suddenly slough off the high dunes and tumble into the hollow, breaking windows and flooding the houses. The villagers would try to clear it out, try to create trenches for the sand to go into, and begin again – but the sand would just keep coming. It was like this relentless force, this invasion they could never repel, no matter what they did.'

'So eventually all the villagers left?'

'After a year, yes. They had to.'

I glance at the photograph she has in her hands, a shot I took from inside one of the houses. I was knee-deep in sand at the time, the walls of the house rising up out of it for only four or five feet, my head almost touching what was left of a shattered roof.

'And this final house is where the three women were filming?'

I nod. 'That's where they vanished from.'

I've only descended about three feet into the hollow when I hit the sand.

I feel my boots submerge, my calves, and when it gets to my knees, I hit some kind of limit. It's not the bottom – if it was the bottom, my eyeline wouldn't be well above the windows, in a space between the tops of them and what was once the roof – but decades of sand have compacted below me, so this is as far as I can sink down.

I take a few pictures and then wade through the house before passing into the torn sides of the next home. It has a chimney breast still standing, an accusing brick finger pointing at the sky.

But it's the last house of five that I need.

With effort, I wade forward, through the crumbling interiors of houses that are drowning in sand. Four houses down, I reach a former garden, a sharp sandbank to my left, dotted with more beachgrass. At the other end of this garden is the final home and, as I approach it, I feel the sand level starting to rise.

It's almost at my thighs.

Irrational as it is, I start to panic, start to see images behind my eyes of suddenly hitting an area of the village where there is no base, no compact layer of sand underfoot, and I start to sink, and the sand is streaming into my mouth.

But that doesn't happen.

Instead, the sand level lowers again as I stop in the doorway and look into the fifth house. Like all of them, it has a chimney breast which, along with the large back wall it's built on to – is mostly intact. It's the chimney where the women's equipment was found, laid out in an orderly fashion as if they were about to call action on a shot. A camera on a tripod; a mic on the end of a boom; a recording pack and pair of headphones; a list of shots they'd had planned. There was a backpack with their personal belongings in it. There were the keys for the car they'd left in the car park.

The only things missing were the women.

'What were the women doing at Porthtreno?'

'Shooting a documentary,' I say to Rebekah. 'They were film-makers.'

She looks again at the photographs I took of the village, at the banks of sand that had poured in through windows and open doorways; at the broken, submerged walls.

'And no one ever found them?'

I shake my head. 'No. CCTV cameras recorded them arriving but not leaving. And if they're in the sea, they've never washed up anywhere.'

'What about footprints?'

'The sand's always been too deep and dry in the houses to make footprints, and outside of the hollow there were footprints everywhere.'

'Did they make any phone calls that day? Send any texts?'

'Not from the island, no.'

'Beforehand?'

'Nothing useful.'

She pauses, looking at the photographs again, and I can see that she's trying to find an angle, an explanation for what happened to the three women back in September 2006. But every angle, every possible explanation for what went on, has already been exhausted.

It's why I've never forgotten their story.

It's why, in my memories, the Lost Women always remain.

Now

Today, a year on from my visit to the cemetery, a year on from that conversation with Rebekah, the only thing I have left to cling on to are my memories.

They're the last pieces of driftwood in the ocean.

Maybe the only things keeping me sane.

I dwell on images of Derryn, of my daughter Annabel, of Rebekah, and of the Lost Women of Porthtreno. And then I think about the cases I've had, of the people who've vanished, and how those cases have twisted and broken me and left scars. I think about the snatches of time I wish I'd made more of, or done differently, or paid more attention to. I think about the regrets I still carry. And I think about the missing person that brought me to this moment.

His name was Preston Stewart.

When I took on his case, I knew I was against the clock from the second I set out to find him, but I still thought I could work it in the same way as all my other missing persons searches.

That was naive.

The more I unpicked Preston's life, the more the search for him metastasized into something worse than a disappearance: something heartbreaking, and terrible, and deadly; something that would profoundly and irreversibly change my entire life.

On day one, I was oblivious to it.

On day two, when I finally understood, it was already too late.

If I'd known the clock was ticking when I'd answered the door on that first morning, I would have tried to work harder, made use of every second I had.

But that was just the problem.
I didn't know I only had forty-eight hours.
And it was why I never saw what was coming.

DAY ONE
Part One

1

. . . 48 hours to go . . .

The car pulled up outside my house at 8 a.m.

It was a black Mercedes with tinted windows.

I watched the driver get out. He was in his early fifties, sharp-suited and square-jawed, and even though it was a cold, grey day in the middle of January, he was wearing a pair of aviators. He was also absolutely massive – six-five, at least eighteen stone – and as he came to the front door, he had to duck slightly to get under the porch roof.

'Mr Raker,' he said, as I opened up.

'Just give me a minute,' I replied, and he stepped off the porch without saying another word and retreated to the car.

I padded upstairs. The door to the spare bedroom was ajar, and through the gap I could see Rebekah facing me, the duvet twisted around her, her unpacked suitcase on the floor.

She must have sensed I was looking in, because a moment later she stirred. A smile crept across her face. 'You're not seeing me at my best.'

'That's the jet lag talking.'

'You old charmer. Are you heading out?'

'Yeah. I'm not sure what time I'll be back.'

'It's fine. I'll be in Cambridge all day.'

Rebekah had been born and raised in England but had moved to the States at eighteen. We'd met by chance in Manhattan when I'd been visiting a friend, and two years ago she'd hired me to find out what had happened to her mother, who'd walked out on her when she was only three. As I'd searched for answers, we'd grown close, and grown even closer in the period since, but we were still taking it slowly, even all this time later. She was separated, and had two daughters under six at home. I lived 3,500 miles from her, had a daughter of my own and my work was all here. Ostensibly, she flew here to deal with legalities related to a house that had been left to her in Cambridge by her mother, but the two of us had been the other reason. Every time I was with her, I felt the kind of buzz I hadn't known since Derryn, but that didn't stop me worrying: we both had roots on opposite sides of the ocean – and those roots were going to be hard to cut loose.

'Get an autograph for me,' she said.

I nodded. 'I'll do my best.'

I headed out of the house and down to the Mercedes. The back passenger door had been left open. As I slid in, the woman seated next to me said, 'Good morning.'

'Morning,' I replied, and glanced at a coffee from Starbucks nestled in a cup holder on the armrest. It had *Matt* scrawled on the side, which I guessed must be the driver's name. It made sense that he'd been the one to go in. If Ellie Snyder had done it herself, she would still have been signing autographs.

'Thank you for agreeing to do this.'

'This is a new experience for me,' I said to her.

'Being driven around?'

'Kicking off a missing persons search from the back of a car.'

She smiled, revealing an immaculate set of teeth, and even as the smile began to drift away, even as a sadness replaced it, it did nothing to erode her beauty. Ellory Snyder – Ellie to everyone, whether they knew her outside of their TV screens or not – was a strikingly beautiful thirty-year-old, the child of a Dutch father and a Nigerian mother. Her features were perfect, all gentle sweeps and flawless skin, her eyes a remarkable blue, and her talents didn't stop at being the lead in the UK's most-watched television drama. The previous night I'd followed links to a podcast network she'd co-founded, to a foundation she'd set up for disadvantaged kids, and to stories about her role as a UN Special Envoy, where 'her powerful voice helped support and build awareness for refugees'. But, despite all of the good she'd done, despite the limo, the fame and the wealth, right now Ellie was going through the same thing as every other person who came to me for help. Someone she cared about was gone.

In the end, grief was the great equalizer.

'Do you mind if I record this?' I asked, removing my phone. 'Taking written notes is going to be hard in a moving vehicle.'

She looked at my phone with a mixture of suspicion and fear. I'd only ever seen snatches of *Church Row Manor*, the Victorian costume drama Ellie headlined. It was itself a spin-off from *Royalty Park*, a mega-hit British–American co-production that had first introduced Ellie's character, Marcella van Straal. If there was an advantage to be gained from not being familiar with her work, it was in the fact that I felt no disconnect between this version of her and the version on billboards, banner ads and talk shows. To me, she was just someone who needed answers, just like all the other people I helped. But there was no denying that, in seeing how she'd looked at my phone, I was also reminded of the differences. It was the reason we weren't meeting at her house and why I wasn't edging past photographers camped at her gates, waiting and hoping for a glimpse of who she was dating: Ellie's life was a constant leaked audio recording away from being front-page news.

Realizing I needed her to feel comfortable, I switched off my phone. 'Why don't you tell me about Preston Stewart?'

She'd called me the day before but hadn't said a lot over the phone, presumably for all the same reasons she didn't want to meet in public or have me turn up at her house. All she would say was that it involved a man she knew called Preston Stewart. When I'd googled Preston, I found out that he was a neurologist at a private hospital in Chelsea called 'The Crest', but apart from his professional credentials, he was basically a blank. According to what I'd read in the media, Ellie was single, and had been for four years, and he wasn't a relative of hers because that had been a dead end too.

When she didn't reply, I gently prompted her again: 'Ellie? Who's Preston Stewart?'

In the front, I saw Matt turn slightly – his eyes going to the rear-view mirror – and a look passed between them. It was brief but it told me everything about the strength of their working relationship and how much she trusted him. It was also obvious from Matt's expression that he didn't much like the idea of outsourcing whatever this was to me; that he might rather have dealt with it himself. In turn, it also made me wonder if the media might have been searching in the wrong place when it came to who Ellie was close to, or even possibly dating. In the world in which she existed, trust didn't come easily, so when you found it, you kept hold of it, were drawn to it, and the bond between driver and star was undeniable, even from this briefest of moments.

I made a mental note of it.

I thought maybe, later on, I might come back to it.

But a second later, everything changed.

2

. . . 47 hours to go . . .

'Preston is my husband,' Ellie said.

I stared at her. 'You're married?'

'Coming up for six months now.'

Though Preston Stewart had been a dead end, I'd spent almost three hours the previous night reading absolutely everything I could find on Ellie, from interviews on YouTube to profiles in glossy magazines, all the way down the slippery slope to stories about her personal life on entertainment and gossip sites. Nowhere did I see anything that even remotely suggested she and Preston were connected, let alone that she was married to him.

'How have you kept it out of the press?'

'We got married in Gibraltar,' she said. 'We flew into Malaga and then drove across the border. The press didn't know that was where we were going, and we didn't have to inform notaries here when we got back, or tour lawyers' offices to get everything signed off and made legal, because it's obviously a British territory. I mean, I love what I do, I really do, and I know I'm lucky, but it can be exhausting. You're sitting having lunch with a friend and suddenly you see someone giving you the side eye at another table, and your first thought is, "I wonder if they're a journalist." It wasn't like that in Gibraltar. No one was looking for me, and the people who married us all agreed to sign NDAs.'

'And the media still haven't figured it out?'

'No. We've been careful. I spend most of my time at his place in the Surrey Hills and only use my home in Holland Park when I'm shooting the show in Ealing. We've had to tell a few selected people, and obviously our families know . . .' Her face became greyer, her expression more sombre. 'Basically, the one thing I've learned is that if you keep the circle tight then you know where the leak comes from.'

We were on the North Circular Road, passing Gunnersbury Cemetery. She swivelled and looked out of her window, the grave plots blinking in and out of view between the skeletal branches of trees stripped for winter.

'I wasn't sure exactly who to turn to for this.' Her eyes flicked to Matt's again in the rear-view mirror. I'd been wrong about them potentially being in a relationship, but I could see I was right about something else: he hadn't wanted to involve me.

'Is Preston missing?' I asked.

'Yes.'

'What happened?'

'He . . .' She stopped. 'He was in a car accident a fortnight ago. He'd, uh . . .' She stopped again, this time for longer, but I could already see where this was going.

'Was he drunk?'

She glanced at me. 'Yes.'

'How drunk?'

'He'd had three pints of beer after work with a couple of colleagues – so, you know, he was over the limit, but he wasn't *drunk* drunk.' She held up a hand. 'Not that I'm saying what he did was right. He should never have got behind the wheel and I told him as much.' She ground to a halt again. 'He hit a lamp post about a mile from his house. Luckily for him, it's all countryside, so there were no witnesses.'

'Was he okay?'

'He was fine – mostly. He cracked an eye socket, bust his nose. Not serious, but serious enough that he needed some surgery. He decided to get it done at the private hospital that he's a partner in – The Crest. It made the most sense. Quite a few of the doctors and nurses there know that we're married, because they've been friends with Preston for donkey's years, and even if they don't, because a lot of high-profile people get procedures done there – you know, celebrities, politicians, sports people – it's extremely discreet. Preston calls it "the vacuum" because nothing ever gets out.'

'When did he go in?'

'Yesterday.'

I looked at her, surprised. I normally worked cold cases because the first port of call for families was always the police. But the disappearance of Preston Stewart was brand new – and that meant it was likely that Ellie had bypassed the cops entirely.

'We got to the hospital at seven thirty a.m,' she continued. 'At about nine, Preston was taken down for his surgery, and I chatted to some of the staff there. The surgery took about an hour – so at ten, ten fifteen, Preston was taken to recovery. I went down to see him there, and he was still coming around from the anaesthetic, but his surgeon friend – the guy who did the op, Robert Lewellyn; he's also Preston's business partner at The Crest – told me it had all gone well and he'd be back to talk to us later.'

She glanced at me – quickly, uncertainly.

'I went and got a tea and then one of the nurses came and found me and told me he'd been moved up to his private room. By that time, he'd been in there, alone, for about twenty minutes. I arrived with the nurse and she started taking his bandaging off so that she could apply some cream. Preston was still groggy, very tired, and the drugs were still in his system, so he was quiet the whole time.'

The Mercedes came to a halt at some lights.

'The nurse,' Ellie started, then stopped again. 'The nurse was new, had never met Preston before – had no idea what he looked like. She just took the bandages off and said that all the swelling and bruising would calm down over the next few days. But I could see straight away. I sat there and I stared at him, and I told her.'

'Told her?' I frowned. 'Told her what?'

'"That's not my husband."'

3

. . . 47 hours to go . . .

I felt thrown, uncertain if I'd heard properly.

'It was someone else under the bandages?'

'Yes.'

'Who?'

'The guy who Robert Lewellyn had operated on *before* Preston. His name was Kevin Neale.' The turmoil in her face was stark, even a day on. 'I said to the nurse, "This isn't my husband," and she looked at me like I was having a breakdown. I told her, "That's not my husband. That's not Preston." And then she scurried off to find Robert.'

'What did Robert say?'

'He walks in, takes one look at the patient – this Kevin guy – and says, "Oh, there must have been a mix-up." I wasn't particularly concerned at that stage, because I thought it would get sorted. I was angry more than anything. The Crest costs an absolute fortune, even with Preston's employee discount, and when you're paying that much, you don't expect them to mix up their patients.' Her voice hitched a fraction. 'Robert started explaining to me that he'd done two operations back-to-back, and then apologized again and started laying into a couple of the staff who were nearby. I don't know whose fault it was – I didn't care – I just said, "Where's Preston?"'

An ominous silence gathered like a storm cloud.

'They couldn't find him?'

'No,' she said. 'My husband had vanished.'

'He wasn't anywhere in the hospital at all?'

'No. I mean, it's genuinely staggering. How the hell does a patient go missing like that? It's not like Preston could have got up and walked out either – he had bandaging all over his face and he was still recovering from the anaesthetic. If he'd got up off the bed, he'd have been flat on the floor in two seconds. He should either have been in recovery, or right there in the room. Plus, there were members of staff around constantly, so how could no one have seen him? I just . . .' She shook her head.

I got out my notebook and – shakily, trying to ride the car's movements – wrote down the names she'd given me. 'So this Kevin Neale guy was operated on first?'

'Yes. He was already in theatre when we arrived at seven thirty.'

That meant, in turn, he would have been further along in his recovery than Preston. But Kevin Neale was still semi-conscious, so at that point Preston would have been even *less* capable of walking out of the hospital unaided.

'Do you know the last time Preston was seen?'

'All I know is what Robert told me. That Preston and Kevin were both in the same recovery room, next to one another, then they were moved to separate private rooms by the same porter.'

'And what has the porter said?'

'That he took Preston to his private room first, then Kevin.'

'So he could have just muddled up the rooms?'

'No. Kevin was in Preston's room, so Preston should have been in Kevin's if it had been a simple mix-up.'

'And no one noticed that Kevin Neale's room was empty?'

'They did, but not until later. The nurse said she was only due to go to Kevin *after* she'd finished with Preston, so no one checked on Kevin's room at first.'

'And the porter definitely brought both men up from recovery?'

'Yes.'

'And he says he delivered them to their correct rooms?'

'That's what he says, yes.'

I tried to make sense of it all and worked through the timings.

There could have been a paperwork mix-up in recovery, whether deliberate or not, and that could have explained why the porter delivered the men to the wrong rooms. Or the porter could have been part of whatever this was and, despite his denials to the contrary, switched the men on purpose. Or some other member of staff was in on it – Robert Lewellyn, the nurse, someone else at The Crest. What seemed much more certain was that neither Preston nor Kevin Neale would have been in any state to walk out of the hospital on their own – and whatever happened to Preston happened inside the twenty minutes he was left on his own after being wheeled up from recovery to the wrong room. But what reason would there be for Preston to just vanish?

Or for someone else to vanish him?

'You didn't want to take this to the police?' I asked her.

She shook her head immediately and, as she did, I saw Matt's eyes shift to her in the mirror. This time, Ellie smiled weakly at her driver's reflection and said, 'Matt thinks I should. Robert said the hospital are obligated to report a missing patient too, even though I'm pretty sure he doesn't want to do that. He's thinking of the reputational damage, I suppose. I asked him to give me forty-eight hours, which he eventually agreed to – and that's where you come in. I don't trust the police.'

'Why not?'

'A few years back, my sister got arrested for dealing. You might have seen it in the press.' I nodded, remembering a story I'd read the night before. 'She made some stupid decisions, got in with all the wrong people. The Met leaked her story to the tabloids.'

'You know that for sure?'

'I know that's what happened, believe me. And if they did that, I guarantee you they'll do the same with this . . .' Anger, frustration.

'I totally understand that,' I said. 'All I'm saying is this is an active case – it's fresh – and generally when families come to me, the missing person has been gone for months, maybe years, and the police have essentially given up on finding them. I don't work many searches like this.'

'I get it,' she said, but there was something in her face this time, a shadow that formed. She held my gaze for a moment. 'There's another, uh . . .' She paused, glanced at Matt. 'There's another reason I don't want to go to the cops.'

'Okay.'

But now the car was silent.

Ellie went to speak and then stopped again, the words mired in her mouth.

'It's all right,' I said.

'Preston studied Medicine at Bristol,' she continued, then faded. It looked like she was steeling herself. 'Something happened while he was at university . . .'

I saw Matt glance our way again.

'He only told me about it for the first time a couple of months ago. He'd never ever mentioned it before then. But one night he got home from work, we opened a bottle of wine – one became two – and we ended up getting pretty pissed. Anyway, I was dozing off on the sofa when I started to become aware of him talking. Whispering would probably be more accurate. I opened my eyes a little – and he was looking at me, right at me, and he was *talking* to me, telling me this whole story.'

'What did he tell you?'

'It was about something he and a friend at university got up to. He didn't tell me who the friend was – at least, not that I remember – but I can't stop picturing the way Preston looked at me. Like, *right* at me. It was so intense. It was as if this was something he'd been needing to say for a long time, to get off his chest – a secret he couldn't keep any more.'

'Like a confession?'

'Exactly. But when I asked him about it the next morning, he laughed it all off and said he was drunk and didn't know *what* he'd been going on about.'

'You think that was a lie?'

'Maybe.' She blinked. 'I don't want to go to the police, because I don't want this all over the tabloids before I've even had a chance to figure it out myself . . .' A pause. 'But I'm beginning to wonder if what he told me is connected to him going missing.'

'Why would you think that?'

'Because he told me he killed someone.'

4

. . . 47 hours to go . . .

'He *killed* someone? You're sure that's what you heard?'

'Positive.'

'You said you were drunk . . .'

'I didn't mishear.' She dabbed a tissue to her eye. 'He said he and this uni friend killed someone in their first year in Bristol.'

'But he didn't say who the friend was or what happened?'

'No.'

'Did he say where this murder took place?'

'No.' Ellie shook her head. 'No, nothing like that.'

No wonder she didn't want to go to the police. If she believed that someone in the Met had leaked the story to the press about her sister's drug charge, how could she trust anyone with the story of her husband going missing? Ellie had done nothing wrong, but she was perpetually in the media's sight lines. That meant her husband's disappearance could lead investigators to his drunken confession – and then any crimes Preston had committed would become hers by osmosis.

'Have you got Preston's phone?'

'Yes.'

'His wallet? His bank cards?'

'Yes, I have those too,' Ellie said. 'He left all of them with me before he headed down to surgery. And his laptop, if you need that, is at his house.'

I took a moment, thinking about the disappearance. He hadn't taken any tech with him, and the means to access his bank accounts were still with his wife. Did that point towards whatever happened at the hospital coming completely out of the blue? And did that make it more or less likely that it might be connected to what he'd told Ellie about killing someone? The quickest way to get to the truth about what happened at The Crest was going to be through their CCTV and by interviewing the staff there. How I proved the veracity of Preston's confession was less clear.

'Okay, let's work through this chronologically,' I said softly and showed her my phone again, telling her that I needed to record what was coming next. She relented. We were past the point at which she needed to worry about being on tape – she'd just revealed that her husband was a drink-driver who may have murdered someone.

'So the confession was when?'

'Around the middle of November.'

Eight weeks ago.

'And, as best as you can remember, what exactly did Preston say to you?'

A painful twist to her face as she went back. 'It was like I told you. He said he did something terrible at university, and that he and this friend killed someone. I took it to mean another student.'

'And, the next day, when he put it down to the drink, you believed him?'

'I mean, it still seemed a weird thing to say, but yes, I did. We'd been married for four months at that point, we'd been seeing each other for a year before that – I'd never had any reason to suspect him of not being totally honest with me. In fact, the opposite, really. Preston tended to overshare. After about two weeks of us first getting together, I knew his whole life story. That was part of what drew me to him. I loved how good and kind-hearted he was, but I really liked how open he was with me, how easy it was to know him. He was atypical like that. Most men I'd been with, most men my friends have been with – in fact, no offence, most men in general – you have to pin down and torture before they start opening up.'

'Had he talked to you about his university friends before?'

'Yes. He talked about them a lot. I've never met any of them, though.'

'Why not?'

'I knew, sooner or later, we were going to have to go public, but I just enjoyed the relative peace that came with not many people knowing about our marriage, even about the fact that we were together at all. I had no real idea who these friends were or if I could trust them. But I promised him that, eventually, we would tell them.' She went to her pocket, took out an iPhone and handed it to me. 'That's his phone. All of his friends' names and contact details are on there. I've been through the texts and emails – every single one of them – looking for some sort of explanation . . .' She grimaced.

I asked her for the passcode and had a quick look through. There must have been a hundred names in the address book.

'So then he hit that lamp post?' I asked.

'Yes.'

'Which was a couple of weeks ago?'

'Yes.'

'And who went and picked him up?'

'Matt. He towed the car back.'

'And between the confession and yesterday at the hospital, you two have never discussed again what he talked about that night?'

'No.' She rubbed at her brow with a painted nail. 'I hadn't forgotten it exactly, but I'd kind of locked it away. Sometimes I would think about it in quiet moments. I would think, "That was a crazy thing to admit to, even drunk." But there's honestly been nothing different about him in the time since, so I guess I never felt compelled to ask him about it. But now . . .' Her voice was getting quieter. 'All I know is that what happened yesterday makes no sense to me unless . . .' Her eyes started to fill up.

Unless he wasn't the man she believed him to be.

Unless he really had done something terrible.

Unless Preston Stewart was a killer.

5

. . . 46 hours to go . . .

We went back over everything we'd talked about, and then, before long, I saw that we were approaching a private airfield. We were somewhere in Hertfordshire, but I'd lost track of what direction we'd gone in because I'd been concentrating on what Ellie was telling me. As soon as she saw me looking, she said, 'Us talking in the back of the car like this – it's not just because I want to try and keep it out of the press if I can. I also have to fly to Amsterdam and then down to Berlin to do some press for the show. I'll be back around nine tonight.'

After passing through security, we followed a road running parallel to the edge of the airfield, down towards a hangar. I could see some of the members of the *Church Row Manor* cast milling around, including Ellie's on-screen lover, as well as a clutch of others on their phones, instantly recognizable as publicists.

'You can call me any time on my mobile,' Ellie said. 'But in the meantime, Matt can drive you where you need to go.'

I saw Matt glance at me again, his face neutral.

Having him drive me back to London wasn't just a practical necessity given the lack of a train station or taxi rank nearby, it also gave me a chance to ask him some questions on the return leg. Ellie had explained that he worked directly for her and Preston and had been hired by Preston after a press photographer had aggressively pursued Ellie's car when she was on her way back from the set the previous September. Matt was an ex-soldier.

'Have you told anyone at The Crest that you've come to me?' I asked her.

'No. But I can call them if that would help?'

'No, don't do that yet. I'll let you know when to contact them.'

I didn't know what was going on at the hospital, but the most effective way to find out was if they didn't know I was coming. Someone in there knew something, because patients in Preston's condition didn't just wander off by themselves, and it would be easier to find the fox in the henhouse if that person had no prep time.

We pulled up outside the hangar.

Matt got out and went to Ellie's door.

But as it opened, she turned back to me and I could see the conflict in her eyes, the expression I'd seen so often in the faces of the families and partners left behind: she didn't know if she'd done the right thing in sharing all of this with a stranger, a feeling exacerbated by her job and the unique pressures that came with it. Deeper down, there was something even worse: the fear that her husband's whispered confession might actually turn out to be true.

'Do you think less of me for not going to the police?' she asked.

I looked at Matt. His expression didn't alter an inch, except when – just for a split second – his eyes flicked to me and away again. He obviously wanted to know the answer to the question himself.

'Look,' I said, 'it's twenty-four hours since your husband disappeared, which means I have the sort of head start that I don't normally get given when I'm trying to locate missing people. We have to make full use of that. After this is over, after I've found him, then you'll have plenty of time to think about what you're going to do and who you're going to tell what. When that moment comes, my opinion on what you've done will remain as irrelevant as it is now. I don't think less of you, Ellie, because we all try to make the best choices we can in the pressure of the moment.'

A smile crept in from the corner of her mouth.

'The second thing you should know is that the police absolutely hate me, so the fact that you're not telling them for the time being – it's not going to keep me awake at night.'

'Why do they hate you?'

'Because I solve missing persons cases they've failed to.'

'So they're jealous of you?'

'It's a little more complex than that, and none of that history is relevant to me finding out where Preston went. But what I *will* say is that, much as I don't like to involve the police – and as much as you don't want to either – at some stage we will probably have to. And even if we don't make that call, as he's already told you, your friend Robert Lewellyn at the hospital will.'

I glanced at Matt.

Maybe a tiny glimmer of approval now.

'Speaking of which,' I said. 'I need to move fast on this, which means being in multiple places at the same time would be very helpful. With that in mind, would you object if I brought someone else in to help me? He's a former detective . . .'

Healy

Yesterday

Healy took a long drag on his cigarette.

He was standing at the bottom of his son's driveway, the front garden — really just a mess of broken concrete and old weeds — behind him, a railway embankment across the street, half hidden by an unattractive steel fence. Every few minutes a train thundered past — a sliver of its roof visible, the noise so loud it was a surprise Alice and Liam ever slept at night — and Healy would wonder if this was really the best they could have done. But they'd worked hard on the inside, concentrating most of their attention there, and because the interior was nice and the back garden had a neat patio, a lawn, and was entirely surrounded by six-foot fencing, sometimes it was possible to believe you weren't in a drab, untidy street in Wembley.

'Ah, there you are.'

Healy turned, following the sound of the voice, and saw his ex-wife, Gemma, emerging from a gate at the side of the house. Like Healy, she was in her late fifties, but unlike Healy she looked pretty good on it: the dark hair that she'd always worn long during their marriage was now chopped into a shorter style that suited her; her green eyes were as bright as the day the two of them had met back in Dublin over thirty years ago. And when she was pissed off with him — which she clearly was now — they'd lost none of their ability to tell him exactly how much.

'You're back on those again, then?' she said, glancing at the cigarette.

The disappointment was heavy in her voice. It took him back to when that was part of their daily routine. At the time, he thought he'd been doing a pretty good job of balancing a career working for the Met and bringing up three kids, but when he and Gemma separated, when their daughter, Leanne, died, when Healy got sacked from the police and his life completely spiralled, he had a lot of time to reassess. The truth was, he'd been a neglectful husband, a mostly absent father and a borderline drunk, and when his daughter had died, he'd got angry and vengeful too, and both of those things had only magnified his flaws. In the end, it had cost him his marriage, his relationship with his two sons, his career and almost his life.

A decade and a half on, he liked to think he was different, and maybe he actually was, but much as he was able to put on a good show for Gemma and was rebuilding a bond with his boys, he knew a part of that anger and vengeance remained. He could feel it like a fire, deep in the pit of his stomach, and knew exactly why it still burned: the man who'd murdered Leanne, who'd murdered eight other women, was still alive. Healy's daughter was in a grave and never coming home, but her killer got a prison cell. He wouldn't ever get released, but that didn't make it right.

Because where he deserves to be is deep in the fucking ground.

'Colm?'

He realized he'd drifted, had tuned Gemma out, and so he looked down at the smoking cigarette between his fingers and said, 'You know me. I aim to disappoint.'

'Here comes the self-pity.'

Healy felt a throb in his throat but pushed down a response. Fifteen years ago, in the dying embers of their marriage, he would never have been able to let that pass.

'Your son and daughter-in-law are wondering where you are.'

He took a drag and held up the cigarette. 'Well, now you know,' he said, smoke gathering in front of his face. 'Is the little lady enjoying bath-time?'

'Why don't you come and see for yourself?'

'I thought I'd give them some space.'

'Liam and Alice get to spend every day with her, Colm. They get to bath her every day. The whole reason they invited you around this afternoon was so that *you* could spend time cuddling your granddaughter and *you* could play with her in the bath. Instead, you're out here letting that head of yours mess things up.'

He looked at her. 'What does that mean?'

'You know exactly what it means.'

'Gem, if I was the greatest grandfather in the world, you'd still –'

'No,' she said sharply, cutting him off. 'This is nothing to do with me. What's going on here' – she looked at him, at his cigarette, at him standing outside while everyone else was in the house – 'this is all you.' She let that settle, her eyes doing the hard work again. 'That baby in there is your granddaughter. She's completely innocent in this. She's not even eighteen months old yet – she knows about ten words, she's only just learned to walk, she can't do anything besides toddle around and feel the love of her family. So I don't care how you do it, but you're going to pull yourself together, and you're going to get inside, and you're going to bath your granddaughter, and you're going to love her. And when you talk to Alice, you're going to stop being an arsehole.'

'I haven't been an arsehole to Alice.'

'It's in what you *don't* say, Colm. I spot you looking at her sometimes and you may as well be telling her to her face that you can't stand her.'

He didn't say anything.

Gemma took a step closer. 'Look at me.'

He tapped some ash from his cigarette, then turned – slowly, reluctantly.

'Alice's father isn't who Alice is,' Gemma said, and Healy was instantly back in David Raker's kitchen weeks before Alice was due to give birth. That was when she'd told Healy and Raker the truth about who she was. She'd told them about how she'd grown up in care since the age of two. She told them how her father had murdered her mother. She told them how she'd just wanted to seek the Healy family out, talk to them, find out about Leanne – just try to get answers and some measure of closure – but had quickly, unexpectedly fallen in love with Liam. And then she'd told them the part that had joined everything together.

She'd told Healy and Raker who her father was.

His name was Glass.

And he hadn't just killed her mother, he'd killed six other women and hidden them in a disused sewer network, disposed of a seventh in a nearby wall cavity, and killed his wife and unborn baby. Nine women, ten victims – and one of them had been Healy's daughter.

'She's a lovely kid, Colm.' Gemma was still talking. 'She loves Liam, and Liam adores her. They have a baby, they have a house. They're happy. Alice doesn't know her father, doesn't *want* to know him, isn't anything *like* him. Please don't punish her for where she came from. Alice isn't the one that took Leanne from us.'

Healy tapped off some more ash. 'Why'd they have to call her Leanne?'

'What?'

'Why did they have to call the baby Leanne?'

'Are you joking? Why do you *think* they called her Leanne?' Her blood was up now. 'It was a lovely thing to do. Don't go and turn it into something negative.'

Those green eyes again, making him feel small.

'No, you're right,' he said, convincingly enough that she seemed to buy the lie. 'I'm sorry. My head's all over the place.' But it was all just a fabrication: he hated that they'd called the baby Leanne. Every time Healy heard his daughter's name, it chipped another piece of him away, and he was back in that moment fourteen years ago when he and Raker had discovered Glass's hideout in a forest nicknamed the Dead Tracks.

He saw the room in which they'd found Leanne.

He saw the stillness in her face.

He was trapped once again in the worst moment of his life.

'Are you coming, then?' Gemma asked.

Healy took one last drag of the cigarette and then flicked it out into the road. As it died against the grey tarmac, he followed Gemma around to the back garden, and then in through the kitchen door. Straight away, he could hear the sound of laughter – splashing, baby talk – coming from upstairs.

Gemma stopped at the bottom of the stairs, gave Healy a look that said, *You're going to go up there and you're going to be the dad and grandad those two deserve*, and then she went into the living room. Healy slowly made his way upstairs.

'There's our beautiful girl,' he said as he entered the bathroom, looking at Leanne, giving her a wave, her red cheeks covered in foam from the bubble bath. Liam immediately made way and Healy dropped to his knees next to Alice, giving her a smile. 'How can Gramps help out?' he asked.

Alice broke into a big smile of her own.

It was warm, totally genuine.

And as he looked at her, despite himself, Healy knew Gemma was right: all Alice really wanted was to be accepted by them. She just wanted to be Alice-Leigh Reddy.

Not the daughter of a serial killer.

And as he played with his granddaughter in the bath, as he made her giggle, as the sound filled his heart and transported him back thirty years to another time and another place when a different little girl – also called Leanne – was in a different bath in another house, he allowed his guard to drop. He let himself think this was normal.

Everything will be fine.

You can relax.

You can just be.

And then it all fell apart again.

Because, an hour later, he found out Alice was lying to them.

6

. . . 46 hours to go . . .

I watched Matt walk Ellie across the tarmac to the plane and texted Healy. I hadn't spoken to him for a week, and a message I'd sent him a few days before, checking in to see how he was, hadn't even been read. I told him to call me.

A few minutes later, I'd switched to the front seat and Matt was nosing the Mercedes back through the gates of the airfield. As he did, I checked my notes, letting the discomfort of a silence settle between us. It was an old police tactic – one they'd used countless times on me – and one that I imagined Matt, given his history in the military, was probably familiar with. That didn't make it any less pleasant to deal with, though, and after a while I saw him start glancing across at my notebook.

'Do you mind if I record this?' I asked, but didn't really give him a chance to respond – I was already setting up my phone. 'Can I ask your full name?'

'Matthew Higgs.'

'And you've been working for Ellie since when?'

'Last October.'

'And you were a soldier before that.'

'I haven't been a soldier for ten years.'

'Which regiment were you in?'

'Does it make a difference?'

'I'm just interested.'

He stared at me. 'Grenadier Guards.'

I wasn't really a military expert, but I knew the Grenadier Guards were one of the oldest regiments in the British Army and its most senior infantry unit. Matt must have been in his early fifties, so he'd probably been on the front line in both Iraq and Afghanistan. I decided not to press him on it for now, though – he clearly didn't want to talk about the army and I didn't need him closing up on me.

'How did Preston come to hire you?' I asked.

'I had a protection job before this, with a patient of his.' He glanced at me and could see I was about to ask who. 'Guy called Clark Sanders. He made all his money in hotels. He got diagnosed with Alzheimer's about two years back and the worse he got, the more his family worried about people taking advantage of him – shoving a form in his hand and telling him he needed to sign it, that sort of thing. So they asked me if I could be around to keep an eye on everything. I mean, at the end, you could have got him to do anything.' A flicker of something different in his face – sadness, sympathy. Those were good things to see. He'd come to care about Sanders. It seemed obvious that he'd come to care about Ellie too.

'What do you think happened at the hospital?'

He frowned. 'Isn't that what Ellie hired you for?'

'You don't have a theory?'

He sighed, like it was all some huge imposition, but I could see his brain ticking over. 'You don't have to be a doctor to know he didn't walk out of that hospital pumped full of anaesthetic. Other than that, I don't know.' He switched on the windscreen wipers. 'No offence, but I told her to go to the cops because they're best placed to find out where Preston went. They've got manpower. They've got the resources. You're just you. I did some reading up last night and some of what you've done, it's impressive, don't get me wrong, but this thing is live. It's happening right now. It's not some dead-in-the-water case.'

'You don't think I can handle it?'

'On your own? No.'

'I've asked a friend to help me.'

'This Healy guy?' Matt smirked. 'Yeah, I saw him mentioned in the articles I read last night. He sounds like a mess.'

He wasn't a million miles away from the truth – or, at least, the truth about a version of Healy I'd met for the first time fourteen years ago – but the Colm Healy of today was different. Or, rather, different enough. I didn't want to get bogged down in history, or why there would always be a small part of me that was waiting for Healy to blow up his life. I preferred to focus on something else.

Healy was a brilliant detective.

'What's Preston like?'

For a moment, Matt seemed thrown by the change of direction. But then he recovered his composure. 'He's a nice bloke.'

'A good employer?'

'Yeah.'

'I'm guessing you spent more time with Ellie than with him?'

He eyed me, like I was implying something. I held up a hand, assuring him I wasn't – although a part of me wondered how far off the mark the idea might actually be. I hadn't once got the impression that Ellie was anything less than totally committed to her marriage, but it was harder to say where Matt's feelings lay.

'I spent time with both of them,' he said.

'And Preston never mentioned this university friend to you?'

'No.'

'Never hinted something may have happened down in Bristol?'

'No.'

'When did Ellie tell you about what she heard Preston confess to?'

'Last night was the first time I'd heard about it.'

'And you helped clean up the scene after Preston hit that lamp post?'

'I did.'

'Has the car been repaired now?'

'Yes. He got it back at the end of last week.'

'Any fallout from that? Anyone come asking questions?'

'No and no.'

I paused, thinking. 'Did he drink a lot?'

Matt's eyes flicked to me and then immediately went back to the road. He watched quietly as the wipers got faster, trying to cope with the rain. Then: 'He never drank when he was working. Preston wasn't stupid. He knew if he drank on the job, he'd get his licence taken away and his career would get flushed.'

'But outside of work?'

He glanced at my phone, at its speaker. 'Will Ellie ever hear this?'

'No. Whatever you tell me stays between us.'

The rain was getting harder, pounding against the roof of the Mercedes, filling the car with noise. 'She doesn't know,' he said.

'"Doesn't know"?'

'How bad his drinking is.'

I waited, watching him.

'In the army, but especially after I left, I saw a lot of soldiers turn to the bottle. I know what it looks like when someone's using it as a coping mechanism.'

'Do you think he was an alcoholic?'

'I don't know, but recently, when Ellie hasn't needed me and Preston's out somewhere – at some business thing, or just with mates – I've been getting calls from him, asking me to pick him up. And when I arrive, he'll barely be able to stand. He'll be absolutely, paralytically drunk. When I drop him home, he'll ask me not to tell Ellie, and he'll sleep on the sofa or in the spare room, and the next day he'll tell her that he didn't want to wake her, which is why he slept downstairs. And she'll believe him.'

'She can't tell he's been drinking?'

'No. He's high-functioning.'

'Earlier, you called the booze a coping mechanism?'

'Yes. And until yesterday I wouldn't have had a clue what he might have been trying to cope with. But now . . .'

Now we know he might have killed someone.

'Now I think he's been trying to forget.'

7

... 45 hours to go ...

As we pulled into Ellie's road in Holland Park, Matt said, 'Wait for it.'

Ahead of us, cars were parked on both sides all the way down, most of them expensive. But then I started to see that dotted in among the Range Rovers and Porsches were much less impressive vehicles.

A rust-spattered Ford.

An old Citroën.

A panel van with a cracked headlight.

In all of them, men were sitting behind the wheel – head down, faces in their phones. As soon as they saw Matt slow down and use a key fob to open the gates to Ellie's driveway, they got out and swarmed our vehicle. Flashbulbs blinked. A zoom lens made contact with the rear passenger-side window. But then, one by one, as they looked at the photos they'd just snapped, they stuttered to a halt.

They'd realized that Ellie wasn't in the back seat of the car.

Matt pulled in through the front gates and then immediately pressed the same key fob as he drove down a slope to a garage at the side of the house.

'Is it like this every day?' I asked.

'When she's on set, yeah, because they know she stays here. When she's not filming, it's not quite as bad, because they haven't figured out where she goes in her downtime.'

He brought the car to a halt.

I got out and took in the house properly.

It was an enormous end terrace, built on four floors and hidden from the road by a mix of high walls, precisely manicured hedgerows and the seven-foot front gates.

Matt unlocked the house.

He went straight to the alarm panel as I took in what was less a hallway and more a foyer: on my left, a staircase twisted up to a mezzanine level and then the first floor; one route on my right took me down to what looked like a living room, another in front of me went to a kitchen; a third entered immediately into a study, in which I could see a glass cabinet with a Golden Globe and two Emmys inside.

I wasn't certain what I hoped to find in a home Ellie barely lived in any more – and had rarely, if ever, brought Preston to – but it was on the way to The Crest, so it made sense to stop off and look around. The hospital and Preston's house in Surrey were likely to be more useful, but as I started going through the rooms, I hoped Ellie's house would give me more of a sense of who she and Preston were.

But none of the photos on the walls was of Preston.

They were of Ellie and her parents, or with her sister and brother, or candid shots of her with friends. They were useful in as much as they showed a side of her I'd seen nothing of as I'd gone through the press stories the previous night; they were real moments in time, not just another sterile, highly organized photoshoot where she had to pretend everything was perfect. But Preston's absence from the walls made this place feel exactly what it was: a house that only existed in the past tense, a place of convenience while she was filming the show, a building that had barely been used in the time she and Preston had known each other.

In the study, I could see a laptop stand but not the laptop itself, which probably meant she had it on her for the trip to Europe, and up in her bedroom I found an iPad in a side drawer. I went through it but there was nothing of note, other than her internet history. Away from acting, she seemed to enjoy cooking and trail running. As I looked at a website she'd gone to which listed the most picturesque routes in the Lake District, I wondered if she ever got the chance to run any trails. There wasn't much point if tabloid journalists were lying in wait for her the whole time.

Matt had remained behind in the foyer.

As I entered, he looked up at me and I remembered Ellie telling me how Preston had hired him after she was pursued from the *Church Row Manor* set by a press photographer.

'Did Ellie ever tell you about the night she was followed by the photographer?'

'Yeah,' he said. 'He was waiting for her on a motorbike when she left the set – basically chased her. She had to slam on the brakes at one stage and hit her head on the wheel. She nearly crashed the car.'

'She must have been shaken up.'

'I didn't start here until a few weeks later – but, yeah, she was.' He shook his head. 'There's always scumbags out front here, and there'll be armies of them when we go to places they know she'll be – press events and premieres and that sort of thing – but most of them know where to draw the line. This one didn't.'

My phone started buzzing in my pocket.

I took it out, saw it was Healy and headed back into the living room, pushing the door shut behind me. 'The Kraken awakes.'

'Meaning?' He already sounded on edge, which wasn't a great start.

'Meaning I'm getting a lot of blue ticks and no replies.'

'Yeah, sorry. I've had some stuff going on.'

It would have been a passable impression of someone who genuinely meant it if it wasn't for the fact I'd had fourteen years to get to know Healy's tics – and I knew instantly that he was lying. But I decided to park any more questions for now.

'I've got something for you,' I said.

'Yeah?'

He immediately sounded brighter. He worked shifts as a security guard, which he absolutely hated, but he'd torched his career as a detective over a decade ago and there was no going back to it now. The work I did, and the cases that I could sometimes afford to fold him into, were like adrenalin shots for him.

'Are you ready to go right now?' I asked.

'I can be.'

'How long will it take you to get to Chelsea?'

'I can be there in thirty minutes.'

Twenty-five minutes later, I called Ellie.

She answered after a couple of rings. 'David?'

'Hi, Ellie. Are you all right to talk for a second?'

'Yes,' she said. 'We're just in a cab.'

'Great. I need you to call the hospital for me now.'

I turned, watching Matt drive off in the Mercedes, rejoining the traffic on Fulham Road. At a zebra crossing further down, Healy was approaching, his eyes switching between me and the Georgian building I was standing in front of.

'Okay,' Ellie said. 'What should I tell them?'

'Tell them I'm right outside.'

8

. . . 44 hours to go . . .

We were put in a meeting room off reception and, as we waited, I filled Healy in on what had happened the day before and what I'd found out so far from Ellie and Matt.

'Basically, there's a missing twenty minutes,' I said. 'Preston is taken from recovery back up to his private room and is alone until Ellie and a nurse arrive to take off his bandages. So what happened when he was on his own?'

Healy nodded, digesting it all. 'I've seen her in that show.'

He was talking about Ellie.

'Yeah? You like it?'

'No, it's a load of pretentious old shite.'

It was a pretty on-message response for Healy and, as we quietened, I took him in properly for the first time. His beard was shapeless and uneven, and he'd come in a blazer but was wearing a wrinkled T-shirt underneath it. His trousers looked a bad fit too. I was guessing it had been a while since he'd been in front of a mirror.

He saw me studying him. 'What?'

'You all right?'

'Why, don't I look it?'

It wasn't just the way he'd dressed. There was something going on behind his eyes; something worrying him. I'd heard it on the phone and I was seeing it here too, a certainty based on fourteen years of reading his warning signs. Healy and I weren't friends in the traditional sense – we rarely, if ever, socialized – but whatever existed between us had endured. One of the main reasons was that we'd both lost someone we loved deeply: Derryn had finally succumbed to breast cancer two years before I met Healy; Healy's daughter, Leanne, had disappeared nine months prior to our first meeting, her murder missed and then hidden by corrupt police officers. We'd found Leanne's lifeless body together, and the memory of her and the other women that the killer known as Glass had taken – and the anger and the grief it had provoked in both of us – was like a sword being forged in a fire.

'How's Leanne?' I asked.

A minor flinch, there and then gone again. 'She's good,' he said evenly. 'Growing up fast. I was there last night.'

'She's – what? – eighteen months now?'

'Almost, yeah.'

'I haven't seen Alice for a while. Are she and Liam enjoying it?'

'Pretty tired, I think, but you know . . .' His eyes went to the window, which had a view out across the high bricked walls of the Chelsea Physic Garden. For a second, Healy seemed caught somewhere else, his eyes trained on the trees in the garden that were gently moving in time to the wind. 'So have you tried looking into this student that Preston reckons he killed?'

As Matt had driven me back to London, I had.

Not that I'd found much.

I'd googled the period in which Preston had been in his first year of medical school – September 1993 to July 1994 – and had searched for disappearances and murders in the Bristol area during that time, but it had been a dead end. It didn't mean there hadn't been any disappearances or murders in the city across that period, just that it was too far back to have been covered online. After thirty years, you had to rely on archived news stories, most likely from the local press, and local press had changed so profoundly in that time, it was basically unrecognizable. Newspapers had closed, the ones that were still going had been downsized; and archiving stories – and the expense that came with maintaining databases full of old articles – were always going to be collateral damage.

The other thing I'd done before getting to The Crest was to go through Preston's phone, looking at his texts, emails and app activity. I'd noted that there was a core of about twenty people that he spoke to most often, and about fifteen that he had more intermittent conversations with. Based on a first look, though, it felt like his texts and emails weren't going to throw up many leads.

A few seconds later, a message from Rebekah buzzed through.

Back home in Britain and taking care of business

It was a photograph of two boxes of Yorkshire Tea balancing in her hand. In the background, from the buildings, I could see she'd made it to Cambridge.

'What's up with you?' Healy asked.

I realized I was smiling.

'Nothing,' I said, and put my phone on the table, face down.

I told Healy we would split Preston's contacts down the middle and that, after we were finished at the hospital, we'd start doing a ring-around. Even if, based on an initial look at his phone, I didn't instinctively feel Preston's address book would lead anywhere, it needed to be done.

'We're against the clock here,' Healy said.

'Yeah, which is why we're going to divide our time here too, so we can go more quickly. I'll take this Lewellyn guy who did the operation and who's Preston's business partner here, you take the nurse and the porter. We can divvy up the rest of the staff later.'

Healy shifted in his seat and, as he did, I caught a whiff of cigarette smoke.

'You smoking again?'

'You sound like Gemma,' he muttered.

I didn't say anything else, but somewhere deep down I felt a minor twist of concern. Healy had spent his whole life in an unending pattern of trying to quit booze and cigarettes, and it had been a couple of years since he'd last smoked, even longer since he'd taken a drink. The smoking itself didn't bother me – he was entitled to do whatever he wanted – it was more what it represented, and what it might be hiding. He only ever started smoking when he was stressed out, or angry, or was wrestling with something big. This was a movie that I'd seen countless times before.

And it always ended badly.

A few seconds later, the door to the office opened and a tall, wiry man in his late forties entered. He was dressed in grey-blue scrubs.

'Gentlemen,' he said. 'Sorry to keep you waiting. I'm Robert Lewellyn.'

9

. . . 44 hours to go . . .

Lewellyn led us deeper into the bowels of The Crest.

Derryn had been a nurse – although not in the private sector – and had spent most of her adult life in and around hospitals. I'd spent most of my adult life trying to avoid them. All they were to me – the identical corridors, the pale lino and off-white walls, the stench of disinfectant and sickness – was a reminder of the years I'd spent driving her back and forth to oncology departments. But there was no denying that The Crest was a different beast from the creaking buildings my wife had worked in, and the places I'd visited on cases in the time since.

It smelt great for a start, the scent of pine in the air, and as we passed a row of private rooms it began to feel more like a hotel. The rooms were plush and light, the floors covered in expensive vinyl that looked exactly like floorboards, the walls scattered with soft uplighting and modern art. Some of the even bigger rooms had floor-to-ceiling glass with views across the hospital's walled garden.

Right at the end of the corridor, outside one of the last rooms, was a whiteboard with a name written on it: *Kevin Neale*. I looked in at the man who had been mixed up with Preston Stewart the day before. He was sitting up in bed, the TV on, his face still covered in heavy bandaging. Lewellyn saw me looking and said, 'Yes, that's Mr Neale. I've told him that you'd probably want to talk to him later on.'

He didn't give us a chance to hang around, marching us into a large nurse's station with doors circling it like spokes on a wheel.

Lewellyn said it was nicknamed the Octagon because of its shape. It was busy, full of staff. A few of them looked up and said hello to Lewellyn.

I glanced to my right, where a corridor ran down to a set of swing doors. I could see a card reader on the wall and MEDICAL PERSONNEL ONLY written above. It must have been where the operating theatre and recovery rooms were.

'Here we go,' Lewellyn said, opening a door.

I'd already told him that my preference was to split duties – I'd talk to him, and Healy would talk to the nurse who'd been assigned to Preston Stewart, as well as the porter – so he directed Healy into the room and told him that both the nurse, who he called Maya, and the porter, Dennis, would be along soon.

Lewellyn and I headed into the next room along.

'Please,' he said, offering me a seat on the other side of an L-shaped desk that was loaded with in-trays full of paper and a new purple iMac.

Lewellyn straightened out the neckline on his scrubs, eyes on me, waiting. I could normally get a pretty quick read on people, but he was harder to gauge. His eyes were bright but they were almost supernaturally still, his expression too.

'Thanks for agreeing to see me so quickly,' I said.

'I have to be in theatre from one p.m.'

'I understand.' It had been coming up to eleven thirty when we'd arrived, but I didn't check my watch again. I kept my focus on Lewellyn and passed a business card across the desk to him. 'If it's all right with you, once we're done with these interviews, I'd like to take a look at the security footage from yesterday. I know you won't have CCTV inside the rooms themselves, but I saw that you had cameras at the front desk, in the corridors between here and there, and next to the nurse's station – and, I'm guessing, there will be more in and around the operating theatres as well?'

'Correct,' he said. 'We have cameras in all those locations – but we've already been through it all. I sat with the security team myself yesterday.'

'And you didn't find anything?'

'No. Nothing.'

'Well, I'd like to take a look at it all the same.'

He seemed distracted by my business card now.

'Mr Lewellyn?'

'Please,' he said, still looking at my card, 'call me Robert.' Finally, his eyes rested on me again. 'You used to be a journalist, is that correct?'

'A long time ago, yes.'

He nodded.

'Is that a problem?'

'No, not at all,' he replied quickly, but there was no change in his face, so it was hard to say if he was being honest. 'It's just surprising to me that Ellie would ask a journalist to help her find out what went on.'

'As I said, I haven't been a journalist for a long time.'

His eyes went back to my business card. 'In the job you do now, you've certainly had some interesting cases.' It was a statement, not a question. In the ten minutes between receiving the call from Ellie telling him I was here and him turning up to collect us from the front desk, he'd clearly spent every available second on Google.

I didn't reply for a moment, just watched him, and as I did, I realized that this was going to be a battle. That didn't necessarily mean he was hiding anything. As Ellie herself had speculated earlier, Lewellyn's biggest worry could easily have been how Preston's disappearance might affect the reputation of the hospital. Certainly, his decision to give Ellie forty-eight hours before he reported the disappearance to the police supported that idea. If I made some headway – even better, if I found Preston Stewart before tomorrow – he would never have to go to the police and this would never go public. Until then, though – including in his dealings with me – caution was the watchword, just in case everything blew up.

He made a few minor adjustments to some paperwork in front of him. 'I'll level with you, David, yesterday was a black day for the hospital. Nothing like that has ever happened here – and any time anything *has* gone wrong in the time since we opened, we've managed to fix the issue quickly and quietly. That's why patients like us. We employ a certain level of' – a pause – 'discretion. As you'll know from Ellie, our client base is made up of a lot of high-visibility individuals.'

He was talking more like a CEO than a doctor.

'The Crest has been open for ten years, is that right?'

Lewellyn nodded. 'Preston and I are the clinical directors, but we also have two guys we brought in to deal with the financial and business side.'

I asked for their contact details and then made him run through the timeline of events the day before, starting from when he arrived at work. His account aligned with everything Ellie had told me.

'How likely is it that there may have been a paperwork mix-up?' I asked. 'Perhaps Preston's notes and Kevin Neale's notes got swapped somehow?'

'I mean, it's possible, but that wouldn't explain how Preston just disappeared like he did. Plus, "swapped" makes it sound like a deliberate act.'

'You don't think it could have been?'

He stared at me, his expression opaque. 'I can't speak to Preston's motivations, but no, I don't think there was a deliberate mix-up with the two sets of notes. I think, if that was indeed what happened – if the paperwork crossed over – it was an honest-to-God mistake by one of our staff. And, as I say, surely the bigger question isn't where the error occurred or why, but how Preston – even if he *was* in the wrong room – got up and walked out of the hospital by himself, given –'

'You don't think he could have had help?'

'I refuse to believe any of my staff are involved.'

'How many people work here?'

'We have eighty-seven employees.'

'And you know every single one of them?'

He didn't say anything for a moment. 'Look, the nurses we had on duty here yesterday are some of our best. I mean, Maya is relatively new, but she came highly recommended and worked in private health care in Brighton. Some of the others have been here since the day we opened.'

Length of service meant about as much as Lewellyn's assurances that he knew his entire staff well enough to vouch for every single one of them. As I'd found out so many times before, anyone was capable of anything in the right circumstances and with the right pressure applied. But I made a note about Maya – the nurse assigned to Preston – being new here. Did that mean anything?

'So what did Ellie tell you about Preston?' Lewellyn asked.

I looked up. He was shifting the chair fractionally from side to side, the mechanism squeaking as it did.

'"Tell" me about him?'

'Yes.'

'She told me a lot of things,' I said.

'Did she tell you what sort of person he was?'

'Yes.'

'So what did she say?'

'She said he was a good husband.'

Lewellyn nodded again. 'Did she tell you he was violent?'

Healy

Now

Healy shook the hands of the nurse and the porter as they entered the consultation room. They both looked nervous, but he didn't read anything into it. It might have been a long time since he'd been a cop, but one of the things he remembered most lucidly from those days was the stark mix of fear and panic that people carried into interview rooms. Even if they were innocent, it was always there.

It made him more suspicious when people were calm.

The nurse, Maya, was in her late twenties, with blonde hair and deep-set blue eyes. The porter was in his early sixties with black hair, very dark eyes and sun-damaged skin, and at a guess – based on the way he looked and the small amount that he'd said so far – Healy would have pegged Dennis as eastern European, perhaps from one of the countries down on the Black Sea.

'Take a seat,' Healy said to them. 'We're just trying to find out what went on here yesterday and gather information from the staff who were on duty.' That seemed to relax Maya, but it was harder to say if it had done much for Dennis. He was still looking at Healy as if he were about to pull on an executioner's hood. Healy decided to softball them for a little longer: 'Where are you guys from?'

'The Netherlands,' Maya replied first.

'I'm from Germany,' Dennis said.

Healy's gaze lingered on him. It was possible, because anyone could be from anywhere these days, but to Healy's ears, his accent definitely didn't sound German.

Healy sat.

'Let's start with you, Maya,' he said. 'As I understand it, you didn't get to chat with Preston before his surgery?'

'No,' she replied. 'I was late starting my shift. I was meant to be here for change-over at six thirty, but yesterday all the trains were cancelled from Brighton. I'm new here, so I haven't found an apartment in London yet, which means I still have to commute. By the time I arrived, Mr Stewart had already gone down.'

'Okay. What about you, Dennis?'

He cleared his throat. 'I talk to him before.'

'I believe his surgery was scheduled for nine a.m.?'

He looked at Healy blankly.

'You don't remember what time he went in?'

'No.'

'What happened when you took him down to surgery?'

He shrugged. 'I just go to the room to collect him, and we talk for a moment about, uh . . .' He paused. His English was pretty good, but he was obviously struggling for a word. *Or, Healy thought again, he's searching for a lie.* 'I think we talk about football. When we talk, always football. I am Bayern Munich, and he is Chelsea.'

'And what did you do once you'd taken him to surgery?'

'I, uh . . .' He stopped. Now it was unclear whether he was delaying or trying to recollect. 'I deal with hazardous waste, and then move furniture for the doctors who need more space in the room. I don't remember what I do.' He looked a little worried now, his cheeks colouring. 'You will see that I am telling the truth,' he added quickly. 'You will see if you check the, uh . . .' He gestured above him.

'The CCTV?'

'Yes, the camera.'

'Okay. So, as I understand it, once Preston's surgery was over and he was ready to be moved through to recovery, Kevin Neale was already *in* recovery, is that right?'

'Yes.'

'Was anyone else in there besides those two?'

'No.'

'Then what?'

'I go away and do more tasks.'

Healy turned to Maya. She was sitting very straight, hands in her lap. 'Nurses must pass in and out of the recovery room all the time if there are patients in there?'

'Yes, there is a nurse's station located inside.'

'So someone's there the whole time?'

'Yes, always. We never leave patients unattended.'

So it was unlikely anything had happened in recovery – unless Healy was willing to believe that two or three nurses were conspiring together. He couldn't entirely dismiss the idea, but it seemed unlikely. The more people you involved, the harder it was to keep a secret. He drummed a pen against the desk, thinking, giving himself a moment to reset. The two patients had been mixed up at some point. If it hadn't happened in recovery, it seemed even more unlikely that it had happened *prior* to surgery, because Lewellyn would have realized if the wrong patient had been delivered to him. And, even if he was in on whatever this was, other staff in the operating theatre would have clocked a potential – or deliberate – mix-up. Dennis couldn't have switched the two men *between* surgery and recovery either, because Neale was already *in* recovery while Preston was being operated on.

Which means what?

He looked at Dennis. 'So you took Preston up to his room first, right?'

'Yes.'

'Why was he taken up first when he went into surgery second?'

'There was a minor problem with Mr Neale's dressing,' Maya said, stepping in, 'so while they adjusted that, the nurses asked Dennis to take Mr Stewart upstairs.'

'Okay, and where were you when that was happening?'

'I was doing my rounds. That took about twenty minutes. Then I headed to see Preston to apply the cream to his face that Mr Lewellyn had recommended. I collected Preston's wife on the way. She'd been waiting for him in the day room. I remember she recognized my Dutch accent and told me her dad was from the Netherlands. Her real surname is Sneijders, not Snyder, but she . . .'

Maya stopped, unsure of the word.

'Anglicized it?'

'Yes,' she responded. 'Yes, anglicized it.'

Healy imagined the information about the surname was right there in Ellie's Wikipedia entry, but he wrote it down for Raker just in case. They were looking for angles and potential suspects, so could there be something to explore in the fact that both Preston's wife and his nurse had a Dutch connection?

'So then you took the bandages off,' he said to Maya.

She nodded. 'Yes. And it wasn't Mr Stewart.'

Healy thought about the missing twenty minutes that Raker had talked about between the two men being returned to their private rooms and Ellie, with Maya in tow, arriving at her husband's bedside. It was the only time the men were left alone.

No nurses. No doctors.

No visitors.

Or none that anyone saw.

Healy returned to the conversation and caught Dennis looking at him. The porter turned away, his gaze dropping to the scarred knuckles of his right hand. As he did, Healy saw a tiny tattoo in the triangle of webbing between his thumb and forefinger, faded to a pale blue.

And that was when Healy knew his instincts had been right.

Dennis wasn't from Germany.

He'd lied.

10

...44 hours to go...

'Preston is violent?' I stared at Lewellyn. 'In what way?'

'In what way do you think?' He shrugged, as if it was obvious.

He's violent towards Ellie.

But if that was true, why hadn't Ellie mentioned anything to me that morning? Had she been worried about how I might react? Did she think it would make me less likely to take on the work? Or was it just something else about her private life that she was frightened might end up in the tabloids? I scanned my notebook, looking at everything she'd told me about her husband. She'd called him good and kind-hearted. She'd said he was open, sometimes over-sharing with her; later on, when we'd gone back over everything, she referred to him as smart and funny, and told me he was patient and fully respected her need for privacy. But then I thought of what Matt had told me.

Preston drank too much.

What if the drink made him violent?

'So he physically abused Ellie,' I said, 'is that what you're saying?'

'I believe so.'

'You believe so – or you know so?'

'I don't live with them, David, so I can't say for sure what goes on when it's just the two of them, alone. But what I can tell you is what I've seen with my own eyes.' He moved forward in his chair, hands flat to the desk. 'In the middle of September, Preston called me and asked me to go to his house in Surrey. We'd already seen each other at work that day, so that was the first thing that didn't make sense. If he needed to speak to me, why not just grab me at work? The other thing that seemed weird was that it was almost ten p.m. when he called. When I told him it was late, and asked if it could wait, he said it couldn't.'

'So you drove down to Surrey?'

'Yes.' He paused, blinked. 'Ellie was there. Her eye had closed up.'

'"Closed up"?'

'A trauma injury. There was swelling, bruising. She had an ice pack on it. She looked like she was . . .' Again, he stopped. 'She looked like she was in shock.'

'What did she say happened?'

'Preston did all the talking. He said she was driving back from the studio when someone started following her on a motorbike. A press photographer. Things got frantic, she had to slam on the brakes in order to stop herself leaving the road entirely, and she lurched forward and' – he clicked his fingers – 'hit her face.'

I recalled Ellie and then Matt telling me of the same incident. 'So what are you saying – you don't believe she was pursued by the press that night?'

'Frankly, no.'

'Why not?'

'Well, in the first instance, why would Preston call me?'

'Why did he *say* he called you?'

'He said he wanted a second opinion on her injuries and trusted me to be discreet. For obvious reasons, the two of them are very secretive.'

Something about Preston wanting a second opinion didn't ring true to me, but I decided to circle back around to it, because there was a more obvious question right now: 'Why would Preston want to show you Ellie's injuries if *he* was responsible?'

'So he could reinforce the story about the press photographer.'

'And Ellie sat there and let him talk, and just went along with everything?'

'I think she was scared of him.'

I studied Lewellyn. 'That night or more generally?'

'Both.'

Pausing for a moment, I tried to fold this new information into what had happened to Preston at The Crest the day before, but the idea of him being violent towards Ellie felt like it had come completely out of left field.

'So you examined Ellie?'

'Yes.'

'And what did you conclude?'

'I'm not an expert in the field, but things didn't add up. Preston said Ellie had been doing sixty miles per hour before the accident, and if you stop dead at sixty miles per hour, you expect multiple facial fractures and a possible brain injury. Her brain function was fine, and she didn't have whiplash or neck damage. And as I left that night, I had a look at her car and the airbag hadn't deployed. I asked Preston about it, and he said it hadn't inflated. I guess it's possible, and I guess it's also possible that she *did* get the injuries from simply hitting her face on the steering wheel, but . . .' He trailed off, the implication clear. *It doesn't seem likely to me.* 'The other thing is, why did nothing appear in the press afterwards?'

He meant if the photographer had been furiously taking photographs of Ellie, why hadn't any of the shots been published in the media in the days after?

I could think of one reason.

Preston, and in particular Ellie, didn't trust the police, so were never going to report the incident to them. But the photographer didn't know that. In fact, he probably *expected* Ellie to go to the cops, given the fact she'd sustained injuries. And if the press had published the photographs, the cops would have been able to trace the person who'd taken them. Maybe the photographer realized he'd gone too far, and the best way to prevent the police turning up on his doorstep was to bin the shots.

I returned to Lewellyn's version of events, to the idea that

Preston was violent and controlling, and whether it might help explain what went on here twenty-four hours ago. He'd admitted to Ellie that he'd killed someone. Now Lewellyn was painting him as an abuser. Those seemed more likely catalysts for him going missing than him being a loving husband and a popular work colleague who suddenly, and without explanation, vanished into thin air.

Except...

Something didn't feel right.

'What else did Preston ask you to do that night?'

Lewellyn frowned. 'Other than assess Ellie's injuries? Nothing.'

'So why did he even need a second opinion?'

'What do you mean?'

'Preston's a doctor, just like you.'

In the swirl of questions surrounding the night he drove down to Surrey – and because it was obvious Lewellyn's ego was massive – the *why* had become lost. Why would Preston even need Lewellyn there? If anything, given Preston was a neurologist, he was better placed to assess a potential brain injury than Lewellyn was.

'I guess he just...' Lewellyn shrugged. 'I guess he just valued my opinion.'

But that wasn't it, I was sure of it.

'I need to make a call,' I said.

11

. . . 43 hours to go . . .

I told Lewellyn to stay put and headed out of the consultation room.

I'd been reluctant to disrupt the interview, especially as the recency of Preston's disappearance didn't afford me the kind of time I normally had to play with in cold missing persons searches. But I needed answers about the night Ellie sustained her injuries before I went any further – and that meant hearing her side of the story.

She answered quickly.

'I need to ask you something else,' I said, 'about the incident last September.'

'The incident with the pap?'

'Yes. Can you tell me what happened?'

'I don't know that there's much to tell, really. It was the second or third day of filming on the new series. This motorbike pulled up next to me as I left the studio, whipped out a camera and started taking photographs. I've had paps follow me before, but not like this. I almost lost control of the car and had to slam on the brakes, and I ended up hitting my face on the steering wheel.'

'Did you sustain any injuries?'

'Yes. To my left eye.'

'Anything else?'

'No, just that. The paps knew what car I drove – make, model, registration plate – so we sold the Lexus and bought the Mercedes. A few weeks after that, Preston went out and hired Matt.' She paused again. 'Matt has been great – very discreet, very professional – but I do miss the freedom. I always liked driving. I liked being by myself after a long day on set. It helped me decompress.'

I wondered for a moment if there was anything in the fact that both Preston and Ellie had been in car accidents over the last five months – and both had sustained injuries to their faces. Could that be related to Preston's disappearance in any way? It seemed more like bad luck, especially as Preston's incident was self-inflicted, but I made a note of it. Nothing was off the table yet.

'I need to ask you something else,' I said.

'Anything.'

'Robert Lewellyn mentioned that Preston asked him to come to the house that night?'

'Yes. Preston was really worried about me and wanted a second opinion on my eye injury. And obviously we wanted to avoid having to go to A&E if we could. If we did that, our visit would have been all over the newspapers the next morning – and our marriage. Plus, Preston had already had a couple of drinks at that point.'

'Okay,' I said. 'This next part is a little delicate.'

'"Delicate"?'

Her response was more cautious now.

I took a breath. 'Has Preston ever been abusive towards you?'

'*What?* No, of course not. Why would you say that?'

'He hasn't ever hit you?'

'*No.* Never.'

'Has he ever been verbally abusive?'

'*No.* Why the hell are you asking me this?'

But then she understood.

'Oh,' she said, 'because of the eye injury.'

And because of his drinking, I thought, but didn't say.

'No, he's never laid a finger on me,' Ellie said. 'He isn't like that. He doesn't hurt people . . .' But then her words fell away – because, a long time ago, as he'd told her himself, he may have done. I've never seen a single part of him that might be capable of that. I mean, he's barely even raised his voice in the entire time we've been together. Like I told you in the car this morning, he's kind, patient and gentle. That night, I hit my face on the steering wheel because I braked so sharply – and that's the truth. Plus, there's no way in hell I would ever let *any* man put his hands on me like that.'

I told Ellie I would call her later, hung up, and then glanced at the room Robert Lewellyn was waiting in.

One of them was lying to me.

And I felt like I had a pretty good idea who.

12

. . . 43 hours to go . . .

Robert Lewellyn looked up from his phone. 'How much longer is this going to take?'

I closed the door of the consultation room and sat down across the desk from him. 'Ellie says Preston never laid a finger on her.'

A slight movement in his brow.

'I just spoke to her. She says Preston has never been violent – and that what he told you happened that night with the press photographer *did* happen.'

He shifted in his seat. 'Well, that's not surprising, is it? Of *course* she's going to say that. If she's scared of him, she's not going to tell you the truth, is she?' But his expression wasn't quite as set now, his demeanour not quite as tranquil.

'I don't believe Preston was violent to her,' I said.

'Well, let's hope you're right.' Picking up a pen and putting it into a pot next to the Mac, he swallowed, smoothed down his shirt, looked at me.

'How long have you known Preston?' I asked.

'A long time,' he said, his voice still tight, cautious. He immediately reached for the pen he'd just put into the pot and took it out again. 'Getting on for twenty years. After he completed his specialist training up in Nottingham, he moved to London and started working at St Thomas'. I was already there; that was where I did my stint as a junior doctor. We met at a Christmas party.' He started clicking the top of the pen on and off, a nervous tic he barely seemed to be aware of as he forced himself to maintain eye contact with me. He was trying to reassure me that everything here was normal.

'What was he like?'

'Preston?' He shrugged. 'We've had a lot of laughs. He's funny, gregarious, dedicated. But he and Ellie . . .' He pushed out a smile. 'Never saw that coming.'

'In what way?'

'I mean he's punching a bit above his weight for one thing.' A second, bigger smile, as if there was nothing to see here, just a gentle ribbing of his friend. But he looked more on edge than at any point in our conversation – and his comment about Preston dating Ellie had left something in his face that looked a lot like jealousy. 'Preston just never dated that much. Ellie kind of came out of nowhere.'

'Did he ever talk about his time at university?'

'At Bristol?' He frowned. 'In what sense?'

'In any sense – his years there, what he got up to, his friends.'

'I'm sure we talked about it,' Lewellyn said, but it already felt like a dead end. He looked like he was fishing for memories, for stories he'd been told, and the fact that there were none suggested Preston hadn't ever talked to Lewellyn about what may have happened in his first year at medical school.

Lewellyn placed the pen back into the pot a second time.

Once he had, I made him wait.

'Was there anything else?' he said, the words coming out fast, a little desperate, as if he couldn't wait for this to be over.

'I just have one more question,' I said.

'Good. What's that?'

'Why are you lying to me?'

Healy

Now

Healy glanced at the tattoo on Dennis's hand for a second time and then told Maya that she could leave. There was a flash of panic on the porter's face.

Maya exited, the door clicking behind her.

'What is happening?' Dennis asked.

'Where did you get that tattoo?'

The porter looked down at his right hand, at the webbing between his thumb and his forefinger, and as he glanced up at Healy, he visibly sagged.

He knew Healy had the answer already.

'You're not from Germany, are you?' Healy asked.

Dennis shook his head.

'I worked a case a long time ago that involved Russian organized crime. I saw tattoos like that everywhere.' Healy gestured to Dennis's right hand. The tattoo was small but intricate: a rose in front of a dagger. 'It's been a while, but if I remember rightly, that means you were sent to prison before the age of eighteen.'

Dennis stared at the tattoo.

All Healy could see now was the top of his head.

'I bet you've got more under your uniform, there, right?'

The porter let out a long breath, looked up, and then pulled the collar of his white shirt away from his neck. Faded ink crept out from the top of his chest: it looked like the domes of a cathedral. The more domes there were, the more sentences a prisoner had served. Dennis had three. He let his collar go.

'Why did you lie about where you were from?'

Dennis shrugged.

'Is it to do with what happened here yesterday?'

'No,' the porter said, and he suddenly looked completely different, horrified at the idea that Healy might genuinely think he had something to do with Preston going missing. 'No, I don't know nothing about that. I am telling truth. Nothing at all.'

'So why did you lie about where you're from?'

'I am not, uh . . .' He stopped.

'You're here illegally?'

A long pause this time, and then quietly: 'Yes.'

Another long breath, and then he went to his shirt again and popped the first three buttons open, widening them into a V so Healy could see more of his chest. It was absolutely covered: as well as the domes there were stars and a spider, and from one shoulder Healy could see the ends of an epaulette too.

The tattoos were everywhere.

'I needed to leave Russia,' he said.

'Why?'

'I could not do the things Bratva ask me to do.'

Bratva were the Russian mafia.

'You mean, killing people?'

'No. I kill people.' Four words, almost whispered, like glass in his mouth. 'No one hate themselves as much as I hate.' He put a hand to his chest, his heart, his history. 'I kill men. Bad men like me. I go to prison for my sin. But I do not kill kids. When they ask me to kill children, I know I must leave.'

'So how did you get a job here?'

He swallowed. 'I have German passport.'

'A fake?'

'Yes.' He looked at Healy, an intensity to his stare that Healy imagined, a long time ago, might have made him very frightening to his enemies. But not any more. He was five years older than Healy, and he was tired, and he was broken, and eventually he seemed to feel all of that washing over him. Softly, the thumb of his left hand rubbing the tattoo, Dennis said, 'I like my life here. It is simple and it is quiet. I like working at hospital. The people are nice. I am happy. If you send me home, I am dead.'

'Well, luckily for you, pal, that's a bit above my pay grade.'

Dennis frowned. 'What does this mean?'

'It doesn't matter.' Healy came forward, tapping his pen against his pad, and, as he thought about next moves, he started to get lost in a memory, in the reason *why* he'd become so familiar with Russian prison tattoos: because Glass, the piece of shit who'd murdered his daughter, had sourced all his formaldehyde through the Russian mafia. Healy had poured over import and export documents and spent hours leafing through Interpol photographs of Russian gangsters, trying to find evidence of where he might be and who he might be interacting with – and in the end it had all been for nothing. His searching, the knowledge he'd built on the Russians, was all wasted effort. Healy had only found Leanne because of Raker.

And by the time he did, it was too late.

As he lingered on that, he thought of something else: what he'd seen at Alice and Liam's house the day before.

'I can go?' Dennis said.

Healy tuned back in. 'If I find out you're lying to me about Preston Stewart, the first call I make will be to the Border Force.'

Dennis nodded contritely. 'I understand.'

Healy gestured to the door.

The porter got up and hurried across, as if the exit might suddenly vanish. Once he was gone, Healy listened to the hum of conversation from next door. He couldn't make out the words – but he could distinguish between Raker's and Lewellyn's voices.

His thoughts started to drift again.

And then he was back in Liam and Alice's house the day before, on his knees playing with Leanne in the bath. The little girl was so beautiful. Big blue eyes, a ruffle of white-blonde hair. As he'd played there with her, bobbing a boat along the surface of the bath foam, she'd looked at him and giggled, and it had filled his heart with so much joy, he was grateful to be on his knees so his legs didn't give way.

After so many years, the memories of his Leanne, his daughter, weren't always as clear as Healy would like, but they were in that moment: he could see the younger version of himself at their old house in St Albans, driving a plastic train around the edge of the bath as his Leanne giggled and drummed her hands on the surface of the water. His daughter's hair had been white-blonde at that age too, and whenever she'd smiled at him, whenever her tiny hands had reached up to him and he'd taken them in his, it would stop Healy's world. As Leanne got older, he'd struggled to rediscover that feeling. But, in the years since, whenever he found some small piece of her to cling to, it was always that image of her as a little girl.

'This thing's going to be a handful,' Healy had said to Alice. Liam had gone downstairs to get Leanne's cup of warm milk ready, and Healy could hear him talking to Gemma.

'She is,' Alice responded. She scooped up some bubble bath and gently blew it in her daughter's direction. As the bubbles rained softly down, Leanne giggled again.

'Liam says she's still waking up a lot at night.'

'She is, yeah, but it's okay.' Alice paused, giving her daughter a look of amazement as Leanne played with the bubbles. 'I don't mind.'

'Leanne . . .' He stopped. '*My* Leanne, I mean. She basically didn't sleep for two years. Me and Gem looked like extras from *Night of the Living Dead*.'

'Gemma mentioned she wasn't a good sleeper.'

'We used to take it in turns giving her the bottle because I wanted to be there, you know? I wanted to be a part of it. But I've honestly got no idea how I functioned.'

'Yeah, that must have been tough with your job.'

'It was. I'd be getting up to feed Leanne in the dead of night, or just to cuddle her for a while – and then I'd crawl into the station a couple of hours later.'

The mention of the station, of Healy's time as a cop, of how that career had brought Alice's father into Healy's life, stalled the conversation. Alice glanced at him, the guilt written on her face, and perhaps for the first time since he'd known her, Healy felt deeply sorry for her; for the responsibility she felt she carried for the crimes of a man she'd barely known. Glass had killed her mother when Alice was two. But that didn't extinguish her father's shadow.

'I'm sorry, Alice,' Healy said.

She frowned. 'For what?'

'For how I've been with you.'

'Oh, you haven't done anything –'

'It's okay. I have. I know I have.' He looked at Leanne again. 'I've never been very good at, uh . . .' He searched for the right thing to say. 'I'm not good with words. Just ask Liam or Ciaran. Or, even better, get Gemma to give you the rundown.' Healy pushed out a smile, trying to camouflage the fact that his wife left him, and his sons checked out, because they never knew what was going on inside his head. 'The irony is, I never used to talk to them about how I felt, but I was terrible at holding my tongue too. I know I can hurt people.'

'You haven't hurt me.'

'It's okay, I know that I have. And I'm sorry. I know you're not your father. I know you've spent most of your life feeling like you're responsible for him when you're not. And I know that how I've been with you, and just how I am generally, hasn't helped.' He painted Leanne's arm with bubbles. 'None of this is you. It's all me.'

Alice blinked, tears welling in her eyes. Healy saw the bracelet she always wore slip down her wrist: it had six daisies on it and a tiny *RIP* engraved on the band itself. There was one daisy for every woman her father had kept hidden at the Dead Tracks.

She'd told Healy and Raker that it was a reminder of the monster he'd been and how she'd been born guilty.

'I was the one that appeared out of nowhere and turned your life upside down,' Alice said, wiping an eye. 'I came looking for your family because I just needed to know who you were, what you were like, how you recovered from him. I never expected to fall for Liam, let alone . . .' She looked at her daughter.

And then they went back to playing with Leanne, and afterwards they all had dinner together, and when Gemma looked at him across the table, she could tell that something had changed.

She smiled at Healy and mouthed the words *thank you*.

And, later on, when Alice was putting Leanne to sleep, and Liam and Gemma were busy talking about some TV show Healy hadn't even heard of, he went upstairs to the toilet. In Leanne's bedroom, he glimpsed Alice on a stool at the crib, gently rocking her daughter, so he didn't disturb her and headed into the bathroom. By the time he came out, Leanne was asleep and he figured Alice was downstairs.

But then he heard something in the main bedroom.

The soft creak of a floorboard.

A drawer being opened.

He stepped back from the staircase and peered around the edge of the door frame. Alice was in there, her back to Healy, leafing through some papers she had in the middle drawer of a chest.

He very nearly said hello to her, but something stopped him: her head was bowed, the papers in her hands slightly vibrating.

Alice was crying.

Eventually, she put everything back into the drawer, covering the papers with underwear. By then, Healy had backed up to the top of the stairs.

As she came out of the bedroom, he deliberately bumped into her. 'Oh, sorry, Alice,' he said, acting as if there was nothing wrong. 'I needed the toilet.'

She seemed none the wiser. 'See you downstairs.'
He headed to the bathroom and locked the door.
He waited for her to join the others.
And then he went across to the bedroom.

13

. . . 43 hours to go . . .

Lewellyn stared at me. 'I beg your pardon?'

'Why are you lying to me?'

He shook his head, apparently outraged, but there was something false about it, as if he'd pulled on a mask that didn't quite fit. 'How dare you suggest that I've –'

'You accused your friend and business partner of physically abusing his wife,' I said, cutting him dead. 'In fact, you offered me that information completely unprompted. But I'm pretty sure you don't think he's ever really laid a finger on Ellie. So the question is, why would you want me to believe that he had?'

Outside, more rain was coming – a steel-grey ceiling over the city – and as the last of the sun was swallowed up, the colour in Lewellyn's face seemed to drain away too. The spark was gone, his skin pale.

His head dropped.

I'd taken a risk, but my instincts about him had been right. Now it was a question of how much of a lie he'd told and how deep it went from here.

'Don't you want your friend found?' I asked.

'It's not that.'

'Then what is it?'

He swallowed.

'Robert?'

'I don't know what to do.'

'About what?'

'I don't want to die.'

I stopped. '"Die"? Why would you think that was going to happen?'

He swallowed again, then again, as if he was struggling to talk now, to breathe. The man he'd been when I'd first entered his office, who'd spent the last half an hour using lies and arrogance as a wall to hide behind, had completely vanished. He was on the verge of tears, somehow smaller, an animal with its belly exposed.

'Robert? Why would you think you were going to die?'

He glanced to the door, as if someone was there, listening, and then he looked at the desk, the Mac, the landline and his mobile.

He reached forward and powered off the mobile.

'What are you doing?'

He pulled the wire for the landline out of the wall.

'Robert?'

He shut down the Mac.

'*Robert?*'

A momentary pause as he waited for the Mac's screen to go dark, and then he double-checked his mobile was off.

'I'm so scared,' he muttered, his voice hushed.

I came forward in my seat. 'What are you scared of?'

No response.

'What are you scared of, Robert?'

'Not what.' He shook his head. 'Who.'

14

...43 hours to go...

He checked everything again – his Mac, his phone, the desk.

'Eight days ago, a patient came to see me,' he said quietly, all his confidence shorn. 'His name was Noah Klein. Because we're private, we have to make something called a Subject Access Request, and that gets us a summary of a medical record. His all checked out.'

'What did this Noah Klein look like?'

'His records said he was forty-nine. He was Caucasian and must have been five-ten, dark hair, dark eyes. He was medium build and in good health, had barely needed a doctor since he was a kid. A nurse took his BP, did a basic health check, and then we talked about why he'd booked an appointment with me. He said he had a deviated septum.'

'Did he?'

'No. In fact, I couldn't find any problem with his nose at all.' Lewellyn rubbed at his face. 'And then he changed.'

'Changed how?'

'He asked me how my daughter was getting on at university. It totally threw me. I said to him, "How do you know Poppy?" He said . . .' A flicker. 'He said he'd got to know her better while he'd been watching her.'

Something curdled in my gut.

'I didn't even get the chance to be angry about it. Almost as soon as he said that, he held his hand up to stop me speaking and he told me to listen to him or my daughter would be . . .' This time there was less of a flicker and more of a flinch. 'He said if I didn't do what he told me to do, he'd go to Warwick, go to

Poppy's room in her halls there, and he'd . . .' Tears welled in his eyes. 'He said he would paint the walls with her blood.'

'What did he want you to do?'

As I waited for Lewellyn's reply, at the back of my head somewhere I felt the faintest sense of recollection. It was hardly even a dot in the darkness, just a mote of light I could barely see – but it was there.

Something had set it off.

'That's the thing.' Lewellyn was talking again, voice unsteady. 'I don't really know *what* I did. He said to me, "A week today, Preston Stewart is coming in for surgery." And then he slid a card across the table to me with a URL on it. That was it. Just a URL. He said, "As soon as you get in that day, you're going to put that into your browser and hit Enter."'

'And you did?'

'Yes.'

'What was the URL?'

'It was just a long string of numbers.'

'Okay. What happened after you put it in?'

'Nothing. It went to a blank white page.'

'That was all he asked you to do?'

'Yes.'

'Have you checked in on Poppy?'

'Yes, she's fine. I've spoken to her every day since.'

I looked at the notes I'd made, thinking.

'I don't know why I told that lie about Preston,' he said. He looked diminished, the ego rinsed from him. 'The whole time you were asking me questions, all I could think about was Poppy, about keeping my mouth shut and keeping her safe. I thought maybe if I got you looking somewhere else, at something to do with Preston, where the answer was impossible to find because it never even happened . . . I don't know, I guess I just thought it was the best thing for my daughter. I'm sorry.' A second later, I watched as the panic set in. 'You can't tell anyone else.'

I held up a hand. 'I won't.'

'I mean it.'

'I know you do.'

I thought about what Lewellyn had been asked to do, about the URL made up entirely of numbers, and then about the memory I couldn't quite get at.

'Why would he want me to do that?' he said. 'Put in that address like that?'

'Because he wanted access.'

'Access to what?'

'To everything,' I said. 'All your patients, their health-care records, your staff, your security – as soon as you put in those numbers and hit Enter, you handed him the keys to the whole hospital.'

15

. . . 43 hours to go . . .

Lewellyn stared at me, horrified.

'I need to go and make some calls,' he said, standing, panicked.

'Before you do, can you log me in?'

I gestured to the Mac.

'You want me to give you access to our *computers*? The information on there is very sensit—'

'Information which is in the hands of the man who came to see you. If you're lucky, it's just this Noah Klein guy who has all your data. If you're not, everything about anything this hospital has ever done is now available online.'

He blanched.

'It's too late to worry about what's sensitive or not, Robert — and, frankly, I'm the least of your worries. You need to find Noah Klein and I can help you do that.'

His thoughts were going at a million miles per hour, he was trying to prioritize on the fly — and he knew I was right. Whether I looked around on the Mac or I didn't, the hospital's network was already compromised.

He powered the computer on.

As he did, there was a knock at the door. I opened it while Lewellyn logged me in. It was Healy.

'There,' Lewellyn said, pointing to the Mac. 'Please don't do anything that will get me into trouble.'

You're already in trouble, I thought.

But, instead, I said, 'I won't.'

I waited until he was gone and then — as I slid in at the desk and started searching the Mac – I filled Healy in on what Lewellyn had told me.

'Noah Klein,' he responded.

I looked up. 'You've heard that name before?'

'Yeah.'

I remembered the feeling I'd had earlier, as if I'd glimpsed a memory but couldn't quite get to it. Could it have been the name Noah Klein?

Healy googled him on his phone but said there were seventeen million search results. He started clicking on stories, but I told him to forget all of that for now and give me a brief overview of his interviews with the nurse and porter. As he did, I kept going on the Mac. I wasn't any kind of expert, but I knew a little, and I was searching for signs the system had been exposed.

'Should we be worried about this Dennis guy?' I asked.

'No.'

'He lied about where he was from, he's got a false passport, and he used to murder people for the Russian mob. None of those things screams *trust me*.'

'I don't think he knows anything about the disappearance.'

'Based on what?'

'It was there in his face. He basically shat himself when I recognized the tattoo. I think the only thing he knows for sure is he can't go back to Mother Russia.'

I let it go for now, opening the hard drive, going through folders, through bespoke software that had been created for The Crest and which housed patient records and information on every member of staff. To the untrained eye, there was nothing suspect. The performance seemed fine – there was no slowdown, nothing was behaving abnormally. I didn't see any rogue files, weird data, or documents that didn't belong.

Not that it really meant much.

If I was right, if the URL Lewellyn had gone to was just a way to gain entry to The Crest's network, it suggested the man we were dealing with was sophisticated. It would need an expert to find out where he was embedded, not an amateur like me.

'Go and talk to Kevin Neale,' I said to Healy.

'Okay. And what are you going to do?'

'I'm going to try and find Noah Klein.'

16

. . . 42 hours to go . . .

The security team was a two-man operation and their office was in the furthest corner of a windowless basement they shared with a supply room and a mortuary.

When I got to the door, I could see both men were inside. One was in his fifties with fair, thinning hair and a pot belly; the other was much younger and built like a weightlifter. At the far end of the office was a wall of monitors, each feed showing a different part of the hospital. On one of the screens in the middle, I could see footage being piped in from the corridor of private rooms that we'd passed through earlier on as we'd followed Lewellyn to the Octagon.

Healy was just arriving at Kevin Neale's room.

I knocked on the door to the security suite.

Both men looked up, but it was the younger of the two that got to his feet. As he opened the door, I saw he had a name badge that said PIPER.

'Can I help you?'

I explained who I was and what I was doing here. The older man, who was called Carston, spent the entire time just watching, letting Piper do the talking. It was only when we were finished that he started wagging a finger at me.

'I know you,' he said.

'You do?'

'Yeah. You were the one that found the Snatcher, right?'

He was talking about an old case I'd worked where the disappearance of a man on the London Underground had pulled me into the orbit of a psychopath the press had nicknamed 'the Body Snatcher'. As memories of what had happened back then flashed through my mind, and I remembered how the aftermath had almost cost me my life, I thought of Healy: the search for the Body Snatcher happened a year after Leanne was killed, when he was still a cop – and his decisions on that case had put the final nail in his career.

'You have a good memory,' I said.

'I was with the Met for a long time.'

Something inside me sank, but I did my best not to show it. I'd never sought out enemies in the Met, but I'd made them all the same, especially in the time after the capture of Leanne's killer, Glass. My work in finding him had revealed endemic corruption inside the organization and a deep police cover-up – and there were still cops there, even now, who hated me for ending the careers of people they'd liked.

Carston smiled. 'You look worried.'

'Well, I'm not on any Christmas card lists at the Met.'

'No, I imagine you're not.' That smile was still there. 'Look, I don't know anything about you, really, other than what I heard at the time and have read in the papers since. But I can tell you what I think of those cops you caught with their fingers in the cookie jar – they're scumbags. You know what I felt when you blew the lid off their little operation?'

I shook my head.

'Relief,' he said.

I'd met cops like Carston before, although not many. Most, even if they were broadly in favour of what I'd done, maintained a basic level of *omertà* because they didn't want to be seen as going against their own in public. But him being friendly was a stroke of luck that I was about to take full advantage of.

'I was hoping to take a look at the security footage from yesterday,' I said.

'You're welcome to, but there's nothing on it.'

I nodded. 'I heard you went through it all with Lewellyn already.'

'Yeah. He came down here and we watched all the videos together. We don't have anything. It's a total dead end.'

Like Lewellyn earlier, he seemed to sincerely believe what he was telling me, but how could there be nothing on the footage? Someone had transferred Kevin Neale to Preston's room, and Preston had vanished from the hospital entirely.

'Okay,' I said evenly, 'well, I'd still like to take a look.'

Carston opened out his hands. *Be my guest.*

'I'm also looking for some footage from eight days ago. Specifically from an appointment Lewellyn had with someone. Is that something you could find for me?'

Carston looked at Piper.

'We keep a week on the hard drives here,' the younger man said.

'Where does the older footage go?'

'To the Cloud. We'd have to download it for you.'

'Could you do that?'

'If you have a date.'

I gave him the day Noah Klein came to The Crest to see Lewellyn.

Piper sat at a computer in the corner. 'Do you want me to download footage from *all* the cameras?'

'How long will that take?'

'For a day's worth of video across the whole hospital? Hours.'

'Okay, well, let's start with the camera that has the best view of where Lewellyn does consultations with his patients.'

Piper said that was most likely to be one of the consultation rooms off the Octagon. 'He does have his own office, but that's on the floor above and he doesn't use that for patients.' Another couple of clicks of the mouse. 'There. It says it's going to take twenty minutes to download.'

'Can I look at the footage from yesterday in the meantime?'

'Do you know which camera you need?'

'Let's start with the corridor where the private rooms are.'

Piper nodded and went to work again, and then a few minutes later he turned in his chair and gestured to the central screen on the wall of monitors. It was showing a feed from the camera I'd wanted. In the corner the read-out confirmed yesterday's date, and the angle of the lens allowed me to see all along the corridor.

On the timecode it was one minute past midnight.

'Can you fast-forward it?' I said. 'Maybe stop it at seven a.m.'

Piper did as I asked.

'Is there any way I could control it myself?'

Piper looked at Carston, who nodded, and then the younger man brought the Bluetooth keyboard across and set it down under the monitor wall.

'Just use the cursors,' he explained.

I pulled out a chair and started the footage.

There was plenty of activity in the corridor – even at 7 a.m. – with nurses going back and forward to different rooms. I shifted the footage on, working out how to switch it to 2x, then 4x, 8x and 16x speed. At 7.28 a.m., I returned it back to normal speed and just watched.

At 7.33 a.m., Preston and Ellie appeared.

I'd only seen Preston before in the corporate portraits I'd found online. Apart from his face, which showed obvious signs of the car accident he'd had a couple of weeks previously, he looked in pretty good nick. Tall. Strong. Broad. Without the bruising, he would be handsome; even with it he carried himself with confidence as he chatted to Ellie and a nurse that must have stepped in when Maya was late turning up to work. Two doors from the end, the nurse directed them into the room opposite the one Kevin Neale was in. Over the next forty minutes, the same nurse came and went, returning to the room with a gown for Preston to change into, then with a blood pressure monitor, then with a coffee, presumably for Ellie. At 8.39 a.m., Lewellyn arrived for the first time. He was in there for ten minutes and then exited again and headed under the camera, to the Octagon.

Finally, at 9.03 a.m., the porter arrived.

I watched him, thinking about what Healy had found out. I'd have to give some thought as to what we'd do with the information about Dennis later on, so for now I just watched. He entered the room and then, a couple of minutes later, re-emerged, pushing the bed Preston was on out into the corridor. Preston was talking again, the porter smiling. He wheeled Preston out of shot, and Ellie headed to the day room.

I accelerated the video to the point when Dennis brought Preston back to the same room he'd collected him from. Preston's face was heavily bandaged, but I could tell it was him from his build. A short time later, Kevin Neale followed, confirming as much: he was smaller than Preston. He was taken into the room we'd seen him in on the way in.

So they were definitely returned to the right rooms.

The question was, what happened next?

This was the twenty minutes that both Healy and I had zeroed in on. Whatever had happened at the hospital yesterday, it had happened here.

I leaned in, pulse quickening.

Doctors and nurses came and went. The porter came back for another patient. Staff stopped to have conversations in the corridors. A family arrived. And then, at 11.22 a.m., the corridor emptied and no one came into shot for a full five minutes until – at 11.27 a.m. – Maya finally appeared from the direction of the day room, Ellie walking beside her. They entered. Even though there was no way to see inside Preston's room, I knew this was the point at which Maya would have started to unwrap his bandaging.

Except it wasn't Preston in that room.

It was Kevin Neale.

And I didn't understand how.

On-screen, Maya suddenly hurried out, checked Kevin Neale's

room opposite, and then walk-ran under the camera, down towards the Octagon. A few seconds later, Ellie came to the door, frowning. She had no idea what was going on but didn't look particularly concerned at this point.

I watched the next twenty minutes play on double speed, trying to get through it as quickly as possible. Lewellyn turned up, so did the porter and a senior nurse. In turn, they all checked Kevin Neale's empty room. At one point, Ellie had what looked like a heated conversation with Lewellyn in the doorway of the room, and then Lewellyn turned to the staff who were unfortunate enough to be there and tore into them. It all backed up what Ellie had told me.

After that, Ellie was returned to the day room.

'Told you there was nothing,' Carston said.

I could have done without the men looking over my shoulder, but there wasn't much I could do about it, so I rewound the video and played it again on 4x speed. Once I got to the twenty minutes in which the disappearance must have happened, I switched back to normal speed and watched the same things play out.

At 11.22, just as I'd seen the first time, the corridor cleared.

I leaned into the screen. This was the five minutes before Maya and Ellie arrived at the room, the five minutes when no one else came into shot – no staff, no visitors. Logically, there should have been nothing in this period to worry about, but something about the lull in activity felt incongruous: either side of these five minutes, there was a constant flow of movement. Inside the five minutes, it was like someone had hit Pause.

I rewound the video to 11:22:01.

What isn't right here?

And then, as I pushed Play again, I spotted something.

It was so small, such a minor detail, that I had to rewind it a few times to even be sure I was right. The third time, Carston appeared at my shoulder.

'What are you seeing?'

'Look,' I said, pointing to the corner of the screen.

And as Carston saw it too, as he pulled out a chair and perched himself on the edge of it, he very softly said, 'What the hell is *that?*'

Healy

Now

Healy entered Kevin Neale's room.

He was sitting up in bed, headphones on, watching something on an iPad, still heavily bandaged on his face.

Healy cleared his throat.

Neale looked up from his iPad and smiled, presumably expecting a nurse – and, by the wattage of the smile, a nurse he'd taken a shine to.

The smile didn't last. 'Yes?'

Healy introduced himself, telling Neale what he was here for. 'I was wondering if we could start by going over your recollections of what happened yesterday.' He grabbed his notebook from his jacket, looking at Neale, waiting for some kind of response. 'Mr Neale?'

'I don't really remember a lot.'

His voice was muted by whatever had been done to his nose, his words a little soft, the inflection slurred. Healy shifted the chair in closer. 'I totally understand. You were coming around from an operation. What did you have done?'

'I had chronic sinusitis.'

'Oh, right,' Healy said, as if that explained everything, but although he knew what sinusitis was, he had no idea how Lewellyn would have attempted to fix it. He changed tack, trying to get Neale to warm up. 'What is it you do for work?'

'I'm an architect.'

'Is there a Mrs Neale?'

'No.'

'Kids?'

'No.'

'A single man, huh?'

'Yes,' Neale said, as if being single in your forties was the greatest thing in the world. But his smile felt painted on and it didn't last very long.

'So, like I say,' Healy continued, keeping his tone upbeat, 'we're trying to figure out what happened yesterday and you're key to us doing that.'

Neale straightened a little in his bed.

Interview 101, Healy thought. *Make them feel important.*

'It's all a bit of a fog,' Neale said.

'Maybe just run me through what you *do* remember.'

He started going over the timeline of events, all the way up to coming out of surgery. 'In recovery, I kind of drifted in and out,' he said. 'Mostly out, to be honest. And then they brought me up here and I slept for a while. Next thing I remember, people were running around panicking. It was only later that I was told a little bit about why.'

'Who told you?'

'One of the nurses. Maya. She said she wasn't supposed to.'

'Mr Lewellyn had asked the staff not to speak about it?'

'Yes. She didn't tell me much, she just said it was to do with Preston.'

'Did you know Preston?'

'No. Never met him before in my life. Maya just mentioned his name.'

Healy could understand why the patients wouldn't have been told very much about what had gone on yesterday, but he didn't think it was suspicious or worrying that Maya had shared some information with Neale. Given everything that had happened here, it would be normal to want to talk about it, because talking about it was a way to try to rationalize it.

'There is . . .' Neale stopped. 'Look, I don't know if this even matters, but ever since yesterday I've been thinking about something weird that happened. I'm just not sure if it was real or if I hallucinated it.'

'What is it?'

'They'd pumped me full of so many drugs . . .'

'What did you see, Kevin?'

He paused, frowned. 'I think I remember a man being in here.'

'Someone came into your room?'

'Yes.' Neale's eyebrows knitted together as he tried to pull the memory back towards him. 'After they brought me up from recovery.'

'Are you talking about *this* room?'

'Yes.'

'Not the one across the hall?'

'No, it was definitely this room – I remember there was the same view out of the window as now. Plus, I don't ever remember being taken to Preston's room. All I remember is being brought here from recovery, and then suddenly I was waking up across the hall.'

'And this person you saw – was it a member of staff?'

'I don't know. I was so out of it. But he asked me if I was awake.'

A low-level alarm hummed through Healy's body.

'What did he look like?'

'It was hard to tell because, like I say, I could barely keep my eyes open. White, I think. Black hair. Dark eyes. He looked like he was maybe in his forties but, as I keep saying, I was so groggy.' A beat. 'Do you think it might have been real, then?'

'You said this guy asked you if you were awake?'

'Yes, and I sort of moaned that I was.'

'And then what?'

'Then he did something to my drip.'

Now it was more than just a low-level alarm Healy could feel.

'It was like he increased my pain medication or something

because all of a sudden I just felt myself go. Before that, I was tired – really, *really* tired – but I was in and out the whole time. After he came in to see me, everything went black. I asked Maya if anyone had been in while I was out, and she said no. That's why I figured it was just the drugs making me see things.'

Healy looked down at his notes again, his eyes drifting back to that name.

Noah Klein.

'I'm sorry I can't be more help,' Neale said.

'No, you've been a big help,' Healy responded, still looking at the same name. Why was it so familiar to him?

He was outside in the corridor, heading down to the Octagon to interview some of the other staff, when the name came back to him again, that sense of familiarity – of knowing Noah Klein from *somewhere* – and this time the feeling wouldn't shift.

Where the hell do I know him from?

Why would that name be so –

He stopped.

The answer had finally come to him.

Healy broke into a sprint.

17

. . . 42 hours to go . . .

I played and rewound the footage, checking it over and over again.

As the timecode hit 11:22:01 – the start of the five-minute lull in activity in the hospital corridor – something happened to the read-out in the bottom corner of the screen. It glitched. The glitch was so minor and so quick I'd failed to notice it at first. But it was there the whole time. And once I'd seen it, I couldn't unsee it.

Except it wasn't that that I pointed Carston towards.

It was something else.

In one of the windows in the corridor, I could see a reflection of the inside of the room opposite. This wasn't the room that Preston had been in, or Kevin Neale. It wasn't even the room itself that was the relevant part. It was the reflection of it.

As the timecode glitched, the reflection changed.

Before the glitch, I could see into the room: the bed, a painting on the wall, a window looking out over the hospital's garden – all of it reflected in the glass.

After the glitch, the door to the room was suddenly shut.

This is why Klein wanted to access the hospital's systems.

He's edited their CCTV.

I gave myself a moment, bringing it all together in my head: the man calling himself Noah Klein had layered a five-minute chunk of video over the top of the real footage from yesterday; the footage that would have told me exactly what had happened to Preston Stewart. If I'd had more time, I might have been able to track the IP address he'd worked from – the address from which he'd uploaded the substitute five minutes. I knew people who could do that for me. But we were against the clock already, and I didn't want to wait around for someone to tell me what I already suspected: the IP address was untraceable.

I looked at Carston. 'Did you check the footage from *all* the other cameras yesterday?'

'Every single one,' Carston said.

'Same deal?'

'Yeah. Preston Stewart and Kevin Neale never leave their rooms.'

Which meant Noah Klein must have plotted an escape route and then altered *all* the footage of those five minutes in all the areas adjacent to Preston's room. It didn't explain how no one at the hospital had seen Preston exiting the hospital with their own eyes – but it explained why no one could find any evidence of it afterwards.

'Are there blueprints for the hospital layout?' I asked.

Carston frowned. 'Why?'

'Someone came for Preston yesterday, moved Kevin Neale to his room, and then walked, carried or wheeled Preston out. I need to try to zero in on how. Your footage isn't going to tell us, because it's been edited, but we might be able to get –'

'CCTV from the buildings outside the hospital.'

I nodded. 'Exactly.'

'Leave it with us,' Carston said. He was getting a taste for it now, the buzz of a case – dormant for so long – in his veins. Now I was going to make the most of it. Requisitioning video from street cameras was a nightmare because it meant dealing with the council, shops and private homeowners without having any legal recourse to make them cooperate. But it wasn't impossible – and out there Klein wasn't going to be able to disappear in the same way he had at The Crest. Gaining access to the hospital's systems was one thing; Klein vanishing himself from every camera on every building in London was another.

I looked at Piper: 'Is that other footage ready?'

'From eight days ago?' He went to check the computer. 'Yes.'

'Can you push it across to here?'

He grabbed the keyboard back, and then, thirty seconds later, the video he'd pulled from the Cloud – of Lewellyn taking Klein to one of the rooms in the Octagon – was ready for me.

Like the previous video, it started at 00:00:01, so I fast-forwarded it to 7 a.m., then 8 a.m., and then 9 a.m., looking for Lewellyn. He appeared for the first time at 9.36 a.m. with a female patient. After that, he saw women all morning. Early afternoon, he returned from reception with his first male patient, but it wasn't Noah Klein; this man was in his seventies and accompanied by his wife.

I watched on, but there was nothing else to see. Once Lewellyn was done with the husband and wife and had walked them out, he didn't come back to the Octagon.

Klein must have done the same thing here.

I rolled the footage back to the early morning and went through it again, this time focusing not on people or staff, but on periods when there were lulls.

At 1.27 p.m., I found it.

Another timecode glitch.

For fifty-five seconds, no one came into shot, and then there was another tiny glitch and people started to appear at the nurse's station again. Twenty-two minutes later, as the last of the nurses left, heading in the direction of theatre, the timecode glitched again. For one minute and three seconds, no one appeared in shot, then there was yet another glitch. I replayed it again, but it was pretty clear what had happened.

Noah Klein had edited over his arrival and departure.

Shit.

Carston and Piper brought a flooring plan across. As Piper unrolled it, Carston looked at the paused image on-screen. 'I take it you haven't found him?'

'No. Same deal as before.'

'Well, here's the layout of the hospital.'

I got up and looked at it, Carston tapping a finger to the room allocated to Preston, and then the one opposite that Kevin Neale had been using.

I leaned closer to the blueprint.

On the western side of the hospital, where Kevin Neale's room was, there was the walled garden. On the eastern side, where Preston's room was, there was something else – but on the blueprint I couldn't tell exactly what.

'This rectangle here,' I said. 'What's that?'

'That's part of the mortuary.'

'It sticks out of the side of the building on the eastern wall?'

'Yes.'

'Preston's room was on the first floor, right?'

'Yes.'

'And how high is the mortuary roof?'

It didn't take Carston long to catch up, but as he looked from the blueprint to me, it seemed like he was trying to work out if I was serious.

'You think our mystery man climbed out of the *window*?'

'Is it possible?'

'What, with a heavily anaesthetized patient in tow?'

'But is it possible?'

Carston's eyes went to the blueprint. 'Yeah, I mean, it's *technically* possible.'

'The mortuary roof is under the first-floor windows?'

'Yes.'

So he could have got out on to the roof, and then escaped via the alley that ran parallel to the east of the hospital. Getting Preston out of the window would have been challenging, though, especially as he was basically a dead weight. And that was before you factored in the process of actually walking him away from the scene. It felt like too much for one man to cope with.

But with help . . .

'You don't seriously think that's what happened, do you?'

I looked at Carston. 'How else did he exit without any of the staff seeing?'

There *was* no other way. Unless multiple members of staff at both ends of the hospital had chosen to remain completely silent about someone walking an anaesthetized patient past them, this was the only route that felt credible. Hard as it would have been to do, if there had been Klein and one other person it could have worked.

Someone knocked at the door.

Piper went to open it and, from the doorway, Healy looked in. His gaze moved from the wall of monitors to the blueprint of the hospital, and then to Carston and Piper.

'Can we help you?' Piper said, an edge to his voice.

'It's okay.' I held up a hand. 'He's with me.'

'Raker, we need to talk.'

Healy waved me towards him, stepping back out of the room. I went to the door and pulled it shut behind me.

'What is it?' I said, eyeing him.

He was flushed: he'd obviously run most of the way down here. But beyond the exhaustion, there was something else.

'Are you okay?'

He blinked.

'Healy?'

I reached a hand to his arm. He flinched at my touch but didn't move away. Instead, his gaze dropped to the floor.

'What's happened?'

'Noah Klein,' he said softly.

'What about him?'

He looked up. 'I know why we recognize his name.'

Naughton

Now

They left the station early because they knew there would be traffic.

They couldn't afford to be late.

Not for this.

In the car, they were quiet for a while, both of them lost in their own thoughts, adrenalin pumping. But then Phillips – in the passenger seat, the casework on his lap, hundreds of pages of history and horror and pain under his fingers – turned to Rosa Naughton and said, 'Did you get the links I sent?'

Naughton nodded. 'Yes.'

'You watched the videos?'

'Yes.'

'All of them?'

'Yes.'

'Good.' Phillips's eyes went back to the road. 'That's good.'

Naughton hadn't just watched them. She'd pored over them, rewound and pressed Play on them tens, maybe hundreds, of times. At 3 a.m., she was still up, face illuminated by her laptop in the shadows of her house. In her twenty years with the Met, Naughton had interviewed hundreds of suspects, she'd been to jails countless times to speak to prisoners, and the vast majority of them weren't that sophisticated. Some handled pressure better than others, but even the best liars eventually got themselves caught.

With this guy, it was different.

She knew he was a liar – he'd lied in his work, he'd lied to the people he'd got close to, he'd lied to the detectives who'd eventually arrested him. She was guessing he'd spent his years in prison lying to everyone in there too. Lying was what he did. In that respect, he was no different from many of the other men who'd sat across the table from her and tried to manoeuvre their way out of the corner they'd been backed into. Except there was one big difference between him and all the other liars.

He was just so good at it.

Naughton had never seen someone like him, someone so adept at manipulation and misdirection; someone who – without you double-checking every line of testimony, every witness statement – could convince you of anything. When Phillips had brought Naughton in, the first thing he'd warned her about was the lying – but there was hearing it, and then there was seeing it. She'd studied the casework for days leading into this. She knew the original investigation back to front. But even last night, as she'd rewatched the videos again, she'd still had to return to the paperwork to verify what she already knew. She would find herself listening to him and casually accepting his version of events, because every word out of his mouth was so convincing. And then a light would flick on, and she'd realize he'd just lied, and she'd have to go back to find the real version of events.

'Are you okay?' Phillips asked her.

She must have looked worried.

'I'm good,' she said.

'It's okay to be nervous. I've been a cop for twenty-six years,' Phillips said, his voice a little muted, his soft Scottish accent barely audible above the rumble of the engine, 'and the thought of him still makes me uneasy.' His gaze went out to the streets, London's buildings, its people and their movements all disguised behind a skein of rain. 'This case . . . it's the one that I think about most.'

Naughton glanced at the detective superintendent, his pale reflection painted in the window as he continued to watch the city pass. She didn't know all that much about him – other than, as a DSU, if it had been any other prisoner, this would have been way below his pay grade – but she'd observed him from a distance, so she knew he was smart, that people liked him, and that he'd broken some big cases before climbing the tree. But she'd also heard the rumours, the persistent whispers that didn't ever go away. The ones that said he'd covered for officers who'd been accused of corruption – and, in his private life, had once laid hands on his wife. Naughton didn't know whether any of that was true; all she knew was that Phillips oversaw the Major Investigation Team she was part of, and last week, when he came looking for someone to work with him, he selected her.

She'd decided against trying to figure out why he'd chosen her above some of the others in her team, because when she started digging into the casework, into the victims, into the people that had orbited the crimes, she began to worry the answer was cynical: that a very long time ago, Naughton had been close to Colm Healy.

And Healy was central to all of this.

'Have you got any questions?'

She glanced at Phillips. 'I don't think so, sir.'

'Okay, good. When we get there, let me kick things off. I know this man about as well as anyone can ever really know him, and that's basically not at all – other than through what we managed to prove in court. He hasn't told us why he wants to meet all of a sudden – not really. He just says it's to do with what went on back then, so I don't know . . .' Phillips paused, flipping open the front page of the file and looking at the face of the monster they were on their way to see. 'My guess is he's probably going to try and negotiate.'

'"Negotiate", sir?'

'He's going to try and trade with us. Maybe offer us something he didn't tell us back in the day. We managed to convict him, but there were a lot of things we had to leave hanging. You would have seen that in the paperwork.'

'I do have one question, sir.'

He looked at Naughton.

'What do we call him?'

Phillips seemed to understand and moved forward in the file. He passed pages of interview transcripts, crime-scene analysis and forensic inventories. He flicked through the victim profiles and, as he did, as she saw their photographs, Naughton started to list the women who were found at the Dead Tracks in her head. Isabelle Connors. April Brunel. Jayne Rickards. Kate Norton. Erica Muller.

Leanne Healy.

And then there was the page with the list of his pseudonyms.

His birth name he almost never used because he hated it so much and, in his mind it was synonymous with the misery of his childhood. In interviews, he told detectives that the name he preferred was Dr Glass, a nickname given to him by the Russian mafia. They were who he'd sourced his chemicals through, and because all they really knew about him was that he was a plastic surgeon – and because he would turn up to meetings with them in a mask – zeroed in on a smooth piece of obsidian he wore on a chain around his neck.

Later, though, after his arrest, the police found evidence of over forty fake identities in his house: passports, driving licences, birth certificates, documents of employment, bank accounts. He said the identities gave him power because he could become anyone at any time, and no one would ever quite know who he was. There were so many different names that, unlike with the victims, Naughton could only recall a small fraction of them – four or five at most.

'I suspect he'll want you to call him Glass,' Phillips said.

Naughton nodded. 'Any idea why this one has been highlighted?' She gestured to an alias halfway down the list which had been coloured by a fluorescent marker.

'Oh.' Phillips looked across at her. 'That one's always been a question mark. It's the only name we didn't find any physical evidence of at his house.'

'So why's it on the list as a pseudonym for him?'

'Because it was a name he used for himself – just the once – in an interview we did with him back then. We hadn't even turned the tape on yet – which is why you won't find it on any of the audio – but I remember he asked me what I thought of it, whether it suited him better than Glass, and then he never mentioned it again.'

'Do you think it's relevant?'

'To our visit today?' Phillips shrugged. 'I doubt it. It was just more of his usual shite. It's all games, all the time, with him – until it isn't.'

Naughton looked down at the list again, at the highlighted name, and tried to commit the alias to memory, just in case.

The name was Noah Klein.

DAY ONE
Part Two

18

. . . 41 hours to go . . .

I told Healy to head home.

He didn't fight me on it, just nodded, wiped his eyes and left. He wanted to be here. He wanted to find out what was going on and why a connection to a crime that had ripped his entire life apart fourteen years ago had just landed in our laps. But he also knew he wasn't thinking clearly. His mind was ablaze with questions.

That was what Leanne's murder would always be.

All his sorrow, all his loss, all his anger.

In truth, I had very little recollection of the name Noah Klein. It was a minor footnote in a case full of false identities and dead ends, but it must have lodged somewhere, half-hidden, at the back of my head for it to spark into life, even if that spark had been small. Healy had been closer to everything: the paperwork, the case, the corruption, the emotional trauma of our search. He'd studied the names on that list of aliases all those years ago. He'd pored over the pages of the case then, and had done so many times in the years since.

In a lot of ways, Glass's actions had defined his life.

After he left, I finished the rest of the interviews. None of the other employees could fill in any gaps about what had happened yesterday. No one remembered anything about the man who'd come to see Lewellyn just over a week ago either. Lewellyn's loose physical description – a white male, dark hair, five-ten, late forties – was too vague to be helpful, and among the hospital staff, the name Noah Klein was a dead end.

I didn't believe in coincidences, especially within the confines of a missing persons case – so the choice of Klein as an alias felt like a deliberate tactic. It meant that, whoever this man was, he must have known that name would eventually connect him to the little-used pseudonym of the psychopath who'd murdered Leanne and eight other women. The question was why? What did any of it have to do with Preston Stewart? And something else too: how could Noah Klein – or whatever his real name was – have possibly predicted that it would be Healy and me turning up here today, not someone else? I wasn't the only investigator in the city – Ellie could have hired anyone.

Except that was the thing.

Ellie *didn't* hire just anyone.

She hired me.

I felt a murmur of disquiet as I headed back down to the basement and then out of a side door that Carston and Piper had left open for me. As I emerged into the rain, I let the water hit my face, trying to align my thoughts. Ellie was an actress. She was a *brilliant* actress. Could she have lied to me? Could it all have been a performance?

But to what end?

If she was working with Klein, it would explain how he was able to get Preston out of his room and through a first-floor window. My suspicion was that the abduction was a two-person job, and Ellie had been in and around the hospital the whole time. But why would she want her husband to vanish? And why would she team up with Klein? Who was he to her?

And then there was the question that worried me more than all of that: was this person just inspired by Glass – or had he actually been in contact with him?

Glass was in a high-security prison in Berkshire and had been for nearly a decade and a half, and visits to him were highly restricted and had to be directly signed off by the governor. The last I'd heard, every request from the media to interview him had been turned down, much to Glass's frustration. I'd seen an article in the papers a few years ago on how he planned to take the government to court, insisting that the excessive control the prison had over his visitor list infringed his human rights – although I'd heard no more since. But while no media got in, Glass had still received *some* visitors, most of whom were groupies. Much in the same way that notorious killers like Ted Bundy and Richard Ramirez had got hundreds of letters, especially from women, the stories were that Glass got sackfuls of mail from his admirers.

Could Klein have been one of them?

Could Ellie?

It seemed pretty outlandish, given that she had one of the most recognizable faces on TV, and I still instinctively felt that everything she'd told me was, from her perspective, a true account of what had gone on. But that didn't change the fact that I didn't believe in coincidences *or* that she was the one who'd hired me.

Unless . . .

I pictured Alice-Leigh Reddy.

She hadn't seen her father since she was two, barely recalled a thing about him, and had spent sixteen years in care after he killed her mother. She'd stood in my kitchen twenty months ago crying her eyes out, and had told me and Healy that she hated her father. His crimes had had nothing to do with her, but she'd carried them nonetheless.

I'd believed her.

Healy had too, even if he'd found the familial bind that would always tether Alice to Glass harder to process and get past. But the timing couldn't be denied.

Alice had entered our lives.

Now Glass was back too.

I put all the questions aside for a moment and refocused on the alleyway. If I was right, this had been Noah Klein's escape route the day before, with Preston in tow, and perhaps a second person too. The mortuary, as I'd seen on the blueprints, protruded from the side of the hospital – a brick square with a sloped roof – the alleyway feeding around it. Directly above, on the first floor, was the window to Preston's room.

I wheeled a dumpster up against the outside wall of the morgue. Climbing up on to it, I grabbed the edge of the tiled roof and then hauled myself up. Through the window to Preston's empty room, I could now see all the way into the corridor beyond, staff passing back and forth between the Octagon and reception. I could see a couple of other things too: one was the window itself. It opened by sliding up and down, with a latch fixed to the outside wall acting as a stopper, preventing the window from going all the way up. Like most upper-level rooms in hospitals and hotels, the idea was to stop people from falling out, accidentally or otherwise. Once the frame hit the latch, there was only enough space to slide an arm through.

Except the stopper had been tampered with.

It was hanging off the wall, attached by a single screw, so the window, when opened, would have bypassed the broken stopper entirely and gone all the way to the top. I lifted the window from the outside just to be certain and then held it in place at its furthermost point.

Now it wasn't just an arm you could get through the gap.

It was a whole person.

The stopper had been dismantled from the outside – there would have been no way to do it from inside the room – which meant Noah Klein, or perhaps someone he was working with, had got on to this roof in the hours or days before the two patients came in for surgery, and unscrewed the latch. There was something else out here too: directly under the window, three of the roof tiles had cracked.

Something had landed on them.

Or some*one*.

Someone like a recently anaesthetized patient.

I got down off the roof and wheeled the dumpster back to

where I'd found it, then headed along the alleyway to the front end of the hospital. There was a gate topped with three lines of barbed wire preventing anyone from accessing this part of the hospital site from the Fulham Road, but something was wrong here as well: the slide bolts fixed to the top and bottom had been removed entirely, the parts left on the ground.

The gate came towards me.

Moving out on to the Fulham Road, I looked at the front of the hospital, and then left and right at the businesses either side. There was a camera on a shopfront on the other side of the street from where I was, but it was a long way away. I headed inside a newsagent next door and saw that they had a camera above the counter. It was facing in the direction of the street – out towards the shop's front window – so it was possible it might have caught Klein, Preston and a third person if they'd headed this way.

The owner wandered out from a back room and I told him what I was doing next door, and then asked if I could look at yesterday's footage.

'No point, mate,' he said.

'Why?'

'I opened up at five a.m. yesterday and all the power was off. Must have gone in the night. I called the electricity board and they said it looked like a – what do you call it? – localized thing. They sent some guy down here and he said the wires had been cut.'

'Cut where?'

'At the main cabinet down the road. The hospital's got a generator, so they were all right. But the rest of us?' The man shrugged. 'All our power was off until six p.m.'

'So every camera in the street was out yesterday?'

'Yeah,' the man said. 'Every single one.'

19

. . . 40 hours to go . . .

When Healy answered his door, I could see he'd been crying.

His flat was on the third floor of a six-storey block in Lewisham and, although he'd been living here for over a year, I'd never been inside before.

As he eased the door open, he didn't greet me, didn't say anything, just headed back along a short hallway that led into a living room. Off to my left was a small bathroom; to the right was a kitchen. One of the cupboards was open in there, revealing a bank of empty glasses. Next to the bathroom was a bedroom, and then I was in the living room: like the rest of the flat it was tiny and cramped, barely big enough for a single sofa, a TV cabinet and a table and chairs. The best part was the view, which took in the ragged rooftops of south London.

Healy collapsed on to the sofa.

On the floor next to him was an open bottle of Jack Daniel's.

He saw me looking at it and said, 'I don't need a lecture.'

I perched on one of the chairs, saying nothing.

He stared out of the window for a moment, like he was searching for answers there, and then sank the entire contents of the glass.

'What did you find out?' he said, playing with the empty glass.

'There's nothing on the hospital feed because he edited over all footage of himself, and he cut the electricity to the street yesterday so we're not going to get anything from surrounding shops or businesses. I think I'm right, though: he took Preston out through the window of that room, on to the roof of the mortuary and down into the alley, almost certainly with help. Given what Kevin Neale said, I suspect that he upped Neale's pain meds so he blacked out, then wheeled him across to Preston's room.'

'But why bother making the switch? If he'd just left Kevin Neale where he was, he'd have got the same outcome – no Preston. What did the theatrics achieve?'

It was a good point and one I'd been thinking about on the journey over here. 'I'm just guessing at this stage,' I said, 'but I don't reckon it was part of the original plan. I reckon it was a spur-of-the-moment decision to put Neale in Preston's room.'

'Based on what?'

'It's a lot of effort to get a man Preston's size out of a window and down into an alleyway, even with help, so once he was outside on the roof, I reckon there was a hold-up. The roof tiles on the mortuary back that up – they're cracked, not smashed, which suggests a heavy, low-impact weight was resting against them, possibly for a while. Moving Preston was hard, awkward work, and it took them much longer than they thought it would – and the whole time the clock was ticking. So while Person Two continues to deal with Preston out on that roof, Klein goes back inside and moves Kevin Neale to Preston's room because that claws him *back* some time. Not much, but enough. I mean, think about it: unlike Preston, who had Ellie in the hospital with him, Neale had no guests. He's a single man, no kids. No family were going to be turning up to his empty room asking questions about his whereabouts. Plus, Maya told you that there was a problem with Neale's dressing in recovery, so if the nurses looked in at Neale's empty room they'd probably just have assumed he was still on his way up from recovery. Meanwhile, across the hallway, no questions were being asked by anyone – not the staff, not Ellie – about Preston or where he was, because as far as they were concerned, he was *right there* in his room. Except that wasn't Preston, it was Neale. And outside, Klein was back on that roof with his accomplice using that time he'd clawed back to get Preston down into the alleyway. And by the point at which Ellie realized it *wasn't* Preston, all of that just worked to Klein's advantage too: while everyone was inside, running around in a panic, Klein was using the confusion to haul Preston out on to the street.'

'Yeah, okay, but why take Preston at the hospital like that? Why go to all that trouble, when this Noah Klein guy could just have grabbed him at home, or when he was out? I mean, from what you said, Preston liked his booze – it would have been easier to wait for him to get trolleyed, and bundle him into the boot of a car.'

'Because Noah Klein had total control at the hospital. He had access to The Crest's entire security system thanks to Lewellyn, so he could go in afterwards and erase all trace of himself. There's no CCTV footage of him anywhere. I looked. No one knows this guy, no one remembers him – other than a general description. If he grabs Preston off the street, it's different. There's nine hundred thousand cameras in London. He's going to get caught on one of them, however careful he is – and he wouldn't be able to edit it.'

'So just do it at Preston's house.'

'If he does it there, he's got Matt to worry about. Ellie too, assuming we think what she's told us so far is the truth.'

Healy poured himself another drink. '*Do* you?'

'I can't say for certain, but my gut says we can trust her.'

'It would make more sense if she was involved.'

'It would fit better, I agree, because it would help to explain why she hired me given that she knows my history with Glass.'

'Exactly. She knew we'd make the connection to Noah Klein.'

'Yeah. But what does she get out of doing that?'

'I don't know.' He looked into his glass, watching the liquid slosh around, and then downed the lot. 'All I know is she's an actress. She acts.'

'I think she's genuine.'

'She lies for a living.'

'I don't think she's lying to us.'

'So you can't ever be wrong, is that it?'

There was a difference in his voice now, a tremor of artificiality that felt like it was disguising something else.

He glanced at me. 'What?'

'What's going on, Healy?'

'Nothing,' he said, frowning, as if he genuinely had no idea what I was talking about.

'Are you sure?'

'What, you think I don't know my own mind?'

I thought of what he'd said about Ellie, and then about something else – the one person in all of this that he hadn't mentioned yet.

'Is it Alice?' I said.

'What?'

'Are you worried that she might be involved?'

'No.'

Too quick.

He filled another glass.

'Yeah,' he said softly.

I eyed him again, trying to get another read on him; trying to see if there was a reason he'd hold off even mentioning Alice's name in relation to this. 'I don't spend as much time around her as you do,' I said. 'The few times I've talked to her, she's seemed authentic, but there's no denying that the timing is a worry. We've only known her for a year and a half. Now this.'

'I agree.'

'So is there anything else I should know about her?'

'No.'

'She hasn't raised your suspicions in any other way?'

'No.' His head stayed down, his eyes on the glass.

'Healy?'

And then in a voice so hushed I could barely even hear it, he said, 'This nightmare will never end for me, will it?' He sniffed;

used his shoulder to brush his face. I was still lingering on what he'd said about Alice, and whether he was being entirely honest with me. But then he finally dragged his eyes up to mine. There were tears in them, his suffering so stark it was hard to even look at – and everything else simply dropped away. 'When you captured Glass that day at the Dead Tracks, why didn't you just cut his fucking throat?'

I stared at Healy, unsure what to say. I wasn't a killer, so I was never going to cut anyone's throat. I didn't take lives. If I started doing that, I became what I abhorred. But the impact of that day, of the decisions I took then and in the hours after, were all ripples on a pond that had never quite stilled. Fourteen years on, Glass – whether he was directly involved in this or not – was still haunting us. His actions were still ripples on that same pond, overlapping with ours.

'What if it *is* him behind all of this?' Healy said.

'Then he's working with someone on the outside and we need to find out why: why he chose Klein, who Klein really is – and what all of this has to do with Preston.'

'And how do we do that?'

'Well, first, you need to stop drinking.'

His cheeks coloured. 'I said, don't lecture me.'

'I'm not lecturing you. How much you drink, how much you smoke, what you do or don't do with your life outside the cases I'm working and that I've asked you to be a part of, I don't give a shit about. But right now, I need your head clear.'

He looked at the glass, tilted it again, swirled the booze around the inside of it. 'I don't even remember the last thing I said to her.' He looked up. More tears. 'Just some argument about something. All I can see is her face, the anger she had for me before she walked out the door. I wish I hadn't been so blind back then.'

I leaned closer to him. 'You loved Leanne.'

'Then why didn't I show her enough?'

I tried to think what to say, tried to come up with some line that would act as a salve. But every word I could think of I'd already said to him, many times over. So, instead, I just watched him quietly break his heart, the pieces of him falling to the floor, and once he was done, he wiped his eyes and hauled himself to his feet.

'If this is him,' he said, 'if he's behind this . . .'

I waited, watching him.

'There'll be no mistakes this time.'

I frowned in a failed attempt to defuse his anger, to make him confront the insinuation he'd just made and see it for its folly.

But soon it wasn't even an insinuation.

It was a promise.

'If he's behind this,' he said, walking away from me, heading towards the bedroom, 'if he's hurt someone else, there'll be no mistakes. This time I will kill him.'

20

. . . 39 hours to go . . .

We arrived at Preston Stewart's home an hour later.

I pulled up at the solid oak gates of a huge Georgian townhouse on a long road full of multimillion-pound properties, buzzed down my window and used a keycode on the intercom that Matt had given me.

Ahead, the gates slowly began to fan open.

I edged through, on to a loose stone driveway that went all the way around to the back of the house – via an archway – to a courtyard. The Mercedes I'd been in this morning – as we'd taken Ellie out to the airfield – was already parked up.

The house was beautiful, built from warm sandstone brick, the sash windows sitting within a sea of vines that climbed from the corner of the house all the way up to the opposite end. The back garden extended away from us, down to a stream and a sweep of fields, and as I took it all in I understood why Ellie might prefer returning here than going to her place in London. It wasn't just that the press were in Holland Park the whole time, it was that we were only eight miles from the city here and it felt more like eighty.

We got out and headed to a back door, which had been left ajar.

Immediately inside was a kitchen, pristine and expensive, the low ceilings and appliances giving it a farmhouse feel. Matt was sitting at the table, a steaming mug of tea in one hand, a laptop open. He nodded at me, and then his eyes went to Healy, taking him in for the first time.

I introduced them.

'You find much at the hospital?' Matt asked.

'Have you ever heard the name Noah Klein?'

He frowned. 'No.'

'You don't remember Ellie or Preston mentioning that name?'

'No, doesn't a ring a bell. Who is he?'

'That's what we're trying to work out.'

I looked around the kitchen. Sitting on a shelf, next to a pot plant, was a small photograph frame with a heart carved into its edge.

It was Ellie and Preston.

I took it off the shelf. It was from their wedding day. Ellie looked stunning in a simple strapless dress, Preston handsome in a black suit with subtle maroon stitching. They'd been photographed somewhere high up on Gibraltar Rock, the skies blue behind them, the tip of the peninsula pointing across the strait to Africa.

'What about the name Alice-Leigh Reddy?' I said to Matt.

I saw Healy glance at me.

'No, never heard of her either.'

I put the photograph back.

'You said to me earlier that you told Ellie to go to the cops?'

'Yes,' he said simply.

'When she told you she didn't want to, do you have any idea what made her pick up the phone to me?'

He shrugged. 'She asked me to dig around and find some names of people who did private work and who we could trust to be discreet.'

'So it was you that suggested me?'

'Don't flatter yourself,' he said. 'I came up with a long list, including some ex-army friends of mine who have actually been trained to find people.'

He said it blandly, as if it wasn't an insult.

'But Ellie chose me?'

'It certainly looks like it, doesn't it?'

The atmosphere had soured.

'We're going to look around,' I said, and led the way out of the kitchen and into a hallway. There were rooms on either side – a bedroom, an office, a toilet, then a living room at the end – and a staircase was midway down, built into a tight and impressive spiral of wood-and-glass railings.

'He seems fun,' Healy whispered. 'You believe him?'

I looked back down the hallway, towards the kitchen. I couldn't see Matt, but I could hear him using his laptop. 'Well, what he says backs up my gut feeling about Ellie. If I'm right, she hired me without knowing there was a connection to Glass.'

'Doesn't mean she's not involved.'

'But it makes it less likely.'

Healy seemed unconvinced.

'Either way, I didn't end up with this case by accident. Someone hoped I would connect Noah Klein to Glass.'

Healy nodded.

'And they knew I would most likely bring you on board.'

He nodded again. 'And if it's not Ellie . . .'

We both looked down the hallway this time.

Matt had told us he'd come up with a long list of names for Ellie, and because Ellie completely trusted him, he wouldn't have had to try very hard to steer her in the direction he wanted her to go.

'I'll take this floor,' I said.

Healy

Now

At the top of the stairs, the landing was in an L-shape. The first couple of bedrooms were smartly decorated and tidy – beds made, furniture expensive – but it was clear no one was living in them. A third bedroom had been turned into a mini gym.

Healy went through the first two bedrooms, looking in wardrobes and bedside cabinets, but found nothing. He checked over the gym, then moved to the bathroom and the final bedroom. It was bright at this end of the house, skylights in the ceilings of the landing and the toilet, and enormous bay windows in the final bedroom.

As he entered it, he looked both ways.

To his left was a walk-in wardrobe with mirrors on the outside reflecting back an image of himself that he didn't spend long looking at.

He headed into the wardrobe.

It was split into two distinct sides, one full of male clothes, the other female. In both were numerous cupboards and drawers, a dressing table on the female side, racks full of shoes and folded T-shirts, even watches. As Healy looked at it all, he felt a pinch of jealousy. He was struggling to pay his bills, could barely afford groceries most weeks, and this guy had a drawer with ten different watches in it.

He returned to the main part of the bedroom.

In the middle there was enough space for a couple of armchairs and a table, the table stacked with the kind of highbrow books on modern art that Healy was pretty sure no one ever read. At the other end of the room was the biggest bed he'd ever seen and a wet room the size of his kitchen.

He moved to the bedside cabinets.

On top of the left one was a script for an episode of *Church Row Manor*. Healy flipped back the cover. Inside, all down the margins, were notes and annotations – he assumed in Ellie Snyder's hand – on her dialogue. He went through the script and then her cabinet, found nothing, and headed to Preston's side of the bed. The cabinet was messier inside than Ellie's: a Kindle, a reading light and creased paperwork were all jumbled together. There were some paperbacks tucked underneath too.

He took everything out.

The books were thrillers mostly, although there were a couple of true crime novels too, one of which looked second-hand, the cover discoloured and torn, the pages browned and curled at the edges. Healy set all the books aside and went through the paperwork and Kindle, but he found nothing of any note.

As he started putting everything back into the drawers again, he heard a creak on the landing, and a couple of seconds later Raker appeared at the door.

'You checking up on me?' Healy said.

Raker just ignored him, his eyes taking in the bedroom.

'What's the matter?'

'I've found something,' Raker responded.

His gaze finally came back to Healy – and then to the junk from Preston's drawers that Healy had placed on to the bed and was busy loading back in.

'Anything there?'

'No,' Healy said.

But Raker was frowning now, his gaze fixed on the junk.

'That was in his drawer here?' he asked, pointing to the old paperback Healy had been looking at only moments ago, its cover torn, its pages curled.

'Yeah. So?'

Raker picked it up off the pile. 'I need to show you something.'

21

. . . 39 hours to go . . .

Twenty minutes earlier, after Healy had disappeared up the staircase, I'd started on the downstairs bedroom. It was large but it didn't look like it was regularly used. The bed was made and it was kitted out with furniture, but the cupboards were empty.

I quickly checked the toilet, then went into the office.

It was tidy and modern, stacks of medical textbooks, biographies and journals on shelves in a bookcase built into an alcove on the back wall. A desk was to the right. Wheeling out the chair, I sat down and opened its three drawers.

The top one was stacked full of paperwork that I went through but could soon see was irrelevant. The next was a mishmash of envelopes and stationery. The last contained an iPad. I looked through it and then set it aside.

A laptop was on the desk and plugged in. The second I used the trackpad to wake it up, a password screen appeared. I went back to the kitchen and asked Matt if he knew what Preston's password was, but he didn't, so I grabbed my phone and messaged Ellie, asking her.

I returned to the office. There were more photographs of Ellie in here, including one Preston had on a pinboard above the desk. She was on a bench somewhere, the sun was out and there were banks of coloured flowers behind her.

My phone buzzed in my pocket, and when I took it out I could see it was Ellie, replying about the password.

> Try Franklampard1976. Favourite player + P's birth year. He's rubbish at changing his passwords

I tried the password and sent Ellie a reply:

> It works. Thanks. Another unrelated Q: Matt says he gave you a list of potential investigators you could use. Do you mind if I ask why you chose me?

As I waited for a reply, I went back to the laptop.

It didn't take me long to realize it was going to be a dead end. Everything on it was work-related, except for his internet activity, which seemed to consist entirely of him being on sports sites or looking at cars and searching for holidays.

I closed it and headed through to the living room.

It was big, running all the way along one side of the house, with a huge bay window at the front and floor-to-ceiling bifold doors at the back. At one end was a dining table, a sideboard and a tall alcove full of wine bottles; at the other were three sofas, a wood-burner inside a stone chimney, and a seventy-inch TV mounted on the wall.

I went through all the sideboard drawers and then, at the end of one of the sofas, found a remote control. Switching on the TV, I looked at the apps Preston had downloaded – Netflix, Amazon, BBC, C4 – and then clicked on each one to see what was in his watch history. I thought it might give me a better idea of the things that interested him and who this man was, other than just a person I was trying to find. The answer seemed to be that he mainly liked US crime shows, Mafia movies and sports documentaries.

Next, I went to YouTube.

As it loaded, Ellie texted me back.

> Why did I choose you? Wdym?

Was she genuinely confused by the question? Or was she trying to dig deeper into the reason I was asking it?

I texted her back:

It's okay. I'll call you later about it.

Preston's YouTube page was now on-screen.

Along the top was a list of videos he was in the middle of watching – red lines at the bottom of each window indicating how far he'd got through them – and under that were recommended videos based on what he'd previously viewed. The recommended tab was mostly in line with his work – science-based TED Talks, swish corporate videos about new hospital tech – but it was obvious that he also had a keen interest in football, cricket and Formula One. When I switched my attention to the videos he'd been in the middle of watching, the subjects were the same.

Except for one.

About ten windows along the line of previously seen videos was one that he'd watched every single minute of, despite it being ninety minutes long. Looking at the rest of his viewing history, I could see that he skitted around a lot, clearly getting bored quickly, and rarely finished the videos he started.

But this one he'd watched beginning to end.

The image on the thumbnail was what looked like the side of a house – except a window was missing and the roof had collapsed.

I took a step closer.

And then I read the title of the video.

Zauna and Marco

Zauna

The day after Zauna's tenth birthday, something bad happens.

The first time she's really aware there's a problem is when she overhears her mum and dad talking in the kitchen. She's supposed to be asleep because it's two in the morning, but the voices wake her up. She stirs and listens.

To start with, the conversation is muffled by the walls of the huge house she lives in, not helped by the fact that Zauna's room is right at the back, on the second floor, and the kitchen is at the front, on the ground, its windows overlooking St John's College. That's where Mum and Dad say Zauna's going to go when she's eleven, even though Zauna doesn't want to. None of her friends will be going there, and whenever Zauna tells them that that's where her mum and dad want her to go, her friends call her *posh* and start speaking like the Queen. Zauna didn't really understand why until her best friend, Sophie, explained that St John's College is a private school and it cost loads of money to go there. Zauna got home that night and asked her mum why she couldn't just go to Cotham, like all her other friends, and her mum said, 'If you want to do as well as Marco has done, you need the best education.'

Marco is her brother.

Her mum and dad are still talking, so she flips back the duvet cover and pads across to her bedroom door. She can hear a little better now, their voices drifting up the stairs. Dad is saying something about not panicking until they find out more, but Mum sounds like she's crying. When she tries to speak, Zauna can't really hear what she's saying. Her words are all muddled up. Zauna edges out on to the landing and moves to the top of the stairs, one hand on the banister, her eyes looking down the steps. There's a plug-in night light at the bottom of them, glowing a very dull orange.

Zauna moves again, descending a little more.

As she looks down the spiral of banisters to ground level, she can see the grey slate tiles on the kitchen floor, and the shadows of her parents as they move around.

She can hear more clearly too.

'He said he would be home three hours ago,' Zauna's mum is saying.

'I know,' her dad responds.

'He wouldn't just not come home.'

'I know. But he's also eighteen, Carolyn.'

'So?'

'So he's a grown adult – a grown adult that also happens to be a teenager who is interested in girls, and going out, and doing the things teenagers are meant to do.'

'He wouldn't forget to call us.'

'He would,' Zauna's dad says, and then, very quickly, 'I'm just saying he would. He's my son, and I love him, but he *would* forget to call if he's having a good time. It's more normal for kids his age *not* to call their parents.'

That's when the phone starts ringing.

Zauna watches her dad's shadow head to where the phone is. It's on a wall at the bottom of the stairs, so Zauna sees her dad now. He's still in his suit. He's a doctor. He must have got back from his shift after Zauna went to bed.

Zauna's dad answers the phone.

He's quiet for a moment. He nods a couple of times and says, 'Okay,' and 'I understand,' and then looks back across the kitchen to where Zauna's mum is. 'Yes,' he says, 'yes, that makes sense.' He nods a few more times, then says, 'Goodbye.'

He puts the phone back on the wall.

'The police are going to send someone round.'

'Good,' Zauna's mum says, relief in her voice. 'When?'

'In the morning.'

'In the *morning*?'

'They need to make sure he doesn't come home first.'

'Nadeem, he was supposed to be home three *hours* ago.'

'I know.'

'Did you *tell* them that?'

Zauna's dad is still where he was before, close to the phone, framed inside the coil of banisters that go from the second floor down to the kitchen. He holds up one of his hands, as if he's trying to calm everything down, and says, 'The police need to be absolutely sure that Marco isn't just out with friends, at a party somewhere. The guy on the phone said he's been through the call-outs and no one has reported a boy –'

'This is your *son*.'

'I know that.'

'Then why don't you care more?'

This time Zauna's dad pauses and she can see he's angry. Most of the time he's very calm, which he says he needs to be in order to do his job properly, though there have been a few times when he's shouted at Marco and Zauna.

'Don't tell me I don't care about my son,' he says quietly.

But it's the kind of quiet that the headmaster at Zauna's school does – the kind of quiet that sounds even scarier than someone shouting very loudly.

Zauna's mum starts crying again.

Sometime after that, Zauna hears her say, 'I'm sorry.'

She watches as her mum's shadow moves again, and her parents hug, and then Zauna shifts, trying to get a better view, and the stairs creak softly under her weight.

She sees her dad's face come back into view. 'Zauna?'

She's been caught, she knows that, so she doesn't bother

hiding. Instead, she gets to her feet and hurries down the two flights of stairs. She wants to find out what's happening.

'What are you doing up, honey?' Zauna's mum says, and comes over and gives Zauna a hug so tight it feels like Zauna's bones might break.

'It's very late, Zee,' her dad says, putting an arm on her shoulder and pulling Zauna into him, so that her head rests against his ribs. 'You should be in bed, angel.'

'What's going on with Marco?'

Her mum and dad look at each other.

'Nothing, honey,' her mum says.

'Then why are you crying?'

'We're just a bit worried about your brother, Zee, that's all,' her dad says. 'But everything's going to be okay. What you need to do is get back to bed otherwise you'll be exhausted for school tomorrow. And how is that *huge* brain going to work then?'

They're putting on a good show.

Zauna is only ten, but she can tell it's a show.

Her mum takes her back to bed before she gives her another long hug as she tucks her in and turns the light out.

'Everything will be better in the morning,' her mum says.

But she doesn't believe it, Zauna can tell.

And in the morning nothing gets better.

Everything gets much, much worse because Marco never comes home.

Her brother still isn't home by the time Zauna goes to senior school nine months later. Her parents don't send her to St John's College in the end. Zauna isn't really sure why to begin with but thinks it might be something to do with her mum. She's sad all the time and cries a lot, and — after Zauna starts getting the bus to and from school — she often arrives back to find her mum asleep on the sofa. Sometimes there's an empty glass on the floor. Sometimes there's a bottle of sleeping pills.

They've already had lessons at school about the dangers of

drugs, alcohol and cigarettes and how people become addicted to them – and, much as she doesn't like admitting it to herself, she often thinks of her mum when the teacher is showing them slides of drug addicts and alcoholics. Whenever her mum speaks to Zauna, she seems distant. After a few months at Cotham, she starts to suspect that one of the reasons she ended up there and not St John's College was because her dad is always working – way more than he worked before – and her mum basically forgot to apply.

Zauna doesn't mind.

She's happy with her friends, mostly. Some days she feels sad, and she misses Marco, and no one can really comfort her. On those days, her friends are cautious around her and don't know what to say, so they tend to just stay quiet. One of her friends, Emily, had a cousin who was knocked down and killed by a drunk driver. But a cousin isn't the same as a brother.

And Zauna *loved* her brother.

Marco was eight years older than her, but he was always so much fun. When she was little, he'd play in the garden with her for ages. He could be annoying like big brothers sometimes are, but mostly he was fun, and funny. He called her Zauny, which she told him she hated but secretly loved.

No one else called her that.

Only Marco.

As she gets older, Zauna is forced to become self-sufficient. Her dad is always home too late to talk to, and he's too tired anyway, and – by the time she's fifteen – Zauna starts to realize that her mum *is* an addict. In the evenings, she'll get Zauna's dinner ready for her, but then she will take a bottle of wine and her sleeping pills into the living room and, after thirty minutes, she'll be lights out. It's Zauna that cleans up. It's Zauna that makes her own packed lunch. It's Zauna that goes into her mum's purse and gets her bank card and walks down to the nearest cashpoint to get the money she needs for the bus at the start of every week. She never steals from her parents, even though she's thought about it, but as she gets older, she gets angry at them. One night, a month before her GCSE exams start, she hears them arguing downstairs while she's trying to revise. She's stressed about her exams and when she can't tune them out, she flips. She storms downstairs and says, 'Just get a bloody divorce!'

That's what they do when she's seventeen.

It's been a long time coming and, when it does, Zauna is almost relieved. They agree to live together in the house, but in separate bedrooms, until Zauna goes off to university. The arguments cease. Her dad gets home later. Her mum drinks more.

At eighteen, she goes to study English and Drama in London.

She got into acting when she was thirteen, mostly because drama was after school and it meant getting home later and not having to deal with her mum as much.

She didn't expect to like it.

She didn't expect it to be her thing at all.

But she loves it.

She reads English at university because everybody at her school kept telling her how hard it is to make it as an actress, and Zauna didn't know what else to pair with Drama. But she's really good at English – she got an A for it at A level – even though she finds most of the texts they have to study boring. It's just a parade of white men from hundreds of years ago writing about things that have no relevance to her life – and at university she soon finds out it's exactly the same, it's just the texts have more pages. But she stays on track with that part of the course – doing exactly as much as she needs to pass – while sinking her heart and soul into Drama. She loves being onstage, loves the theory side of it too, especially when they do modules on cinema.

Halfway through her first year, they study film noir and, when Zauna turns up to the lecture, she discovers her class and the Film Studies students are all in together.

That's where she meets Anna.

Anna wants to be a director.

They hit it off straight away. Anna is so different from Zauna. She's tall, pale and blonde, quite plain but incredibly funny, and both her parents are from Sunderland; Zauna's dad is from Pakistan and her mum's grandparents were Italian, so Zauna is dark-haired and dark-eyed, strikingly beautiful, quiet away from the stage, and – according to other people's opinions, anyway – often quite serious. Anna grew up on a sprawling council estate but loves her parents to bits; Zauna grew up in a multimillion-pound townhouse and isn't sure if she ever wants to go home again.

Zauna feels comfortable with Anna in a way she's never felt comfortable with anyone else in her life. It doesn't take long before she's telling Anna all about Marco.

'And no one ever found out where he went?' Anna asks.

'No. Never.'

'Someone needs to look into it.'

'The police already have.'

'The police are shit,' Anna says matter-of-factly. Zauna has worked out fairly quickly that Anna, her family and the people in the area that she's from have little to no faith in the ability of the police to do or solve anything. 'Your poor mum and dad.'

And poor me, Zauna thinks, but doesn't say. Down the years, a few people have said the same thing about her poor mum and dad, and she's old enough now to understand that losing a child is uniquely painful. But her life was ruined then too. If Marco hadn't disappeared, Zauna might have had a normal childhood like Anna.

After university, the women keep in touch. They don't see each other quite as often, but they're always calling one another. Zauna tries to get acting work and goes to what feels like a billion auditions, but the best TV job she can get in the first twelve months is in an advert for a supermarket. She pays the bills with small theatre roles.

On a warm evening, a year after they graduate, she meets Anna for a drink.

They talk for a while and catch up, and Anna tells Zauna that she's got a job at a small production company called Scenic View which make factual programmes and documentaries. She mentions a couple of things they've had commissioned, including one exposé for BBC Two about prisons, but Zauna hasn't heard of or seen the shows, and she hasn't heard of Sydney Roder either, the woman Anna says runs it.

'I hope you don't mind,' Anna says, 'but I told Sydney about Marco.'

Zauna frowns. 'What do you mean?'

'It's an absolute bloody tragedy that no one's ever looked into what happened to him,' Anna says, leaning closer to Zauna. 'Someone needs to get you answers.'

Zauna blinks. She doesn't know what to say.

'Would you let me look into it for you?' Anna asks. 'Sydney suggested I start to dig around and gather information – but I wouldn't do it without your blessing.'

Again, Zauna is quiet.

'Sorry,' Anna says. 'Sorry, forget I said anything.'

But Zauna takes Anna's arm, and this time she starts to cry. Twelve years of pain, of pushing down her sadness over Marco going missing, of growing up in a house where her parents were only ever adjacent to her life, just pour out of her. She's smart enough, even upset as she is, to know that Anna and her boss see this as a story, a chance to tell a tragedy on the small screen, and that Zauna and her family will be conduits. But she also knows Anna is doing this because she genuinely cares.

'I didn't mean to make you upset,' Anna says.

'Please find out where my brother went.'

The two women hug.

After that, she doesn't hear anything from Anna for a while. Weeks pass with only occasional texts, and then weeks become a month, and a month becomes three.

But then, one evening, Anna calls Zauna.

'We've found something,' she says excitedly.

'What?'

'I think we've got a lead on Marco.'

Zauna is so thrown she can't think of what to say.

'Zauna?'

'Yes, I'm here. What have you found?'

On the line, Zauna can hear pages being turned.

'It's a place in Cornwall,' Anna says. 'Have you ever heard of Porthtreno?'

22

. . . 39 hours to go . . .

I led us back down to the living room.

Paused on the television was the title screen for the ninety-minute programme Preston had watched in its entirety. 'This is the only thing he's sat through recently,' I said.

Healy looked at the title of the video.

'*The Lost Women of Porthtreno*,' he read off the screen.

For a moment I was transported back eighteen years, to the journey I'd taken down to Cornwall when I was a journalist, trying to figure out what had gone on and how three women could disappear into thin air. I could almost smell the salt on the breeze; almost hear the whisper of the sand shifting constantly inside the old village.

'Where the hell is Porthtreno?' Healy asked.

'Cornwall. It's a small tidal island.'

He eyed me. 'Have you been there?'

'Back when I was a journalist.' I held up the book. It was also called *The Lost Women of Porthtreno*. That was what they'd become known as. 'I know the woman who wrote this. We came up together at *The Times*.' I turned the book in my hands, looking at the small black-and-white photograph of Marla Campbell on the reverse. The book was seventeen years old now – and out of print – which explained why the copy Preston had in his drawer was so discoloured and damaged.

Healy looked at the photographs of the three women on the TV, their faces set inside Polaroids. Each Polaroid looked like it was in the process of disappearing.

Sydney Roder. Anna Casey. Zauna Roy.
'Who are they?' he asked.

'They disappeared in September 2006. I took a drive down to Porthtreno the following April to write and research a story on them. I remember it clearly because Derryn was going through chemo at the time.' I stopped, the words stalling in my throat even all these years on, because now I had the clearest view possible of what had followed. 'Those women had been a massive story for a while – but then it had fizzled out. I wanted to dig into it and get it going again.'

'Why had it fizzled out?'

'Dead ends. The cops had absolutely nothing. They sent search teams down there, boats out into the water. They never found a trace of those women.'

'What's on the island?'

'Mostly it's just sand and beachgrass, but there's a tiny village right in the middle of it called St Petroc. It hasn't been lived in for years; it was abandoned in the 1870s. The dunes on Porthtreno, they're like this force of nature, this perpetually moving wave, and tons of sand kept swamping the properties. That was where the women were filming. All their equipment was still there when the cops turned up.'

I went to the book and flicked to the centre, where there was an insert with eight pages of colour photographs. 'Look,' I said, and showed him a picture that the police had taken shortly after arriving at the scene. It was the remains of one of the houses in St Petroc, the sand like a sea washing against the walls, the top half of a former chimney breast poking out. On a wooden platform placed flat against the surface of the sand was a camera on a tripod, a boom mic and a recording pack. Hanging from jagged bits of brickwork were the women's coats, power cables and one of their backpacks.

'It looks like they were just there,' Healy said.

I nodded. 'There and gone.'

'They weren't under the sand?'

'No. The cops used radar.'

He eyed some of the other shots. They were a mix of police photographs and portraits that Marla Campbell had taken during her research for the book. I hadn't seen her for over a decade – the last time had been at a former colleague's wedding – but I remembered talking to her about the book then, and the case as a whole. By Marla's own admission, the book hadn't interested people in the way she'd been hoping. She'd put it down to the fact that, as detailed as her account was, she couldn't definitively say what had happened to the three women and that had niggled at those who, according to her, liked 'life to be tied up in a neat little bow'.

'So the book came first?' Healy asked.

'Yeah, and then National Geographic did a documentary on them that came out four years later.' I went to the documentary and confirmed the date in the end credits.

'So, wait,' Healy said, trying to get everything lined up in his head, 'the women themselves were *also* making a documentary at the time they disappeared?'

'Yes.'

'What was *their* documentary about?'

'Zauna Roy's brother, Marco.'

'What happened to him?'

I looked at the TV again, at the book.

And then I thought of Preston Stewart's confession to Ellie.

'Raker?' Healy said. 'What happened to this Marco kid?'

'He disappeared in Bristol in December 1993.'

23

. . . 39 hours to go . . .

Healy stared at me.

Bristol. December 1993.

'Wait, are you saying that this Marco kid was at university at the same time as Preston?'

'Yes,' I said. 'Same university, same city, same year.'

Healy glanced at the TV, looking for answers.

I thought back to the fruitless search I'd done earlier in the day, trying to zero in on crimes and disappearances that had happened during the first year that Preston had been at university. I thought the reason I'd come up short was because it had been too far back. And maybe that *was* the reason that Marco Roy's disappearance had never appeared in my search. But I realized there was another reason too: there had been no conclusion. Marco was never found. And with no conclusion and no leads, there was no new angle to sustain media coverage. The Lost Women's story was different because it had happened in the internet age, thirteen years later, they were female, all photogenic, and they'd gone missing in headline-grabbing circumstances. Those things were powerful tools when editors were cynically pursuing clicks and circulation bumps. But Marco was different – and so his story, like him, had simply vanished until Sydney Roder and Anna Casey had offered to tell it to the world.

'First this Noah Klein shite,' Healy muttered. 'Now this.'

He was right: even if I'd been willing to believe the use of the name Noah Klein was a coincidence – which I wasn't – this put paid to that. Preston Stewart was now linked to two old cases in which I'd played a part.

I glanced at the book Marla Campbell had written on Sydney, Anna and Zauna and then at the YouTube video, the title card showing an image of one of the broken, abandoned houses at St Petroc. I'd thought about the village of sand often in the years since I'd written about it. The unanswered questions. The families of the women, who had gone so long without answers. I'd shared it with others too, including with Rebekah.

But when I'd started digging into Preston's life – and even when I'd listened to Ellie telling me this morning about his drunken confession – I hadn't once thought to connect the dots from the date that Preston had started medical school – September 1993 – to Marco going missing three months later. They were two different cases.

Except now they weren't.

Now they were all part of the same thing.

Healy stepped closer to the TV, bringing me back into the room. 'So, are you going to say it or am I?' he asked.

But neither of us needed to say anything at all.

Because the question we'd been left with was obvious.

Was Marco Roy the person that Preston and his friend had killed?

24

...39 hours to go...

I hadn't read Marla Campbell's book for years, so I went to the index at the back to see where Marco Roy was mentioned. There were thirty-seven references to him. Handing over the book to Healy, I said, 'Find out as much as you can about Marco.'

He took the book and started going through it.

I grabbed the remote control, returned the documentary to the start, and then – after selecting subtitles – put it on mute and began playing it at 2x speed. Ten minutes in, Marco was mentioned for the first time. The business partner of Sydney Roder, who ran the tiny production company called Scenic View that Anna Casey had also worked for, was being interviewed. He called Sydney 'immensely driven' and 'incredibly smart' and said, 'She wanted to tell stories that were important, but the story always had to connect with her on an emotional level.' He went on to explain that Sydney's sister had died when Sydney was young, which was part of the reason she was so interested in Marco Roy's disappearance.

Part of the reason, but not all.

Zauna Roy was the other reason.

What I remembered most clearly about Zauna were two things: the first was that she was absolutely stunning, her Pakistani-Italian heritage creating a face that was hard to forget; the other was that, even in pictures when she was smiling or appeared to be happy, there always remained just a hint of sadness. When I'd been researching the story, and especially after I'd been down to Porthtreno, I would often come back to Zauna's expression, to what lay behind it. Later, I found out that her childhood – in the years after Marco went missing – was very unhappy, her father deliberately burying himself in work, her mother addicted to booze and antidepressants. Carolyn Roy died from an overdose the year after Zauna went to Porthtreno.

As I watched old camcorder footage of a teenage Zauna playing in the documentary, I wondered if her looks, the way she carried herself, might have been one of the other reasons – perhaps a more cynical reason – why Sydney Roper wanted to tell Marco's story. Based on the test footage Sydney and Anna had shot, and around four hours of initial interviews they'd done with Zauna that police had recovered from the Scenic View production office, it was obvious that Sydney had decided to put Zauna front and centre of her documentary. She looked the part. She was articulate, speaking eloquently about Marco. But there was also that hint of sadness, that image of a beautiful, slightly broken woman that pulled you in and made it hard to turn away.

'Have you found anything?' I asked Healy.

'Not really,' he said, flicking back and forth to the index. 'I'm guessing most of this is stuff you already know.' He landed on a page about halfway through. 'Marco went to Bristol University in September 1993 to study Biochemistry. He was born in the city – his parents lived in the Clifton area – so he didn't move out, just kept living at home.' He turned a few pages. 'He went out with friends one night in December 1993, the friends confirmed he arrived and spent a couple of hours with them in the pub, and then he left at ten thirty p.m. No one ever saw him again after that.'

I looked at the television. There was a shot of Marco Roy on it now, then camcorder footage of him on a swing in a park, with his eight-year-old sister on the swing next to him. Like Zauna, he was very good-looking, tall and slim.

'Why was Preston looking at all of this now?' I said, my mind racing. 'I mean, he must have watched it in the last couple of weeks otherwise it wouldn't be sitting in his recently viewed list. We also have to assume, given his possible involvement in Marco Roy going missing, that Preston has watched this documentary before at some point. I mean, if this is your crime' – I gestured to the TV, to the images of Marco on-screen, and then the ones that followed of Sydney, Anna and Zauna – 'then you're going to watch a documentary about it. You're going to want to find out what's being said and whether anyone's managed to get close to the truth about what actually happened.'

Healy nodded. 'Yeah, that makes sense.'

'So, let's say Preston read Marla's book when it first came out, and watched this when it first aired – why would he reread and rewatch them both now, years later?'

'Something's changed.'

'Right. The women have been back on his mind – and so is Marco.'

'Which would explain why he confessed to Ellie that he killed someone.'

'Correct,' I said. 'But if Preston was *also* why the three women disappeared, if they were digging too deep and getting too close to the truth about Marco, and Preston and his accomplice got rid of the women as well, then why didn't he mention *that* to Ellie? If you were drunkenly confessing to one murder, you'd confess to them all, surely? He's either in denial about what he did to the three women and has locked it up somewhere so deep he never talks about it. *Or* he had nothing to do with Sydney, Anna and Zauna going missing.'

My gaze drifted back to the TV, to some test footage National Geographic had got hold of: Sydney going back and forth to the camera as she set up an interview segment; Anna busying herself in the background, dressing the set; Zauna making notes in the corner, getting ready to be interviewed.

Healy stepped forward. 'So we're saying a possible version of this is that Preston and a friend killed Marco after he left that pub in Bristol. They got rid of the body. Thirteen years later, the three women went to Porthtreno, following some new lead on Marco. We don't know what that lead was or why Porthtreno was relevant to what happened to Marco up in Bristol, but whatever it was, it must have been big, because that was when someone – either Preston, or this accomplice of his, or both of them – intercepted the women before they got the chance to tell the world what they'd found. And now nineteen years on from *that*, Preston is going back over old ground, reading and watching this stuff.'

'Yeah,' I said, 'all of that makes sense.'

'But why would Preston kill Marco? Plus, where does Noah Klein fit into all of this? Why was Preston targeted yesterday?'

I shook my head in response, frustrated.

The questions were piling up fast.

'So no one knows what exactly the women were hoping to find in Porthtreno,' Healy said quietly, almost to himself, his focus back on the documentary. 'Maybe they thought Marco's body might be buried there.'

'Maybe. But the police scanned the area with radar when the women went missing, so they would have found Marco too. And why would Marco disappear in Bristol and end up in Porthtreno?'

'The women didn't have any notes? Any research?'

'Some at the Scenic View production office, but nothing that led anywhere.'

'Doesn't that seem weird to you? That no one knew what the women thought they'd find in Porthtreno, or what their lead on Marco was?'

'Yeah,' I said. 'It does.'

'Do you think someone cleaned house?'

It was a theory I'd spent a lot of time thinking about at the time, and one that the police and media had speculated on too: that whoever was responsible for the women going missing also went through all the research they'd done in preparation for making the documentary on Marco and destroyed anything incriminating. As far as I could remember, no one had been able to prove that was what had happened, but the missing link between Marco and Porthtreno, and the reason the women had driven down there, was noticeable by its absence from any evidence the police had collated.

On-screen, the documentary continued to play, alternating between interviews with people who'd known the women, and Marla Campbell, who knew the case better than anyone. I went to my phone, seeing if I still had a number for her, and when I saw that I did, I wondered if it was the number she was using now. I hadn't spoken to her in a decade. When I googled her, I found she had a website, but it looked like it hadn't been updated in a long time.

'We need to try to find out who Preston's accomplice was,' I said.

'Agreed.'

'We still haven't called the names in Preston's address book. Maybe we should start there.' I got out Preston's phone and went to his contacts. 'Let's split it down the middle. I'll take A to M, you take N to Z. We need to try to –'

Healy's phone started ringing.

He grabbed it from his pocket and looked at the caller, frowned, then turned the screen around for me to see. 'You recognize that number?'

It had got gloomy in the house, daylight starting to fade outside as another winter night stalked towards us. But I could see the number on his phone clearly.

Central London.

'No,' I said, eyeing him. 'Should I?'

'It's my old number.'

'What do you mean?'

'This is the number I used to have.'

'Used to have where?'

He looked at the phone again. 'Used to have at the Met.'

Healy

Now

Healy glanced at Raker, who was watching him closely, clearly concerned about why the Met would be calling.

'Are you going to answer it?' he said.

Healy did, bringing the phone to his ear. 'Hello?'

'Colm?' A woman's voice. 'Colm, it's Rosa.'

Rosa Naughton. They'd worked together a long time ago when Naughton had been a detective constable. She'd been in her twenties then, a petite powerhouse who used to do weight training and bodybuilding. Healy had taken her under his wing.

Then they'd had a case that had gone south.

They hadn't spoken since.

He looked at Raker. *Everything's fine.* Raker pointed to his own phone as if to say he was going to make some calls, then paused the documentary and headed out of the living room.

'It's been a while,' Healy said.

'Yeah, it has.' Naughton stopped. He imagined her thoughts were back on that same, disastrous case – and all the ways it had driven a wedge between them.

The Red Woman.

That had been the nickname that Healy and Naughton had given to the girlfriend of a low-level gangster they'd interviewed after the gangster had vanished. Completely believable and apparently deeply concerned about her boyfriend's disappearance, soon after the girlfriend left the station the entire case had gone sideways. Naughton had returned to interview her and had found the girlfriend no longer existed. There was no trace of a woman with her name, nothing at a flat she'd cleaned out, and her entire employment history had been fabricated. But the two of them kept digging, and – in the pitch-black of an abandoned building – the Red Woman had held a knife to Naughton's throat and been seconds away from using it. The experience had affected her so profoundly, Naughton had ended up transferring out of Healy's team. Naughton had said it was because every time she looked at him – every time he even as much as spoke to her – she was reminded of the worst day of her life.

'How are you doing, Colm?' she asked.

He tried to figure out why she would be calling him after so much time – and why she was calling from his old extension. 'Are you on a comeback tour?'

'What do you mean?'

'This is my old number.'

'Oh. Yeah, I'm back where it all started. I'm a DI now.'

'Congratulations.'

'Thanks. They gave me your old desk.'

Healy didn't say anything. He felt annoyed about it for some reason. It wasn't his desk any more – it hadn't even been his desk when he'd been a cop; it belonged to the station, not to him personally – but Rosa had hurt him deeply when she'd put in for a transfer. Much more than he'd ever let on.

'I was sorry to hear about what you've been through,' she said.

'Which part?'

He wasn't being facetious, because there were so many things that had gone wrong since he'd worked with Rosa Naughton. She'd probably read about some of his troubles in the press, and she would have definitely heard about them from his enemies at the Met.

'I did what I thought was best back then,' she said.

'Good for you.'

'You have no idea what it was like.'

'Oh, I don't?' Healy could feel the heat prickling in his skin.

He took a second, trying to calm himself. It didn't work. 'My daughter was murdered, my wife left me, my sons hate my guts. I got sacked from the Met, I had a heart attack, spent weeks in a coma, and got sent to prison for faking my own death. You had a knife held to your throat for a couple of minutes. I can take a guess at how hard it's been for you.'

He heard her let out a frustrated breath.

'Why are you calling me, Naughton?'

'I need to ask a favour.'

Healy almost laughed.

'I'm serious,' she said.

'And what favour would that be?'

'I want you to tell me everything you know about Alice-Leigh Reddy.'

25

... 38 hours to go ...

I headed outside, into the dwindling light, to make the call to Marla Campbell.

In the courtyard at the back of the house, Matt was vacuuming the Mercedes. I moved past him, on to the lawn, trying to get clear of the noise, and ended up going all the way down to the end, where low, neatly cultivated hedgerows separated the garden from the stream and fields beyond.

Once I did, I glanced back at Matt.

Doubts were playing on my mind, even though my gut feeling about Ellie hadn't shifted. My head was telling me that she could easily be playing me; that she knew from the start that the search for her husband would lead me to Noah Klein, to Glass, and then to Marco Roy and Preston's interest in the Lost Women. But my heart, my instinct, was telling me something else. I'd been tricked by liars before, but not often. One of the things I'd become good at was understanding what inauthenticity looked like – and that wasn't what I saw when I watched and listened to Ellie. Her heartache and confusion felt completely real.

Which means someone else needed me to take this case.

Matt glanced in my direction, but I managed to turn away before he caught me staring. With the setting sun at my back, I selected Marla Campbell's mobile.

It rang out and went to voicemail.

I'd barely finished leaving a message for her when my phone started buzzing again, Marla's name flashing. She was calling me back on FaceTime.

I accepted, and after a pause she appeared on-screen. She was in bed, propped up on some pillows, slatted light cutting across her face and body. I didn't show any reaction to her appearance, even though it was like looking at someone completely different from the woman I'd known years before. She was emaciated, her face hollowed out and jaundiced. She had no hair. The only thing that remained the same were her eyes. They still sparked; were still playful.

'David Raker,' she said.

'Hey, Marla.'

She smiled, her way of telling me that she was handling her situation as best she could, but it was a smile cut through with so much pain and fear it was like I was sixteen years younger, sitting on the edge of the bed in my old house in Ealing, holding my wife's hand.

'Well, you look sickeningly good, Raker. Don't you ever age?'

'That's sweet, Marla, but creaky knees and a dodgy hip say yes.'

Marla started chuckling, and then the chuckle became coughing. Slowly, she reached for some water.

'I'm so sorry, Marla. I had no idea you were ill.'

'Oh, don't be silly. Why would you?' She shrugged. 'I mean, when was the last time we saw each other? Must have been Diamond Dave's wedding, right? Didn't we sit next to one another?' I told her that we did. 'I should have got you drunk that night, Raker, and had my wicked way with you.'

I laughed.

'This crap has been the last five years of my life' – she touched her hand to her head, to the medical equipment out of shot – 'and now I've got four months left, so whatever you're calling me out of the blue about, it'd better be very, *very* exciting, because this is a pile of shit and I deserve a little excitement before I go.' Her matter-of-fact, almost nonchalant analysis of her situation was painful to watch.

'I wanted to talk to you about the Lost Women.'

A look of surprise. 'Shit. Raker does it again.'

'Does that pass the Excitement Test?'

'It does. Don't tell me you're looking into the women?'

'Not exactly.'

I gave Marla a brief overview of Preston's disappearance. I told her that he was missing, but left out any mention of the hospital and of Ellie.

'So this guy Preston had an interest in the women?'

'It looks that way.'

'Damn,' Marla said. 'Do you think he could be the man responsible?'

'Hard to say at the moment.' I hadn't told Marla about Preston's confession to Ellie, or my suspicions that the person he killed might have been Marco Roy. Sick as she was, Marla was a terrier, a journalist through and through – it was in her blood, far more than it had ever been in mine – and, much as I liked her, I didn't one hundred per cent trust her not to pick up the phone to someone.

'So what is it you wanted to know?' she asked.

'I've got a copy of your book here, and I've just been through the documentary, and there's nothing in either about how the women connected Marco to Porthtreno.'

'That's right.'

'Is it possible they *weren't* down in Porthtreno because of Marco?'

'It's possible, I guess.'

'But you don't think so?'

'The documentary they were making was *about* Marco. Admittedly, there was some material back at the Scenic View office that suggested the women might also have been taking a wider look at why young people disappear, but fundamentally this was a search for answers in the Marco Roy case. I mean, Zauna was the star of the documentary from day one. The only footage they'd recorded at the time they vanished was of her talking about Marco, about their childhood, about how miserable her home life was after he went missing. I know she had a face for TV, but you don't put that many hours into an interview unless the interviewee is going to play a huge part. Plus, I looked into whether Porthtreno had any history of disappearances – because I wondered if they may have been down there for another reason, digging into some other case – but it hasn't. Marco *had* to have been why the women were there.'

'Except there was never anything to confirm that?'

'No.' She shook her head. 'That whole line of enquiry was probably one of the biggest mysteries. I spent months chasing my tail, trying to find out what the link was – what made the three women *so* sure the answers about Marco lay in Porthtreno – and I never even got close. There was nothing in the records they left behind, nothing on any of the test footage they shot, nothing in the interviews they'd conducted with Zauna. It was just a vacuum of information. And it wasn't just me. I had some friends at the Met – and made some friends in stations down in Bristol and Cornwall too – and they had no idea either. There *was* one thing, though: the cops turned the Scenic View office over and one of my sources said it felt like things were missing.'

'I remember. It was like someone had gone in there, right?'

She nodded at me.

'But there was no evidence of a break-in at the office?'

'None. It was all locked up.'

'So what sorts of things were "missing"?'

'One example I got given was these notes Anna Casey made. They went to, like, forty or fifty pages, but there were just these weird jumps at certain points. Like, one page would end halfway through a sentence – but the next page would start with a *new* sentence, or part of the way through a different sentence altogether.'

I paused, thinking. *Could it have been Preston that had got into the office and removed those pages?*

'I don't remember there being many suspects either,' I said.

'There were none. When the women went missing, the cops went back to the Marco case and dug into it. But Avon and Somerset had done a pretty good job with what they had. There's a very fuzzy CCTV shot of Marco Roy walking up Whiteladies Road in Bristol, on the way back from the pub – but that's the last time he was ever spotted. The cops in Bristol talked to everyone who was in the pub that night and the friends Marco had at university. No one knew anything.'

'And it's not possible that the women could be under the sand?'

'No. The police did a search with ground-penetrating radar, and then air tests, and then a third search with cadaver dogs.' Marla took another sip of water. She looked tired all of a sudden, her skin pale, her eyes heavy. Eventually, she said, 'I hate to cut you off in your prime, Raker.'

'It's okay, Marla. I understand.'

I looked at her and thought of Derryn. There was an echo of my wife in the expression on Marla's face; in that sharp, rooted sadness that lingered because a call she'd enjoyed was ending, and she knew she didn't have many more of them left.

'If you crack it, will you FaceTime me again?' Marla asked.

'I will. I promise. Thanks, Marla.'

'All right, handsome.'

I ended the call and stood there for a moment, the sorrow I felt for Marla like a residue on my skin.

And then I glanced back at the house.

The Mercedes was parked in the same place, its doors open, but the vacuum cleaner was on the ground now, tipped on to its side, the nozzle snaking off across the grass. Despite that, it was still on, its motor whining. I couldn't see Matt: he was no longer at the car, and it looked as if the back door of the house was shut.

I moved a step closer.

Something isn't right.

The sun had almost gone down, the sky a dark blue, the house gloomy and still. I saw a shadow in one of the ground-floor windows. Healy maybe, or Matt. But why was the back door closed? Why was the Mercedes still open? Why was the vacuum cleaner switched on but lying on its side?

A light blinked once in the living room.

And then a split-second later, a noise ripped through the air.

It was a gunshot.

26

. . . 38 hours to go . . .

I sprinted to the back door.

It had been pulled most of the way shut, only a sliver of the kitchen visible in the gap between door and frame. Night was moving in fast, the sun gone from the sky, and it created shadows everywhere. I pulled the plug on the vacuum, the silence that replaced it deafening, and then slowly pushed the back door open. It creaked away softly on its hinges to show the kitchen.

I let my eyes adjust and inched inside.

Everything ahead of me was shrouded in the twilight: the worktops, the table, and then the door on the far side that led to the hallway and down to the living room.

I listened.

Somewhere on the roof, a crow squawked, then I heard the beat of its wings – and then it was gone and there was nothing. No sounds from deeper into the house. No voices.

No Healy.

No Matt.

I moved into the kitchen, quietly removed a knife from a block on the worktop, then stopped at the door. As I looked along the empty hallway, I realized how worthless a knife was going to be if someone in here had a gun, but I forced myself forward and listened again.

Who could have had a gun?

One thing was for certain: it wouldn't be Healy.

And that was exactly what I was worried about.

As I approached the doors on my left and right, I slowed, not wanting to be surprised, but when I peered in, I found the rooms unchanged. At the staircase I looked up, through the spiral of steps to the landing – but if there was someone up there, it was impossible to see.

My gaze returned to the living-room door.

Now, finally, I could hear something.

A dull *bumph-bumph* sound.

Keeping the knife up in front of me, I edged forward, my heart beating so hard it was like my bones were vibrating.

I held my breath as I got to the door.

And then I could see where the sound was coming from.

In the middle of the living room, Matt was on his back, blood all over him – it had soaked through his shirt, his jacket; spattered up his neck and over his face.

Healy was kneeling next to him.

The *bumph-bumph* sound was his hands on Matt's chest.

He was giving Matt CPR.

'Healy?'

He looked up, blood over his hands, over his lips as well where he'd had his mouth on Matt's, giving breaths. His face was beaded with sweat and he was panting.

'What the hell happened?'

Healy's eyes went to the door, then back to me.

'I don't know,' he whispered. 'But whoever did this is still here.'

27

. . . 38 hours to go . . .

I spun around, looking back down the hallway.

No movement anywhere.

No flicker of a shadow on a wall.

The only sound was Healy behind me, doing compressions on Matt, on a man that we both knew wasn't going to make it. Even if paramedics were on their way, it was going to be too late for him. His chest was a ragged mess. I could see tiny, singed circles in the walls at that end of the room, where shotgun pellets had gone through him and peppered the plasterboard.

I glanced at Healy and whispered, 'Who did this?'

'He had a mask.'

'Where did he go?'

'I don't know.' Healy was out of breath, exhausted. 'Matt came in here to get something,' he said, his voice barely even a whisper. 'And then he turned around and . . .' He pointed to the living-room door.

The gunman was suddenly just there.

The shock was hitting him. He'd paled, quietened, his breathing slowing. He was staring at the doorway, realizing how easily he could have been dead too.

A floorboard creaked above us.

Both of us looked up.

I waited for another creak, another sound, but there was nothing. Moving out of the living room into the hallway, I stopped at the foot of the staircase. Placing a foot on the first step, then the second, I tried not to make a sound. At the fifth step, because I was tall, my eyeline was level with the floor of the landing, and I could see from room to room.

The house creaked again.

It wasn't movement or a person.

It was the cold.

'Raker!'

I hurried back to the living room.

Healy was looking out through one of the far windows now, its view of the garden and stream, of the fields around us, of the place I'd called Marla from only moments ago.

Someone was at the bottom of the garden.

And he was making a run for it.

28

. . . 38 hours to go . . .

I raced to the bottom of the garden.

Over the hedgerows, a patchwork quilt of green and brown fields rolled ahead of me, either side of a narrow, V-shaped dent in the valley. In the dent was woodland, a thick ribbon of trees that was slowly starting to fade into darkness.

He was already halfway there.

I used a wooden stile to get up and over the hedgerow and then took off after him. There was a trail – part stone, part mud – but as the gloom set in, and especially as I started to descend into the valley, it became harder to make out the path. A couple of times I slid on a patch of dirt, almost losing my footing entirely. But I kept going, pushing on, my eyes trained on the movement ahead of me. I couldn't see much of him because he was mostly in black, but his T-shirt was a pale grey, and every time the wind picked up, it rippled like a tail behind him.

He has a gun, I thought.

He has a gun and you have nothing.

I'd left the knife back at the house; had put it down when I'd found Healy and forgotten to pick it up. Now I was trailing a killer into the night, unarmed.

Up ahead of me, I saw him stop, and then I realized he was getting up and over a gate, entering the woodland, awkwardly carrying the shotgun with him. It looked double-barrelled in a side-by-side configuration, like the type of gun a farmer might have. Even from where I was, I could tell it wasn't pump-action or semi-automatic – so it would only hold two shells.

And he'd already fired one.

As he landed on the other side, he glanced once in my direction, the mask he was wearing standing out against the night as it caught what little light made it down here. And then the mask and the man were gone again.

Into the woods.

Into the dark.

I felt a hitch in my stride and slowed, but it was too late: I was already at the gate. On the other side, a well-worn path snaked between high walls of oak trees. But only so far. The path faded, and it faded fast, the winter night swallowing it whole.

A little way down, it became pitch-black.

I'm going to be totally blind.

With a swift movement, I put one foot on the fence and then vaulted it, on to the other side, landing as softly as I could. I kept my eyes fixed on what was ahead of me, even as underfoot I felt the ground shift and slide, the mud slick, the trees forming a canopy above so that no sun got in during the day and no light bled in after dark.

I listened.

It was the middle of winter, so there were no birds. Any animals that might be here were hibernating. The night was still, only the hushed rustle of branches and a few dead leaves scattering. It was bitterly cold now too. The second the sun went down, the temperature had plunged. As I inched forward, trying to force myself to see into the dark, my breath started to form in front of me. I tried to slow my breathing, tried not to exhale as often, in case it helped him to find me.

This is suicide.

You have no clue where he is.

My hand went to my pocket automatically, to my phone, knowing I could solve the problem in a second by turning on the light. But the dark wasn't just my problem.

It was his too.

I couldn't see him.

That meant he couldn't see me.

I glanced across my shoulder, back towards the gate. I could barely make it out now – the top of it was a vague horizontal line; above that was the slope of the valley, reduced to little more than grey-black grass and the undefined contours of the path.

A noise.

I whipped back around, looking ahead of me.

I heard it again.

Now it sounded like it was coming from my right, away from the muddy trail I was on, inside the forest of oaks. I searched the gaps between trunks for any sign of the man, but I couldn't see anything.

It was like staring at a jet-black wall.

But then the noise came a third time.

It's twigs, cracking underfoot.

I stayed where I was, trying to isolate the sound, trying to decide where exactly it was coming from. It came again, a pause, and then again. I tried to still the sound of my heart, or at least tune it out. The noise from the twigs was so soft it could almost not have been there – except it *was* there, and I *could* hear it, and I knew it was him.

And now I knew what he was doing.

He was circling me.

29

. . . 38 hours to go . . .

I closed my eyes, trying to isolate the sound.

Another twig cracked.

The wind, so soft until now, roused, passing through the trees – branches creaking, undergrowth crackling. For a second, it disguised the fall of his steps.

Which means it'll also disguise mine.

I moved.

Keeping my eyes on the ground, trying to see where my feet were landing, I stepped off the trail and into the woods. I couldn't see very much, but I could feel it: everything was denser, more unruly, branches and brambles coming at me from all sides. I put a hand up in front of me and the flat of my palm hit the ruffled wall of a tree trunk.

The wind fell away again.

A tiny pinprick of light was escaping through the canopy, maybe ten feet from me. That was when I saw him, right on the very edge of the light.

His pale grey T-shirt.

I didn't move; held my breath.

I could see the shotgun.

He'd stopped, as if he'd sensed something had changed. The undergrowth was so thick here, so uneven underfoot, roots breaking out of the earth everywhere, that he had to readjust in order to land his foot somewhere flat.

His head moved.

The mask came around in my direction.

To start with, it was hard to get a sense of what exactly he was wearing on his face, because it appeared to be changing shape and colour the whole time.

The light caught it, just briefly, as he looked the other way.

I focused on his position, and then the wind came again – and when the trees moved, so did I. I took a big step forward, another, then a third – and stopped.

He was still in the same position.

He had no idea where I was.

I sized it up: there was maybe seven feet between us, maybe less. I had a better angle on him too: I was looking at his back, at the flap of grey T-shirt that had escaped from his waistband. The shotgun was at his side, barrel facing the ground.

One more rush of wind and I could get to him.

But then he started moving again, very slowly lifting a leg and placing it down, like the ground in the woods was made of porcelain. He'd figured me out: he knew I'd heard the crack of the twigs, knew I was somewhere else – not on the trail – and now he had to find out where. He took another step, so far beyond the patch of light that he was little more than a streak of grey paint.

I dropped to my haunches and felt around.

Twigs. Leaves. Mud. Grass.

A stone.

I picked it up and then tossed it in his direction. It landed exactly where I wanted it to, between him and the trail. It only made a soft pop, but in the silence of the woods, it was enough: he instantly swivelled, stiffened, the shotgun up.

His back was to me again.

I didn't move; hardly breathed.

And then, very gently, the wind returned: it stirred the branches and I saw him tilt his head slightly, as if trying to tune it all out.

By then I was already moving.

I smashed into him, hitting him with everything I had, the impact so hard, the shotgun spun away from him and we left the ground entirely. We careered past the treeline, out on to the trail – and when we landed, he was underneath me, face down.

All of my weight was on him.

His mask crunched against the mud, against his face.

The air left his body.

He hadn't even had a chance to catch his breath by the time I'd flipped him over, on to his back, one hand on his throat pinning him to the ground, the other ripping off the broken mask and tossing it aside. There was blood over his face, his nose busted.

I grabbed my phone, flicked on the torch.

The light blinded him, a groan passing from his throat to his lips. I started to realize his shoulder was dislocated. He moaned again, his eyes squeezed shut – and as I kept him pinned down, I washed the light over his face.

He was just a kid, no more than twenty.

I'd never seen him before in my life.

'What's your name?'

He blinked.

'*What's your name?*'

'That's not important,' he croaked.

'Why did you shoot Matt?' When he didn't answer, I shifted my knee and pressed it into his shoulder, and his scream of pain told me I was right: it was dislocated. Releasing the pressure, I leaned in: 'Who *are* you?'

Under the stark glare of the phone's light, I looked at his face again – his blue eyes, his blond hair, his straggly, untidy beard. My first thought was he might have been the man who'd posed as Noah Klein. But that man's description was totally different: forty-nine, five-ten, dark hair, dark eyes.

So maybe he's the one who helped Klein at the hospital.

'I can't breathe,' he choked.

'That's the whole point,' I said, and took my hand off his neck. He let out a gasp, bringing his hand up to his collarbone, his Adam's apple.

'You're going to talk to me,' I said.

He nodded; rubbed his windpipe.

'Who are you and why did you shoot Matt –'

Suddenly, he yanked a chain out from under his T-shirt.

On the end was a small, tube-shaped piece of plastic. I registered it, registered how cheap the chain and the pendant seemed, how odd it looked on him, and how disposable all of it appeared – but by then he already had the pendant in his mouth.

'No,' I said, trying to stop him, '*no.*'

He bit down on it.

The pendant shattered between his teeth.

I tried to get my hands into his mouth, to fish out what was left of the pendant, but it was too late: foam started bubbling at his lips – but even as it did, he kept his gaze fixed on mine, his eyes watering but absolutely alight, all of that pain forgotten.

'David Raker,' he croaked, his body shutting down.

And then he smiled.

Blood on his teeth.

Death foaming on his tongue.

'You have no idea what's coming . . .'

DAY ONE
Part Three

30

. . . 37 hours to go . . .

The house was crawling with cops inside thirty minutes.

A stern, monosyllabic scenes of crime officer from Surrey Police immediately separated me and Healy, bagged our clothes, took DNA swabs, then moved us into the back seat of two vehicles parked side by side on the street. From there, we watched everything unfold from a distance. Eventually, one of the detectives came over, introduced himself as DI Dougan and asked if I could walk him back into the valley and go over what had happened. I knew, given my history with the police, that suspicion would fall on me, which was why I'd left everything untouched down there.

We'd already given initial accounts of what had happened at the house, but now Dougan made me run through it all again, making notes as I talked. Techs circled the body of the young man I didn't know, bagging what little was left of the necklace he'd bitten down on, the shotgun, and the mask I'd torn off and tossed aside.

And it was the mask I couldn't stop looking at, the mask that slowly filled me with a creeping dread.

It wasn't just the way it looked.

It was what it was made of.

With lamps washing across the trail while the forensic team worked, I watched as a tech picked the mask up off the ground and guided it into an evidence bag. The inside was plain white plastic, but the outside was different. As soon as it was moved, bits fell away from the front, tiny shards dropping into the mud.

They were pieces from a broken mirror.

Hundreds of them had been stuck to the front, overlapping, all different sizes, all thicknesses and shapes. Except for the black of the eyes and two nose holes, everything was a jagged, uneven, monstrous-looking visage that reflected back a fractured image of the forest. And given everything that had happened over the last eleven hours, it felt like another deliberate message.

Worse, it felt like absolute confirmation of what I'd feared.

I thought of the man who'd abducted Preston Stewart and had chosen the name Noah Klein.

And then I thought of the killer who'd gone by that very same alias fourteen years ago – along with many others – as he'd murdered seven women.

His name was Glass.

And that was exactly what the mask in the woods was made from.

31

. . . 35 hours to go . . .

By 8.45 p.m., I was in a police station in Guildford.

I didn't have my mobile phone because it had been bagged as evidence at the house, but the cop who'd interviewed me, Dougan, had seen messages popping up on it and had informed me that Rebekah had been texting me. The fact that he mentioned anything was surprising. It wasn't the kind of welcome I usually got at police stations, and I took it as a positive sign.

I called her from a phone in a small, nondescript room at the back of the building with no windows and – as I waited for her to answer – tried to think how long it was since anyone had been this concerned for me.

Too long, I thought.

Rebekah picked up after a couple of rings.

'Hello?'

'Bek, it's David.'

'Oh hey. Are you all right?'

'I'm fine. Sort of. I'm in a police station at the moment.'

'Shit. Are you in trouble?'

'No.' I thought of Dougan mentioning Rebekah's texts when he didn't have to. What if it was all some game to him? A way to lull me into a false sense of security? 'I don't think so, anyway.'

'Is there anything I can do?'

'No,' I said. 'No, I'm just sorry I'm not there. I don't know what time I'll be back.'

'It's okay. The most important thing is you're all right.'

I felt that same spark; the warmth I'd forgotten I needed,

forgotten how to feel, when someone other than your family cared this much about you. 'I'm fine,' I replied. 'I promise to make it up to you.'

'You don't have to make anything up to me,' she said softly. 'If it wasn't for you, I would never have found out where my mum went. And if it wasn't for you . . .' She stopped, went quiet. 'If it wasn't for you, I wouldn't have travelled three thousand miles to take care of something I could just as easily have done over Zoom.'

That same warmth again, like heat in my blood.

And even deep in the bowels of a police station – even in the middle of a case that felt like it was spinning further away from my control with every second – it brought home to me again how much I'd missed that feeling since I'd lost Derryn.

'Well, I'm glad you decided against the Zoom option,' I said.

'Yeah.' I could hear the smile in her voice. 'Yeah, I am too.'

Pausing there for a moment, the phone still against my ear, I closed my eyes, trying to retain some of the feeling I was getting from the call with Rebekah. But it didn't last long. Everything slowly faded in around me: the hum of the air conditioning, the dim lighting in the cramped room, the presence of an officer right outside the door. The shooting. This case. The unanswered questions.

Next, I called Ellie.

'I just landed,' she responded immediately, her voice taut. 'The police are here.'

'At the airfield?'

'*Yes*. What's going on? Where's Matt?'

I paused, the image of Matt's broken, bloodied body burned on to my eyes, the dull noise of Healy's chest compressions like a heartbeat I couldn't still.

'Why are the police here, David? I specifically *told* you I didn't want them anywhere near this –'

'Ellie, I need to ask you some questions.'

'Okay.' She still sounded angry, but now there was confusion too.

'Was Matt the one that suggested you hire me?'

'What? Yes. Well, he gave me a list of names.'

'But what made you choose me?'

'I can't remember exactly,' she said. 'I think your name was at the top and he told me you were meant to be good. Why, what's going on?'

'Did he talk about any of the other names on the list in that way?'

'What do you mean?'

'I mean, did he say any of the others were any good?'

'No, not that I recall. Why?'

Because he told me some of the others were ex-army friends of his. He told me his friends had found missing people before and were better at this than me. But if he knew they were better than me and they were friends of his, why didn't he suggest them to Ellie first? Why would he big me up and not them?

The answer seemed obvious.

Matt wanted her to hire me. He wanted me to find Noah Klein. He wanted me to make the connection to Glass. But why?

'Have you ever heard the name Noah Klein?' I asked.

She took a moment. 'No.'

'What about Marco Roy?'

'No.'

'Zauna Roy? Sydney Roder? Anna Casey?'

'No. No, none of them. Who *are* these people?'

'They're names I've come across in the search for Preston and I'm trying to figure out why and where they fit in. I'm sorry to bombard you like this, but I'm at a police station with no access to my phone – and this will be my one chance to call you for a while.'

'A police station? What's happened?'

'It's Matt.' I swallowed. 'He's been killed, Ellie.'

'*What?*

There was a horrified silence as I explained what had happened earlier at the house — and then after the silence came the muted sound of sobbing. As I listened, there was a knock at the door. Through a glass panel I could see Dougan, tapping his watch. I held up a hand, telling him I was almost done.

'Can you think of any reason Matt might have been targeted?'

'No,' she replied. 'No, I wouldn't have the first idea.'

'And he's seemed okay in the last few weeks?'

'Yes.'

Dougan knocked on the door again.

'This is going to be all over the bloody newspapers,' Ellie said quietly.

She was probably right. Even if Surrey Police weren't as porous as the Met had been, sooner or later the details of Matt's murder were going to be made public. And those stories would talk about his history, and his job, and who he was working for.

'One last question,' I said.

I could hear Ellie's heels clacking against what must have been the runway's tarmac. The more she walked, the more other things slowly began to fade in — car engines idling and the muted crackle of radios. She was nearing the police.

'Have you ever heard of someone called Dr Glass?'

'No,' Ellie said. 'Does he work at The Crest?'

'No, he's in prison.'

'Oh.'

'Fourteen years ago, he killed seven women.'

I heard Ellie slowing down.

And then she stopped completely.

'Wait,' she said, 'was he that plastic surgeon?'

I tensed. 'Yes.'

'The one that was kidnapping all those women and trying to . . .' She paused again, not knowing how to articulate Glass's work. 'Was trying to . . . change them?'

'Yes. What do you know about him?'

On the line, I heard a male voice say, 'Ms Snyder?'

'Just give me a second,' she responded, and then must have angled her body away from the police because the peripheral sound dulled just a little. 'A couple of months back, I was at the Barbican. It was nothing special – it was just this thing for the podcast business I co-founded. Marian – my business partner – had arranged a load of press. Anyway, I was late leaving the last interview, and Matt had texted me to tell me where he'd wait for me, so I headed down to the car. And when I got there, he was on his phone – and that was what he was reading about.'

I frowned. 'What do you mean?'

'That guy you mentioned. The one who killed the women.'

'Matt was reading about Glass?'

'Yes. I could see the headline.'

'You're sure?'

'Yes, positive. It lodged with me because I'd never seen Matt reading anything except sports stuff – it was always biographies, or books about football. That was all he *ever* read. That plastic surgeon thing, it was really unusual.'

'Did you ask him about it?'

'I did, but he just brushed it off as nothing.'

'And you never saw him reading about Glass after that?'

'No, never,' Ellie said. 'Is this why he's dead?'

Dougan opened the door to the room. 'Time's up.'

'David?' Ellie was still on the line. 'Is this why Matt's *dead*?'

'I don't know,' I said to her, because that was the easiest answer for now. But as I looked at Dougan, his face grim, I wondered if I was about to find out.

32

. . . 34 hours to go . . .

Dougan took me to an interview room and was soon flanked by another cop called Bodie, and the two men made me go over my account of what happened at the house yet again, this time for the tape. I'd asked for the duty solicitor – who was in the seat next to me – even though Dougan had assured me, as of now, that I wasn't a suspect.

But I'd heard that song from the cops before.

It took an hour to go through everything. I had no choice but to tell them I was working for Ellie. I had to give a reason for us being at the house, and that meant talking about Preston and about his disappearance, and how I'd ended up working it.

'So Ellie doesn't trust cops?' Dougan asked after I was done.

'Well, she doesn't trust them not to talk to the media.'

'Weren't you a journalist once?'

'That was a long time ago.'

Dougan nodded. 'These days you're an investigator.'

I studied him, trying to decide if it was a statement laced with the usual contempt detectives held for me. It was difficult to tell, Dougan's fifty-year-old face opaque. Even back at the house, he'd rarely deviated from the same expression, same voice, same manner. I imagined it made him an effective cop, someone who people underestimated because there didn't seem to be much to him. Bodie, next to him, was much less mysterious: about the same age as Dougan but far easier to read.

'This Matthew Higgs,' Dougan said. 'What did you find out about him?'

'Not much.'

'As I understand it, he was an ex-soldier?'

'Yes.'

'He was in the army. He'd been to warzones. He'd spent time around guns and men who knew how to use them. Do you think his death is connected to his history in the military?'

'I don't know.'

It wasn't a lie. I didn't; not for certain. But somehow I doubted it. Matt was the one who'd directed Ellie to hire me. He was the one who'd been looking at a news article on Glass only a couple of months before he was killed. The kid who'd shot him had worn a mask of broken glass, and Preston – Matt's employer – had been abducted by a man using one of Glass's pseudonyms. This wasn't to do with his time in the army.

Dougan removed a photograph from a folder he'd brought with him and slid it across the table towards me. It was Matt's killer, his skin cut from where the hard plastic interior of the mask had cracked against his face as I'd landed on top of him. Dougan tapped a finger to the picture: 'Who's this?'

'I don't know.'

'You've never seen him before?'

'Never.' I studied Dougan. 'Do you know who he is?'

Dougan shook his head. 'Nope. No ID on him, no sign of a car parked close by, so he either walked all the way from the train station in Gomshall, got a bus in, or got dropped off. Maybe we'll get lucky with the DNA swab and he'll have a record. Maybe the dental records will come up trumps. Or maybe the gun will take us somewhere – registration, ownership – *if* this gun is either legal or actually belongs to him, which, if I had to guess, I suspect will be a no on both counts. After that, it'll be a CCTV trawl to try and see if we can pick up a trail.'

Dougan glanced at the man in the picture, then at me.

'Why?' he continued. 'I mean, that's the million-dollar question here. Why was this kid at Preston's house? Why did he shoot

Matt and not you or Healy? Why did he take a necklace full of poison with him? Was it a last resort in case everything went tits up – or was it always the plan to bite down on it at the end of this whole . . .' He faded out.

This whole what?

'I don't know about the poison,' I said, 'but I think Matt might have been working with whoever Noah Klein is.' I told them about Matt drawing up a list of investigators for Ellie and pushing her towards me.

'Why would he and Klein want you to connect the dots like that?' Dougan asked.

'I don't know,' I repeated. 'Maybe they're toying with us. Maybe it's a message.'

'A message?'

'Maybe they're telling us history's about to repeat itself.'

'What, that this Noah Klein guy's going to pick up where Glass left off?'

I shrugged.

'Glass murdered people,' Dougan said, 'he didn't make them disappear.'

'He made them disappear before he murdered them.'

'So you think this could be a copycat?'

'I don't know what it is,' I said, 'but if I was in your shoes, I'd be asking Lyegate Prison to send across a list of all the visitors Glass has had over the last few months.'

'As I understand it, Glass doesn't get many visitors.'

'It's still worth checking.'

Dougan's gaze remained on mine. 'Do you think Klein and the kid in the mask killed Matthew Higgs because he was no longer aligned with their plans?'

'Why else would you turn a shotgun on someone?'

'There are all sorts of reasons why people get kill–'

'Within this context, I mean.'

Dougan didn't respond.

'If I had to take a guess,' I said, 'and it's just that – a guess – I'd say that Matt was having second thoughts, and that became dangerous for them.'

'Why would he start to wobble like that?'

'I think he liked Ellie. I saw it in the car this morning. I heard it in his voice.' Next to Dougan, Bodie rolled his eyes. 'Look, you can believe me or not,' I said, 'but that's the sense I got. I think, whatever role in this he had, he'd started to lose faith in it because he could see it would hurt Ellie. Maybe he started pushing back against this Noah Klein guy and the kid in the woods, not wanting to do whatever it was they were asking him to do. That would certainly explain why they shot –'

'This is just wild speculation,' Bodie said, cutting me off.

These were the first words he'd spoken for an hour.

'It's speculation,' I said calmly, 'but I don't think it's wild. Have you been through Matt's phone? His texts? His emails?'

'Whether we have or we haven't is no concern of your–'

'Go through his phone. If there's nothing on there, then you can come back and call me a fraud.'

Dougan had started softly rubbing his thumb and forefinger together. It felt like a reaction to Bodie cutting his rhythm dead. 'Okay, let's park that for now,' he said, and came forward, letting Bodie know that he was in charge and he was going to dictate the pace of the interview. 'Tell me about the Lost Women of Porthtreno?'

'What about them?'

'When was it you realized that Preston might be interested in them?'

'When we got to his house. I saw he'd watched the documentary and then Healy found a copy of the book in a bedside cabinet. It's another reason why I believe I was deliberately chosen for this job. The Lost Women was a story I covered, and spent a lot of time on, back when I was a journalist. I mean, if you can't get behind the idea that Matt was a part of whatever is going on here, then you have to believe that it was a complete coincidence that Ellie hired me to find Preston – *and* that Preston just happened to be interested in a story I'd covered back in the day. You also have to buy into the name Noah Klein being chosen completely at random.' I looked between them. 'This is all deliberate. It's the only way it remotely stacks up.'

'What about this?' Dougan said, and slid a photo of the mirror mask across the table. The picture had been taken in the woods, the individual pieces of broken glass shining under the lights that had been set up down there. Hundreds of versions of the same image – the forensic tech with their camera up – were reflected back, repeated over and over in the fractured mask. 'Have you ever seen anything like this before?'

'No.'

'And you said you didn't know what the kid meant at the end when he told you, "You have no idea what's coming"?'

'No.'

'So Noah Klein is a total mystery, so is the kid wearing the mask, and so is his warning about you having no idea what's coming.' It was a statement, not a question, and Dougan's delivery meant that it was difficult to get a handle on where exactly his thoughts had landed. 'Is that everything?'

The one thing I hadn't talked about was Preston's drunken confession to Ellie and the suspicion that the person Preston killed might have been Marco Roy. In truth, I wasn't exactly certain why I'd chosen to keep that part back. Maybe it was so that I could retain a little control; have something of worth to offer as a bargaining chip later on, if I needed it. Maybe it was territorial: this was my case, and I hated the idea of not being able to finish it. Or maybe it was because, when I'd got back to the house from the woods, I'd told Healy we needed to go easy on what we told the cops, and Preston's confession seemed an obvious thing to hold back. It was possible – somewhere else in the station – he'd bowed to pressure and had mentioned what Preston had told

Ellie, but it seemed unlikely. It was the cops who'd got in his way when he'd tried to find Leanne.

He hated them more than I ever could.

Dougan was quiet for a moment, studying the notes he'd made and tapping his pen against the page. Bodie was still slumped in his seat, arms crossed, staring at me.

Someone knocked at the door.

Bodie stood to open it.

I couldn't see who was there, could just hear Bodie talking in a low whisper. But Dougan seemed to know who Bodie was in conversation with straight away, because he ripped his gaze from his notebook, got up and went to the door.

He pulled it all the way back.

Now I could see who else was out there.

And as I did, my stomach dropped.

Naughton

Six Hours Ago

The room they were in at the prison was small and dingy.

One window, high up.

A table and four chairs, all bolted to the floor.

A bland shade of magnolia had been used everywhere and had darkened over time. As Rosa Naughton went to her phone and set up the recording app, she noticed a hole above the skirting board, next to the door. It looked like someone had put a boot through the wall. Insulation was spilling out, dust specking the carpet.

Next to her, Phillips was testing the tape player he'd brought with him. It was an insurance policy. If there was some technical problem with either of their phones, they could fall back on the tape. Whatever happened, they needed this on record.

After that, they waited in silence, Phillips checking his watch, his fingers playing with the corners of the file he'd brought with him. Naughton glanced at it. She knew what was inside, because Phillips had shown her. It was a cross-section of a fourteen-year-old case; carefully selected pages that Phillips thought might be useful for whatever was coming. Interview transcripts. Evidence inventories. Crime-scene photographs from the Dead Tracks. Naughton had looked at every single one of those photographs, and at the hundreds of others back at the station, and it occurred to her what a shot in the dark it was for Phillips to have selected pictures he thought might be useful. How could he possibly make an informed choice when they didn't have a clue what *this* was? Glass had sent out the message that he wanted to talk. They'd dropped everything to accommodate him. But it could just as easily have been a trick.

Images from the Dead Tracks flashed in her head. It was in that forest, out in east London, that six women had been found in clear plastic coffins filled with liquid formaldehyde. A seventh had been found in a wall cavity nearby, and Glass had kept all of them hidden in a disused sewer network thirty feet under the earth. As she went through the pictures of the women in her head – of how six of them had been found and lined up, weirdly peaceful as they floated inside the coffins – she realized her leg was vibrating nervously under the table. She stopped. Phillips noticed. 'I know it's hard,' he said, 'but don't show him.'

Don't show him you're nervous.
Don't show him you're scared.
Don't show him anything.

'Don't think of him as a killer,' he went on. 'It's counter-intuitive, but if you think about him in terms of his crimes, it'll be harder. He's like a shark. He's constantly moving forward, looking for the smell of blood in the water. If you think of him as a killer, if you look at him across the table and see the man who did this shite' – he gestured to the file – 'you're done. It will throw you off your game and he will sense it the second that happens.'

Except he isn't any other man, Naughton thought.

She tried to keep her mind clear, but soon, like animals stalking in from the shadows, the images were back in her head, and she was seeing the coffins and the wall cavity, and the faces of the women, and she started thinking about Leanne Healy, a woman she'd never known, except through her dad. And then Naughton thought of the last time she'd spoken to Healy.

It must have been seventeen years ago.

She remembered the months when they'd worked together, and then the way it had ended between them in the aftermath of the Red Woman investigation. Naughton had never been able to get beyond her memories of that case, of having a killer's knife at her throat and of Healy being only feet from her, unable to do anything. When she slept, she could feel the blade against her skin. When she was on other cases, that one would flash back to her. But it was always around Healy when she would spiral the worst: every time she looked at him in the weeks and months after it happened, she was back in the dark, and the Red Woman was behind her, and there was no escape.

Voices outside the room brought her back.

Three-quarters of the way up the door there was a small glass panel, three inches thick and reinforced. A prison officer's face appeared from the right of it, his eyes settling on Phillips and Naughton. He looked back the way he'd come, and said, 'Remember the rules.'

He's speaking to Glass.

'Don't mess around,' the officer continued, 'and don't give us a reason to pull you out of this room and drag your arse back to the floor. If you do that, I'll be upset.'

The prison officer entered.

A second officer appeared in the doorway, then took a step back, watching as the prisoner moved towards him.

Finally, he appeared.

Glass.

Fourteen years ago, and in all the photographs Naughton had seen of him, he was – it pained her to admit – very attractive. Dark brown hair, brown eyes, fit, slim. Now he was much thinner, paler. He was fifty-two but looked older, the weight loss ageing him. Most of his hair was gone, just a hint of it in a horseshoe between his ears. Yet, as he entered, his wrists handcuffed, in a hoodie, trainers and a pair of tracksuit trousers, Naughton could see some things hadn't changed.

It's those eyes.

They flicked to Naughton, taking her in for a split second, and then settled on Phillips. They stayed there – the intelligence behind them so obvious now, his brain working – and he said, 'Aiden.'

Phillips nodded a hello and then said, 'And what can I call you?'

'I didn't realize I was so mysterious.'

Glass glanced at Naughton and gave her a *What's he like?* look.

'Well, you've had a few names down the years.'

'That's what they say about the devil.' Again, Glass looked at Naughton – but, this time, his eyes lingered on her. 'I don't mind,' he said, talking to Phillips but looking at her. She was finding it hard not to turn away. 'Just call me Glass if you prefer.'

His attention switched back to Phillips.

Naughton took a breath.

Glass slowly pulled a chair out from under the table and eased himself down, and behind him the officer said to Phillips, 'One of us will be outside at all times if you need anything.' Phillips said thank you and the officer exited.

Glass glanced at the plain, brown card cover on the file, then his gaze returned to Naughton. She held it as best she could – but she realized now that she hated his eyes, hated how dark they were, how bottomless, how every time he looked at her it felt like she was sitting here naked with every thought in her head projected on the walls.

He smiled at her. 'And who do we have here?'

'Detective Inspector Naughton,' she said.

The words came out strong enough.

But he looked at her like he knew it was an act.

'You got us in here to tell us something,' Phillips said.

Glass pulled his gaze back from Naughton.

'Yes, Aiden, I did.'

'About what went on at the Dead Tracks fourteen years ago?'

'In a way.'

'So what do you want to tell us?'

Glass sat back in his chair, hands together on his lap, his tongue moving along his teeth as if he was trying to dislodge a sliver of food.

Phillips gave him a couple of seconds and then said, 'No, this isn't what's going to happen. If you want to talk, talk. If you want to piss around and play games, we're getting up and we're leaving right –'

'Let me ask you something.' Glass said, cutting him off.

And then he looked between them both, drawing it out.

'Have either of you heard of Porthtreno?'

33

. . . 33 hours to go . . .

Detective Superintendent Aiden Phillips entered the interview room.

'Hello, David,' he said, the greeting to me so neutral it might have sounded like we barely knew each other.

But we did know each other.

That was just the problem.

He'd been the SIO on the Glass case fourteen years ago and he'd actively come after me and Healy in the aftermath. When I'd exposed police corruption, Phillips hadn't been one of the cops who'd been outed, but he'd been a senior officer and had ignored the warning signs, and that had made him guilty by association. He'd been temporarily suspended before eventually being reinstated, but it had damaged his reputation, and his anger towards me had festered. He'd patiently pursued me in the time since – trying to get something to stick, trying to expose me as a dangerous charlatan – and almost had me cornered a few years ago. But then a mistake in his personal life – and a leaked story about him and his wife – had broken the surface and I'd managed to get away from him again. The leak hadn't come from me, it had come from another cop, but he'd blamed me all the same.

He moved further into the room, pulling the chair Dougan had been using out from the table. As he did, a woman in her forties followed him in – dark hair, petite but solid – a lanyard around her neck announcing her as another cop.

'This is Detective Inspector Rosa Naughton,' Phillips said.

She took the second chair as Dougan and Bodie reappeared, carrying seats of their own. Neither of them said anything.

'What the hell's going on?' I asked, looking between them all.

Phillips got out a notebook, making me wait.

I glanced at Naughton again. *Rosa.* That was the name of the person who'd called Healy at Preston's house from his old landline at the Met. As I thought of that, I thought of the feeling I'd had at Healy's flat, the vague sense that he may have been keeping something hidden. I'd given him the benefit of the doubt – but what if that had been a mistake? What if it had been something to do with Naughton?

'Tell me more about Porthtreno,' Phillips said.

I frowned. 'What?'

'Porthtreno,' he repeated.

My solicitor – who I'd almost forgotten was here – came forward at the table and said to Phillips, 'Mr Raker is under no obligation to answer your questions, especially since you haven't even done him the courtesy of introducing yourself.'

Phillips stared at me like the solicitor hadn't said a word.

'Mr Raker and I know each other from way back, don't we, David?' He finally glanced at the solicitor. 'DSU Aiden Phillips.'

I saw the solicitor shift, and knew what he must have been thinking: he'd been in many interview rooms down the years, representing many different people, and he had rarely, if ever, seen a cop at Phillips's level turn up and do the interview himself.

Except this wasn't an interview.

Phillips hadn't read me my rights, hadn't reached for the tape, hadn't bothered ticking any of the boxes he needed to if this conversation was going to be used at any point down the line.

He was here for another reason.

He's fishing for information.

'Why are you asking me about Porthtreno?' I said.

'You've been telling Detective Inspector Dougan all about it for the past hour.' He shrugged like it was obvious. 'I'm just interested in finding out more.'

'I don't believe you,' I said. 'Why are you really here, Phillips?'

'It's Detective Superintendent Phillips.'

'I don't give a shit what it is. I know you're not here officially – at least, not yet – because if you were, you would have been forced to read me my rights, or actually explain what's going on, and this wouldn't still be off.' I gestured to the recording equipment. 'So why don't we lay our cards on the table and get it all out in the open?'

Phillips stared at me, unmoved.

Naughton had glanced up from her notebook, her eyes moving between me and her boss, as if she'd never heard anyone speak to him this way before.

'You know something, David,' Phillips said finally, voice low, simmering, 'every day since you and I first met, I've been waiting for the moment when everything goes spectacularly wrong for you. The moment when that silver tongue of yours just can't *quite* get you out of the latest hole you're in, or you don't get to jump through the world's tiniest loophole, or you can't persuade a piece of shit like Colm Healy to side with you. I wait for that day – I wait for it patiently – and it has never come. And, let me tell you, that's *so* frustrating. But I'm a professional so I've learned to let it go. I just keep my focus on the positives. And the biggest positive is that, since I became a DSU, I get to drown in paperwork and politics, and utterly tedious as both of those things are, they mean that I have never, ever had to cross paths with you on cases, and that makes my day one hundred per cent better, one hundred per cent of the time.' He stopped, looked around the room. 'And now you've even gone and spoiled that.'

Before I had a chance to respond, he turned to Naughton and she got up and went to the door. Opening it fully, she stood there for a second, watching someone approaching in the corridor outside.

It was a uniformed officer.

Next to him was Healy.

'So,' Phillips said. 'I guess it's cards-on-the-table time.'

Healy

Two Hours Ago

'Have you talked to Raker yet?' Healy asked.

Dougan came forward in his seat, hands on the table in front of him, fingers laced together. In the chair beside him, Bodie had been making some notes, but now he looked up and both of them stared at Healy.

'I spoke to him at the house,' Dougan said. 'We'll talk to him again once we're done with you.' Dougan, his expression still, tilted his head slightly. 'Why, is there something in particular I should ask him?'

Healy looked at the empty seat alongside him. Raker had asked for a solicitor and had told Healy to do the same, telling him it was worth having someone in the room to keep the cops in check. But Healy had passed.

'*Is* there something I should be asking Mr Raker?' Dougan repeated.

'No.'

Healy's thoughts shifted to what he'd found in Alice-Leigh's drawer the day before; the papers he'd seen her going through and that he'd gone through himself once Alice had joined the others downstairs.

He still hadn't mentioned what he'd found to Raker because . . .

Healy stopped. *Because what?*

Because Raker would go nuts if Healy told him what he planned to do with the information he'd found in that paperwork.

Dougan gathered up his notes. 'Can we get you anything to eat? A sandwich? Do you want a drink?'

'Coffee would be good.'

'Black, right?' He gestured to a cup in front of Healy.

'Yeah,' Healy said. 'Thanks.'

The two cops left.

In the silence of the interview room, Healy retreated to what he'd found in Alice's drawer. But then the door to the interview room opened again, disturbing his train of thought, and a uniformed officer came in, cup in hand. Healy thanked him and watched the officer head out.

He didn't close the door.

Healy wasn't under arrest, so he was free to leave at any time – but if he bolted now, it might make them question why he was in such a hurry to exit the station. Even so, interview rooms were always closed if they were in use.

Unless . . .

Healy heard footsteps.

Unless this is the start of something else.

Rosa Naughton appeared in the doorway. 'Hey, Colm.'

'What the hell are you doing here?'

She came further in. It had been a very long time since they'd seen each other in the flesh, but while seventeen years had altered Healy profoundly – physically and emotionally – Naughton had changed far less. Her face showed a few more lines, a few freckles on her nose and cheeks, but not much else. Healy imagined, in return, Naughton was looking at him, thinking the total opposite: he'd lost a ton of weight, he'd shaved off his hair, he'd grown a thick, red beard, and looked about a hundred years older.

'I have some questions,' she said.

'About?'

She came to the table, put down her notebook and a phone. 'I want to follow up on Alice-Leigh Reddy.'

'I already told you everything I know earlier on the phone.'

'No, you told me to go fuck myself – and then hung up.'

'Maybe you should take the hint, then, Rosa.'

She just smiled at him.

'Alice is my son's girlfriend,' he said.

'I know.'

'She's the mother of my granddaughter.'

'I know that too.'

'So, if you want to talk about her, you need to tell me why.' Healy paused. He wanted to know why – he *really* wanted to know why – Rosa had decided to pick up the phone to him after seventeen years to talk about a girl who'd only entered Healy's life twenty months ago. Was it to do with her father? Was it to do with what Healy had found in Alice's drawer? Or was it something else entirely? He craved the answer but, at the same time, didn't want to give Rosa the satisfaction of his desperation. He shifted in his seat. 'I don't discuss my family with people I don't trust.'

'Is that what she is, Colm? Family?'

'You going to tell me why you're here or just sit there grinning like a Cheshire cat?' Over Naughton's shoulder, someone else appeared in the doorway. Healy hadn't even heard them approaching.

His stomach plunged.

'You've got to be fucking kidding me,' he muttered.

'Colm,' Aiden Phillips responded. 'It's been a while.'

Healy glanced at Naughton.

He felt like he'd walked into a trap.

Naughton gave him nothing, just kept her attention fixed on him, as Phillips came further in and pushed the door closed behind him. It was the first time Healy had laid eyes on him since Leanne had died; since he'd had to sit in an interview room and listen to Phillips's bullshit questions. He'd been relatively gentle with Healy in those first days, because even a robotic arsehole like Phillips could imagine what it was like to lose a child. But once the dust settled, and especially after Healy served his suspension for teaming up with Raker to track down Glass, Phillips had set his dogs loose. Healy had gone back to work, and his life had been made a living hell. Phillips was one of the major reasons Healy got sacked, one of the major reasons he'd spiralled into depression after. His lackeys had pushed Healy's buttons, banking on him self-destructing, and they did it knowing he was vulnerable and grieving.

Phillips sat down, straightening his tie. His hair had thinned and his face was older, but he still dressed like he shopped on Savile Row, and his aftershave was still too strong. 'I imagine you have questions.'

Healy laughed. 'You think?'

'Where do you want to start?'

'How about why the fuck *you're* here?'

'When Rosa called you earlier to ask you about Alice-Leigh Reddy, we were on our way back from Berkshire.' A pause. 'We'd just been to Lyegate Prison.'

'What?' Healy felt like he'd been hit by a truck. He wasn't sure what he'd been expecting, but it hadn't been this. 'You went to see him?'

'Yes,' Phillips said.

'*Why?*'

'He requested a meeting with us.'

'He "requested" one?'

'Yes.'

'"Us"? Do you mean the police – or you personally?'

'The police. And for obvious reasons, it got passed to me.'

Healy looked between Phillips and Naughton.

'*And?*'

'He's lost some weight,' Phillips said, 'and we've all got a little older, but otherwise it was pretty much what you would expect. A lot of games. Little comments. Lies and half-truths.' Phillips's voice rarely went much above a highly controlled hush, but as he described Glass, Healy could hear the distaste. It was maybe the one thing that Healy actually had in common with him. 'He knows about Alice.'

'So? He murdered her mother when she was two. It's not like he never knew he had a kid.'

'No, you misunderstand me,' Phillips said. 'I meant, he knows about Alice *now*. He knows she changed her surname. He knows what she does for a living. He knows where she lives, and *who* she's living with, and he knows that Alice has a little girl.'

'And how the fuck does he know that?'

Phillips looked at Naughton and then watched as she unclipped her notebook and opened the front cover. Inside, on top, was a piece of paper, folded quarter size. Naughton removed it, unfolded it, then slid it across the table to Healy.

It was a list – split into three columns – with surnames and first names in the first column, and times and dates in the second and third. Healy only knew it was people's names because FULL NAME was printed at the top of the first column. He wouldn't have known otherwise, because every name had been redacted.

Or, at least, every name except one.

'What's this?' Healy said.

'That's all the visitors Glass has had in fourteen years.'

Healy looked at the list again.

Ten people in almost a decade and a half.

And at the bottom, unredacted, was Alice.

34

. . . 33 hours to go . . .

They brought a chair in for Healy.

'We went in to see Glass earlier,' Phillips said once we were all seated.

I glanced at Healy, next to me, who showed no reaction to the news.

He already knows.

'He told us he wanted to talk, including about the Dead Tracks.'

I turned to Healy a second time. He was staring ahead, deliberately so, trying not to show anyone in the room anything. Not the pain, not the misery, not the loss.

I waited for more.

But Phillips just stared at me.

'So what you're telling me is, totally out of nowhere and after fourteen years, Glass decides to pick up the phone because he fancies chatting about his crimes?'

'In a nutshell,' Phillips said, simply.

'And that doesn't smell off to you?'

'I'm not naive.'

'So what did he say?'

He tapped a finger against his notebook. 'You held out on us, David.'

'What are you talking about?'

'When DI Dougan was asking you questions about Preston Stewart, you didn't tell him about Preston's drunken confession to his wife.'

In everything that was going on, I'd almost forgotten that Ellie had been met off her plane by the police. She must have felt like she had no choice but to tell them.

'I wasn't holding out on –'

'You and Healy knew that was a key piece of information,' he said, cutting me off, 'and neither of you thought to mention it. It makes me reluctant to trust you.'

I smiled humourlessly. 'I think we're a little past that, don't you?' I looked at Dougan. 'Don't take it personally. I'm sure you're one of the good ones, but when I've put my faith in cops in the past, it's tended to end badly.' I turned to face Phillips again, the implication clear. 'We're not under caution and – as far as I can tell – Healy and I aren't under suspicion for the shooting, so I had no obligation to tell Dougan, or you, or anyone in this room, anything. However, I went ahead and *did* tell Dougan ninety-nine per cent of what I know, because I was trying to help, and the rest of it I held back because I don't know how it fits in.'

'That's a load of shite and you know it,' Phillips replied. 'Because here's the other thing, David: we did some digging around and we discovered that Preston Stewart and Marco Roy were at university at the same time as one another – in the same *year*, in fact.'

'And?'

'That's cute. They were both down in Bristol at the same time Marco disappeared. Preston says he and an accomplice killed someone. It's easy maths.'

'What did Glass say?'

'He said a lot of things.'

'Meaning?'

'We're still trying to make sense of it all.'

'Alice-Leigh went in to see him.' Healy this time. I looked across at him, then back to Phillips. 'She went in before Christmas. They just told me in the other room.'

Healy looked away from me, shifting fractionally in his seat. It was such a tiny movement it probably hadn't even been noticed by anyone else. His eyes were fixed on a patch of carpet in the middle of the room, fingers twisting and re-twisting a knot of red hairs at the end of his beard. I waited for him to look across at me again, to make eye contact, because I knew if he did I'd be able to get a read on him. I'd be able to see what had made him shift slightly; whether it was to do with what he'd been told in the other room, or if it was related to my suspicions in his flat earlier that he was holding something back. But he just kept staring at the ground.

'You didn't know Alice had been in to Lyegate?' I asked Healy.
'Do you think I would have forgotten to mention it if I did?'
I don't know, I thought. *Maybe.*
'That's all I know,' he said. 'That's all he would tell me.' The *he* was Phillips and – just from that one word and the way it was delivered – I was reminded again of how much they loathed each other, their enmity a level above Phillips's and my own.

'Have you spoken to Alice?' I asked Phillips.
'Yes.'
'What did she say happened when she went in to see him?'
'She said Glass apologized to her.'
'For what?'
'For killing her mother,' Phillips said, and flipped back in his notebook. He began reading off a page packed with his handwriting. 'He told her he had very few memories of that period – that it was a "fugue state" – but he deeply regrets what he did, the pain he caused her, and knows fully well the burden he's left her with.'

Phillips kept his attention fixed on his notes. When I looked at Naughton, she turned away. When I glanced at Dougan, he stared back as blankly as always. But in Bodie's face I saw something; a momentary oscillation in his expression.

'What's really going on here?' I said to Phillips.

He snapped his notebook shut and went to the pocket of his coat, removing his mobile phone. 'One of the other things Glass told Alice was that he still had something belonging to her mum.

It's how he persuaded her to go to Lyegate in the first place. He told Alice that he wanted her to have it.' Phillips set his phone down on the table. 'The item was being kept at a bank in Mayfair. Glass gave her the address, and she went and collected it from a safety deposit box there. Glass's solicitor met her.'

'His solicitor? *What* solicitor?'

'On an unredacted visitor list we got from the prison, two men have been in repeatedly over the past nine months. They claim to be his lawyers. Jonathan Pope and Daniel Schubert. Pope was the one who met Alice at the deposit box. But these two men . . .' Phillips glanced at Dougan, at Naughton. 'We can't find them.'

'They don't exist?'

'No. There's no law firm in London employing solicitors with that name, and as far as we can tell, the only other legal representation that Glass has had in the entire time he's been inside is when he hired a firm for a few months a couple of years back to take the government to court. You might have seen it in the press. He said the prison was infringing his human rights by controlling his visitor list. The case got thrown out. The firm he used back then was legit. We called them earlier. But this Pope and Schubert, we think they're aliases.'

'Did Alice give you a description of this Jonathan Pope guy she met?'

'White, five-ten –'

'Medium build, dark hair. It's got to be Noah Klein.'

'The physical description matches, yes.'

'Which makes the other lawyer the kid from the woods.'

'Possibly. We've asked the prison to get us CCTV of the men.' Phillips's hand was still across his phone. 'We'll see for sure if you're right once Lyegate show us the footage from the days these "lawyers" visited.'

'What was the item Alice was left by her mother?'

'That's just the thing,' Phillips said. 'I don't think it *is* from her mother. I think Alice was just being used as an unwitting messenger. I think Glass and Klein guessed that, as soon as you took on Preston's case, you'd bring Healy on board, and they knew that once Matt was killed, the police would get involved too. Specifically, when the connections to Glass were made, I would be brought into the fold. And then we'd all start digging around, and we'd talk to Alice about her father – and from Alice, we'd follow the lines of enquiry and end up at the deposit box. And this gift they told her is from her mother is just a way to remind us that they're the ones in control here – because it's a message from Glass.'

'A message?'

He picked up his phone, tapped it a couple of times, and then put it back down again. He swivelled it around so I could see properly.

'This is what was in the safety deposit box.'

It was another mirror mask.

35

. . . 32 hours to go . . .

Healy got out of his seat and came across to the table to look.

It wasn't identical to the mask the kid in the woods had been wearing – the mirror pieces were different, stuck on at different angles – but it was very similar and obviously made by the same person.

'Does Alice still have it in her possession?' I asked.

'No,' Phillips said, 'it's with our forensic team now.'

'I doubt you'll find anything on it.'

'And you know that how?'

'This Noah Klein guy got an anaesthetized patient out of a first-floor window, accessed a hospital security system to overwrite video footage of himself, and then cut the electricity to an entire street in order to disappear yesterday. You really think he's going to leave his DNA all over something he *wanted* us to find?'

'Well, we'll see, won't we?'

'Yeah, we will,' I said. 'And we'll see whether he walked into Lyegate Prison to speak to Glass and somehow forgot there's a billion CCTV cameras in there.'

'You can't just disappear inside a prison.'

'This guy knows what he's doing. He's smart.'

'Even smart people make mistakes.'

It was a statement loaded with subtext.

I shook my head. 'Really? This tedious shit again?'

Phillips held up a hand to me. 'Our number-one priority right now is to figure out what's going on here and how it connects back to Preston Stewart.'

I zeroed in on his choice of word. *Our.*

He was making us a part of the same team now – so he definitely needed something. And whatever it was, he could only get it from us.

'Alice said that all Glass did – other than give her the details of the mask – was apologize to her?' I asked.

'Yeah,' Phillips replied, pocketing his phone.

'Well, we can ignore the apology. That's bullshit. I doubt there's been a single second in his entire life when he's felt regret about something he did. So it was really about the mask.'

Phillips nodded. 'About sending a message with it.'

'Right. He's telling us he's working with Klein and the kid in the woods, and the mask is just a way for us to join the dots. Noah Klein was the one who took Preston. He was most likely the one who met Alice at the deposit box. And the mask in the box was the same type that the kid was wearing when he shot and killed Matt. The masks loop everything together – Glass, Noah Klein, Alice, Preston, Matt.'

'But why would Glass want to tell us he's working with Klein?' Dougan asked from the back of the room. 'What's this doing for him?'

'He's never getting out of prison,' I said, 'so I imagine it'll be doing plenty.'

Again, Phillips nodded in agreement. 'Power, ego and control.'

'That's what he cares about,' I said. 'It's what he cared about back when he was killing people. And he can find all of those things through Noah Klein and the kid in the woods. You don't just kill yourself like that kid did without being an absolute believer in your cause. The kid's cause was Glass.'

'Those two are his followers,' Phillips said.

'Followers, believers, zealots, cultists – maybe a little of all of them. And when he can't brainwash them like Klein and the kid, he bends them to his will instead.'

'That's what you think he did with Matthew Higgs?'

I eyed Phillips. The question felt loaded. I glanced at Bodie in the corner, who – earlier on – had taken down my suggestion that Matt had started to push back against Noah Klein's blackmailing. Bodie had called it wild speculation.

But now, in his face, I could see I'd been right about Matt.

'Matthew Higgs's younger brother has multiple sclerosis,' Phillips said. 'Badly, from what I've been told. Matt was his primary carer – they don't have any other family – and, based on texts and emails we've found on Matt's phone, we think Noah Klein initiated contact with Matt at the end of October, about three and a half weeks after Matt started working with Preston and Ellie.'

'Any chance of tracing Klein's location from their texts and emails?'

'We've got digital forensics on it, but we've followed a couple of IP addresses already and they just lead us to a bunch of proxy servers.'

It wasn't surprising. Phillips knew, as I did, as everyone in the room did, that Klein wouldn't have gone to the trouble of setting up something this elaborate only to send out a bunch of emails that could be traced back to him in a couple of minutes.

'What did Klein say in the messages to Matt?' I asked.

'Basically, it looks like he'd done his due diligence: he knew Preston liked a drink, and he guessed – rightly – that if he started drinking, he'd start talking. He told Matt to ask Preston about medical school and his friends back then. It's why Preston must have mentioned the murder to Ellie the night they both got drunk: Marco Roy was on his mind because Matt had been asking him about it.'

'And why would Matt agree to do that?'

'Noah Klein had started illegally importing Colazone for him. It's an MS medicine that the Russians developed last year and claim is some wonder cure. It's not been approved anywhere else in the world apart from China, Belarus and Iran because it's

Russian, obviously, and because initial testing has shown it has next to no effect over and above existing MS medication. But Matt's brother is having a tough time, Matt was desperate for him, and so obviously he said yes. You talked about Glass and Klein bending people to their will. This was how they bent Matt.'

'Until he pushed back?'

'Yes. He told Klein he was done. That was two days ago.'

But, by then, Matt had found out enough from Preston – about what he'd done at university, about Marco Roy, perhaps even about Preston's potential culpability in the disappearance of the Lost Women – for it to be a problem. Whatever Noah Klein's ultimate plan was, Preston was intricately woven into it, and he couldn't afford for Matt to walk away knowing as much as he did.

'But why would Glass give a damn about the fact that Preston may have killed this Marco Roy kid thirty years ago?' Healy said. 'Glass is a murderer . . .' He paused, swallowed; that same tremor of pain. 'He killed my girl, those women, Alice's mum, his wife and unborn baby – it's not like this guy's got any conscience. He doesn't care about an unsolved crime. If he cared so much about Preston confessing, about Marco, about the Lost Women, why not send Noah Klein around to Preston's house, put a gun to his head and get him to spill the beans about what happened to Marco that way? It would have taken ten minutes and is a hell of a lot easier than abducting Preston at The Crest.'

It was a good point.

Glass – via Klein – had chosen something far more elaborate.

'Maybe Glass didn't want to reveal his part in this too soon,' I said. 'Maybe he wanted us to be this far in before his involvement was discovered.'

'Because?' Phillips asked.

'Because it's harder to walk away when you're already deep in the swamp. If we'd picked up his scent at the start, we would have had choices. Healy and I could have thought about whether it was a good idea to get involved with him again. We could have recused ourselves; you could have too. You could have brought someone else in at the Met to work this, someone who has no history with Glass and no baggage. All of us would have had options. But now we don't. He's very carefully led us to this point – through Matt, through Preston's confession and his disappearance, through the shooting, the masks, through hiring me and asking for a prison visit from you – and now it's impossible to turn around. I mean, is anyone here going to turn their back at this point? We all want the truth – and finding Preston Stewart is how we get it.'

'Except only Glass and Klein know where Preston is,' Dougan said.

'Exactly. Glass is in prison – unable to do anything himself – but inside two days, he's put himself front and centre when it comes to whatever happens next.'

'Power, ego and control,' Phillips repeated again, his voice distant, his eyes on the blank page in front of him.

Suddenly, something was different about him.

I looked at Dougan, at Bodie, at Naughton.

Something's different about all of them.

'What aren't you telling us?' I asked Phillips.

It took him a moment and then he looked up from his notebook. 'Glass told us he knows where the Lost Women are.'

I felt my blood run cold. 'What?'

'He says he knows where they're buried – *and* who killed them.'

I looked between Phillips and Naughton. 'So who killed them? Preston?'

'He wouldn't tell us.'

I shook my head. 'Of course he wouldn't.'

'He also says he knows where Marco Roy's body is.'

'And you believe him?'

'I can't just ignore what he says.'

'But do you believe him?'

'I believe that if there's even a tiny possibility he's telling the truth, we need to take it.'

I dragged my gaze across to Healy, but he was still staring into space, lost in a deluge of questions – and when I finally returned my attention to Phillips, he'd paled, his skin almost grey.

This is it, I thought.

This is where all of this has been heading.

'He says he'll tell us everything,' Phillips said, his voice muted. 'Where the women are, where Marco Roy is, where Preston Stewart is being kept, how it all connects . . .'

I studied him. 'But?'

'But he'll only talk to you and Healy.'

Zauna and Marco

Zauna

They reach the coast just before midday.

It's been a seven-hour drive from London, and Zauna can feel the exhaustion in her bones. She's not good with early starts; never has been. One year, when she was eight or nine, Marco bought her a poster for her wall that had the words *Mornings aren't really my thing* across the top and a photograph of a sleepy-looking sloth underneath. A few months later she got home to find that her brother had cut her face out of an old photograph and stuck it over the sloth's.

Briefly, she sees a reflection of herself smiling in the back-seat window of Sydney's car, and then they're pulling into a parking space. Zauna straightens, trying not to show Sydney and Anna that she's tired. Sydney, especially, seems to be a perpetual ball of energy – never tired, always on form. She's almost thirty years older than Zauna, but she doesn't look anywhere close to it. She's pretty, very tall, and can be fierce when she's angry. Anna says Sydney doesn't take any bullshit, especially from 'the awful men in the TV industry', and Zauna can imagine that being the case – although Sydney has been nothing but kind to Zauna so far.

At the studio in Soho, they've already recorded four hours of Zauna talking about Marco – the type of brother he was, the night he disappeared, what it was like at home in the years after – and Sydney has been endlessly patient. Zauna was apprehensive to start with, worried about how she would come across, but Sydney set her mind at rest and made it feel more like a conversation. After a while, Zauna started to tune out the studio, and her memories of Marco began pouring out of her.

Sydney switches off the engine.

The tide is in, splashing up and across the walkway that connects this side of the coast to the island. Zauna has seen pictures of Porthtreno – Anna has stuck them up all over the office – but it looks so different today. Sydney and Anna had said it would.

That was what this place did.

It changed.

Five weeks ago, when she'd met Sydney for the very first time – and Anna had explained the connection they'd found between this place and Marco – Anna had talked about the island as if it were a living, breathing thing. At first, it had seemed weird to Zauna; a little childish even. But then she looked at the research Anna had done for Sydney, at the photographs she'd sourced, and Zauna understood. This island really *did* change. In light winds, in heavy storms, in rain, in sun, when waves crashed on its shore and even when they didn't, its lines and contours altered.

Zauna has seen it in Anna's pictures.

And, as wind rolls in off the sea now, she sees it for real.

Sydney gets out of the car and goes to the barrier separating the edge of the car park from the banks that slope down to the water. Anna follows her, and then so too does Zauna. It's only the middle of September but the weather is cool, the air frigid, the wind making a constant, low moan. Zauna does up her coat as Sydney looks around, seeing who else is here. It's a Wednesday, so the only other car belongs to a mother and her young son. Zauna can see them playing at the spine of the island, where the sand forms a natural apex, like the ridge of a mountaintop.

From here, they can hardly see the village.

'I think we go across there first and suss it all out,' Sydney says to Anna, 'see where we can set up, go through the shot list.'

Anna agrees.

'They'd better not be late,' Sydney says.

She's talking about the council's Road Works team. It's part of the reason it's taken the women five weeks to get to this point. Anna has had to apply to Cornwall County Council to shut off the road into the car park, allowing them the run of Porthtreno for six hours. Sydney chose a 3 p.m. start because the sun goes down at 7.30 p.m. and that means they can make use of the 'golden hour', a film term for the periods just before sunrise and just after sunset. It will give them a richer colour palette, more atmospheric shots, and an hour to film in the dark afterwards. Zauna didn't really understand why Sydney would want to film in the pitch-black, but then Anna had told Zauna, 'We want the audience to see how it was.'

'How it was?'

Anna had grimaced. 'How it was the night Marco was here.'

Marco

The party is at a big house about twenty minutes west of Penzance.

It belongs to the parents of a girl called Emma on Marco's Biochemistry course. She tends to be more talkative when her boyfriend isn't around – he's in his second year studying Economics, is a rugby meathead, spends most of his life pissed up, and, to Marco's mind at least, seems like a strange choice for Emma to have made. He's asked her a couple of times – as subtly as he can – what she sees in Derek, and the best Emma seems to be able to come up with is, 'He's really fun.' Marco would never admit it to anyone except his best friend, Joel, but he likes Emma – maybe a little more than he should – and he often finds himself wanting to impress her. Part of that is trying to understand what it is Derek is doing that so attracts Emma, because as far as Marco can see, he isn't good-looking, he isn't funny and he's got the emotional intelligence of a snail. Joel puts it down to either Derek being insanely rich or having a massive cock. 'And he's not insanely rich,' Joel adds.

Despite all that, or perhaps because of it, when Emma asks Marco if he wants to come down to Cornwall for the weekend, to a house party at her parents' second home, he doesn't even think twice before saying yes. She tells him to invite Joel too, but Joel can't make it: he plays football for Bath City in the Vauxhall Conference, and they have a match at Kidderminster Harriers. So either Marco goes alone to Emma's house party, or he doesn't go at all.

He speaks to his mum about it when he gets home, and she instantly tells him he should go. Marco's mum worries about him more than she should, and, although he doesn't tell her this, he thinks having Zauna has changed her. Marco loves his little sister to bits, and he loves his parents too, even when they annoy him, but his mum has become more protective over Marco since his sister was born. Sometimes his mum forgets to switch from parenting a child to parenting an adult. Most of the time, he just ignores her overprotectiveness, or he holds back on certain things. It doesn't surprise him that she wants him to go to the party, though: aside from the inevitable worries that will surface about him borrowing the car and driving down to Cornwall, or getting drunk and going night-swimming, or drugs, or sex, or falling into the sea, Marco's mum also worries about his social life. She worries about the fact that he hasn't had a serious girlfriend and whether living at home, rather than in halls like everyone else, is affecting his personal growth. Going to one party for one weekend with hardly anyone he knows might fix all those problems, she thinks. It's why she encourages him to go, despite the fact that he's worried about not having Joel there.

But, in the end, he goes.

He asks Emma if he can follow her down, and she says, 'Why don't you come with us?' She means her and Derek, and Emma's best friend, Fran. Marco is unsure – he doesn't like Derek and he doesn't really know Fran – but then Marco's dad is called in for a surgery and he has to take the car, so the decision is made for Marco.

The journey turns out to be fine.

Derek mostly talks about himself for the first hour and goes on about how late he was out boozing the night before and how he has a hangover. But then a couple of hours in he falls asleep, and for the rest of the journey it's just Marco, Fran and Emma — she's doing the driving — talking about uni, their friends and their families. To his surprise, Marco finds himself liking Fran. She's always been a little standoffish with him, a little cold, but now he realizes it's because she's shy. Like Marco, she also has a much younger sister — but, unlike Marco, she hates hers.

He thinks of Zauna.

As he was leaving the house that morning, he heard a knock on the glass behind him and turned to see her at the window of her room. Because she'd liked the sloth poster so much, he'd bought her a toy sloth for her next birthday. She was holding it in her hand as she waved him off.

They arrive at Emma's parents' house four hours later.

It's basically a mansion, set on a sharp incline above a sweeping, horseshoe-shaped beach. Marco asks her what her parents do, and Emma just waves a hand and says, 'Something in finance.' It's not too long before others start arriving. Marco only knows most of them peripherally, but, as the afternoon becomes evening and Emma lights a fire pit at the back of the house, Marco manages to find a little group of people he likes: Fran, a friend of hers called Lynda, and two others — one is called Stuart, who barely says anything but seems inoffensive; the other introduces himself as Oliver.

'Marco,' Oliver says, 'that's such a cool name.'

'Thank you. My mum's family are Italian.'

'Awesome. I'd love to be even a *little* Italian.' Oliver starts doing an impression of Marlon Brando in *The Godfather*. '"A man who doesn't spend time with his family can never be a real man."'

Marco laughs politely.

The first night is fun. Marco gets a bit tipsy, and he and Fran stay up until 4 a.m. talking about films. They spend most of the second day together too, just sitting around talking as others drift in and out of the house. The time passes so quickly that neither of them are really aware that it's got dark until Emma bursts into the conservatory and says to them, 'Who fancies a night-time walk?'

Marco and Fran look at each other.

Neither of them wants to. But then Emma says, 'You two lovers can't stay in here the whole day.' The *lovers* part embarrasses them enough that both Marco and Fran say yes, and Emma hands them torches and tells everyone to follow her outside.

'Where are we going?' Marco asks.

Emma winks at him. 'You'll see when we get there.'

Zauna

Inside twenty minutes, the women have Porthtreno to themselves.

They stand on the highest point of the island, looking down at the remains of the village, hidden in the hollow and drowning in an ocean of sand. The wind has picked up, and it moves the beachgrass and the sand, and Zauna can see Sydney taking it all in, thinking about the shots she needs, and how she's going to use the weather – the breeze, the sea, the skies – to create the atmosphere she's seeking.

It's beautiful here, Zauna thinks, but there's also something lonely and even a little ominous about the island. Zauna wonders if it might be its location. They're literally as far down the country as they can go, as far west as it's possible to get, so there's nothing beyond Porthtreno except the endless grey sweep of the Atlantic.

Or maybe it's the village, she thinks, staring at its half-consumed walls, the broken roofs, the gaping doorways and windows.

Or – and it seems more likely it would be this – perhaps it's just that Anna told Zauna that Marco was here a week before he disappeared.

Vaguely, Zauna has a memory of waving her brother off from the top floor of their house in Clifton the day he left for Cornwall – and then, somewhere in her head, she has a memory of him getting home again. She'd been too young to see it then, but he'd carried something back with him.

Something bad.

Before they drove down, Anna explained how they'd connected Marco to Porthtreno: 'We've managed to track down all the people who were at that house party. We're asking them to go back thirteen years from now, but the story from those who remember is pretty consistent. The one woman, Emma, whose parents owned the house, said they went to Porthtreno after dark, a whole group of them, and they were all drunk. The next morning, Marco left without even as much as a goodbye and got the train home. It was out of character.' Anna had looked at Zauna grimly. 'This Emma says it was too long ago to remember why Marco left like that.'

'But you don't believe her?'

Anna had shrugged. 'Sydney thinks she's lying.'

'Surely the police would have interviewed these friends, though?'

'The police spoke to the people Marco met at the pub the night he went missing. It was most of the same people who were at the house party a week earlier – but the cops were focused on Bristol, on Marco's life there, on his university, on the pub, not on the weekend before at Porthtreno. If the house party even came up at all, it didn't get looked into, because Marco had returned to Bristol safe and sound, and had been home for a week by then. But Sydney says we need to dig deeper into the party. This Emma woman didn't want to be interviewed by us. She told us she didn't like appearing on camera – which makes no sense at all.'

'Why not?'

'She's on camera all the time these days,' Anna had said. 'She's a local TV reporter.'

Marco

They start along a trail that weaves down a sandbank, the beach-grass shimmering in the starkness of their torchlight. There's ten of them, Emma out in front, Marco towards the back, with Fran in front of him and Stuart behind him. There's an eruption of laughter up ahead – one of the guys has stumbled and fallen over and spilt half a can of beer all over himself.

It's Oliver.

They all stop, waiting for him to get to his feet, and from behind Marco, Stuart shouts, 'Stop being such a bloody lightweight, Ollie!'

More laughter.

'There's a village over here,' Stuart says.

Marco realizes he's talking to him.

'Sorry?'

'I said, there's a village on the island.'

'A village? What do you mean?'

Marco can't see any lights or people.

'Wait until you get there,' Stuart says. 'The sand's almost waist deep in places.'

Marco isn't sure what he's talking about, but as Emma leads Fran and the others along a narrow coastal trail and closer to the island – the sound of giggling, songs and drunken shouting confirming their path – Marco starts to follow them again.

Then he feels a hand on his shoulder.

Marco turns.

It's Stuart for a second time.

Marco shrugs the hand off his shoulder and feels a flutter of disquiet. Something's different about Stuart. He's tall and handsome, and from the little the two of them have spoken so far, Marco had believed them to be quite similar in personality: quiet, preferring to watch rather than take part; better in smaller groups.

But now he's not so sure.

Stuart has changed.

His gaze holds Marco's for a while longer and then he says, 'I want to give you a piece of advice. It's about Fran.' His voice is hushed. 'Stay away from her.'

Marco frowns. 'What?'

Stuart steps in closer to him. He has three or four inches and a couple of stone on Marco and is looking down at him now.

'Stay the fuck away from her,' Stuart says.

And then from somewhere ahead of them, they both hear Fran shout, 'Are you two coming or what?' and Stuart steps past Marco, smiling, like he's a completely different man once more. 'Oh, and it's not Stuart,' he says over his shoulder to Marco.

Marco just stares at him.

'You must have misheard. That's my surname, not my first name.' He heads off towards the others. 'I'm Preston.'

DAY ONE
Part Four

36

. . . 30 hours to go . . .

We got to Alice and Liam's house at 1 a.m.

There were still lights on inside and, as I pulled up at the driveway, both of us could see Gemma, Healy's ex-wife, between the curtains of the living room, Leanne in her arms, asleep. In the passenger seat, Healy looked at them. It wasn't hard to know where his head was at, because mine was in the same place: Glass had told the cops that he had all the answers – but he would only give them to me and Healy.

'You doing okay?' I asked.

'Not really.'

Turning off the ignition, I waited for him to say something else, but he just kept looking at Gemma and Leanne.

I used the silence to go back over everything we'd talked about in the interview room in Guildford. We were meeting Phillips, Naughton, Dougan and Bodie again at 10 a.m. I'd agreed to do the interview with Glass. Healy, though, had said nothing. His silence had been interpreted as a confirmation, but I could see the conflict now, the confusion and doubts and fury coming off him like heat. This was exactly the opportunity Healy had been waiting for. He'd dreamed about being in the same room as his daughter's killer over and over since the moment we found her body at the Dead Tracks. But in the version in his head, they were always alone, and Healy had Glass up against the wall, his hands on the killer's throat, choking the life from him. Or he was on top of Glass, punching and punching until there was no sound except the wet, dull thump of flesh. His version wasn't what was coming. He hadn't envisaged a highly controlled interview with Glass dictating the flow, or the certainty that, hidden in his request for us to speak to him, was some sort of embedded plan; a way to switch everything in his favour.

Between the curtains, Alice came into view.

She took Leanne from Gemma, smiling at the sight of her sleeping daughter, and then, very gently, kissed her on the head.

Healy opened his door.

'I don't know if I can do this,' he said softly.

'Look, whatever happens with Glass later, that happens later. In this moment, you just need to make sure you're around for your family. That's all you can do.'

'What the hell am I supposed to say to Gem and Liam?'

'The police have been here tonight talking to Alice, so Gemma and Liam will know about Alice's prison visits already. The part about us going in to see Glass – you just have to be straight with them. Don't lie and don't try to dress it up.'

'I'm not good with words.'

'You don't have to be.'

'"Hi, everyone, how was your night? By the way, Gem, I'm going in to have a chat to the man that killed our daughter."'

'Gemma will understand you have no choice.'

'When was the last time you spoke to her?'

The answer was eleven years ago, in the aftermath of Healy's own disappearance, where he'd made the world – and me, for a while – believe he was dead.

'You don't know her any more,' he said. 'I'll walk in there and she'll look at me like it's my fault, and she'll probably be right.'

'It's not your fault.'

'Maybe it is.'

'It isn't, Healy.'

'Glass is coming for us.'

'We don't know what he's –'

'Don't dress it up, Raker. I know you're thinking it as well: this is revenge. We cost him his freedom back in the day, and later on you and I are going to walk into that prison, and he'll let off the fireworks, and when we come out the other side, he'll have taken something else from us. And afterwards people are going to look around for someone to blame. And that's when Gem is going to think of Leanne – *our* Leanne – and the argument I had with her before she disappeared, and how, if I'd just kept my mouth shut all those years ago, if I'd just been more patient with our kids, or more available, or less obsessed with my work, our girl would never have stormed out of the house, and she would never have been taken by Glass. So it doesn't matter whether *you* think it's my fault or not, *she* will think that. And because she thinks that, so will the boys.' He stared at me, waiting for me to come back at him.

But I didn't know what to say.

Gemma had been the only parent on the scene for Ciaran, Leanne and Liam at the time Healy was working at the Met. She'd pretty much been the only parent after as well. She'd dealt with the fallout from Leanne's murder as Healy had imploded. She was there for her boys after they thought he was dead. She was and always would be their port in a storm. And so, if she blamed him for going to see Glass – if she blamed him for anything at all over the next few days – Healy was right: Liam would drop anchor, and so too would Ciaran.

All they knew about Healy was that he had abandoned them.

'Do you want me to come in with you?' I asked. He shook his head. 'Okay. Well, I'll pick you up at nine.'

He didn't move. It was starting to get bitterly cold in the car now, the heaters failing to repel the frigid air coming in through the door Healy had open.

Finally, he said, 'Make it seven.'

'Phillips and Naughton are in Brixton.'

'Yeah.'

'The station's only eight miles from your flat. I don't need to pick you up three hours early.'

'I need to show you something.'

I eyed him. 'What are you talking about?'

I thought of being in his flat the previous day and then of the moment in the interview room when it had felt like Healy had stopped short of saying something.

He hauled himself out of the car.

'What have you done, Healy?'

But he just said, 'Pick me up at seven.'

Healy

Now

Liam let Healy into the house and then hurried back through to the kitchen, where he was in the middle of getting Leanne some warm milk. Healy shut the door and then started taking off his shoes. A moment later, his son headed upstairs. Healy could hear Liam and Gemma talking in hushed tones in Leanne's bedroom.

Alice appeared on the landing.

Healy stayed where he was, watching her. She didn't spot him to start with as he was partly hidden by the shadows of the hallway, but then, halfway down the stairs, she stopped, put a hand to the railing and said, 'Hi.'

'Hey, Alice.'

She came down to Healy's eye level. 'Look,' she said, 'I, uh . . .' She rubbed her face. 'I don't know if . . .'

'It's okay,' he said to her. 'I know about the prison visit.'

She dropped back, on to the step; sat at its edge. 'I wasn't trying to keep it a secret.' The words rushed out of her in a single breath. 'He said he had something of my mother's. That was the only reason I went.'

'It's okay.'

'I never meant to hurt anyone –'

'It's okay, Alice,' Healy said again, raising a hand. 'Knowing he's your father . . . it's a lot. The fact you've turned out how you are . . .' He remembered Gemma ripping into him and thought, *Tell her exactly what she needs to hear in this moment.* 'If it makes a difference at all, I think you're pretty amazing.'

It did make a difference.

Her lips trembled and her eyes filled, and Healy realized for the first time just how lonely Alice was. She had Liam and Gemma and – somewhere much further out – she had Healy, but the only two people in the world who shared her blood were a baby daughter she wouldn't be able to tell a thing to for years, and a psychopath who had killed nine women, including her mum. She'd spent her entire childhood looking for a home, for a space to fit into, and even when she finally found one, Healy had been chipping away at its foundations. Alice had just wanted to belong, and he'd ruined it, and as simple as his words to her were, they were everything that she needed to hear.

Suddenly, he felt a prickle of guilt as he pictured himself going through her drawer, through the paperwork she'd kept in there.

'Do you mind if I ask you a couple of questions?'

'No,' she said. 'No, of course not.'

'This Jonathan Pope guy – the solicitor – who met you at the safety deposit box: did you ever speak to him on the phone *before* you visited Glass?'

'No.'

'The date and time were all arranged through Glass on your visit to him?'

'Yes.'

'So you never received any letters from Glass, or from his solicitors? There was no . . .' A beat. 'There was never any physical paperwork?'

'There were no letters or anything like that – but when I got given the mask, I was given some paperwork. It was just a form the bank made me fill out. You know, because Jonathan Pope said they would be closing the deposit box after I left.'

That was the form Healy had found in her drawer.

'Did you show the cops the form from the bank when they were here tonight?'

'No.' Alice looked worried now. 'No one asked me and I forgot to mention it. Do you think I'll get into trouble?'

'No, you aren't in any trouble. I'm sure if the police need to see the form, they'll ask you for it.'

Healy had already guessed – from the conversations they'd had at the police station earlier – that the cops hadn't been aware of the form – and their oversight worked in his favour. It would give him and Raker some breathing room when they met at seven. As he thought of that, he went back over the reasons he'd kept it secret from Raker until now, and about his original plan for how he was going to use the information on the form. But the second Glass had actually requested a meeting with the two of them, Healy's plans had been razed. And now, when he met Raker in the morning, Healy was going to have to be honest about the form, about his original intentions – and about what else was on it that the police hadn't seen yet.

Raker was going to hit the roof.

Gemma emerged from the bedroom at the top of the stairs, and Liam followed her down, a quarter-finished glass of milk in his hands.

'Hey,' Healy said to Gemma.

'Hi,' Gemma responded.

Liam looked at Alice with concern, as if a conversation with Healy might leave bruises on her. Healy tried not to let it annoy him and said, 'I was just asking Alice a couple of questions. I have to go back to the station in a few hours.'

'To do what?' Gemma asked.

He looked at her. *To get ready to speak to our daughter's killer. I have to sit across the table from him and watch him spin his lies as if everything he did to us – the way he broke us, the way he broke me – is ancient history.* He remembered what Raker had told him in the car about being straight with his family. But how he could be straight with them? How could he tell Gemma he was giving that murdering piece of shit the time of day? So he shrugged and said, 'It's just more questions, that's all.' Gemma looked at him like she knew that wasn't quite the truth, but before he could give anything else away, he turned to Alice again. 'When did you go in to see him?'

'Just before Christmas. December the 9th.'

'Can you describe what it was like?'

'Do you really need to do this now?' Gemma asked.

He didn't respond, just smiled at Alice. 'I know it's late, but it would help.'

Alice shifted. 'Some of it's kind of a blur,' she said quietly. 'But the first thought I had was that he was different from how I imagined him being. I'd only ever seen photos of him back when he was arrested. That was all I had to go on. But, in there, he'd got old. I mean, obviously. But he was skinnier, he'd lost a lot of his hair. In the media reports, it said he was six-one, but he didn't seem it. He was less . . .' She trailed off. 'Less intimidating, I guess. And when he spoke, he spoke so softly.'

'The police said he kept apologizing to you?'

'Yes.'

'That was all he did, apart from direct you to the deposit box?'

'Yes. He just kept repeating himself; kept telling me that he was sorry for what he'd done to my mother, to the other women – and to Leanne.'

Healy saw Gemma react to their daughter's name.

This is why I can't tell you I'm going into prison to talk to him, he thought. *You're as angry as I am, you just disguise it better.* Going in to talk to Glass would be a tacit act of forgiveness on Healy's part. That was how Gemma would see it.

'What do you remember about this Jonathan Pope guy?' Healy asked.

'I gave a description to the police.'

'I know. I meant, aside from how he looked. Did he say anything or talk about anything that you remember as being particularly memorable?'

'Memorable how?'

'I don't know,' Healy said. He was tired. 'Just anything you remember from that conversation.'

'Not really. He seemed nice.'

'Okay. And when you saw the mask for the first time?'

'It seemed an odd thing for my mother to want me to have,' Alice said, and glanced at Liam. He moved across to her and reached for her hand. 'I mean, I barely even remember her, but I took that mask out of the deposit box, and I looked at it, and I know it sounds very after-the-fact, but I genuinely thought it was a bit . . .' She came to a halt. 'It was creepy. That was why I put it in a box and left it at the back of the wardrobe upstairs.'

'The police took the mask away tonight, is that right?'

'Yes.'

'And what did this Jonathan Pope say about the mask? I mean, did he feed you some story about why your mother would want you to have it? Or maybe Glass mentioned something to you himself?'

'No, not really. Although Jonathan – or the guy I suppose I thought was called Jonathan – joked that the mask could help me see the future.'

Healy paused. 'What?'

'Yeah. It was such an odd thing to say.'

'What do you think he meant by that?'

'I asked him and he laughed it off and said it was some silly comment that . . .' A pause. 'It was a comment that, you know, *he* had made.'

'Glass told Jonathan Pope that the mask could help you see into the future?'

'Not me specifically, just anyone.'

'Okay . . .'

'"When someone looks at the mask and they see an image of themselves in the mirror pieces on the front, they're seeing the future." That's pretty much the direct quote.'

Everyone's eyes were on Healy now, as if he might be able to interpret what this meant. All he knew was that Jonathan Pope, or Noah Klein, or whatever the hell his actual name was, wouldn't have relayed those words to Alice by accident.

'And – what? – Pope just laughed it off?' Healy asked.

'He laughed it off, but I don't know . . . It kind of felt like he didn't *actually* find it funny. There was nothing in his eyes, you know? No light. It was more like . . .'

'More like he believed it too?'

'Yes. And then he said the same thing again – you know, that you could see the future – except, this time, he framed it differently and said you could see the future version of *yourself*.' Alice squeezed Liam's hand a little tighter, unsettled and clearly confused. Gemma and Liam had turned to Healy again, looking for answers.

Healy shrugged.

He was pretending he was as perplexed as they were. But he wasn't. He knew Glass. He knew how he thought. And he knew what message Alice had carried from Glass to Healy without her even realizing it: when you looked at the mask, you saw the future, broken version of yourself.

And that was what was coming.

That was what Glass was going to do to them.

He was going to break them.

37

. . . 29 hours to go . . .

Rebekah was asleep on the sofa when I got in, the lights all off, the TV on mute. In the silence of the house, I listened to the soft sound of her breathing, then padded through to the kitchen, poured myself a glass of water, and collapsed into a chair at the table.

Every part of me felt weary.

Physically, emotionally, I was exhausted.

Even so, my head still hummed with noise, with questions I didn't have answers to, with tethers I was trying to connect, and I knew if I went to bed, I'd just spend the night staring up at the ceiling. Healy wanted to meet at seven, which gave me about four and a half hours, so I had to try to get some sleep. But as I thought about his request to meet early – and what his reasons might be for doing so – it did nothing to still the waters. If anything, I could feel the dread calcifying at what might be coming.

'Hey.'

Rebekah was standing in the door to the kitchen now, blanket at her shoulders, her head tilted slightly as if she was studying me.

'Hey,' I said. 'Sorry if I woke you.'

'You didn't, don't worry.'

'A long day.'

'Yeah.' She glanced at her watch. 'Did you just get in?'

'A few minutes ago.'

She drew the blanket tighter around her, her head still at an angle, her eyes on mine. 'You look absolutely knackered.'

I smiled, pulling out a chair for her.

'What?' she said, sitting down, smiling herself now.

'*Knackered*. You don't hear many Americans saying that.'

'I'm not American, I'm British.' It was true: she'd been born in Cambridge and had gone to school in London and had only moved to New York at eighteen. 'Well,' she added, 'maybe a bit of both these days. It'll be twenty-five years in the US soon.'

'Wow.'

'Yeah. Why does time speed up when you get older?'

'I don't know, but if you find a way to slow it down, make sure you tell me.' I rolled my neck. It was a little stiff, maybe a little jarred, from where I'd crashed into the kid in the mask. I'd landed on him, and he'd taken the brunt of my weight, but I'd still hit him hard, and I could feel it in my muscles, my joints, in my bones. Rebekah was right: time accelerated as you got older, and it only took a night like this one to remind you how fast. 'How was the trip to Cambridge? Did you sort everything out?'

'Yeah, everything's good. Mum's estate isn't that complicated, really. It was weird going back, though. I got a cab to the house I grew up in and I don't know . . .' She was quiet for a second. 'It feels like it was someone else's life.'

'Going back can be like that.'

'Yeah, I guess. I saw my half-sister too.'

I kept my expression neutral. 'How was that?'

'Fine. She seems nice.' A frown. 'She said she knows you.'

When I'd been searching for Rebekah's mother, I'd been drawn into the orbit of a sister that Rebekah never even knew she had. Her sister was no threat to Rebekah – in fact a benign threat to pretty much everyone – but that didn't mean she was harmless. She and I shared a secret and sometimes, like now, she liked to remind me of our pact.

'She knows me?' I said to Rebekah innocently.

'Yeah, she told me she met you once, on a case a long time ago.'

'Oh.' I felt a part of me collapse as I lied to Rebekah's face.

We've barely even begun and I'm already keeping secrets. 'Yes, we may have done.'

'You don't remember her?'

'I've had a lot of cases down the years.' As the guilt needled at me, I moved the conversation on. 'Did you talk to your girls tonight?'

'Yeah. They're all good. Gareth was a spectacularly average husband but he's a good dad, so they seem happy.' She blinked. I could tell how desperately she missed her daughters, even though she was doing her best not to show it. This was the peak we had to scale at the heart of whatever it was between us: her ex-husband, and her girls, and her friends, and her life, and the roots she'd grown across twenty-five years in a country 3,500 miles away; and what I myself had, small as it may have been, on this side of the world: a grown-up daughter I loved deeply, a life I'd built in the aftermath of Derryn's death, and the missing people that had become my oxygen.

'Did you want to talk about what happened tonight?' she asked.

'I think I'm still trying to figure it out.' I rubbed my eyes. 'Do you remember – when you came over to visit me a year ago – you asked me about my journalism days?'

'I asked you which story you never stopped thinking about.'

I smiled. 'You've got a hell of a memory.'

'It's the doctor in me.'

'Do you remember what I said?'

She frowned, casting her mind back. 'Not everything. But . . .' She paused again. 'Wasn't there something about a village of sand?'

'You really do have a great memory. Porthtreno. It's in Cornwall. Back in 2006, three women vanished while making a documentary down there. They were looking into this kid that *also* disappeared.'

'Yeah, I remember the women. Was that what tonight was about?'

Rebekah had buried her own traumas – if you could ever really bury anything – and those traumas were every bit as profound and deep-rooted as mine. In many ways, what she'd had to go through in her life and the pain she'd had to endure may have been worse than anything I'd been through myself. So I wasn't reticent to tell her because I didn't think she could handle it. I knew she could. I was hesitating because I still didn't have a clear view of what was going on myself, and that made it hard to articulate my thoughts, especially at two thirty in the morning.

'In part it was about the women, yes,' I said, finally. 'I was thinking on the drive home, I don't do a lot of talking in the press, certainly not since my days as a journalist, but when I have, I've often talked about that case. I went on this podcast a few years back. *Echo World.*'

'I know it, yeah.'

'They've won two Peabodys, all these other awards, have had something crazy like three-hundred-and-fifty-million downloads – but I always liked the podcast, even before it became massive. It's just the type of journalism you don't see so much any more: well researched, compassionate, responsible. They asked me on to talk about missing people after this case I was on caught fire in the media, and I told them about those women, about Porthtreno, about how I thought of that story often. Anyway, I never really thought about that interview again until today; about it being beamed out all over the world, or who might be listening to it.' With my hand flat to the table, I saw that I still had some dirt under my nails from the woods. 'I never thought about who might have been listening to me.'

Rebekah watched me. 'And who was listening to you?'

'That story's a way to control me, because I want answers. I've always wanted answers. I've wanted them from the minute I drove to Cornwall eighteen years ago. And now that desire I have, it's been weaponized. He's got exactly what he wanted . . .'

'"He"?'

'Glass.'

She frowned. 'The serial killer?'

'Yeah.'

'The one who . . .' She trailed off.

Who killed Colm Healy's daughter.

'I think I might have told you about him too, but the last time you were here he was just a bad memory; a terrible piece of history. Although he's neither of those things any more. He was most of what tonight was about. And I've been trying to figure out how he managed to pull himself back into focus like this, and I'm starting to think it might be because he listened to me talking on that podcast, or he saw me mentioning those women in the media at some point, and he knew that was the opportunity he'd been waiting for. This was how he regained control. So he started digging, or he got someone else to – or maybe more than one person – and he found something new about the women. And now all of us – me, Healy, the cops – are dancing to his tune.'

But I didn't say the rest out loud.

I couldn't.

I didn't want to acknowledge it.

We're dancing to his tune.

And this is going to end badly.

Because with Glass, it always did.

Naughton

Now

Naughton left the station and headed to her car.

As her heels clicked on the concrete, she realized how quiet it was. It was 3 a.m. in the depths of winter – skies dark, air bitter – so there was no birdsong yet.

Naughton unlocked her car and saw Bodie exit the station behind her. He looked up, spotted her, and made his way over. She was parked in one of the bays furthest away from the station, on the near side of a closed security gate. There was a high wall hemming everything in, with barbed wire along the top. In the dark, it felt more like a prison yard than a car park.

'Well, I'd better get home for the world's shortest sleep,' Bodie said.

Naughton smiled. 'I think it's going to be another long day.'

'I think you're right.'

They'd only met for the first time a few hours ago – and had said almost nothing to each other while Raker and Healy were in the station – but, as they'd both been getting ready to leave, Bodie had started chatting. Naughton had to admit that he was nice to look at: tall, sculpted, well dressed in a tailored charcoal-grey suit.

'Where do you call home?' he asked.

'Chertsey.'

'Oh, not too far, then. I'm in Woking.'

Naughton had been married once and had a six-year-old son, Frankie, but now they both lived with her boyfriend, Todd, who she'd been with for a couple of years.

'Well, see you back here at eight,' Naughton said.

'Bright and early.'

They got into their cars.

Naughton popped the cap off a bottle of water she'd left inside, took a mouthful, and then Bodie passed her, waving as he stopped at the security gate. It began rattling across. He accelerated out before it had even got all the way over. He clearly couldn't wait to get home and Naughton didn't blame him.

She started up her own car and nosed through the open gate, down towards a junction at the bottom of a ramp. Ahead of her, Bodie was going right, the tail lights of his Audi blinking against the dark. Naughton turned up her music, trying to keep her concentration going, the exhaustion weighing heavy on her. She'd done late nights all the time when she was in uniform, but as a detective her hours had become more regulated, unless she was in the middle of a big case – and she hadn't had one of those for a while.

She arrived at the junction, braked, and saw Bodie disappearing into the distance. The streets of Guildford were empty.

'You're going to turn left here.'

Even before she'd had a chance to do anything, before she'd seen the movement in her rear-view mirror, she felt a knife at her throat. An arm was against her right shoulder, a black sleeve visible out of the corner of her eye. She couldn't see a hand, but she could feel it against her neck – a leather glove, the rounded end of a handle – and the point of the blade was at the left-hand edge of her jawline, on the opposite side.

Her heart thumped against her ribs.

'Give me your phone.'

It was a man, but his voice was suppressed somehow, muted, as if it were coming from a distance away. It made her think of what had happened earlier, the shooting at the house, the kid in the woods.

The mask.

She glanced in the rear-view mirror again.

Whoever was behind her adjusted position, coming forward into the light, the mask on his face, its mirror pieces, echoing back a hundred different versions of her.

Oh fuck.

'I said, give me your phone,' the man hissed.

'Okay,' she replied, her voice fractured and scared. 'Okay.'

Naughton reached into her pocket.

'Slowly.'

Over her left shoulder, his other arm came out of the shadows, the fingers opening out like a spider unfurling its legs. The gloved hand waited while she placed her phone there, and then it moved again, to the front of her.

Her face unlocked the phone.

As the hand withdrew, Naughton tried to get another look at who was behind her – the eyes, the hair, anything that might help her identify him – but he'd managed to raise himself up now, almost definitely deliberately, and all she could see from her position was the bottom of the mask.

'Rosa.'

Her name, whispered.

She could hardly breathe.

'This must bring back some memories for you.'

The worst moment of her life flashed in her mind: staring across the darkness of an abandoned building and seeing Healy.

She'd felt that knife at her throat for months after.

Now, seventeen years later, it was happening again.

And no one's going to save me this time.

'What do you want?' she asked.

She tried to sound firm, strong – as if the sheer terror she was feeling wasn't making it hard for her to even speak – but her words tripped at the end of *want*. The second they did, whoever was there reached past her, and – with his spare hand – took hold of the rear-view mirror and tilted it downwards.

Now she couldn't see him.

She could only hear him.

She could feel the sharp edges of the mirror pieces on his mask brush against her face as he leaned into her ear. Even as he changed position, the knife at her throat didn't move an inch. She couldn't lean away from him. She couldn't even squirm. If she did either, the blade would cut her jugular.

'You're going to turn left here,' he said again.

She could feel his breath on her ear, could hear it whistling slightly as it passed through the slit on the mask where the mouth was; through tiny, uneven nose holes.

'Why?' she said.

'You'll see.' His breath again, dancing across her face, the smell of coffee and mint coming from him; of scented soap on his skin. 'This is where it all begins, Rosa.'

'What does?'

'Your part in all of this.'

38

. . . 26 hours to go . . .

My alarm woke me from a dead sleep at 5.30 a.m.

The house was absolutely pitch-black, the bedroom freezing cold. I jumped in the shower and let the hot water wash the grit from my eyes. As I got dressed, I wondered again why Healy wanted to meet me so early.

Nothing I could come up with brought me any comfort.

I sank a mug of coffee and wolfed down some oats, and then left a note on the fridge for Rebekah. As I pinned it in place with a magnet, I had a sharp sense of déjà vu, a moment when I was suddenly twenty years younger, and in my old house in Ealing, and doing the same for Derryn when she was at the hospital, working a shift.

Outside, the winter air hit me like a wall.

Frost sparkled on the front lawn, on the roofs of the houses around me, on the pavements and the roads. I slid into my car, started it up and got the heaters going.

A message from Healy chimed through.

Meet me here

He'd sent a pin. When I opened it, I could see it was a coffee shop in Paddington Basin, right on the canal, close to the northern entrance to the train station. I zoomed out, trying to get a sense of what else was nearby, but I had no idea why he'd chosen it. We'd never met there before, it wasn't close to Brixton station and it was ten miles across London from where he lived in Lewisham.

I'd been worried before.

Now I was starting to panic.

I found a space in an underground car park on Edgware Road and then cut through to Paddington Basin at the corner of Praed Street and Harbet Road. It was just before seven and still quiet, the surface of the canal dotted with lights from the hotels and office buildings that flanked the water. I found Healy waiting for me a little way down, hidden by the shadows beside the coffee shop.

'What's going on?' I said by way of a greeting.

He gestured to the shop. It was getting ready to open, the staff inside unstacking chairs and busying themselves behind a long wooden counter.

'It's freezing cold and I need coffee,' he replied. 'I'll tell you inside.'

He glanced across the canal in the direction of a five-storey office building. I followed his gaze and could see the office had a ground-floor entrance set back under a roof supported by pillars. Inside, the lights were just flickering into life.

'You coming or what?' Healy said, heading into the coffee shop, which was now open. I followed him in, ordered and then we took our drinks to the far corner.

As soon as we sat, I said again, 'What's going on?'

He took out his phone, opened it and found something on it, then placed it on the table. But he kept his hand across it, deliberately covering the screen.

'The day before yesterday, I was at Liam and Alice's,' he said, and then stopped. He seemed tentative, and it immediately set me on edge. He was only ever like this when he'd done something he knew I'd hate. 'It was nice. I bathed Leanne and then, later on, I went up to the toilet, and I saw that Alice was up there. She'd just put the little lady down.' Another pause. 'Alice was in the bedroom, had a drawer open, and was looking at some paperwork.'

I glanced at the phone again. 'Okay. And?'

'She was crying. I wanted to know why.' He finally lifted his fingers away from the screen and swivelled the handset around so I could see it properly.

He swiped between three photos.

It was a three-page form, headed with the name of the bank in Mayfair where Alice had collected the mirror mask from. I pinch-zoomed in on the first page. At the top was the name of the company that was looking after the box for their client.

Pope & Schubert.

Under that was the name of their client.

Glass.

Below that was Pope & Schubert's address.

I glanced up at Healy, then out of the front of the coffee shop. It was the address for the office building on the other side of the canal.

The same one I'd seen Healy looking at earlier.

I felt myself sag. 'So you knew all about Alice being given the mask before Phillips told us last night?'

'No, I swear. Look, there's no mention of a mask anywhere on this form. I just saw this paperwork and guessed she must have been in contact with Glass because his name was at the top of the first page.'

'You went through her things?'

'Save me the morality lesson, Raker. Her old man killed my daughter. She was upstairs, on her own, going through paperwork and crying her eyes out. Something felt off, so I did what I did. How was I supposed to smell what was going on?'

'Did she show this form to the police?'

'No. She says they never asked.'

I resized the picture. 'Why didn't you mention this to me yesterday?'

'It didn't come up.'

'Don't give me that crap. You had all day to mention this and chose not to. I *knew* you were keeping something back. And that worries me, Healy, because when you get secretive it tends to mean you're dreaming up some insane plan that's going to ruin our lives.'

'Wait a minute –'

'No.' I shut him down. 'Why didn't you mention this?'

He made me wait, sipping from his coffee, his eyes moving from me to the canal, to the office building across the grey water. More lights were coming on inside, but the top floor remained dark.

'I don't know,' he said finally, his eyes still on the canal, on the frost-specked rooftops and windowsills; on the commuters passing in a fog of steaming breath. But he did know, that was the thing. He knew exactly why he'd done it, and as he turned towards me again, putting his coffee down in front of him, something shifted: a colour change in his skin, the slightest tremor at the corners of his mouth.

'Ah shit,' I muttered, seeing the answer now.

Healy said nothing.

'You were going to try to use Alice to get you in on a visit to Glass – is that it?'

Again, he said nothing.

'And do what? *Kill* him? You tried this exact same shit thirteen years ago and got yourself fired from the Met.'

'You don't get it,' he said.

'It didn't work last time, why was it going to work now?'

'I don't *know*,' he shot back, his voice sharp, too loud, the staff glancing in our direction. 'I never thought I was going to get the chance to be face-to-face with him. I didn't know we'd end up sitting in that room with Phillips last night. So that was why I didn't tell you, okay? I thought Alice would be my only chance to get across the table from him and look him in the eye. I just needed to hear him say it.'

'Say what?'

'Say why he killed Leanne.'

'Because he's a psychopath, Healy.'

'I need a reason.'

'Even if he gives you one, it's not going to bring you any comfort.'

'How the hell would you know?'

'Because it's Glass. It's who he is. This thing with him later – the whole reason he wants you in that room with him – is because he *knows* you're a powder keg. He's going to wait for you to blow up. That way, *he* looks like the calm and rational one, not you. And if he looks in control in there, like he's reborn – if all this shit he told Alice about being sorry for what he did looks like it's real and you're in there ranting and raving, and trying to grab him across the table – he's going to get exactly what he wants. Whatever his reasons are for needing to talk to us, whatever he *really* knows about Preston, and Marco, and the Lost Women – if he even knows anything at all – it's not going to matter if you're in there losing your shit.'

Healy shook his head.

'You know I'm right,' I said. 'The cops will be saying the same thing to you later. My bet is they'll ask you to avoid even speaking to him.'

'*He killed my girl*,' Healy said through his teeth.

He leaned back, blinked.

And as he calmed, his eyes filled with tears.

'You know,' he said, his voice quiet now, 'every morning I open my eyes and, just for a second, I hope I'm still dreaming. I hope I'm still fast asleep. I hope that all of this – him, what he did, Leanne – is just this terrible nightmare that I need to wake up from. And when I do, I'll go downstairs and she'll be in the kitchen, helping herself to breakfast and spilling cornflakes over the worktops because she was always so messy.' The emotion took his words from him. 'I'll say, "Lee, you've left more cereal on the counters than in your bowl," and she'll roll her eyes and say something. Except . . .' He swallowed. 'Except I can't remember her voice any more. It's gone. It's . . . It's just gone. And so every day, when I get out of bed and nothing has changed, that's when I know for sure: I'm never waking up from this fucking nightmare.'

It was hard to know what to say.

Grief became easier.

Guilt didn't.

I stayed quiet, letting him slowly gather himself. And then, finally, he took a long, deep breath, his shoulders rising, and said, 'The firm of Pope & Schubert doesn't exist. We know that already. And these two pricks pretending to be Glass's lawyers – one of them's dead and the other's in the wind. We know that too. But the question is, why would Noah Klein and the kid in the woods write the address of that office on a form' – he pointed across the canal – 'when there was every chance it would be seen?'

I looked across the water to the office.

The top floor was still dark.

'It's because it's not an address,' Healy said. 'It's a clue.'

39

. . . 24 hours to go . . .

We entered the office building.

The foyer was narrow but long, with polished black marble floors and a curved walnut counter to the right. Behind it was a silver-haired man in his sixties.

'Morning,' Healy said.

The man looked up. 'Morning.'

As Healy dug around in his jacket pocket, he glanced at the lanyard around the man's neck. 'Joseph,' he said, 'my name's DI Grantley.' I didn't react to the lie but had to try hard not to when he took out a black wallet and flipped it open to reveal a police warrant card. It looked completely legitimate.

'This is my colleague DS Moon,' he added, gesturing to me. 'Do you know who's renting the office on the top floor here?'

Joseph frowned. 'No one.'

'No one's up there at the moment?'

'No. It's empty.'

Healy glanced at me and feigned surprise. 'How long's it been empty?'

'About nine months. The last company went bust.'

'Okay,' Healy said, 'well, we're going to need to take a look.' He leaned back, looking down towards the lifts. 'Can you take us up?'

Joseph hauled himself away from the desk and we followed him as he swiped his ID through a card reader. Once the doors fanned open and we got into the lift, Healy said, 'We appreciate it, Joseph. Thank you.'

'I used to work for British Transport Police.'

'Oh yeah?' Healy said, convincingly interested. 'I used to know a couple of guys there, at HQ in Camden.' He listed a few names. I didn't know if any of them were real, because Joseph didn't recognize the names, but sometimes it was easy to forget how good Healy was at adjusting to the temperature of the room. I'd only really got to know him properly once he'd been fired from the Met, but I'd seen a little of him before that and enough since to understand why he'd closed so many cases.

The lift doors reopened.

At one end was a window showing views of Paddington Basin, down towards the station side. At the other end was an entrance with the name of the company who'd previously occupied the office stencilled on to the glass. Joseph used a set of keys to unlock the doors.

'Thanks so much, Joseph,' Healy said warmly, once they were open.

'Well, you know where I am if you need anything.'

'We do.'

Joseph stepped back. Healy thanked him again, and we both smiled at him as he returned to the lift.

The second he was gone, Healy looked at me and the smile dropped away. He knew what I was going to ask. As he handed over the warrant card, he said, 'It's the work of a guy I know on the Old Kent Road.'

'How long have you had it?'

'Couple of months. This is its maiden voyage.'

It made me wonder why he would pay for a fake ID in the first place – and if I should be worried – but then we headed inside.

The first room was a reception area. Chairs had been stacked up in one corner, there were two leather sofas, and the front desk was empty. Everything was covered in a fine layer of dust.

Off the reception were four doors.

Two went through to male and female bathrooms. As Healy

checked those over, I tried the third. It was a meeting room: a table with ten chairs and a whiteboard.

I heard Healy trying the lights in the bathrooms.

I tried them in the meeting room.

Nothing.

We came back out into the reception area and moved towards the fourth door. It was wide, set into the wall to the right of the front desk, and had a glass panel in it.

All we could see on the other side was darkness.

Healy opened it.

It looked like there were desks in two islands of four, a small kitchenette to the left and a second, smaller meeting room on the far side.

It was hard to tell for sure, though.

The windows were all covered in black card.

We moved further in, eyes on the windows, on the silver duct tape used along the edges of the card to further prevent daylight escaping in. As Healy inched down the side of the office where the kitchenette was, I went between the banks of desks and headed across to the meeting room.

I waited until Healy came over to where I was, and then placed my hand on the door of the meeting room. Its windows were covered in black card too.

I thought of what Healy had said in the coffee shop.

It's not an address.

It's a clue.

I opened the door.

Zauna and Marco

Marco

Marco follows the others across the wooden walkway to the island. The tide is in and it's sloshing up and over some of the slats. As it does, under torchlight, he can see Fran – five people ahead of him – giggling as her boot lands in a puddle of water, and then a second wave comes and, once it hits the walkway, it turns into spray and dots the coats of some of the other people between them. One of them is Preston. Marco can't quite hear what he's saying – his voice keeps getting lost in the wind – but whatever he's saying is making everyone ahead of Marco laugh.

Marco feels a twist of anger.

He keeps returning to what Preston said about Fran. *Stay the fuck away from her.* The threat came completely out of nowhere. Marco has basically said nothing to Preston all day. It's why Marco mistakenly thought that Preston's first name was Stuart – he heard one of the other guys call him that, and Preston didn't correct him. But a mix-up over a name is a simple misunderstanding. The thing that Marco *really* doesn't understand is why Preston got so aggressive about Fran. Marco has spent most of the day with her, and at no point did she or anyone in the group mention that she was in a relationship. He hasn't seen her hanging around with Preston, hasn't seen them exchange a word. For some of the day, Preston wasn't even at the house, he was at the beach playing touch rugby with the others.

Up ahead, Fran laughs again.

She's talking to Oliver now, the one who did the Marlon Brando impression; who fell over drunk a few minutes ago. He's still staggering, slurring what words Marco is able to hear over the waves, and while Oliver has a torch, it's pointed out to sea, so he keeps tripping on the slats.

Eventually, they reach the other side.

Marco is last to get there and, as soon as he does, Emma – somewhere up ahead – says, 'Hide-and-seek!' and everyone scatters. Marco stands there, unsure what to do. Out of the darkness, Emma shouts, 'Marco, you're seeking!'

Marco's heart sinks.

He's wishing now that he hadn't agreed to come to Cornwall at all. For a second he thinks about just heading back to the house, but he knows it will make him look weird, so he starts moving through a canyon of dunes in front of him. It rises from the shoreline, where the walkway is, up to the spine of the island. When he gets there, he stops. He can hear giggling from somewhere close by, but the wind is a little stronger up here, and it alters the direction and volume of the sound. He waits for a lull in the breeze and listens again: more giggling and then some movement from below him.

He looks down, into the hollow.

All he can see down there are broken walls and empty windows.

He remembers what Preston said to him, about there being a village here, and then he starts to walk-slide down a cascading river of sand, trampled out of the beachgrass by decades of tourists and visitors. Ahead of him, someone has left their torch on, and Marco can see the light beyond one of the windows. Whoever it is must hear Marco coming because the torch snaps off.

In the dark, he hears a girl laughing.

Marco's legs begin to disappear into a knee-high sea of sand. As they do, the wind dies away. He's in a high-walled crescent of dunes now, protected from the breeze, and he can hear much better: most of the group who have sought a hiding place here are doing a terrible job of keeping quiet.

He wades through the sand to the first window.

'Boo,' he says gently, leaning through the window frame, and the girl he heard earlier squeals and starts laughing. Marco illuminates them with his torch: he doesn't know the girl, but the guy is someone he said a passing hello to in the kitchen earlier on. There's another guy a few feet away.

He moves around the broken and crumbling exterior wall, into what was once the inside of the house – interior walls rising up, out of the sand, in various states of disrepair – and then realizes it's the first of five houses. He can see all of them to some degree, although the ones further down the slope are more obscured by the night. As Marco inches from one former house to the next – torchlight skittering as he fights against the weight of sand – everything shifts around him. Sand sloughs off the surface and runs past him in rivers. More comes from behind him, like an avalanche.

He spots another couple he doesn't know hidden in the third home. They say something to him, but he can't quite hear what, because more sand is running down the slope towards him, whispering softly.

Marco starts to shiver.

He didn't bring a coat.

But it's not just that.

There's something strange and a little unsettling about this place now. He may well not be alone in what remains of the village – there may be others in the group who've sought cover behind its fractured walls – but he can't hear them and he can't see them either, and it suddenly feels like he's totally alone.

I just want to go home, he thinks.

That's when he hears Fran.

He isn't sure exactly where her voice is coming from to start with, but then he turns to face down the slope. He lifts his torch, trying to direct it past the fourth of the houses, towards the one furthest away. The torch isn't strong enough, so he shifts forward, thighs pushing hard against the sand, and feels more of it peel away from him in a powdered lake. After half a minute, he's level with the fourth house. He thinks he can see Emma inside one of its broken rooms, a pale face peeking out. He directs his torch at her and says, 'I can see you, Emma,' and she starts to drunkenly wade out.

'How many of us have you found?' she asks.

'Six, I think.'

Marco looks down the slope, to the last house, and as he does, he hears Fran for a second time. Her voice is clearer and so is the tone of her voice.

'Please,' she's saying. 'Please don't do that.'

Marco glances at Emma, who surely must have heard Fran too – but Emma doesn't move. She doesn't even react. She just stares at Marco.

'Don't get involved,' she says quietly.

Marco frowns.

Emma is drunk but, in this moment, it's like she's stone-cold sober.

'She told me she likes you,' Emma says, 'if that's any consolation.'

'The two of them are together?'

Emma takes a moment to reply. 'Yes.'

Marco looks down the slope again.

He thinks of Preston.

Stay the fuck away from her.

And then he hears Fran again.

It sounds like she's crying.

He takes a step forward and then feels Emma's hand on his arm, stopping him from going any further. When Marco looks back at her, she's shaking her head.

'Honestly,' she says, 'don't. She won't thank you for it.'

'We should –'

'No. We shouldn't. She won't want you involved – and he definitely won't.'

Emma tears her eyes away from Marco for the first time and glances down the slope. There's no sound coming from the last house any more.

Just silence.

'You're a good man, Marco,' she says. 'But not all men are like you.'

40

. . . 24 hours to go . . .

We entered the meeting room.

It was very dark, the card at the windows fitted precisely to the frames. At first, I thought the room was completely empty – there were no chairs, no table, no cabinets, no shelves – but then both Healy and I took out our phones and switched on the torches.

On the back wall, there were photos. Hundreds of them. They climbed up in columns, one after the other, some of them taken only seconds apart.

The photos were of me.

They were of Healy.

They were of Alice, and Liam, and Gemma, and baby Leanne. They were of Phillips and his wife, Naughton and her young son, Dougan and what must have been his three teenage children, and Bodie and what looked like his girlfriend. They were of Rebekah.

Every photo had a date-stamp on them.

They'd all been taken in the last twenty-four hours.

I felt my stomach clench as I saw a long lens photograph of me getting into the Mercedes yesterday, Ellie visible inside, Matt standing at the door. In the column next to it were shots of me and Healy outside The Crest, getting ready to go in and speak to the staff there. There were zoomed-in shots of Naughton and Bodie in the car park at Guildford station – just a few hours ago – talking to one another at their cars. There was a shot of Dougan and Phillips at a window, Phillips perched on the sill, Dougan typing something on his phone. There was me and Healy talking in the car when I'd pulled up outside Liam and Alice's place at 1 a.m. Healy entering the house as I drove away. Healy in the hallway, Alice on the stairs. More shots showing their misshapen silhouettes through the glass panels of the closed front door as they talked. Another one, next to it, taken through the living-room window of Alice holding a sleeping Leanne, with Gemma and Liam close by. And then five consecutive shots of Rebekah walking to her train at King's Cross when she'd gone to Cambridge.

Picture after picture.

Row after row.

In the middle of the wall of photographs – as if the pictures were the planets and it was the sun – was a clock. It was analogue but there was a digital readout right in its centre. Six red digits glowed dimly against the dark of the room.

Except the digital display wasn't confirming the time.

It was a countdown.

Out of the corner of my eye, I saw something flutter to the floor from the top of the door and, when I looked up, a piece of silver thread was hanging off it.

A makeshift tripwire.

The moment we'd opened the door, the timer had started.

Hours. Minutes. Seconds.

Suddenly, our phones chimed in unison. I took mine from my pocket. Healy removed his. We both had text messages.

The sender was listed as unknown.

But the message was exactly the same.

Now you have 24 hours. Tick-tock.

DAY TWO
Part One

41

... 19 hours to go ...

Lyegate Prison emerged from the rain.

It was huge, a vast, red-brick Victorian building that had originally been built in the 1800s as a sanatorium. More modern extensions had been added at the back and along both flanks, sprouting like artificial limbs, but as we approached the turn-off, it was the front that dominated the view from the road. If it hadn't been hemmed in by high-security gates and razor wire, if the sash windows weren't barred and there weren't CCTV cameras everywhere, its steeply pitched roofs and ornate gables wouldn't have looked out of place behind Ellie in an episode of *Church Row Manor*.

We slowed, taking the turn.

I was on the back seat, Dougan beside me. In front of us were Healy, Bodie and Naughton. Up front, a uniformed officer was driving and Phillips was in the passenger seat. No one had said a word for the entire journey.

We arrived at the perimeter gate, a security guard emerging from a hut. The uniformed officer buzzed down his window, but Phillips did the talking.

'Detective Superintendent Phillips,' he said. 'Gary is expecting us.'

Phillips's use of the governor's first name in an attempt to assert some measure of authority was met with complete indifference. The security guard just ambled back to the hut without saying a word.

Thirty seconds later, the gates fanned open.

We moved along a cracked carpet of tarmac to the main building. The car park was virtually empty because there were no visiting hours today.

Or, at least, not for anyone but us.

Earlier, instead of meeting at the police station in Brixton, the cops had come to the office building at Paddington Basin. As they'd arrived, we'd watched the slowly dawning horror in the faces of Phillips, Dougan, Naughton and Bodie as they'd seen the photographs on the wall of the meeting room, each of them pictured with their loved ones. Phillips told us he'd received the same text as we had, just after 8 a.m.

Now you have 24 hours. Tick-tock.

I listened to him launch into a frustrated rant to a couple of people on his team about Alice's paperwork from the bank slipping through the cracks. If the officers had asked her the right questions, they would have got the form themselves and the cops would have been in Paddington way before me and Healy. When Phillips finished, Dougan and Bodie went down to the foyer to kick-start a search of security footage. But everyone seemed to know already that a CCTV trawl and the subsequent hunt for forensic evidence at the office would be as fruitless as it had been at the hospital.

Healy slid the passenger door to one side, returning my focus to the van, and got out. I watched him, his back to me. He was pretending none of this had got to him; that he was just taking in the prison, the entrance, the three storeys of windows and bricked-up doorways. But the cold gave him away: his breath was coming fast, gathering in clouds in front of his face, even as the rain continued to fall.

Phillips moved past him and led the way down to the Visitor Centre, the rest of us following. As soon as we entered, we hit a metal detector and X-ray machine. Phillips had brought reams of paperwork, while Bodie and Naughton were holding a video camera, a tripod and a power pack between them. Dougan had a Dictaphone and a laptop and, after Phillips had called ahead, we had all been cleared to take our mobiles in. But everything still had to be disassembled and then reassembled by the officers as they checked batteries, tapes, equipment slots and power leads for anything suspect.

Once the checks were over, we were led deeper into the prison.

We passed the Visitor Centre, which had been built inside one of the modern extensions, and through a series of security doors, into the gloomy hallways of the original, Victorian building. There was little in the way of natural light, everything painted a sickly glow by the ceiling lamps. At one point, we were able to see through to the cells, but then the view was gone again, until finally we reached two rooms facing each other at the end of a corridor. A number 1 had been stencilled on to one door, 2 on to the other.

The prison guard opened the door to Room 1.

'We'll bring him here,' he said to Phillips, and then opened the door to Room 2. 'Those of you not meeting with him can watch from in there.'

The rooms were almost identical and – judging by the size of the tables in each, and the whiteboards and pinboards on the walls – must have been used for internal meetings by prison staff. In Room 1, there were just three chairs, though, and while the pinboard in Room 2 was still full of employee information, the one in Room 1 was empty; even the pins had been taken away.

Everything was a potential weapon.

A door opened behind us and a man in his late fifties emerged. He was holding a laptop, wearing an expensive-looking three-piece suit, had a shaved head and a thick beard, and smiled as he made eye contact with Phillips.

'This is Gary Yates,' Phillips said to us.

Yates looked around, his gaze lingering on Healy and me.

'Nice to meet you all,' he said.

Dougan and Bodie nodded a greeting in response.

But Naughton's face remained a blank.

Yesterday, as we'd talked about visiting Glass, she'd looked shaken. Now she was showing absolutely nothing. It was like she was part of a meeting discussing who was next on the roster for traffic duty.

'We're going to handcuff him to bring him down here,' Yates said, 'and those handcuffs are going to have to stay on at all times, I'm afraid.'

From his expression, it was clear that Phillips didn't like the idea. His reasoning was probably that the more relaxed Glass was, the more likely he was to talk, and being handcuffed wasn't a good way to get him to loosen up. But with Glass I doubted it would make much difference. Most of what was about to come out of his mouth would be a swirl of lies and half-truths, and him not being in handcuffs was unlikely to change that.

'But there are a couple of things we need to talk about before we can bring the prisoner down,' Yates said, his voice tighter now.

Phillips eyed him. 'Is everything okay?'

'I pulled the footage off the system that you asked for, of all the times that these lawyers, Pope and Schubert, visited him.'

Phillips glanced at Yates's laptop. 'Is there a problem?'

Yates didn't reply for a moment.

And when he did, he said, 'It's probably just better if you see for yourself.'

42

... 19 hours to go ...

We gathered around Yates's laptop as he hit Play on the first video.

It was from a CCTV feed at the main entrance, the camera just above the metal detector and X-ray machine. In the corner of the screen was a date and time stamp.

The morning of 3 May last year.

Two men in suits were queuing to come in.

'That's the kid from the woods,' Dougan said, placing a finger against the face of the first man in the queue. He looked older here, his hair slicked back, his suit expensive. We still didn't have a clue who he was. Earlier, Phillips had said a rush job on the kid's DNA, fingerprints and dental records had gone nowhere.

The man who'd called himself Noah Klein — here pretending to be a lawyer named Jonathan Pope — entered Lyegate just behind. The description given by witnesses at The Crest appeared to be fairly accurate: dark hair, five-ten, medium build. But it was impossible to tell if he was in his late forties, impossible to say if he had the dark eyes people had described, because his head was down and he'd turned away from the camera. In real time, I doubted any of the staff at Lyegate had noticed anything odd about the movement. In a paused image, it was easier to see the truth.

He was hiding his face from the CCTV.

'He knows where the camera is,' I said, remembering Phillips's declaration the previous night that it would be impossible to avoid all surveillance.

We were about to find out if he was right.

Yates closed the video and opened another. It was the next part of the prison. Klein and the kid from the woods were being directed to a door on the far side of an empty Visitor Centre. Again, there was no clear view of Klein's face, his head tilted so we could only see his hair. To anyone watching at the time, it would have looked like he was simply glancing around.

The next video was from the corridor beyond the door: the two men entered a room on the right, almost directly under the camera.

Again, the only view we had was of the top of Klein's head.

'This is where lawyers meet their clients,' Yates explained, 'so there's no video inside the rooms.'

'What about when he comes back out?' Phillips asked.

'He does the same thing – but in reverse.'

'There's no angle on his face at all?'

'No,' Yates said, 'nothing in any of the videos. We can make all this footage available to you and your team, but I've spent an hour this morning going over all of these recordings and I still have no idea what he looks like. It's the same the other four times he came in.'

Phillips glanced at me and then returned his gaze to the footage, a twist of frustration in his face. 'How could he possibly know where the cameras are?'

'Because he's been to the prison before.' Everyone looked at me. 'If this is his first time here, he should be searching for cameras in order to avoid them. The fact he doesn't once turn to see where the cameras are means he already *knows* where they are.'

'But this video is from the first time these two ever came in,' Dougan said.

'It's the first time they ever came in posing as his lawyers,' I replied. 'That doesn't mean it's the first time they've been in.'

Phillips eyed me.

He knew exactly where my thoughts had landed.

I looked at Yates. 'Has Glass had any other male visitors while he's been inside?'

Yates shook his head. 'Until this, it's been exclusively women. Groupies.'

'So, to my mind, there are three ways Klein knows where the cameras are. One is that he's been into the prison before – under whatever his real name is, or using another fake ID – but came in to visit someone other than Glass. Two, he sent someone else in to do the camera reconnaissance for him so he would know the layout before his own visit. Or three, he was a prisoner here and learned where the cameras were during his sentence. Short of Klein gaining access to the prison's security system, or getting hold of a complete blueprint for every camera position across the entire facility, how else would he know how to do this?'

I gestured to the laptop, to the paused image of Klein with his head ducked – his face hidden – as he made the turn into the room he'd be meeting Glass in.

'But why wouldn't the kid conceal his identity too?' Healy asked.

It was the first thing he'd said since we'd left Paddington.

I stayed silent and looked around the room, waiting for a response from one of the others. No one said anything. Eventually, the gaze of everyone but me and Healy drifted back to Phillips, as if every response and every theory needed to be fed through him first. 'Could have been inexperience,' he said, 'or an oversight. Maybe he was meant to hide his face – maybe that was the plan – but he panicked and forgot to.'

'Or maybe, unlike Klein, he knew no one would find him.'

Phillips's jaw clenched.

'The search for the kid has gone nowhere,' I said, 'so whether he showed his face on video or not, he clearly felt that it wouldn't make any difference.'

'But with Klein it would,' Healy added.

Phillips shook his head, the frustration evident. 'If Klein was a prisoner here, why aren't the guards reacting to his visit? They're not even giving him a second look. You don't think a single one of them might think it's weird that an ex-con is now acting as Glass's lawyer?'

'The officers who staff the Visitor Centre – where the meetings rooms are – aren't the same officers who staff the floors,' Yates said. 'It's possible these employees may never have come into contact with this Klein/Pope guy.'

'*If* he was a prisoner here,' Phillips added.

'Right,' Yates responded.

'Even if it turns out that he wasn't,' I said, 'Klein knows the layout somehow – and he's hiding his face from us. And whether he's been in here before as a visitor, or whether he sent someone else in to do the recon, or whether he *was* a prisoner, there's a reason he's doing that.'

Healy stepped forward, eyes glued to the laptop. 'He thinks we might recognize him.'

'Exactly.' I looked at Klein myself. 'Maybe all of us here know who he is.'

43

. . . 19 hours to go . . .

The room was quiet for a moment.

'The kid is here on film showing his face to absolutely everyone,' I said. 'Why wouldn't Noah Klein be comfortable doing the same?'

'*Because*,' Phillips replied, 'he doesn't want to get caught.'

It was true: it may just have been an insurance policy on Klein's part, reducing the possibility of him ever being identified to near zero. But every time I looked at the kid – his face, the openness of his stance – and then at Klein, I saw two people, working closely together, who had two entirely different perspectives on being recorded. The contrast wouldn't stop niggling at me.

'Where would we have come across him before?' Dougan asked, stepping in.

I opened out my hands. 'At The Crest? In the disappearance of the three women? In Marco Roy's case? In the original investigation into Glass? In all four?'

'Why does he have to be in any of them?' Phillips said.

He was right. From the outside looking in, if you were coming in cold to the case, this whole angle might have felt like a shot in the dark. But we *weren't* coming in cold. We'd seen enough already to know that Noah Klein left nothing to chance. 'There's a reason he's not showing his face,' I said. 'And it's not just out of an abundance of caution.'

'So you're saying this is another one of your gut feelings?'

I looked around the room. Dougan's face showed very little, but I could tell from his questions that he had gradually begun to trust my instincts. Bodie tended to follow Dougan's lead, which meant he was probably onside as well. Naughton had said almost nothing all morning, so it was hard to say what was going on in her head.

'The hospital, the Lost Women, Marco Roy and Glass are orbiting the search for Preston Stewart,' I said, keeping my voice as even as I could. 'Noah Klein is central to that search. I just think it would be worth seeing if we can find him in those four cases somewhere. If I'm wrong, I'll hold my hands up.'

'We haven't found him so far,' Phillips said.

'Doesn't mean he's not there.'

'I've got a team of thirty people on this.'

'Doesn't mean he's not there,' I repeated. 'We're talking about four different cases, thousands of pages of police work – and we have no actual idea who he is and only a rough idea of what he looks like, so we don't even know in which parts of these cases we should be searching.'

But Phillips was shaking his head again. 'It's a stretch, Raker.'

Yates, who'd just been watching us, snapped his laptop shut, ending the back and forth. 'I'll return in ten minutes with an update.'

He headed out of Room 2.

One of the prison staff started setting up the video-conferencing equipment, pulling down a projector screen to cover the whiteboard, before doing the same in Room 1. Soon, a live feed was up and running between the two different cameras.

No one spoke until the staff member had left, and then Dougan looked up from his phone and said, 'We've just checked in with everyone.'

He meant our families and friends.

He meant Rebekah.

He meant my daughter, Annabel.

She lived in south Devon and hadn't appeared in any of the photos pinned to the wall of the office, but I'd called her all the same, and then so had the cops. Like the rest of the families, like Rebekah, she'd been ordered to stay at home. It was unclear whether the photos were a direct threat, a suggestion that Noah Klein was going to come after the people we cared about, or just a way to show how close he could get to us without us being aware. What was more certain was that, in order for him to take that number of photos – and print them out – he'd have needed some help.

And not just from the kid in the woods either, especially as he'd been on a mortuary slab since yesterday evening.

He would have needed help from others.

Others we knew nothing about.

44

. . . 18 hours to go . . .

No one spoke for a while as we waited for whatever came next. Finally, it was Bodie who broke the silence: 'How long's your son in Spain for?'

He was talking to Naughton.

I watched her as she adjusted herself. The boyfriend she lived with wasn't in any of the photos at the office, but the police had sent someone around to watch his house anyway. Her son had flown out to Spain with her ex-husband and his girlfriend early this morning, which – in the estimation of the police – made the boy less of a target.

Not that Naughton seemed to have sought much solace in the fact.

She'd been subdued all morning, her expression set, and even at the mention of her son, it didn't move. 'They're out there for a week,' she replied to Bodie.

'What part are they going to?'

'Majorca.'

'Nice.'

'Yeah.' Naughton finally pushed out a smile. 'He'll have fun.'

No one else in the room seemed to have noticed the slight stiffness to her gait, the tautness of her smile, and as she returned to her phone, I started to talk myself back: Phillips and Healy knew her much better than me, so if they didn't think that something was up with her, maybe there wasn't.

'Are you two clear on everything?'

Phillips was looking between Healy and me.

I nodded. 'Crystal.'

Healy didn't move or say anything.

'Healy?'

He dragged his gaze up from the tabletop. 'You only went through everything about a hundred times this morning, Phillips. Yes, I'm clear.'

'Don't let him play games.'

'How am I going to do that if I'm a fucking mute?'

The two of them glared at each other. As I'd predicted to Healy this morning, one of the first rules Phillips had laid down was that I had to do all the talking. I was no fan of Phillips, but I would probably have made the same decision in his position. Glass wanted Healy there to try to stoke a reaction. And as he picked at the wounds, Glass wouldn't be using a sledgehammer, he'd be using a scalpel. It would be a slow, subtle, painful dissection of Healy's grief and anger until something inside Healy finally went pop.

'If you react, he wins,' Phillips said.

'I get it.'

'I hope you do, because we need to find out what happened to those three women, to Marco Roy, and we need to know where Preston Stewart is. If your head goes in there, then we're not going to get that. He's just going to keep –'

'Holy shit, Phillips, I *get* it. Okay?'

The atmosphere in the room cooled.

That was when Governor Yates appeared in the doorway.

'The prisoner is on his way down.'

Naughton

Now

Naughton watched as Raker, Healy and Phillips headed through to Room 1, and then got to her feet and grabbed the tripod. Bodie picked up the video camera and the leads, and the two of them followed the others across the corridor. As she set the tripod down and stepped away to allow Bodie to plug everything in, she saw Raker glance in her direction. Casually, she turned her back on him. She didn't want Raker to look her in the eyes.

He was smart.

He saw things.

She'd noticed him studying her earlier on, and it had felt as if he were peering right into her head, reading her thoughts. When he did, it was like he'd been there at 3 a.m. in her car as the knife had been held to her throat.

It's like he knows I'm lying to everyone.

It's like he knows what I'm being forced to do.

She'd done some background on Raker before she and Phillips had visited Glass, because Raker was as fundamental to understanding Glass's history as Healy was. She'd pored over the accounts of what had happened at the Dead Tracks, and she'd been through news stories about the missing people Raker had found in the years since. Some of his investigations had passed almost entirely unnoticed, others had blown up, but the through-line in all of it was Raker's desire to remain out of sight. There had been one or two occasions when he'd spoken to the media – including a podcast that Naughton had listened to – but mostly he existed between the lines in articles and outside the frames of press photographs.

That made him harder to know.

When she'd listened to him on the podcast, it had been obvious that he had an emotional attachment to his work, an empathy with the families he worked for, that made him different from most cops Naughton knew. But empathy was just one part of what made him successful. The other was his ability to watch people, interpret them.

That was the part that scared her.

She headed back to Room 2.

Dougan was still at the table, tapping out an email on his laptop. Naughton sat and looked at the video feed being piped in from the other room. Phillips was once again talking to Healy about not losing his head.

Eventually, Raker interrupted him. 'I think he gets it, Phillips.'

'Yeah, well, we can't afford any screw-ups,' Phillips responded. 'Neither of you have spoken a word to him in years, whereas I spoke to him yester—'

'That prick killed my girl,' Healy said, 'so I don't need an education on what he's like. What I need you to do is shut the fuck up.'

Dougan glanced at the video feed, then at Naughton.

In the other room, Bodie had frozen.

'Just don't go and mess things up like you normally do,' Phillips said as a final retort and then left the room. Bodie followed.

Phillips entered Room 2 seething, but Dougan and Naughton pretended not to notice. Bodie closed the door and sat two chairs away from Phillips.

Naughton looked at the video feed again, at Raker and Healy settling into the two seats on the right-hand side of the table. It was clear that they'd spent a lot of years together. You could see it in their mannerisms, in how comfortable the silence was, in the fact they didn't need to say anything to one another about Glass. She wondered if that was part of the reason Phillips seemed to be so threatened by them, and she was more convinced than ever that it was the reason he'd asked Naughton to be a part of this. He was using her to try to drive a wedge between the two of them, to unpick the solid nature of Raker and Healy's relationship by getting Healy on to her side, so that Phillips could exert more control.

It wasn't going to work.

Phillips was still under the mistaken impression that Naughton and Healy were close. But Healy hadn't said a word to Naughton since the interviews at the station in Guildford the night before, and Phillips obviously hadn't dug down into the reasons why.

Her phone buzzed.

She immediately felt on edge because she knew who it would be, but she made the movement to her pocket look relaxed. None of the others noticed.

It was a message from an unknown number.

You know what to do

Almost on cue, out in the corridor, she heard the security door buzz.

Low voices.

The metallic rattle of handcuffs.

Naughton glanced at the text message again, swallowing down tears that were close to the surface.

And then she put her phone away.

She looked at the feed from next door.

And she watched as Glass entered the other room.

45

. . . 18 hours to go . . .

He paused in the doorway and looked in at us.

Phillips had prepared me for the physical change in him, but it didn't make it any less stark. Gone were the looks he'd traded on as a highly qualified plastic surgeon; now he was a balding middle-aged man who looked too thin for his body shape. Prison food – or perhaps the lack of it – had drawn his cheeks in and created dark crescents under his eyes. He moved quietly to the table, his expression neutral.

Next to me, Healy didn't move an inch.

It sounded like he was barely even breathing.

'Good morning,' Glass said to me, his handcuffed wrists in front of him as he obediently let one of the guards sit him down.

The guard took a step closer to him. 'Remember what I told you. You do anything in here that we don't like the look of, and this ends straight away.'

'I understand,' Glass replied, still looking at me.

The guard left, pulling the door shut. As he did, Glass finally took in the room, his gaze settling on the camera above the projector that was being used to feed video through to Phillips and the others. He stared at it for a moment and then, slowly, returned his attention to us. Except he didn't look at me this time.

He looked at Healy.

'I'm sorry for what I did to Leanne.'

It felt like the entire room tilted on its axis.

Healy's hands moved to his lap, fingers entwined, body rigid.

His cheeks had started to flush. He stared at Glass, who stared back: pale, dark-eyed, expressionless.

'I really am sorry,' Glass said again, his voice quiet. 'I've had a lot of time to think about what I did . . .' He stopped. 'It was unforgivable.'

'What are you doing?' I said.

He continued looking at Healy for a moment and then his eyes flicked to me. He examined me, as if he'd forgotten there were three of us at the table, and he needed reminding of who I was. Minutely adjusting his wrists, the handcuffs clattering against the tabletop, his fingernails bitten and broken and ringed with grime, he said, 'David. It's been a while.'

'I'm not playing games with you.'

'An apology isn't a game, surely?'

'You didn't ask us here to apologize.'

'I wanted to say to Colm that I was —'

'You don't regret anything you did.'

'How would you know? We haven't spoken for fourteen years.'

'You're a psychopath.'

'I am what I am,' he responded, and then turned to Healy once again. 'That doesn't mean that I can't feel regret about what I —'

'Enough,' Healy said, cutting him off. 'Enough.'

Glass blinked.

I shifted forward. 'You told Phillips yesterday that you —'

'*Phillips*,' he said, spitting the name out, and then looked towards the camera above the projector. 'He's a worm. All three of us know that. I told him what I needed to tell him in order to get you two in here.'

'So this *is* a game?'

'No. No, it's not a game, David. I want to help you.'

Healy got to his feet.

I glanced at him. 'What are you doing?'

'What do you *think* I'm doing?' He waved a hand at Glass. 'This is bullshit. You really think this lying little prick wants to *help* us?'

'Fine,' Glass said. 'I'll rephrase it. I want to be honest with you.'

'Honest about what?' I said.

'About what's going on here.'

I studied him. 'And what's that?'

'I expect Detective Superintendent Phillips and his colleagues in the other room have, among their paperwork, a list of prisoners whose sentences have coincided with mine. I mean, it's a fairly obvious furrow to plough. They'll be looking for angles of investigation – you know, possible connections, etcetera.' He looked into the camera above the projector. 'May I suggest you bring that list in here?' He then returned his attention to Healy. 'Are you going to sit, Colm?'

'Don't call me Colm.'

'What would you like me to call you?'

'Nothing. I don't want you to call me anything.' Healy looked at me and I could see everything was different now: being in a room with Glass was *all* he'd wanted when he'd been going through the drawer in Alice's bedroom. It was all he'd wanted since the moment he'd found Leanne's body. But not any more. Now he'd walked into the darkness that had stalked him for years, and realized he didn't have a map. He didn't understand Glass. He couldn't read him. It was like Glass had sucked all the air out of the room.

'Please, Colm,' he said to Healy, 'sit.'

'Fuck you.'

'I have some things to tell you both,' he replied, his face showing absolutely no response to Healy's retort. 'We can start as soon as Phillips brings that list in.'

'Do you know where Preston is?' I asked.

'Let's start with that list, shall we?'

'What about Marco Roy?'

'The list.'

'The Lost Women?'

The door to the room opened.

Phillips entered, trailed by Dougan.

'If this is a game, there'll be consequences,' Phillips was saying, coming around to Glass's side. But Glass didn't even acknowledge him. 'Did you hear what I said?'

Again, he got no reply.

'*Glass*, did you hear what I said?' Silence. Phillips glanced between us, the frustration and anger colouring his face, and tried again: 'You will be punished severely if this turns out to be some wild goose chase.'

The very corners of Glass's mouth twitched. Everyone in the room knew it was an empty threat. Phillips had no control over how prisoners were treated, or what punishments were meted out, and the impotence of his statement seemed to annoy him even more.

'Are you listening to me?'

For a fourth time, Glass acted as if no one had said anything.

I looked at the sheets of paper in Phillips's hand, a prison emblem at the top, a long list of names on the first of what looked like three or four pages.

'Why do you want this list?' Phillips asked Glass.

Nothing.

'Oh, we're really still doing this, are we? Stop being such a bloody child.'

This time, Glass shifted an inch, his head tilting towards Phillips, his eyes fixed on a space between Phillips and Healy. 'I think it's you that's behaving like a child. I told you yesterday I had information about the case that David and Colm have been working, and that I would give it to them personally.'

'You're not dictating the terms –'

'I find you so uninteresting,' Glass said quietly, evenly, as if he were discussing the weather. He still hadn't made eye contact with Phillips.

'Is that supposed to upset me?'

'I mean, you briefly stopped being mediocre a few years ago, but even that didn't last long.'

Phillips frowned. 'What the hell does that mean?'

'I think you know what it means.'

'No, I don't.'

'Do you really want me to say it out loud? In front of everyone?' Glass glanced at me. 'Except, of course, everyone in this room already knows, don't we?'

Healy seemed genuinely confused.

But I knew where this was going.

I'd heard the rumours from my sources at the Met.

'Come on, David, don't be shy. I can see you know.'

'I don't know what you're talk—'

'You know exactly what I'm talking about,' Glass said. 'All of us here know what I'm talking about.' He leaned a little closer to us, the pressure of the table at his ribs stopping him halfway, and then he whispered, 'Detective Superintendent Phillips likes to beat women.'

The air chilled.

Phillips took a step closer to Glass, his face burning, his jaw clenched. 'You're talking shite.'

Glass ignored him.

'Did you hear me? You're a *liar*.'

Finally, Glass moved, turning and looking up at Phillips for the first time. 'The most interesting thing you ever did in your life was push your wife into a kitchen cabinet.' The words were slow, deliberate, like the steel edge of a blade. 'But even then you couldn't grab her by the throat and choke her. You couldn't pin her against a wall and break some bones. You couldn't do something *really* interesting. All you did was shove her a little, and then shit your pants like a toddler.' Glass's gaze seared into Phillips – and Phillips wilted. He blinked, looked at us. He was lost, completely unmoored. '"I'm so sorry I got angry,"' Glass moaned in a cruel imitation of Phillip's accent. '"I'm so stressed at work. I'm so sorry I pushed you, my darling, I –"'

'Stop,' I said.

Phillips glanced at me, at Healy.

It looked like a part of him had broken.

Glass continued glaring at him for a second longer, and then he turned in his seat and stared across the table at me and Healy. 'You're nothing,' he said in a hushed, controlled voice, looking at us but still addressing Phillips. 'All I see is a fly buzzing against a window. *Tap. Tap. Tap.* You can't get out of the box your life has become, and you don't have the intelligence or the wit or the invention to be in here – so why don't you hand over that list and let the grown-ups do the talking?'

I saw Healy's eyes moving between Phillips and Glass, waiting for whatever came next. But Glass had gone too far. He hadn't just broken Phillips, he'd annihilated him. Phillips was raging and now he wasn't thinking straight.

'This circus ends right now,' he hissed.

'Phillips, wait –'

'No,' he spat back at me. 'We're done here.'

He stormed towards the door, list still in his hands.

'Look under V,' Glass said.

Phillips stopped next to Dougan, who was unsure whether to look at him, Glass or us. Reluctantly, Phillips half-turned and said, 'What?'

'The list,' Glass replied. 'Look under V for Vessler.'

Zauna and Marco

Zauna

The men from the council arrive about fifteen minutes late, but they do what they've been paid to do, and close off the route into Porthtreno. Once they've gone, Sydney leads Anna and Zauna down a path to the wooden walkway that crosses the water.

It's an awkward descent, because they're all carrying more bags than they can ideally cope with, and Anna is also trying to balance a tripod on her shoulder, but as they get to the walkway, water lapping at its edges, the skies clear and the sun comes out, and Sydney starts to become visibly excited. She gets even more excited once they've ascended to the apex of the island and peered down at the village itself.

'Look,' she says to Zauna, and points to some of the shadows the old, broken homes are casting across the sand. 'Those angles will be fantastic.'

They dump their equipment on the ridge and then carry it down to St Petroc, piece by piece, wading through the deep sand to the last house in the village. It takes them almost thirty minutes and, by the time they're done, Sydney is humming with impatience and begins going through the shot list with Anna.

As Zauna waits for the two women to get organized, she looks around the village, thinking about her brother and what Anna was telling her earlier about Emma – one of the women who'd come here with Marco a week before he disappeared – and how she didn't want to be interviewed for the documentary. Soon, Zauna's thoughts drift further and she's ten again, in the week after Marco returned from Cornwall.

Frustratingly, her memories of those seven days aren't as clear as she would like. Mostly, if they come to her at all, they do so in brief, snatched moments: when Zauna gets home from school and Marco is at the kitchen table, and it looks to her like he's been crying; a few days later, when Zauna gets up in the early hours to go to the toilet, and she finds him wide awake and sitting at the open window in his bedroom, staring out at the night. But mostly her recollection of that week is more of a feeling than a picture, an ominous sense that something was out of kilter with her brother. Before he went away to Cornwall, he was a light that burned and rarely went out, but in the week before he vanished, Zauna hardly saw him. It was like he didn't want to be home at all and, later, as Zauna got older, and her thoughts matured, she wondered if Marco had avoided the house because somehow he felt like he was contaminating it and everyone inside; as if he were carrying something infectious. And it wasn't until she met Sydney and Anna, and they started to talk about how they thought something had happened at the house party a week before he went missing, that she started to realize she was right.

'Zaun?'

Anna is talking to her and, after apologizing, Zauna wades through the sand to where Sydney and Anna have sorted out all the equipment, using broken, protruding pieces of the last house's chimney breast as makeshift shelves.

'So, Zauna,' Sydney says, dragging her legs through the sand, 'what we're going to do is have you stand here' – she points to a cove in a former living room – 'and then you're going to look around here, as if you're seeing it for the first time. As you do, we'll pan around from you and . . .' Sydney stops.

Her hand hangs out in front of her for a moment, pointing up the slope of the village to the frill of sand that runs along the ridge of the island. It's well above their eyelines and they have to look into the evening sun to see it.

Someone is up there.

'You can't be here!' Sydney shouts.

Whoever it is, is a silhouette against the sky.

'This whole area is off-limits!' She pushes through the sand. 'That's what those signs in the car park were for!'

The silhouette doesn't move.

Sydney's blood is up now, Zauna can see it.

Sydney pushes forward again, shielding her eyes from the sun so she can see the person more clearly.

But the person remains a silhouette.

'Did you hear what I said?' Sydney shouts.

No reply.

'Did you hear what I *said*?'

'You're Sydney Roder, right?'

Sydney stops moving, glances at Anna, who has moved closer, and then looks back up the slope. It's a man. Zauna watches as Sydney adjusts her position again, tilting her head, attempting to transform whoever it is into more than just a black smudge against a blue sky.

'Who are you?' Sydney shouts up to him.

'Sydney Roder, Anna Casey, Zauna Roy,' the man calls out in response.

Zauna looks at Sydney and then at Anna. Sydney's gaze remains on the man, but Anna glances in Zauna's direction: confusion – and the first flicker of unease.

'Okay,' Sydney says to him. 'You know us, so who are you?'

Marco

Marco looks down the slope of the village to the last of the houses, and then glances at Emma again. What she said to him only moments ago is still playing in his head.

You're a good man, Marco.
But not all men are like you.

He looks towards the darkness of the final, broken home in St Petroc, right at the bottom of the sea of sand. It's where he heard Fran giggling with Preston, and then arguing, and then crying. Now there's just silence. He can't see them and he can't hear them.

'Let's go back,' Emma says.

But, just as she says it, Marco clocks movement and, a second later, Fran emerges from behind one of the walls. She's masked by the darkness for a while, only one side of her – painted by the moon – visible to Marco. She's struggling against the weight of the sand, trying to wade through it on her way up the slope towards them.

'Are you okay?' Marco asks her.

Fran is too far away to hear.

'Let's leave them to it,' Emma responds, and touches Marco's arm, giving the sleeve of his coat a tug, trying to turn him around.

But Marco stays where he is and watches Fran coming slowly towards them. As she does, there's more movement in the darkness of the last house.

Preston.

Something balls in Marco's chest as he sees him, and Emma attempts to take him by the arm again, to lead him away.

'Let's go, Marco,' she says.

But Marco shrugs her off a second time, and as Fran gets closer Marco can see she's wiping tears from her eyes.

He looks past her, to Preston.

Except that's when Marco realizes he's got it all wrong.

He realizes that neither he nor Emma ever referred to Preston by name when they were discussing what was happening down there.

It was Marco who assumed it was Preston with Fran.

He'd assumed it because Preston had been the one who had told him to stay away from Fran. But now Marco is beginning to understand.

Preston wasn't threatening Marco.

He was trying to protect him.

Oliver – the one who said he loved Marco's name, who did *The Godfather* impression, who fell over drunk on the way down here – forms in the darkness.

He's quick and effortless through the sand.

Marco takes him in, his smooth movement, the expression on his face, and thinks, *He doesn't even look drunk any more.*

He looks stone-cold sober.

Was it all an act?

Fran – pale, sobbing – aims a crooked smile at Marco as she gets to him.

'Are you okay?' he asks her.

'I'm fine,' she says, but her words feel as fake as her smile and she doesn't wait for a response from Marco, just moves past him and up the slope.

When Marco returns his attention to Oliver, he feels a surge of anger, and then an instant cooling of his ire. Oliver isn't huge, but there's a subtle, unspoken threat coming off him; the way he looks at Marco, the way he carries himself.

Emma says, 'You're an arsehole, Oliver.'

'I didn't even do anything,' he replies.

'Then why's she crying?'

But almost instantly Emma glances away, towards the blackness of the water, as if she doesn't want to have to look at Oliver once he gets to them.

Oliver smiles at Marco – as if they're best friends, as if there's some inside joke that only they would understand – and he shakes his head and opens out his hands. But even though he's smiling, even though he says, 'I just told her I loved her and then she burst into tears and ran off,' Marco takes a step back. He finds himself a little frightened of Oliver.

Oliver stops.

He's shoulder to shoulder with Marco – Marco facing down

the slope, Oliver facing up. For a moment, Oliver does nothing, just stands there watching Fran, her legs moving slowly against the tide of sand, her sobs audible as she climbs.

Finally, he leans into Marco.

'Women,' he whispers. 'Am I right?'

Marco swallows.

'Am I *right*?'

Marco nods – once, twice.

And then, with one, last lingering look, the tip of his nose almost touching Marco's cheek, he moves past them.

That's when Marco finally breathes.

46

. . . 18 hours to go . . .

Phillips placed the prisoner list down on the table.

It was four sheets stapled together, a long list of names, in alphabetical order, of everyone who'd served time during the fourteen years Glass had been inside. He flipped the pages to V, and it became clear that someone in the other room had been going through the list because every name on the first and second page, and half of the third, had been highlighted. I was guessing the names were being cross-checked against the police database.

But V was on the fourth page.

'Who's Vessler?' I said to Glass.

'Oliver Vessler,' he responded. 'That's who you want.'

'Why do we want him?'

'Well, you're looking for Noah Klein, aren't you?'

I glanced at Phillips; he looked back at me.

'You're saying this Vessler guy is Noah Klein?'

'That's exactly what I'm saying.'

'So this is the man who abducted Preston from The Crest yesterday?'

'Yes.'

'The man who's been pretending to be your lawyer?'

'Yes.'

'And you're telling us this why?'

'As I stated before, I want to be honest with you.'

'What can we find out about Vessler?' I asked Phillips.

'Bodie,' Phillips called across the hallway. Bodie came in a couple of seconds later, glancing between us all, his gaze settling on Glass, wary of him.

'Jump to the end and find out what you can about this Vessler,' Phillips said to him, confirming that Bodie had been the one going through the list of names.

Bodie hurried off again.

'I can tell you what *I* know about him,' Glass said to me. 'But I think I'd rather continue this conversation with just you and Colm.'

Phillips didn't move for a moment, his eyes narrowing – and then, reluctantly, he exited the room with Dougan.

'Oliver Vessler was at university with Preston Stewart and Marco Roy,' Glass said. 'He was also at the pub that Marco went to on the night of his disappearance. The police down in Bristol even interviewed him. He said he didn't see or know anything about Marco going missing. They believed him.' He paused, looked between us. 'Your friends in the other room will check their database and Vessler will be in the Marco Roy paperwork somewhere. Probably only a couple of lines among all the witness statements that the police in Bristol took from the students at the pub that night, but there nonetheless.' He adjusted himself at the table, drawing his hands in towards him. 'Phillips and his minions will do their best to track him down, but they won't get far. Oliver doesn't have a mobile phone or a registered address. He's also had no paid employment since he was released from prison last year. So anything you find on Oliver Vessler will pre-date his conviction. A dead end.'

'But – what? – you know where he is?'

'Yes. I can give you his current address.'

'So give us the address.'

'Aren't you curious about why he's doing what he's doing? Who he is? Where he's come from?'

I stared across the table at him.

'Please, Colm,' Glass said to Healy, still standing. 'Won't you sit?'

Cautiously, Healy did as he was asked.

'Vessler was in here doing fifteen months for medical manslaughter and seventeen months for assault,' Glass continued. 'He was an oncologist. Five years ago, he injected a toxic cancer drug into the spine of an eighteen-year-old who'd undergone treatment for leukaemia. The victim was in remission, so she didn't require the drug. At trial, the prosecution argued that Vessler did it on purpose – that he had a God complex, and wanted to see what would happen – but Vessler always maintained it was an innocent mistake. A few days after the teenager died, her dad confronted Vessler outside the hospital. Vessler pinned him up against a wall and almost choked the poor man to death. In court, Vessler argued that it was self-defence, in response to the father's extreme level of aggression. The father said all he did to Vessler was swear at him and the next minute Vessler had him by the neck.' Glass stopped again, his forefingers pressed together in a V. '"I will end your fucking life,"' he said matter-of-factly. 'That's what Vessler told the father.'

Healy was googling Vessler on his phone.

'Like I told you,' Glass said, 'you might find pictures of him online, but not recent ones. No one knows the real him, the *current* him. Well, no one except me.'

Healy put his phone down on the table.

A photograph of Oliver Vessler looked out.

It had been taken during his trial, Vessler caught mid-stride as he entered the pillared entrance at Bristol Crown Court. He looked smart, had dark, slicked-back hair and a shading of grey stubble. The caption underneath said he was the same age as Preston – forty-six, which made him late forties now – but without confirmation of that it would have been hard to take a guess at exactly how old he was. The grey stubble added some years, but the rest of his face was unblemished and smooth: no lines, no age spots, his jaw square, his hair full. A few other things stood out: he had dark eyes, a medium build and was listed as being five-ten.

'What happens when the countdown clock gets to zero?' I said.

Glass frowned. 'What?'

'The clock in that office. What happens in eighteen hours?'

That same confusion on his face. 'I'm afraid I have no idea what you're talking about, David.'

I saw Healy glance in my direction, but I kept my focus on Glass. Was he playing us? Or did he genuinely not know what I was talking about?

'What I'm going to tell you about Oliver Vessler,' he said, 'and about how we ended up here is the truth. Like I say, I want to be honest with you.'

'Why would you help us?'

A smile traced the corner of his lips. But then his eyes stayed on me, taking in my face again, and the smile fell away. 'Oh, you're being serious.' He adjusted himself, handcuffs jangling, his eyes showing no light from the room — no reflection, just darkness — and for a second I was back in a police station fourteen years ago facing the younger version of him. 'Well, I thought that would have been obvious. I want some things in return.'

'I don't think you're in any position to make demands —'

'Thirty minutes south of Bristol is a place called Hillgrove Woods,' he said, cutting me off and then pausing deliberately to glance at the camera, looking into the lens, into the next room. 'It's on the Mendips. I believe they used to mine lead there once, which is why the grassland and heather is so undulating around the woods. Not that I've been down myself, for obvious reasons.' He looked at Healy and lifted up his wrists. 'I'm told the woods themselves are on the south side of the mines.' He stopped again, making us wait — and then he angled his head away once more and talked directly into the lens above the projector, to the cops in the other room: 'That's where you'll find him.'

I leaned in. 'Who? Oliver Vessler?'

'No, not Vessler.'

It took a second, his eyes lingering on the camera.

And then he faced Healy and me again.

'*Who* will we find in those woods?'

'Marco Roy,' Glass said. 'That's where his body is buried.'

47

. . . 18 hours to go . . .

A devastating silence passed across the room.

'You don't look convinced, David,' Glass said.

'How do you know Marco is buried there?'

'How do you think? Oliver Vessler told me.'

'And Preston?'

'What about him?'

'Did he and Vessler kill Marco together?'

Glass flattened his lips. 'Maybe it's best if you ask Preston that part.'

'Tell me where he is and I will.'

'Vessler and I grew close in here.' He'd just ignored my question entirely. 'We shared a lot. He knew who I was, and he wanted to talk about the things I'd done in the past. It wasn't so surprising. When I looked at him, I could see he was a partial reflection of myself. He didn't feel anything. He didn't care that he'd hurt people. He thought he could impress me because I suppose I was like that for a long time.'

'But now you're repentant,' I said.

He made a point of looking at Healy. 'Yes, I am.'

Healy shook his head in disgust.

'I really am, Colm.'

'Shut the fuck up.'

'Sometimes, in the medical field, you need that kind of detachment,' Glass responded, unaffected. 'It helps you make logical, unbiased decisions. But I could see that Vessler was more than simply detached. There was a darkness to him, and I used that.'

'"Used it"?'

'I don't like the term "brainwashed". I prefer "reprogrammed".' He smiled at me. 'Vessler latched on to me when he arrived here and, once he started opening up, I realized I could use him. He was academically clever, but that doesn't mean he was smart. In fact, in many ways, he was quite simplistic. Deep down, he wanted to do something that would get him noticed, something that people would really remember him for, and he liked taking risks. Unfortunately, his ego was too big for his intellect, which is why he got caught.' He glanced at Healy. 'I mean, why else would a doctor with his experience give a kid medicine she didn't need? He thought he was clever enough to get away with it – and when he didn't, when he got sent here, he was belittled and angry. And, wow, that darkness he carried, that *anger*. It was so easy to see once you'd dug under the skin a little. I opened him up, and I found out what made him tick, and pretty soon after that, he was my lapdog. He spilled everything and confessed to killing Marco Roy. The police interviewed him back then because he was in the pub the night that Marco disappeared, but it never went further. He didn't tell me the full story about *why* he'd felt the need to abduct and kill Marco, he just told me he did.'

'You didn't ask for the full story?'

'They went to a beach house down near Porthtreno a week beforehand – this big group from the university. Marco was there, Preston, Oliver Vessler. Marco saw something there. What I mean is, something happened at the beach house. And whatever it was, he carried it back to Bristol with him for the next week – and then finally he confronted Vessler about it. Vessler told me he'd done what was necessary.'

'Are you seriously telling me you didn't ask Vessler what Marco saw or what happened at the beach house?'

'I asked, but he wouldn't tell me.'

'You're lying.'

He took a long, frustrated breath. 'I'm not lying, David. I've told you where Marco's body is, but I'll go a stage further to reassure you.' He glanced to the camera. 'Latitude 51.258995, Longitude −2.644101.' Back to us. 'See? No lies.'

'Do we really have to sit here and listen to this shite?' Healy said to me.

'What's the matter, Colm?' Glass asked.

'You're a fantasist.'

'What else did Vessler tell you?' I said.

'We can get to that. But, believe me, he shared a lot.'

'And now you're selling him down the river.'

'Do you care? Do you feel sorry for the man who murdered Marco? Who ended the life of a young woman in remission and told her grieving father that he would kill him? Do you care about a man who – over the past day and a half – has had you and Colm chasing your tails, trying to find out what happened to Preston Stewart?'

'Do you *really* know where Vessler took Preston?'

'Yes.'

'Because Vessler told you?'

'No. Because taking Preston Stewart was my idea.'

I frowned. 'What?'

'Actually, this whole *thing* has been my idea.'

He stared across the table at me, his face a blank, as if he were describing what he'd had for lunch. But disguised in the banality of his tone, in the unembellished nature of his delivery, was exactly the truth that I'd dreaded was coming.

He's behind everything.

'Surely you guessed that already, David?'

'The abduction of Preston Stewart was your idea?'

'Yes.'

'The killing of Matthew Higgs?'

'Yes.'

'The use of the name Noah Klein, and the masks –'

'Yes.'

'– and having Vessler follow our families?'

He paused. 'Follow your families?'

'The photographs of our families in the office.'

He said nothing, his expression indifferent, and I thought back to when I'd asked him about the countdown. He could have been lying, but he didn't appear to know anything about the clock – and now he seemed to be in the dark about the photographs pinned up alongside it too. I tried to think what it meant and, if this wasn't just another elaborate lie, there only seemed to be one answer.

The office in Paddington was never a part of his plan.

It was Vessler's idea.

He'd gone rogue.

If Glass was as successful in controlling him as he seemed to be, Vessler would only have created the trail from the deposit box to the office because he thought it would get Glass's approval. He must have thought Glass would like the theatre of the photographs and the countdown clock. The question now was what Vessler believed the clock was ticking down to.

'Why would you want to abduct Preston Stewart?' I asked. 'Why would you send Vessler out to do that for you?'

'We can get to that in a moment.'

'Why don't we get to it now?'

'Timing is everything.'

I eyed him. 'Meaning?'

'Patience, David.'

'What about Alice-Leigh then?'

'What about her?'

'You manipulated her into visiting you.'

'I didn't manipulate her. I genuinely wanted to see her.'

'No, it's pretty clear now the only reason you asked to see her was so you could send her to that deposit box to find the mask. You used her to send a message to us.'

'It doesn't mean I didn't want to see her. Men can change,

David. I mean, look at Colm here.' Glass's eyes went to Healy. 'You look good with less weight on, my old friend. The beard suits you too. And it's so wonderful that you're a grandfather now.' And then, like a light going out, his face instantly neutralized. 'It was a lovely touch by Liam and Alice to call her Leanne. I'm sure that meant a lot.'

'Don't ever talk about my family,' Healy said through his teeth.

'*Our* family, you mean?'

'No.'

'Leanne is my granddaughter too. We're both lucky like that, aren't we, Colm?'

'*No.*' Healy smashed the flat of his palm on to the table.

Glass smiled and then turned, looking into the camera. 'Christopher Pockman. Pop his name into the PNC and you will find your "kid in the woods".'

'Pockman?'

'Yes,' he said to me. 'Big fan of mine. He used to write me letters telling me how much he admired me. I didn't even really have to try with him. He was young and angry, raging at the world because his childhood was a total fucking horror show. I gave him safe harbour. I made him feel like he belonged to something. Inside a few weeks, he was all in. I mean, he bit down on that poison because I told him to have a back-up plan in case he ever got caught. I suggested wearing a necklace like that, and so that was what he did. He would have done anything to please me.' Glass blinked. 'Sweet boy, really.'

'You never got letters from him,' Healy said.

'I did.'

'The prison have been monitoring your mail every single day for fourteen years and you've never received any correspondence from a "Christopher Pockman".'

'Don't be naive, Colm. Prisons are leaky. There are ways to bypass checks.' He glanced at the camera again. 'Not that Governor Yates doesn't run an *extremely* tight ship. But if you go back through my mail, you'll find a series of codes hidden in love letters from fictional women. The letters all came from Christopher. I do a favour for someone, someone does a favour for me and smuggles in a mobile phone. I put the codes I've been sent into a URL, and – boom – I'm suddenly on a secure messaging platform chatting with Oliver and Christopher. Christopher was extremely good with technology. I mean, you would have noticed that yourself at The Crest. His work got us access to the hospital's security system.'

'Why the hell are you admitting to all of this?' I asked.

'My life here is miserable. My visits are controlled to the point where I spend most of my days alone. My reading material is still highly restricted, and I only get to visit the library twice a month. I've never had one decent job in all the time I've been inside. I'm highly educated. I could be teaching fellow inmates how to read, how to write. Instead, Governor Yates has me scrubbing down toilets. Yes, I've managed to cut corners to pull some favours here and there – but those are small, rare moments. I want to make my life better.'

'So all of this just because you don't like mopping floors?'

'In part,' he said. 'It's also been about messing with you and Colm a little.' His mouth flattened. 'I fucking hate you both.' He delivered the line with no emotion.

'So this is revenge?' I asked.

'Messing with you was just a happy bonus. As I said, I can tell you everything you need to know – I've already given you Marco, I've given you Christopher's name; I can give you Preston's location and I know where the Lost Women are buried.'

The news that the Lost Women were dead wasn't a surprise. They'd been missing for almost as long as Zauna Roy had been alive. But confirmation that their bodies were hidden somewhere was no less jolting. It was more lost lives; more women whose lights were extinguished at the hands of awful, violent men – and the bleak, depressing irony was that any closure for the three women's families would be coming from a man who had cut short the lives of nine innocent women himself.

'Did Oliver Vessler kill the Lost Women?'

'All in good time. I imagine the officers in the next room have already picked up the phone to their colleagues down in Avon and Somerset Police, and a team in Bristol are on the way down to Hillgrove Woods as we speak. All of you here will, I'm sure, want to make certain I can be trusted on the location of Marco Roy's body. After that, you'll want to ensure I'm telling the truth about Christopher Pockman too. I mean, what's a negotiation without credibility?'

'And then?'

He opened out his hands. *That's the big question.* 'I'll give you everything – so you have the whole story, start to finish – and, in return, my demands are really very simple. I don't want to have to mop shower floors and scrape down toilet bowls. I want better access to the prison library. I want to educate. I want to teach my fellow inmates how to read and write.'

I waited, saying nothing.

Giving Glass the opportunity to manipulate and corrupt vulnerable prisoners didn't feel like a smart move, but there wasn't time to worry about that for now – and I didn't have the power to decide whether it happened or not, anyway. Ultimately, in this moment, all that mattered was the recovery of four bodies and a missing person.

Except I could see from Glass's face that there was more.

His eyes were alive now.

Power, ego, control.

'Oh, and just one more thing,' he said. He blinked, making us wait. 'I've been in here a long, long time now and not a single one of my cells has ever had a window.'

'So you want a cell with a window?'

'I want to watch a sunrise.'

'I'm sure Governor Yates can look into that.'

'Oh, no, you misunderstand me, David,' he said, and then stopped, drawing it out. 'I want to watch a sunrise out *there*.'

I stared at him. 'You mean, outside the prison?'

'Yes. I want to watch the sun rise at Porthtreno.'

48

. . . 17 hours to go . . .

Healy was the first to speak. 'Are you taking the piss?'

'It's a beautiful part of the country, Colm.'

'So it's not because that's where the Lost Women were last seen? Not because you claim it's the place where something happened to Marco a week before he vanished? Not because Preston spent the time before he disappeared watching TV shows and reading books about that island? Those have nothing to do with it.'

'Of course they have something to do with it. Reading about those women was when I first became interested in the island. Now I actually want to see it.'

Healy pushed back from the table. 'I'm done.'

'What's the matter, Colm?'

'You're out of your mind,' he said to Glass, 'that's what the matter is.'

'Why?'

'Why do you *think*? This shite about watching a sunrise. You do realize that no one with a brain cell is going to let you out of this prison, right? Not now, not ever.'

'Well, that's not your decision to make, is it?'

'They're not going to let you out to watch a *sunrise*.'

'Why, do you think that's unreasonable?'

'Yeah, I think it's unreasonable. In fact, I think every single thing that comes out of that hole you call a mouth is unreasonable. If all you wanted was to watch a sunrise, you'd have been happy to sit on the roof of the prison and watch it from there. You're not being honest. You're not sorry. You're a fucking cockroach.'

'It's unfortunate that you feel that way.'

'It's unfortunate you're still breathing.'

I tried to wade back through the deluge of information Glass had offered up, but he was deliberately overloading us. He was handing us genuine, case-changing lines of enquiry like Marco's burial site and the identity of the kid in the woods, and both of those things were almost definitely accurate: I already knew Marco would be in those woods, exactly where Glass said; I already knew that he wouldn't be lying about the name Christopher Pockman. I knew it because Glass needed us to think he was credible and honest, and this was how he did it.

But it was a Trojan Horse.

He was trying to smuggle something else past us.

'David,' he said, 'perhaps you feel differently from Colm?'

'I don't trust you.'

'I didn't think you would, and I understand your reasons why. Let's go back a little way.' Glass moved himself a fraction. 'Once Oliver Vessler told me how he'd killed Marco, I used one of my all-too-rare visits to the prison library to look up Marco's disappearance. That was when I read about the Lost Women for the first time. And that was when I discovered you wrote about them as a journalist.'

I waited to see where he was going.

'That's when the idea first hatched; the idea to set all of this up. I could see in the words you wrote about the Lost Women how deep that case ran for you. It was one you weren't going to be able to let go. Afterwards, on one of the phones I had smuggled in, I listened to a podcast you did where you talked about them. The more I listened to you talk, the more I started to realize I could use those women against you. I wanted to mess with you. I wanted to mess with you both, in fact. I wanted to *hurt* you. You two are why I'm in here. I wanted to make you suffer.'

Again, it felt like a marriage of fact and fiction.

I'd suspected he'd seen my work on the Lost Women, had even speculated to Rebekah the previous evening that he might have listened to the podcast. And I didn't doubt the events of the last two days were, to some extent, an act of retribution. But revenge wasn't his prime motivator. He'd already called that part a *happy bonus*.

'I'm glad you both came, though.' He looked between us. 'I mean, I know you were always going to, David, but I did wonder about you, Colm. Would you agree to see me when you realized there was no way for you to sneak a knife in?' He lifted his wrists to his throat and vividly mimicked a knife being repeatedly stabbed into his jugular. 'I'm assuming that's crossed your mind at some point.'

Healy just stared at him.

'I played the long game with you, David. I found out about your connection to the Lost Women – I realized how much their fate mattered to you; more lost souls you felt you needed to bring home – and once Vessler got released from prison, I realized I could finally begin.'

The door to the office opened again and Phillips came in, followed by Dougan. 'We're pressing Pause on this until we can prove he's telling the truth about Marco,' Phillips said. 'No,' he added quickly when he saw that I was going to try and suggest we kept the conversation going. 'You're going to go to the other room.'

Reluctantly, I stood.

Glass showed no reaction to us leaving, no change in expression. He just angled himself slightly and said, 'I look forward to your return.'

I felt a hum of panic, deep in my bones. He appeared so much older than he was, drawn and colourless, the shadows of prison life playing out in the tint of his skin and the lines on his face. He'd lost his definition, his looks cast off to time, his physique shapeless. But I was starting to realize that concealed the biggest lie of all.

He'd let his body go, but not his mind.

His mind was stronger than ever.

And that meant he'd never been more dangerous.

49

. . . 16 hours to go . . .

Fifty minutes later, Healy and I were taken back through to Glass.

Phillips and Dougan followed. I hadn't seen much of Phillips since he'd interrupted the interview. He, Dougan, Bodie and Naughton had been using a second, smaller meeting room, so they could talk out of earshot of us.

As we re-entered Room 1, Glass looked like he hadn't moved an inch.

He stared straight ahead until we were seated across from him, and then his eyes went to me, to Healy, and then to a card file Phillips was holding in his hands.

'He's telling the truth about Christopher Pockman,' Phillips said to me.

He flipped the front cover of the file and placed a photocopy down on the table. It was Pockman's driving licence.

He was the kid in the woods.

I glanced at Glass, who had the same blank expression as before.

Phillips handed me a second sheet of paper: a printout of a photograph. In the corner were lines of metadata: where the shot was taken, what day and what time, as well as the name of the police officer whose phone was used to take the photo. It was today's date and the time was seven minutes ago.

The location was Hillgrove Woods.

The picture was of a grave site, deep in the woods. Portions of a skeleton were visible in the earth: half a skull, an elbow, a knee, the fingers of both hands. The rest was soil and leaves, moss and pine needles. On the middle finger of the right hand was a silver ring, dirty, dulled, with a subtle black mesh pattern engraved on it.

Marco Roy had been wearing the same ring the night he vanished.

'You care about the Lost Women,' Glass said, talking to me, 'and because you care about them, you care about Marco. That's why I had Vessler take Preston at the hospital yesterday, why we lured you all the way in until you were too far along the road to turn around. Preston and Vessler both know what happened to Marco, and Vessler definitely knows what happened to those three women. I sold Vessler a lie when he was in here with me. I told him all of this was part of some baroque plan to make you pay. But the truth is far more mundane. I was manoeuvring them both into position so I could hand them over to you gift-wrapped. And all you have to do to get to Preston and Vessler, and to get the answers about Marco and the Lost Women, is give me what *I* want.' Glass pointed at the picture in my hands. 'I mean, look at that poor boy. What a waste of a young life. Do you really not want Vessler and Preston to answer for their parts in his death?'

'So you're saying Preston *did* kill Marco?'

'I'm saying he knows what happened to him. I'm sure Preston can explain it much better than I can.'

When Glass saw my frustration, he opened out his hands. *You give me what I want, I give you what you want.*

'We'll put a rush on the DNA,' Phillips said, stepping in, 'but forensics think it's Marco. He came off his mountain bike when he was sixteen and broke the ulna in his left arm.'

'The remains show evidence of that?' I asked.

Phillips nodded. 'Yes.'

Every pair of eyes was on Glass now and, finally, like a mask breaking, the corner of his mouth turned up and his eyes widened a little, and he said, 'I told you.'

'So you want to negotiate a deal?' Phillips asked him.

'If that's what you want to call it, Aiden.'

'What do you want for Oliver Vessler's location?'

'As I stated already, I want improved access to the library. That means daily visits for a minimum of an hour a time. And, separately to that, I want to take classes in there, teaching people to read and write. I don't want to mop floors or clean toilets again. Not ever. Not once.'

'Is Preston being kept where Vessler is?'

'Daily access to the library. No mopping, no toilets.'

'Fine. And in return for Preston's location?'

'There are cells on Twos with windows. I want one of them.' *Twos* was the nickname inmates gave to the second floor of the prison. 'I want to be facing west as well. I want to be able to see the sun going down in the evenings.'

'Okay. And for the location of the Lost Women?'

'That's a biggie,' he said.

'What do you want, Glass?'

'I already told you. I want my sunrise.'

'We're not taking you to Porthtreno.'

He shrugged, grimacing. 'That's a shame, Aiden, because it's kind of a dealbreaker for me. I want to breathe fresh sea air. I want to see the sun come up. I want to be on the coast for an hour, that's all. And then you can return me to my new cell on Twos, and I will work happily in the library for the rest of my life.'

'You think you can escape at Porthtreno – is that it?'

He looked at Phillips like he'd lost his mind. 'How would I escape, exactly? It's an island. You will, presumably, have a whole army of police officers there. Plus, Pockman is dead, I'm handing you Vessler, so there's no one left to help me. And even if there was, I'd need ten, fifteen, twenty people to best the manpower you will be throwing at this. Unfortunately, I'm just not that popular.'

'We're not driving six hours to Cornwall just so you can watch a sunr—'

'You'll kill two birds with one stone if you do.'
Everyone stilled.
'Porthtreno is where the Lost Women are.'
Phillips immediately shook his head. 'The three women aren't on the island.'
'They are.'
'No. That island has been searched multiple times.'
'Then it hasn't been searched well enough.'
'The cops down there used radar. They used dogs.'
'Be that as it may, the women are there. I will take you to their bodies once you've signed on the dotted line and driven me down to Porthtreno.'

No one moved for a long time. I watched Phillips, trying to read his expression – and then his eyes flicked to me and away again.
'No,' I said to him.
He held up a hand to me. 'Not here.'
'It's a trap.'
'I said, not here. If you want to talk about this, we can move to the other –'
'He already knows everything we're going to say. He's spent months bringing us to this point.'
Phillips paused, looking between me and Glass. 'We have a duty to recover those bodies.'
'This isn't what it seems –'
'And we need to find Preston. He's how we do it.'
'This is part of some plan he's –'
'He's one man and we'll have thirty police officers there.'
'We don't know who else he's working with –'
'Every single element will be highly controlled.'
'It doesn't *matter*, Phillips.'
'You've made your feelings clear, Raker, but the decision has been taken.' He glanced at Dougan. 'Go and get Governor Yates and call a lawyer. We need to draft a legal agreement and get it in front of him as soon as possible.'

I dragged my gaze back to Glass.

He'd angled his head slightly, deliberately, so that neither Phillips, Dougan or the two prison officers at the door could see him. Only Healy and me. And once he did, once he knew he couldn't be seen, he started mouthing something silently to us.

Tick-tock.

Tick-tock.

Tick-tock.

Healy

Now

Healy leaned in, staring at Glass.
Tick-tock.
Tick-tock.
Tick-tock.

But he didn't get a chance to respond. Neither did Raker. A second later, Yates entered and the prison officers moved in on Glass, flanking him at the table, and then Phillips was asking Healy and Raker to leave the room.

'This is a mistake,' Raker said, but Phillips ignored him and, next minute, Raker was being ushered out of the room by Dougan, and Healy was following.

They entered Room 2.

Naughton was in the corner, phone in her hand, her attention flitting between that and the live feed of Glass. Bodie was on the far side of the table, a police file spread out in front of him, photographs of Glass spilling from it. He was writing something down, his laptop open and showing pictures of Oliver Vessler.

Naughton looked at Healy.

He waited for her to say something to them, a reaction to what had just gone on, but she went back to her phone.

'So?' he said to her.

She looked up again; Bodie did too, until he realized Healy wasn't addressing him. Naughton frowned. 'What?'

'You haven't got any comment on what went on in there?'

Bodie looked up again, sensing the tension.

But then Raker moved alongside Healy, his attention fixed on

Rosa – and suddenly she seemed to wilt, almost shrinking in on herself.

'What did you make of it all?' she said to Healy.

The question felt false – fabricated, too upbeat, too friendly.

Bodie glanced at Naughton, obviously noting the strangeness of her delivery too, patently wondering what was going on between them all.

'Your boss has lost his mind,' Healy said, 'that's what I make of it.'

'He's doing what he thinks is best for those families.'

'Oh, is that what he's doing?'

'There are no good choices here, Colm.'

'He doesn't care about their families. He cares about himself. His reputation, his career, what *he* can get out of it. He's thinking of the headlines at the end of this, when his photograph is on the front pages and he's being celebrated as the hero cop who brought the Lost Women home and arrested Oliver Vessler.'

'That's not fair.'

'It's fair.'

'It's cynical. You're not seeing clearly.'

'I've been able to see clearly for fourteen years – ever since your boss decided my daughter wasn't important enough to find because it didn't suit his agenda.'

'That's not what happen—'

'Don't tell me what happened. You weren't there.'

Naughton didn't come back at him this time. She just glanced at Raker again. In the feed from the next room, Glass was still sitting at the table, the prison officers either side of him. Phillips, Dougan and Yates were talking in the far corner.

'I need to piss,' Healy said, and headed out.

A single bathroom was at the end of the hallway. He slammed the door shut, locked it and then pressed his back against the door.

His heart was hammering.

His blood was up.

But it wasn't just anger he was feeling. If it was just anger, he could have dealt with it, could have stayed in that room – could have shouted Rosa down until she withered into silence – because anger was nothing.

Anger he could cope with.

But not the grief.

Not the guilt.

Both had been intensified by being across the table from Glass, and even as Healy squeezed his eyes shut and sought safety in the darkness, they remained there, smouldering, the ashes of them still burning from the pit of his stomach to the dome of his head. They'd burned the same way every day for the last fourteen years.

This was his burden.

This was the deepest, most despairing, most irreparable loss a parent could ever feel, and all of it gathered in his throat now. As he kept his eyes shut, he saw Glass looking at him from across the table, telling Healy he was sorry, using his daughter's name, wielding it; Healy saw himself kneeling at the bath a couple of nights before, painting his granddaughter's perfect pink skin with bubbles; he saw Liam and Ciaran as adults, as men who'd spent years hating him, and then as young boys for whom Healy had once been everything; and then, out of the smoke, forming from the rubble of his life and his choices, came Leanne – twelve or thirteen, her blonde hair long, her smile so pure it could stop time.

I'm so sorry, sweetheart, he said to her.

I'm so sorry for who I am.

My heart is broken and I deserve it.

Suddenly she was older – the young woman she was at the end, twenty years of age and every bit as beautiful as when she was a kid – and started speaking to him. But her voice wasn't carrying across the dark; the sound of her was lost in the forever between then and now.

I don't understand, Lee.

I don't understand what you're saying.
She spoke again.
He still couldn't hear her.
'Why can't I remember your voice?' he whispered.
In his head, she reached out her arms to him.
That face.
That smile.
'Why can't I remember your voice?'
And then, gradually, his daughter's image started to fade.
Don't go.
Please don't leave me again.
Healy started to cry.

50

. . . 14 hours to go . . .

I watched from across the other side of the prison car park as he emerged from the yawning mouth of the side entrance, the same two prison officers flanking him, Phillips trailing in his wake. Glass was dressed in a grey sweatshirt and blue trousers and, as he was walked the short distance between the gloom of the prison interior and the open doors of an unmarked white van, he looked across the car park, seeking us out.

In front of me, I saw Healy shift. He was seated next to Naughton and Bodie. Beside me was Dougan. When I glanced at him, he looked back at me and, for a fraction of a second, I could see the concern playing out on his face.

It was coming up to 6 p.m., the sun long gone, the cold of January biting. The heaters were all going in the van, but they did nothing to warm me up. As I watched Phillips on the other side of the car park, talking to the prison officers under the jaundiced glow of the prison's exterior lights, I felt a knot form in my chest.

The legal agreement was relatively simple and had been drafted, checked and signed inside three hours. What Glass was asking for at the prison wasn't complicated. Gary Yates's only stipulation was that the education classes that Glass got to run at Lyegate were overseen by staff at all times. Glass had agreed immediately. Phillips had suggested he might want to run the agreement past a solicitor of his own, but Glass had just scrawled his name across the bottom of the page and pushed the agreement back across the table.

'Vessler is using an abandoned flat in Camberwell,' he'd said.

Healy and I had been watching on the feed from the other room.

'Where in Camberwell?' Phillips asked him.

'Willowtree Grove. The Sampson estate.'

Phillips knew it, and so did I. It was a series of interconnected tower blocks on the south-western corner of Burgess Park.

'Which block?' Phillips said.

'Cook House.'

'Which floor?'

'Tenth. Flat 278.'

'Is he armed?'

'I don't know the answer to that,' Glass said, scratching the underside of his wrist, the handcuffs rattling. 'Assume he is. Vessler can be . . . unpredictable.'

'And Preston?'

'Most likely in the flat with Vessler.'

'"Most likely"? So you don't know for sure?'

'The plan was to take Preston to the flat.'

Phillips shook his head. 'You realize you've voided this whole thing about two seconds after signing it, right?' He gestured to the agreement, still sitting on the table between them. 'You said you knew where Preston was.'

'I do. He's in that flat.'

'You said he's "most likely" there. That's different.'

'The plan was to take Preston to the flat.'

Phillips paused, taking a long breath. Glass sat at the table, hands out in front of him, completely motionless. Finally, Phillips had looked at the prison officers. 'Start getting him ready,' he'd said.

And now he was ready.

Phillips returned to our van.

As he got in, he looked across the seats at me, then at Healy, then pulled his door closed. Glass wanted the two of us to travel down to Cornwall with them. Phillips had tried to refuse, but

Glass had insisted that if we weren't there, he wouldn't show them the grave sites.

On a human level, I understood Phillips's decision to take Glass to Cornwall. I understood his desire to push forward – to ignore all the misgivings he must have been feeling – because bringing families of missing people an ending was one of the most moral and profound things you could do. But everything he was doing, every decision, every part of what was going to happen, was tainted by the presence of Glass. Human, moral choices crumbled to dust when you were dealing with a monster.

'Just follow them out,' Phillips said to our driver.

Across the car park, one of the prison officers got into the back of the van and I saw him perch on the edge of a moulded bench. The other officer was already inside. He was leaning forward, only his legs and waist visible. I imagined he was securing Glass to whatever fixings they had inside. Once he was done, he looked out of the rear doors of the prison van and gave us the thumbs up.

The doors closed.

I thought about how many people had already been dragged into this. Three prison officers. Four cops. Me. Healy. When we got down to Porthtreno in five and a half hours, we were going to be met by a team from Devon and Cornwall Police, comprising uniforms, detectives, body-recovery specialists and an armed response unit. That would be at least another twenty.

Thirty people, all dancing to Glass's tune.

I thought of Ellie, waiting by the phone for updates. Dougan had called her earlier to fill her in, talking around some of what was happening, then I'd followed up with a second call to reassure her that we would have more details soon. As I'd made the call, I'd felt conflicted, as if I'd abandoned the search for her husband. I'd had no choice but to bend to Glass's demands, but my lack of options didn't leave me feeling any less guilty.

'Is Preston alive?' Ellie had asked.

I didn't know the answer to that and neither did anyone else. Not yet, anyway. A second armed response unit was being assembled and sent to the tower block in Camberwell. They would be arriving imminently.

'As far as we know,' I'd said to Ellie, 'yes, he's alive.'

I'd listened to her cry then, the line filled with the relief that she must have been feeling for the husband who'd been missing two days.

I didn't voice the rest of my thoughts.

Because even if Preston *was* alive, even if he *was* in that flat with Vessler, the aftermath looked stark for him and Ellie if Preston was involved in Marco's death.

Fifty minutes later, on the motorway, Phillips got a call.

It was hard to hear a lot of it, his voice lost in the roar of the heaters and the chop of the windscreen wipers scraping back and forth. But when he was done, he dropped his phone from his ear to his lap and just stared at it. I glanced at Dougan. He looked at me. 'What's going on?' I said softly.

Dougan shrugged, as in the dark as I was.

Eventually, Phillips dialled the noise of the heaters down, and slowly turned in his seat to look back at us. 'They just got to the flat in Camberwell,' he said.

'Was Preston there?' I asked.

'No,' Phillips replied quietly.

No Preston.

What did that mean?

'What about Vessler?' Naughton this time.

Phillips didn't seem to have heard her; didn't really seem to be taking in much of anything at all. But then he raised his phone above the level of the seat and showed us the screen, and we could see that it was paused on a video.

'What's that?' Healy asked him.

'It's body-cam footage from the team at Vessler's flat.'

51

. . . 13 hours to go . . .

Naughton took the phone from Phillips. All of us gathered in a half-circle around her.

She tapped Play.

There are three vehicles.

They glide in convoy — quickly, silently — into the Sampson estate, making almost no noise at all. As soon as the first vehicle pulls up to the pavement in Willowtree Grove, the doors on its right flank slide open and three armed officers from the Met's Specialist Firearms Command — MO19 — hurry from the road to the low-lit stairwells of Cook House, the tower block Vessler is hiding out in.

It's raining, coming down hard, the weather and the advancing twilight an advantage: as a second team of armed officers join the others, three detectives get out of the last of the three vehicles and start checking windows and doorways.

Because of the storm, no residents are outside.

No one has seen them arrive.

There are two stairwells, one running parallel to the other. A walkway at the apex joins the two together.

The six armed officers ascend.

They move through the huge spiral of pebble-dashed concrete, the lights flickering in and out. It takes one team a minute and a half to get to the tenth floor, the officers breathing hard by the time they get there. The other team arrives ten seconds later. The sergeant running point leads the way to the eastern flank of Cook House and then moves to the front of the pack. The other five follow. They're in another walkway now, flats on the left, a balcony on the right with views across the city. Distantly, drifting like a ship in the mist, is the vague shape of the London Eye.

At Flat 278, they stop.

Two men move either side of the door, the sergeant faces it front on, and the last officer moves in front of him, swinging the MOE – on a shoulder strap – around to his front. The Method of Entry tool is a compact, jet-black Enforcer, a sixteen-kilo steel tube with a handle at the back and the top and a thick, flat plate at its nose.

It impacts with a weight of 3.5 tons.

In five seconds, this door will fold like paper.

The officer holding the MOE glances back at the sergeant, who gives him a single nod of the head, and then the officer moves to the door.

A second check with the sergeant.

The sergeant nods again.

The officer swings the Enforcer at the door and it buckles immediately and whips all the way back, slamming against an interior wall. The MOE operator steps aside and the four officers flood the flat.

'Armed police!' one of them shouts.

Another does the same.

They shout it again as they fan off in different directions. The flat is gloomy, its corners daubed in shadows. The hallway runs all the way down to a kitchen at the back. To the left is a bedroom and bathroom. To the right is the living room.

There's no one in the kitchen.

It's narrow enough to see that the worktops are scattered with food cartons and dirty plates. There's a first-aid kit in here too, its contents a mess.

The bathroom is small, nothing in it – no accessories, no

toiletries, the absence of both emphasizing something that's become obvious.

This flat isn't supposed to be occupied.

In the bedroom there's nothing at all, just a carpet; spidering out from the highest corners and into the centre, there's a speckled atlas of black mould on the wall.

There's black mould in the living room too, but that's not what any of the officers are focusing on. Instead, they're looking at a man slumped on a wooden chair in the middle of the room, the legs slightly bent under him.

His arms are hanging down at his side, his body sloped, his head forward – chin against his chest – a mix of blood and saliva on his lips and clothes.

'Sir!' one of the officers shouts at the man.

He doesn't move.

'Sir, armed police, can you hear me?'

The officer moves in, slowly, cautiously, and then lifts the head of the man away from his chest. It's a dead weight. His glazed eyes stare off, pale and cloudy.

A second officer checks the man's neck for a pulse.

He's dead.

'Looks like he's taken something,' the officer says, before gently returning the man to the position they found him in. 'There's a lot of saliva around his mouth.'

The team look at the rest of the room.

Apart from the mould, there's nothing on the walls. There's no furniture except the chair the man is sitting on. There's not even any carpet.

'Better send a forensic team,' the sergeant says, talking into his radio.

'Visual ID on the deceased?' the response comes back.

The sergeant looks at the dead man. 'It's Oliver Vessler.'

'No sign of Preston Stewart?'

'Negative.'

The sergeant searches the flat again, going back to the other rooms, double-checking them. He's doing a third sweep when one of the officers comes through from the living room and says, 'You'd better see this, boss.'

The sergeant follows the officer out.

The two teams are gathered around the body of Oliver Vessler. He has a shirt on, dirty and bloodied, with a breast pocket on the front.

Inside is a mobile phone.

It was easily missed until now, not least because it's old-fashioned and small. The front of the phone – a clamshell design – is blinking blue.

Someone is calling it.

Vessler was dead.

It looked like he'd committed suicide.

But there was barely time to process any of that. Because everyone in the car except Phillips was still watching as the sergeant radioed Command.

He needed instructions.

Did they want him to answer the ringing phone?

The response came back: *Answer it.* The sergeant looked nervous, as if he were standing next to an unexploded bomb, but then he reached inside the pocket with his thumb and forefinger and pulled out the phone.

Around me, in the van, I felt everyone tense.

The sergeant held the phone up to the rest of his team and – almost to a man – they instinctively took a half-step back.

A small digital display was under the phone's blinking light.

It was where a number should have appeared.

Instead, it said unknown.

The sergeant opened the lid of the clamshell. He pressed a thumb to his Motorola so Command could hear both sides of whatever conversation was coming.

'Hello?' he said into the phone.

'Glass is just a pawn,' a voice said.

It was digitized, robotic.

The caller's using a voice changer.

'He's just a piece on the board that I'm moving around.' Fractured, mechanical breathing. 'It's me you should be worried about.'

And then the line went dead.

DAY TWO
Part Two

52

... 7 hours to go ...

In the darkness, Porthtreno moved.

I watched it from the windows of the van, the ruffled ridge of the island, pale under a half-moon, like the spine of some huge, dormant creature. The beachgrass – growing out like tufts of hair – swayed and danced, the sand swelling and shifting and gathering around it. And then, as the wind gradually died down again, the creature settled, the dunes having changed shape once more.

My watch softly chimed. It was 1 a.m.

All I could see were police vehicles – cars, and vans, and huge incident trucks. Temporary lights had been set up and open-sided awnings erected, officers gathered under them looking at laptop screens and pointing at maps.

All of it was for one man.

Phillips, Dougan and some of the officers from Devon and Cornwall Police had been in to the van to speak to him three times, presumably to find out the precise location of the women's bodies, and to try to figure out Preston's whereabouts. My gut told me that Glass had known all along that Preston wouldn't be found at the flat with Vessler, but if he stuck to the story about it being where Preston was *supposed* to be, it was unlikely to invalidate the agreement he'd signed. Preston's absence helped throw further shade on him too, which may or may not have been Glass's intention. Could Preston have killed Vessler himself? And if he did, was this the re-emergence of the man who'd murdered Marco Roy and buried him in woodland?

Phillips wasn't going to worry about those questions for now. His immediate priority was the recovery of the women and conducting a forensically flawless operation that ended without incident. The maps he and the other cops were studying were topographical: the island, the coastline, the contour lines; the depths, flats, cliffs and slopes. It was the cops back in London and Surrey that would be focused on Preston, on hunting him down using the scraps that Glass had fed them.

After the first of the three conversations Phillips had with Glass, he, Dougan and a body-recovery team had headed across to the island. The unit had ground-penetrating radar and sniffer dogs, but the entirety of their work had been conducted out of sight, on the reverse side of the island's ridge, so it was hard to say what they'd found. When they'd returned, no one had come to update us.

From just watching, though, I could infer enough.

The fact that the operation had gathered pace – and not stalled the instant Phillips and the recovery team had returned – suggested they'd found the hint of something, or someone, deep beneath the sand. Except the idea that Glass could have been telling the truth about the women – just as he'd told the truth about the location of Marco Roy's body and handed over the address for Oliver Vessler – brought me no comfort. All it did was raise more questions. If the radar or the sniffer dogs had zeroed in on a body, why had it only happened now? Radar, dogs, even chemical analyses of the air around St Petroc, had been incorporated into a search in the same spot nineteen years ago. Why hadn't any trace of the women been found back then?

And that wasn't the only thing playing on my mind.

Oliver Vessler and Christopher Pockman were dead. Both had committed suicide, in almost exactly the same way. *Or had appeared to.* I'd watched Pockman bite down on the poison he'd been carrying, but Vessler's demise was less certain. Had he ended his life out of choice – or could it *really* have been Preston, or someone else entirely, who made it look that way? The truth would come out eventually, perhaps in his autopsy, but the results of that were hours – more likely days – away.

And there were no immediate answers as to who had made the call to Vessler's phone either. I'd barely spoken to Phillips on the journey down, a deafening silence greeting the end of the body-cam footage, but I knew forensics would be concentrating on the phone itself, rather than the voice of the caller. They'd be using the phone to find out where it was bought, by whom, what activity was on it, if any, and whether they could reverse-engineer a route back to the person at the end of the line.

But the caller was one thing; what they'd said was something else. *Glass is just a pawn. He's just a piece on the board that I'm moving around. It's me you should be worried about.* Was it the truth? Another lie? Was the caller working with Glass or against him? I imagined Phillips had spent some of his time talking to Glass trying to seek an answer. And I imagined he was as in the dark now as he had been before.

I resurfaced from my thoughts as, in front of me, Healy moved. We were the only two remaining in the police van and neither of us had spoken for a long time.

'You all right?' I asked him.

It took a moment and then he said, 'Glass will be loving this. In there, hearing it all, listening to the whole circus.'

I nodded. 'If I had to guess, I reckon he's given them the location of one of the women – or, at least, a body, anyway – and he's promising to tell them where the other two are once he gets his sunrise. This whole thing is about control. Always has been.'

We returned to silence.

Time ticked over.

And then, at one thirty, something changed.

53

. . . 6 hours to go . . .

It was subtle. The slight alteration in atmosphere. The stiffening of the gait in the officers surrounding the awnings.

I watched Phillips move from one awning to another, and then Dougan talking to him and showing him his phone screen. Shortly after, Dougan went to someone from Devon and Cornwall Police, signalling to a laptop, and the officer brought it over. Phillips got on the phone to someone, gesticulating, animated in a way I hadn't seen all night. After he was done, a group – Phillips, Dougan, Bodie and Naughton, plus two local detectives and a uniformed officer who, from what I could see of the epaulettes on his shoulders, looked like a chief inspector – gathered around the laptop. Their expressions were bleak.

'What do you think's going on?' Healy asked me.

'I don't know, but it can't be good.'

Whatever they were studying held their attention for almost ten minutes, then Phillips began talking to the chief inspector, the others listening.

Then the chief inspector looked at us.

So did Phillips.

So did everyone else.

There was a brief pause before Phillips said something to Naughton and she headed across the car park towards us, sliding the side door open.

'The boss wants to talk to you two.'

She glanced at me, a flutter of something in her face, and

then she was heading back to the awning. Healy peered over his shoulder at me. 'We going?'

'Is Naughton all right?'

'What do you mean?'

'You don't think she seems different today?'

'From yesterday?' Healy looked at his former detective, a frown on his face. 'What do you mean? Different how?'

'It doesn't matter,' I said, and led the way across the car park, the wind off the dark Atlantic bitingly cold.

Phillips stepped forward as he saw us approach.

'Is this to do with Preston?' I asked. 'Have you found him?'

'What do you know about Robert Lewellyn?'

It took me a second to pivot. 'What?'

'Dr Robert Lewellyn. Preston's friend and business partner.'

I paused, thinking back to my interview with Lewellyn. I remembered how he'd batted off my questions until I'd cornered him – and then it had all come out. The visit he'd received from Oliver Vessler, pretending to be Noah Klein. Unwittingly handing over the keys to The Crest's entire security system. Doing it because Vessler had told him if he didn't, his daughter would get hurt. Had I missed something?

'What do you mean "what do I know about him"?'

'Do you know what reason he might have to disappear?'

I frowned. 'Lewellyn has disappeared?'

'Or gone on the run.'

'What?' *Maybe I really did miss something.* 'Why would he do that?'

'I don't know, but he's not answering his phone and no one can find him.'

Phillips spun the laptop around. On-screen was a photograph – marked with the Met logo – of what must have been Lewellyn's office at The Crest. I could see photos of himself and his daughter, and certificates with his name hanging on the walls.

I noted the time the photograph was taken.

Thirty minutes ago.

Phillips reached forward to the cursor keys, his finger poised above the right arrow. There had to be more pictures from Lewellyn's office after this one.

But, for now, he didn't tab forward.

He just said, 'Digital forensics have traced the source of the call that was made to the phone discovered on the body of Oliver Vessler.'

He tapped the right arrow down.

A second photograph appeared.

'The caller was Robert Lewellyn.'

54

. . . 6 hours to go . . .

I stared at the second photograph, processing what Phillips had said.

The picture was of the top drawer in Lewellyn's desk, which had been pulled all the way open.

Inside was a mobile phone.

It was almost an exact match for the one that had been found on Oliver Vessler: a clamshell design, with a thin display on the front showing the time and date.

Next to that was something else.

I'd seen one before on a case I'd worked a few years ago. It had the appearance of a compact, thin-strapped breathing apparatus.

But it wasn't.

It was a voice changer.

'When we found out he was the caller,' Phillips said, 'we sent officers to the hospital and his home. We can't find him at either location and he's not picking up.'

'But – what? – when you turned up at The Crest, these just happened to be in the top drawer of his desk? This has got to be a set-up.'

Phillips didn't say anything.

'It's way too convenient. You went to that office in Paddington, just the same as I did. Pockman was dead by the time most of those pictures were taken and, as far as I'm aware, Vessler can't teleport, so it would have been impossible for him to have taken all those shots himself, because the locations were miles apart. Someone else is involved that we haven't identified yet. It's the same person who made that call to Vessler's phone. The same person who put those things in that drawer.'

'And that person couldn't be Lewellyn?'

'If Lewellyn's in on this, why has he made it so easy for you?'

'Maybe he's careless.'

I shook my head. 'Glass isn't careless.'

Phillips didn't say anything for a second time, just edged the laptop closer to me, and then tapped the right arrow again.

This time, a video appeared.

It was from a CCTV camera in The Crest, and a read-out in the left-hand corner showed yesterday's date, the time 6.17 p.m.

It was the corridor that Lewellyn's office was on.

As the footage ticked over, I could see all the doors were closed. It looked like everyone had gone home for the day.

'What am I supposed to be seeing here?' I said to Phillips.

But almost as soon as I'd spoken, he walked into shot.

Lewellyn.

He entered the corridor at the far end, from a fire exit staircase that I knew went all the way down to an emergency door adjacent to the operating theatres.

Straight off the bat, he was acting oddly.

He paused as he entered the corridor, looking back down the stairs he'd come up – once, twice – and then, as he approached his office, the room nearest the camera, he tried every other door.

He was checking to see if anyone else was still working.

When he got to his office, he stopped, looked both ways, and then – taking a set of keys from his pocket – unlocked the door. As he did, he went to his pocket again.

This time he took out a phone.

It was the one that had been found in his drawer.

Lewellyn headed into his office.

'This doesn't prove that he made that call to Vessler.'

'Just watch,' Phillips said to me.

A minute passed and then Lewellyn re-emerged from his office.

He opened the door and leaned out, then walked to either end of the corridor for a second time, trying doors, double-checking that no one was coming up the stairwells to his floor.

But that part I barely noticed.

Instead I was looking at what else was in his hands now.

The voice changer.

He hurried back to his office and then slowly, awkwardly, attached the mask to his face, straps feeding off above his ears, a small square device with a meshed front over his mouth.

I glanced at the timecode in the corner. Barely sixty seconds after this, the phone that had been found in Vessler's breast pocket had burst into life.

'The call to Vessler's mobile came from The Crest,' Phillips said. He picked up some print-outs from a nearby table. 'Forensics broke the encryption. They triangulated the call. The phone in Lewellyn's hand is the one that called Vessler.'

'But why would he put the voice changer on outside his office? Why would he risk being seen by someone with that thing strapped to his face? Why not –'

'Why not do it out of sight, *inside* his office?' Phillips said, cutting across me and finishing my question. 'Why leave the phone and the mask in his drawer?'

I eyed him. 'So you think it's a set-up too?'

'All I know is Lewellyn is currently unaccounted for – and that's a legitimate concern.'

'You haven't got any leads on his location?'

'No. That's the whole reason I shared this with you. You went in to see him yesterday, so we thought you might have some insight into his motivations.'

'I think his only motivation is protecting his daughter,' I said.

Phillips nodded and then used the cursor key to tab the video back a couple of frames, trying to get the best angle he could on Lewellyn as he stood in the doorway. He then went to the menu and used the magnifier tool. The quality broke up and became more pixellated as he zoomed in – but now nothing was in frame except the side of Lewellyn's face.

'We spotted this earlier,' Phillips said, and pointed to Lewellyn's ear.

Healy leaned in. 'Is that an *earpiece*?'

'Yeah.' Phillips used a finger to trace the edges of a small cream circle deep in Lewellyn's ear canal. 'Someone's telling him what to do.'

55

. . . 6 hours to go . . .

I studied the magnified image of Lewellyn and then turned to Phillips. 'Whoever's speaking to him through that earpiece has told him his daughter will get hurt if he doesn't do what they ask. It's the simplest way to control him.'

Phillips nodded. 'We're checking ANPR cameras on the motorways between London and her university campus. We're hoping where he's "disappeared" to is Warwick – but so far, nothing.'

Everyone quietened.

The only thing that made a sound was the wind.

'What did Glass say about Preston?' I asked.

'At this point, we're going to have to treat Preston Stewart as an unknown.'

The implication was clear.

Glass hadn't given them anything else and, wherever he was, they didn't know where Preston's motivations lay or what his story was. He could have been abducted or he could have been the person who was talking to Lewellyn.

He could be a victim.

He could be a suspect.

Or he could be dead.

'Did you find anything under St Petroc?'

Phillips took a moment, glancing at the chief inspector from Devon and Cornwall Police, then at the other cops who were under the tent with us, as if weighing up whether to share anything else with me.

'We've found one body. Glass says the other two are close by.'

I stopped, returning to the question I asked myself before: how did they get missed the first time?

'The sun comes up at one minute past eight,' Phillips continued, looking at all the officers gathered around him, trying to sound confident, 'but twilight starts just after seven. So, at seven a.m., we're going to go back across the water there – and we're not leaving the island without bringing those women home.'

'I think something's going to happen when you get there,' I said.

Phillips looked at me.

'The clock we found in the office was put on that wall for a reason – and it hits zero at eight a.m., when the sun comes up.'

'Glass didn't know anything *about* the clock when you asked him.'

'I think Vessler, or whoever this third person is, put it up on that wall – and took all those photos – because they thought it was the type of thing Glass would like. But he didn't. It's too blunt an instrument for him.'

'I agree,' Healy said. 'Way too much of a giveaway.'

'Glass is far subtler, so he will hate that they've done that, but just because he hates it, it doesn't mean the countdown clock is meaningless. When we were in the interview yesterday, Glass mouthed "tick-tock" to us. That's the game *he* wanted to play, because you can't infer anything specific from him just saying those words over and over. But we can infer plenty from a clock actually *counting down* from twenty-four hours. So whoever put it on that wall has done it because they know Glass has something planned – and I think it's going to happen at eight a.m.'

'So what does he have planned?'

'I don't know. But what I know for sure is that, when that countdown hits zero, you and your group are going to be on that island with him.'

I looked around.

A few of the faces paled.

'He'll be one man versus many,' Phillips said, trying to sound reassuring.

'Which he will have factored in.'

'He'll have a rifle trained on him the whole time.' Phillips gestured to the armed response unit. 'If he tries something, he'll end up in the hospital or the morgue.'

I sighed. 'This isn't a Hollywood movie, Phill—'

'Thank you, Raker.'

'He *wants* you on that island at eight o'clock –'

'That's *enough*.' His face flushed, he looked at the body-recovery team. 'Let's get everything set up.' Then at Bodie: 'And take Raker and Healy back to the van.'

Naughton

Now

Raker and Healy were returned to the van, then Phillips kept the rest of them busy for a few hours. Once everything had been set up, all they could do was wait.

They needed light.

As soon as there was light, they'd head across the water.

Naughton found a quiet corner of the largest awning and tried to suppress the terror she felt in every part of her body. This was it. This was what she'd been waiting for. Once they got to the island, her life was going to change forever.

Just before 5 a.m., Dougan wandered across to her.

'You okay?' he asked.

She forced out a smile. 'No one tells you that the waiting is the worst bit.'

Dougan responded with a smile and moved to the laptop Phillips used earlier – the one with the video of Robert Lewellyn on – and peeled up the lid. The laptop was still paused on the footage from The Crest.

Dougan started dragging the timeline back.

'What are you looking for?' Naughton asked him.

'I just figured it was worth another watch.'

Something fluttered in Naughton's chest.

Dougan worried her. He was pleasant, polite, easy to talk to. He seemed interested and was skilled at conversation, always pitching his questions on the right side of non-intrusive. But he was also opaque. She couldn't get a handle on him. There had been a couple of moments – a flush of colour; a pushing together of the lips – when Naughton had felt certain he hadn't agreed with Phillips's decision-making, but those were few and far between. In some ways, he reminded Naughton of Raker. In fact, sometimes – especially in the way he would ask Raker questions – Naughton wondered if Dougan might secretly trust Raker's instincts more than Phillips's.

Under the other awning, Bodie was moving around.

He was easier to interpret and didn't concern Naughton as much. He had an eye for detail, a talent for eking out tiny trails in dense paperwork, which was why Phillips had entrusted him with things like the list of prisoners who'd been serving sentences at the same time as Glass. But he also had almost no ability to conceal his feelings and was a born subordinate. In private, as they'd driven out to meet Raker and Healy at the offices in Paddington the day before, Phillips had called Bodie 'a nodding dog'. It was why Naughton guessed Bodie wouldn't be part of the group going to the island. Phillips's plan was to keep the group small, and while Bodie was good at following a paper trail, he was unsophisticated, and a lack of guile was a weapon Glass could use.

Not that Phillips was bulletproof either.

He was clever and, for the most part, pretty rational, except where Raker and Healy were concerned. Whenever they were around, he became more impetuous. Naughton could see that he was self-aware enough to realize it was happening, but he seemed incapable of stopping it. That was why Raker and Healy would be left behind too. Even if Glass insisted, Phillips had a bargaining chip now. He could throw back the fact that Glass hadn't delivered Preston Stewart. The parameters of the deal had changed – which meant no Raker.

Naughton felt some small measure of relief at that.

'I'm just going for a smoke,' she said to Dougan and, as he nodded at her, she headed off across the car park, the breeze drifting in off the ocean, the air bitter. From her pocket, she took a pack of cigarettes, flipping open the lid.

Inside was a single cigarette and a lighter.

Stopping in the shadows of a long bank of oak trees, their trunks blown almost horizontal by the perpetual power of the wind, she stared at the cigarette.

She hadn't smoked since she was a teenager.

She *hated* smoking.

Pulling the cigarette out, she checked no one was approaching her. She was about twenty-five feet from the nearest vehicle, a mobile incident unit with two uniformed officers outside it, half-disguised by the low light. One of them may have been looking at her. She propped the cigarette between her lips and lit it.

She almost started coughing straight away.

Calm down, she thought.

You don't have to smoke it.

You just have to make it look like you are.

She took out her phone, checking the time.

The text would be here in one minute.

As she stared at the screen, her mind went back to the early hours of the previous day, to the moment she'd realized someone was in the back of her car. She remembered the mirror mask, and the man wearing it — who she now knew must have been Oliver Vessler — as, knife poised at her throat, he'd told her about the text.

'Make sure you're alone at five a.m.,' he'd said quietly.

'Why?'

'Because that's when you'll get your instructions.'

'Why *wouldn't* I be alone?'

'Well, I imagine the car park's going to be busy.'

'What? What car park?'

'At five a.m., you'll be waiting to take him to the island.'

Him. Glass.

'To the island? What are you talking about?'

'Just be alone at five a.m.'

Naughton closed her eyes, trying to rid her head of his voice, of his mask, of all of this. When she opened them again, she was still here.

This nightmare was still suffocating her.

Vessler was dead, so she didn't even know if the text was still coming. But she couldn't take the chance. Raker had told Phillips earlier that at least one other person was still out there, working with Glass, which meant if she didn't do what Vessler had asked her to do, and the text arrived, and she didn't answer, something just as bad was going to happen.

She stared at her phone screen, waiting for the time to tick over.

Waiting . . .

Waiting . . .

And then the clock hit 5:00.

The moment it did, a text pinged through. It was from an unknown number. As she saw the message – the instructions Vessler had promised would come, the instructions from whoever was now in control – her eyes filled with tears.

It was only eight words.

But they were about to ruin her life.

Look in the chimney of the last house

DAY TWO
Part Three

56

. . . 59 minutes to go . . .

The sky began to change just after seven o'clock.

It was only a hint to start with – the black of the sky becoming a deep mauve – but as it altered, the group moved into place around the prison van.

Healy and I watched from the sidelines, Bodie close to us, as Phillips, Dougan and Naughton fanned out in a semicircle and two prison officers started to unlock the rear doors. Officers from the Devon and Cornwall Armed Protection Unit stood sentry in the shadows, weapons across their chests.

Earlier, we'd watched as two separate teams had done another sweep of the car park, looking for spots where a potential trap could be launched from, including an old, long-shuttered lifeboat station further along the coast to the right. The same two teams had then moved across the walkway to the island and circled it twice. Porthtreno was harder to sweep because it was undulating and rugged, but after ninety minutes on the island, the two teams returned to Phillips and told him everything was clear.

'Good,' I'd heard Phillips say.

He projected an air of confidence, but I could hear the anxiety in his voice, even as he tried to hide it.

The clunk of the prison van brought me back into the moment as the first of the Lyegate officers clambered out, folding one door back, then pulling out a set of extendable steps from underneath the rear bumper. He waited, looking into the darkness. The second prison officer emerged, a hand trailing behind him. He was holding on to something.

Or someone.

The officer took the first step down and looked back.

Glass came forward. He paused, glancing out at the crowd gathered in the car park, at the faces under the awnings, and then he found me and Healy.

The second prison officer said something to him that I couldn't hear, Glass nodded, and then he was guided down the steps and on to the tarmac of the car park. His arms were in a downward V in front of him, tightly handcuffed. He looked small next to the officer, who must have had three or four inches and about three stone on him, and then Phillips moved in and started speaking to him. Again, I was too far away to hear, the wind a low, steady moan, the waves along the shoreline relentless.

Phillips called Dougan and Naughton in closer to him, then two of the body-recovery team – one man, one woman, both carrying packs and dressed in forensic suits, the man holding a dog on the end of a leash – and then, finally, a paramedic. It looked like the second prison officer was going too.

The door to the van was open, the cold air drifting in, and to the left of us was Bodie. I glanced at him, wondering what he made of being relegated to guard duty – but it didn't take me long to work out. His arms were crossed and his face was showing every second of every thought he was having about being left behind.

Phillips began to lead the group away.

Briefly, the eight of them were reduced to silhouettes, but then they changed direction, heading to the path that went down to the walkway, and then to the island, and – as they did – the pre-dawn light began to illuminate them in a low, soft blue.

The armed officers spread out behind.

Two stationed themselves on the edge of the car park, looking down the slope to the walkway. The third stayed with the group, following at the back.

'This must really piss you off,' Healy said.

I glanced at him and then realized he was talking to Bodie.

'Shut up,' Bodie responded.

'I guess Phillips thinks you're good for adding up numbers and looking at lists but not good enough to join the grown-ups for the big-boy stuff.'

'I said, shut up.'

'It's all right, pal,' Healy said, holding up a hand. 'I'm on your side.'

Bodie waited a second longer, as if considering his next move, then reached to the slide door of the van and shoved it hard.

It slammed shut in Healy's face.

I sighed. 'What was the point of that?'

'I was just having some fun.'

'It's wasted energy.'

Healy glanced at me. 'Well, it's a good job it's mine to waste, then, isn't it?'

'What's the matter with you?'

'What do you *think's* the matter with me, Raker? We've just spent most of the night sitting in this shitbox. We may as well have not come at all.'

'I know. I get it. But if they *can* recover those three bodies –'

'Then everything will be hunky-dory.' He shot me a withering look. 'You go home to your American lady friend, with your Lost Women case all wrapped up in a neat little bow. I go home to a tiny flat and a shite job and kids that hate my fucking guts. I don't much like the look of that bigger picture.'

'What difference is it going to make to you or your life if you go to the island or not? Whether he leads them to those bodies without you, or he leads them there and you're standing right next to him, it's not going to get you a better flat or a better job.'

As an ethereal version of him formed in the windows of the van, I started to wish I'd bitten my tongue. More often than not I did, because it was the quickest way to defuse the moments when this older version of Healy – the angrier incarnation of him, the one who had imploded his career at the Met, and who had made terrible life decisions after that – emerged from cover, trying to blame anyone but himself for what he'd done.

I should have, but it had been a long, frustrating night.

And, in truth, in being left behind, in having the search for Preston Stewart – and everything connected to it – ripped from my grasp, I was angry too.

'Look, Healy –'

'No, it's okay,' he said, voice softer. 'You're right.'

'Your boys aren't going to come back to you quicker because you're down on that island tonight. You trying to be a cop again, that's not what matters to them.'

In the window, his reflection nodded at me.

I sat back, glancing out of the front of the van, and saw the outline of the lifeboat station a little further down the coast, a sloped ramp at its front. The windows were boarded, the entranceways padlocked. It must have been thirty years since it had been used. Moss grew in thick coils along the roof and down the edges of the windows, and the boards secured to them had all bleached white from sea salt.

Healy said something to me.

'What?' I responded, but my attention was still on the lifeboat station, on the ramp slick with seaweed at its front, at the rusting metal roof that the early morning had turned a deep red.

There was something about the building.

Something that had started needling at me.

'I said, I need to get some fresh air,' Healy repeated.

He reached for the handle, slid the door across – the cold pouring back into the van – and then he ducked his head and climbed out.

That was when I saw it.

It was coming from a space next to one of the windows. A tiny section of the brickwork had broken and fallen away, revealing the darkness of the interior. The lifeboat station was old, decaying, decades past the point when anyone should have occupied it, so there shouldn't have been any working electrics; no light of any kind.

Except a light was what I could see.

A tiny pinprick of white against the blackness.

Something – or someone – was inside.

57

. . . 48 minutes to go . . .

I moved, trying to get a better angle on the light.

But now I couldn't see it any more.

Getting out of the van, into the cold, I glanced at Bodie. He was slightly ahead of us, his attention centred on the other side of the car park, where the two armed officers were stationed. They were still looking down the slope to the walkway, Phillips and the others crossing the water now out of sight.

I turned to the lifeboat station again.

I started to doubt myself, started to disbelieve I'd seen anything at all, and then I talked myself back again.

I saw a light in there.

I know I saw it.

'I need to take a leak,' I said to Bodie.

There was a toilet block at the back of the car park, two uniformed officers on either side of it. Bodie studied me for a moment, as if I might be playing him, before slamming the van door shut.

'Don't be long,' he said.

I glanced at Healy, whose eyes narrowed, seeming to sense that something was up. But I couldn't take him. It would instantly raise suspicions.

Moving across the car park, I kept my eyes on the toilet block, not wanting my gaze to stray, to give away where my intentions really lay. When I arrived at the men's, both officers eyed me, and then I headed inside.

There was a window in one of the cubicles.

I moved into the stall, locked the door, dropped the toilet seat and stepped up on to it. The window was frosted glass, but it could be opened and latched in place.

Softly, I inched it out from its frame.

Through the gap now, I had a perfect view of the lifeboat station. The sky was changing all the time, the ruffled edges of the clouds visible high above the ridged metal roof. The sun was about fifty minutes away from breaching the horizon, but its light was ahead of it, spilling along the coastline like a wave.

I zeroed in on the gap in the lifeboat station's brickwork.

No light.

Come on, I know what I saw.

I didn't move, didn't even breathe.

I know I'm not mistaken.

I know –

The light blinked.

On. Off. On. Off.

I tensed, trying to establish what it was. And then, as the white dot winked inside the station, I suddenly thought of something my dad had taught me a long time ago. I'd been a teenager, a kid who would rather have been out with friends – but I'd also been a kid who had loved his dad and recognized, even then, how important it had been to him that I listen.

The light started up again.

It's following exactly the same pattern every time.

In my head, I went back, returning to the room I'd grown up in on my parents' farm, to the scruffy, browning pages of the book my dad had given me; the one that had been handed down to him by his father. I tried to picture the alphabet at the back of that book, and the key that had run in a column next to the letters.

And, as I watched the pattern start up again, I knew I was right: there was a message coming from inside the lifeboat station.

Two words, in Morse code.

Help me.

58

. . . 43 minutes to go . . .

I unlocked the cubicle door and looked around the toilet block.

There was a second window at the far end, above the basins. It was bigger and opened from the left-hand side, which meant I could get through it. I rushed across and inched the window out. Climbing up on to the basin, I slipped through the gap and landed at the back of the toilet block.

I moved in the direction of the lifeboat station and then stopped at the corner, where the block finished. From where I was now, I could see the van, Bodie a step away from it.

Every head in the car park was turned towards the island.

About thirty feet from me, cut into the rock face, were some steps that ascended to the level of the road that wound up and out of the peninsula. I made a dash for them, taking them two at a time, following their bend all the way to the road. It was a single-track lane that ran a mile and a half inland. Fifty feet from the top of the steps, facing out on to the road, was the entrance to the lifeboat station.

Crouch-running below a bank of yellow gorse, I reached it quickly.

Two huge, rust-speckled double doors had been padlocked and chained. A window to the left of those had been boarded, the boards secured in place with immense rivets. I tried the doors and then the window but there was no give.

Heading along the right flank of the building – everything and everyone in the car park to my left – there were two other windows ahead of me. Both had been boarded and riveted shut. I double-backed, returning to the front, and looked along the left-hand edge of the building. Two more windows, both secured.

Next to the first window was the gap in the wall.

That was where the message was being sent from.

'Hello?' I said quietly.

Nothing.

No sound but the wind and the sea.

I tapped gently on the double doors, my knuckles making a dull chime against the metal, the chains shifting and clanking.

'Is anyone in there?'

Nothing again.

Out of the corner of my eye, I saw the two officers outside the toilet block start moving towards one another, talking about something. One of them gestured inside.

They're getting twitchy.

I wanted to look in through the gap in the brickwork, wanted to stare into the darkness there, but I'd immediately reveal myself if I walked along the left side of the lifeboat station.

Not that it would make any difference before long.

Pretty soon they were going to realize what I'd done – and I probably only had a minute before they did.

Hurrying back around to the right of the station, I headed all the way down to the end and peered along the front. Another huge set of double doors – also chained and padlocked – opened out on to the ramp as it descended directly into the water.

Next to the doors was a ladder.

It was welded to the front of the station and led to a small, open-sided viewing platform about three-quarters of the way up. Back when this had been operational, the men that had worked the boats would have been up there with binoculars, spotting any vessels or people in trouble during storms.

I darted to the ladder and headed up.

The platform at the top was slick with rainwater and seaweed, its iron railings oxidized in orange and red. It stank of fish, and age, and sea salt.

'Hey!' A voice carried in on the wind.

I glanced towards the car park. One of the officers was staring up at me, already speaking into the radio at his collar. Beyond him, Bodie turned.

Then Healy.

Then everyone else.

'Raker!' Bodie shouted, running now. 'Stop whatever you're doing!'

I looked to my feet.

On the platform, under my boots, was a hatch.

I bent down and opened it up.

59

. . . 35 minutes to go . . .

Immediately inside the hatch was a second ladder.

It dropped down into pitch-blackness.

I took my phone out, switched on the Torch function, and directed it into the opening. A cone of white light washed across a patchwork of rotten floorboards.

'Raker!' I heard Bodie call again.

The wind picked up, the shouts of other police officers in the car park carried off by it. When I looked, I could see a swarm of them – Bodie at the front – sprinting in my direction. He mouthed something else, but I couldn't hear, and I zeroed in on Healy instead. He'd moved around to the front of the van, eyes on me.

I dialled his number.

Wedging the handset between my ear and shoulder, I grabbed the handles of the ladder in the hatch. As Healy's number rang, I placed a foot into the darkness, on to the first rung – rust flaking away beneath my boot – and trusted it would hold.

Healy picked up. 'What the fuck are you doing, Raker?'

I placed my foot on the next rung and then tilted my head as best I could with the phone in place, trying to see what lay below me. It was hard to see anything at all. Vague outlines. Nothing else.

'*Raker?*'

'You need to try and get a message to Phillips.'

'A message?' Healy said. '*What* message?'

I took another step down. 'There's someone in here.'

'What?'

I looked in the direction of Porthtreno. From the top of the lifeboat station, I could see more of the island: its long ridge of dunes and beachgrass, the very top of a chimney on the other side, part of the most elevated house in St Petroc. The group that Phillips was leading had just reached the other side of the walkway. Glass was in the middle. From where they were, with the wind and the sea, they'd be oblivious to the movement and noise from the officers flooding towards me at the lifeboat station.

'I think Glass has set this up,' I said.

'What?'

'Just tell Phillips to abandon the search.'

I hung up and shone the torch the rest of the way down the ladder. *Four rungs.* Lowering my phone as far as I could, I pointed it towards the rear doors of the station and in the vague direction of the gap in the brickwork. All my phone picked up were more floorboards, some of them long gone and showing through to rocks and seawater below. Halfway across the room was a crumbling partition wall.

I couldn't see anything beyond it.

Taking the four steps fast, I paused at the bottom of the ladder, probing the boards beneath me with the toe of my boot.

They were soft, decomposing.

I glanced at the partition wall again. Next to it was a doorway – no door, just the frame. As I stepped off the ladder, I felt the floor bend, the old bones of the lifeboat station creaking so much I wasn't sure if it was coming from under me or around me.

'Hello?' I said, looking to the doorway.

Nothing.

The missing floorboards between me and the door ran in a zigzag, and their absence revealed a criss-cross of iron struts, built on to the rock and supporting the entire weight of the station. Seawater sloshed up through the gaps, past the struts and into the station, spreading across the floorboards in a lake of foam and water. I kept my gaze fixed ahead of me and moved forward.

At the doorway, I peered around the edge of it. There was a smaller room beyond the partition – what looked like a former office – a desk still in place in one corner, and then the double doors facing the road.

I could hear voices now.

Radios crackling.

The cops were outside, checking the padlocks on the doors, the chains rattling as they did. I heard someone say, 'We're going to need bolt cutters.'

But, by now, I wasn't listening.

My entire focus was on the centre-right of the room, four feet from where the gap in the brickwork was. The light was so poor in the lifeboat station, its corners so shadowed, I'd almost forgotten it was morning outside, the sun coming up.

But there was a single spear of light arrowing through the gap.

It perfectly cut across what was in here.

A man, his back to me.

His ankles were duct-taped to the legs of a metal chair, his wrists tied to the arms. It was too gloomy and my angle too acute to see his face.

Both his hands had something in them.

I angled my approach to him, coming around in an arc, attempting to get a better look at him in the low, grey light of the lifeboat station.

'Hello?'

The man immediately flinched, reacting to my voice.

He's alive.

He turned to me as best he could, head whipping around – and that was when I saw the duct tape on his mouth.

Two huge silver strips of it, stuck there in an X.

I'd found Preston Stewart.

60

. . . 27 minutes to go . . .

I rushed towards him.

He appeared so different from the photographs I'd seen, so different from the man Ellie had described. His face still held all the stitches and the bruising from his operation, his skin flushed and angry, but he seemed smaller too, diminished.

'It's okay,' I said, the fear in his face suddenly so stark, eyes wide, skin beaded with sweat. He started saying something to me, repeating it over and over, and I could hear it clearly, even through the gag.

Help me.

Reaching forward, I tore the duct tape from his mouth.

'Get me out of here,' Preston said immediately.

'Calm down –'

'*You need to get me out of here.*'

'Preston, calm down.'

I looked at his hands again. They'd been taped in place so many times, I could only see the tops of his fingers poking out – and then, encased in more tape, I noticed the edges of what looked like small black boxes pressed against either palm.

'You need to get me out of here.'

I took another step forward.

'Did you hear me?' Preston shouted. 'I said, you need to get me –'

'Don't move.'

It must have been the forefinger of his right hand that he'd used to send the message, because the right box had an LED on it, and his finger was hanging over it.

But that wasn't what I was looking at.

I was looking at a thin wire running across his lap from one palm to the other, and a second one snaking off towards the darkness in the corner of the room.

'Stay still,' I said to him again.

'You need to get me out of here.'

'I will. But, right now, I need you to stay absolutely still for m—'

'Get me out of here!' Preston screamed, not listening to me, his voice breaking up, tears filling his eyes. The chair rocked under him. '*Get me out of here!*'

In the shadows, something lit up.

It was a mobile phone, stuck to the wall in the far corner with more duct tape, everything on it covered but the display.

10 . . . 9 . . .

All I could see were numbers.

8 . . . 7

They were counting down from ten.

6 . . . 5 . . .

'Get me out of here!' Preston screamed again.

4 . . . 3 . . .

Except it was already too late.

2 . . .

It was too late for Preston.

1 . . .

And it was too late for me.

Healy

Five Minutes Ago

Raker's words were an echo that wouldn't still.

Get a message to Phillips.

Healy looked at the officers streaming across the car park, Bodie leading the charge. Above Healy's eyeline, Raker disappeared into the lifeboat station.

Healy turned and hurried in the direction of Porthtreno, weaving a path through the awnings and vehicles to the two armed officers stationed at the top. One, to the right of the path down to the walkway, glanced back across his shoulder and saw Healy approaching first; the other reacted almost immediately, swivelling around, hands tensing on his weapon.

'Stop,' the one on the right said.

Both of their eyes flicked to what was going on at the back of the car park, seeing the commotion properly for the first time. There had been thirty-five cops here ten minutes ago – now at least ten of them were heading up to the lifeboat station.

'Get back,' the same officer said to Healy.

'I need to get a message to Phillips.'

'I said, get *back*.'

Healy took a subtle step forward, opening up his view of the path down to the walkway, and he could see Phillips and the others heading through a gap between the dunes, following a trail that would take them out of sight. Naughton was bringing up the rear.

They were just about to vanish from view.

'Phillips!' he shouted. 'Rosa!'

The wind instantly defused his voice.

No one could hear him.

'Step *back*,' the same officer said, and this time he slid his hand to the end of his rifle, a finger to the trigger.

Healy reset, looking around. Attentions had split: some eyes were on him, some on what was happening at the lifeboat station, some across the water on the island.

Under an awning to his right, in the middle of a phone call – his eyes on what was happening with Raker – was the chief inspector from Devon and Cornwall. Healy fished for his name. He hadn't bothered learning it, had barely even bothered listening to what the guy had to say when he'd talked earlier, because Healy knew straight away he and Raker weren't going to be taken seriously by him.

But now I have to try to get him to listen to me.

Healy rushed across to where he was standing. As Healy got closer, he could hear more of the chief inspector's conversation.

It sounded like he was on the phone to Bodie.

'They were supposed to have checked the roof too,' he said into the phone. 'I didn't know anything about a hatch . . .' He trailed off as soon as he saw Healy approaching. Taking his phone away from his ear, he said, 'What do you want?'

'Phillips is walking into a trap.'

'What?'

'Raker says Phillips is walk—'

'*Raker?*' The chief inspector smirked. 'Your pal Raker's the reason all of this is going on.' He gestured wildly to the cops heading to the lifeboat station. 'I'm not taking advice from a man who has no respect for –'

Healy didn't hear anything else.

All he heard was the explosion.

61

. . . 21 minutes to go . . .

The doors of the lifeboat station blew outwards.

They were torn from their frames – propelled in the direction of the road – brutally cutting down the police officers who'd been standing there. I heard a split second of sound – the dull, wet thud of bodies thumping against the immense doors; the clatter and ping of the padlock and chains as the blast turned them into lethal projectiles – and then there was nothing.

My hearing was ripped from me.

Debris spattered my face.

Dirt and dust.

The ferocity of the explosion – even one directed the other way – pitched me back. I stumbled, landing on Preston, the two of us tumbling to the floor of the lifeboat station. As I tried to scramble to my feet again, my balance affected by the damage to my ears, I saw the wires trailing off the detonators that had been placed against his palms: they'd been completely severed and were now snaking out of Preston's taped hands like torn veins. He was still on the ground, stunned by the blast, but alive. I reached down and hauled him up – still secured to the chair – then checked him for injuries.

Other than the ones from the operation to his face, he seemed okay.

I glanced at the mobile, still secured to the wall with duct tape, its screen scorched from the explosion, and then to the metal frame that surrounded the space the doors had occupied only seconds ago.

The frame was mostly gone now.

Under it, packed into the wall cavity, was where the explosives must have been placed – and when Preston had started violently rocking the chair, he'd set the timer going.

I hurried out on to the road, my head a turbulent fog. There were police officers scattered everywhere. Debris was burning, the stench acrid. Most of the cops seemed to be alive, dazed but breathing, some already sitting, some slowly hauling themselves up off the tarmac. Some were injured, rolling around on the floor, teeth gritted, grasping parts of themselves.

But not everyone had been so lucky.

Two officers in uniform, one with a set of bolt cutters a couple of feet from his outstretched arm, were dead, their bodies a bloodied, mangled mess.

Bodie was lying close to them.

He was almost perfectly central to the doors, on his back in the middle of the road, eyes closed, face coated in blood. It looked like he was choking.

As I rushed across, he coughed up some blood.

I glanced around me. A uniformed cop was staggering towards me, rubbing an eye, his legs barely carrying him.

'We need paramedics,' I said to him.

He looked at me as if he hadn't heard me, as if he didn't know what he or I were even doing here, and I realized he was concussed.

A new wave of officers was starting to arrive.

'We need paramedics!' I shouted at them.

My voice still sounded dull to my ears.

My hearing was still shot.

I looked down at Bodie, and his eyes stared up at mine. They were wet, glazed. He blinked once, sluggishly, as if moving in slow motion. There had been two paramedics in the car park – one had gone to Porthtreno with Phillips, one had remained behind. But even if both of them were here right now, it wasn't going to be enough.

I glanced at the strewn bodies.

We don't need two paramedics. We need ten.

Bodie's eyes closed.

For the first time, I noticed that he had a deep, bleeding laceration above his hip. It had been disguised by his jacket. Metal had embedded itself in him.

'Bodie?'

I leaned down.

He'd stopped breathing.

I placed the heel of my hand in the centre of his chest, my other palm on top, and started to give him chest compressions. As I counted to thirty, I looked around again. More police were here now, some on their radios, some on phones.

After I got to thirty, I gently tilted Bodie's head up, lifted his chin with my first two fingers, and then gave him two breaths.

'*Raker.*'

Someone was saying my name.

I turned, thinking it might be Healy.

It was the chief inspector.

I glanced beyond him, not stopping the compressions, and saw Healy come to the top of the steps. The horror in his face was lucid.

The chief inspector stepped forward. 'You're responsible for –'

'People are *dying*.'

The ringing in my ears increased, rising every time I had to shout. The chief inspector just stared at me, a mixture of incredulity and shock as – for the first time – he properly took in the scene he'd walked into.

That was when it seemed to click.

Now wasn't the time.

Now he needed to save lives.

He hurried off behind me and I could hear him shouting instructions, and as I got to thirty compressions, I leaned in and blew into Bodie's mouth again.

'What the fuck happened?'

Healy was at my side now, his voice distant to my ears.

I blew again and then pointed to Preston, a pale, traumatized face among the shadows of the lifeboat station.

'Did you get a message to Phillips?' I said to Healy.

He shook his head. 'No, I tried.'

I looked from Healy to the chief inspector, to the officers who were lying on the ground injured or dead. I saw the sole paramedic sprinting from the top of the steps, radioing for help as he did.

Everyone's pouring up here.

No one's in the car park any more.

No one's watching the island.

'This is the trap,' I muttered softly. 'This is the trap he's set.' I glanced at Healy. 'All the focus is here.'

He looked around himself, blanching, but then he started trying to reel it back in, to reason with himself, to deny what he knew in his gut was true. 'There's eight of them on that island,' he said, 'and one of him.'

'Has anyone tried *calling* Phillips?'

'Yeah, he just tried on the way up here.'

He pointed to the chief inspector.

'And?'

Healy blinked.

'*And?*'

'And Phillips isn't answering.'

'What about Dougan?'

'Same.'

'Naughton? Anyone else?'

'No.' Healy shook his head. 'No one can get through to any of them.'

Naughton

Ten Minutes Ago

As the wind picked up, the waves boomed against the shore of the island.

Naughton followed at the back of the group, Phillips at the front, Glass between him and Dougan. A different boom carried across the air, deeper and more resonant than the ones the waves were making, and she saw Phillips look back over his shoulder, as if he too had noted the distinction.

But he didn't stop, and neither did anyone behind him.

The normal route to the village, the one the team had taken the first time they'd come across, was up again – ascending through the dunes to the crest of the island – but in front of her, Glass said something to the prison officer beside him, who passed on the message to Phillips. Everyone stopped.

Naughton was close enough now to hear.

'We're not going up?' Phillips said to Glass.

'No.' Glass's hands were still secured at his front, the cuffs so tight, his wrists pulled so close together, it had forced his shoulders to hunch.

Phillips eyed him with suspicion. 'You said the bodies are in the village.'

'No,' Glass replied immediately, 'I told you *one* of them is in the village – that's the one I gave you this morning. The other two are close by, just beyond the end of it.'

Phillips looked ahead to where the path split in a V: one branch moved upwards to the ridge; the other stayed at ground level and went to the right, between the sloping peaks of the main dune and the shoreline. When Naughton took a half-step and looked along the right-hand path, she could see the outline of the last house in the village at the very end, where the shoreline path finished. Phillips was talking to Dougan about something, leaning in, whispering. The armed officer moved closer to Glass.

Naughton's heart started hammering.

Were they having second thoughts?

Please don't turn us around.

Please don't take us back.

'It's longer along the shoreline,' Glass said to Phillips, 'but it's easier.'

Phillips stopped his conversation with Dougan.

'We won't have to wade through deep sand if we take this path,' Glass continued, 'and it brings us out adjacent to the last house, near to where the other bodies are.'

It was obvious to Naughton what was going on now.

Glass didn't care whether they waded through the sand or not. What he cared about was avoiding the ridge of the dune. Because from up on the ridge, they had a 360-degree view – and they'd be able to see the car park.

And something's going to happen there.

Or it's happened already.

She thought of the boom she'd just heard, the rupture in the morning that didn't sound like another wave pounding against the coast, and then Phillips started moving again, heading right, along the trail Glass had directed him to. After a while, the last, lowest house in St Petroc started to come into view, its back wall still standing, a crumbling but largely intact chimney breast in front of that. All its other walls could be seen too, at least in part – including the internal ones that had once marked out its rooms – but most of those were now in an advanced state of decay. If there were windows in the house, they were empty of glass. If there had been doors, they were just memories now.

As they walked, Naughton thought again about the boom

sound. If something had happened at the car park, why wasn't anyone radioing through?

She took her Motorola out.

The signal was dead.

Confused, she cast her mind back to earlier, when they'd come across to Porthtreno to do a recce. Everything had been fine with her signal then.

She went to her jacket and took out her personal phone.

No bars at all.

'Hey,' she said to the armed response officer in front of her, a big guy in his late thirties called Dover. The paramedic was between them. 'Hey, Dover.'

'What?' Dover said, without looking back.

He was keeping his eyes ahead of him, on Glass.

'Everything all right with your comms?'

This time, Dover glanced back across his shoulder. 'What?'

'Are your comms working?'

'Yes.' He sounded annoyed, as if these questions were pointless and badly timed. He didn't check his radio, just returned his gaze to the back of Glass's head.

'What about you?' Naughton said to the paramedic.

As they continued walking, the paramedic went to the radio at his lapel and – angling his head down – tilted the handset towards him.

A glitch in his stride; a noticeable pause.

His comms are down.

Naughton felt a flutter of disquiet in her chest as she looked along the line towards Glass.

He's walked us into a black spot.

Something down here was jamming their signals and no one except Naughton and the paramedic even realized there was a problem. The paramedic turned to her again, about to say something, when, up ahead, Glass called out, 'This is it.'

They'd arrived adjacent to the fifth and final house in St Petroc, the place where the Lost Women's equipment had been found nineteen years ago. Phillips took in his surroundings: the view up the sloped sea of sand to the crest of the island, all five of the houses running upwards on one side of it; the path they'd taken along the shoreline; and then the Atlantic everywhere else.

His eyes settled on Glass. 'Where are the other two women?'

'Beyond the last house, there,' Glass responded.

He was pointing to an area on the other side of the back wall and chimney of the final home. Phillips moved to where the sea of sand began sloping up towards the central ridge of the island; at the bottom, where the group were, it flowed into and then became part of a small frill of beach. Phillips crossed the lowest part of the cascading sand river and then disappeared behind the final home.

Naughton couldn't see him now.

After thirty seconds, he re-emerged, gesturing to the body-recovery team. One of them had hauled the ground-penetrating radar all the way down here – a piece of equipment that looked like a lawnmower – and the other had a large kit bag over one shoulder and the Alsatian on the end of a lead.

All of them followed Phillips back in, behind the house.

Slowly, the rest of the group began to shift around, trying to get a better angle on what was happening. Behind the house it was just sand and densely packed scrub: a mix of beachgrass, gorse and big chunks of fallen masonry. The wind had picked up, so Naughton was finding it hard to hear what was being said, but she could see they were all in the centre of a circle of undergrowth, a patch of white sand in the middle.

Phillips looked back and asked the armed officer to bring Glass over. As he did, Naughton said to the paramedic, 'You'd better get close too. Just in case.'

The paramedic nodded.

Naughton could see in his face that something didn't feel right to him, but she flashed him a reassuring smile.

As soon as he moved in front of her, Naughton darted to the left – using the crash of the sea to cover the sound of her movements – and into the foothills of the sloped dune. As she waded up towards the chimney of the last house, the sand quickly became deeper. She heard voices on the other side of the house's back wall, Phillips saying something to Glass, Glass calmly responding. There was so much sand piled against this side of the house, it was a wonder it hadn't collapsed.

Naughton stopped.

She was facing the chimney now, the sand almost up to her knees. Looking to her right, down the incline, she could see the paramedic's back, the green of his coat and his trousers just behind the back wall. Everyone's attention was on Glass. She could hear him talking again, on the other side.

He was keeping them occupied.

He knew this was Naughton's moment.

She shifted her weight, trying to get even closer to the chimney. Pieces of it had fallen away over time and become submerged under the sand, and she could feel them beneath her feet – hard, awkward, uneven. The erosion of the back wall had left behind a random series of platforms and she knew that, along these makeshift shelves and coves, the women had temporarily placed some of their equipment as they'd set up.

In the very centre of the chimney was a partially intact stone fireplace.

Everything above its mantelpiece was gone, but the bottom part remained, and behind the mantelpiece was a small, concealed section.

She leaned closer, following the instructions from her 5 a.m. text, and reached under it.

She ran her hand right to left.

There was something three-quarters of the way along.

It had been duct-taped to the inside. As she felt its shape with her fingers, the familiar grooves and patterns of it, her throat pulsed.

Why is this nightmare happening to me?
Why can't I just wake up?

She gripped the object and ripped it away, bringing it out from the chimney into the light, silver duct tape still stuck to its body.

No one had seen her do any of this.

But they would soon know about it.

She tore off the duct tape and tossed it away.

And then, tears in her eyes, the fear tremoring through her bones, she waded back down the sea of sand and raised the gun in front of her.

62

. . . 9 minutes to go . . .

Bodie sucked in a long, rasping breath.

His eyes flicked opened.

I rocked back on my knees, exhausted, my hands and wrists aching from doing the chest compressions. As he sucked in more air, nose flaring, mouth open, the paramedic rushed over. Bodie blinked, looked at me, at my hands, at the blood that had been smeared on my skin from the wound at his hip.

His face held a mix of trauma, shock and gratitude.

I looked around. It was carnage. Bodies. Officers administering CPR. The paramedic trying her best to move between all the injured. Somewhere far off in the distance – beyond the cries of those in pain, the orders being barked, and the burning crackle of debris that lay smoking on the tarmac – I could hear sirens.

More police.

More paramedics.

I watched as, out of the lifeboat station – limping, Healy's arm around his shoulder – came Preston. Healy had cut through all the duct tape with his penknife. He brought him out to where Bodie and I were and sat him down on the ground.

'Raker.'

I turned.

The chief inspector was coming towards me.

'Look what you did,' he said, pointing at me, getting so close I felt the end of his finger touch my chest. 'People have *died* because of you.'

I glanced towards the island.

My head was full of static.

I still couldn't hear properly.

I was jittery and angry and confused.

Had people died because of me? If I'd never got into the lifeboat station, would any of this have happened? Would the explosives have gone off if Preston hadn't reacted so desperately to me, rocking his chair, trying to get me to help him out of the binds? Or was the bomb always going to go off?

Preston looked back at me, shaken, his skin still raw from the duct tape.

Was he a killer?

Was *I* a killer?

I closed my eyes, trying to tune out the chief inspector, so close to me now, shouting so loudly, so aggressively, I could feel his saliva flecking my face.

No, this lifeboat station isn't on us.

We didn't set those explosives.

We didn't turn this building into a bomb.

I opened my eyes again.

'If you need to arrest me,' I said, swatting his hand away, putting mine to his chest and pushing him back, 'you can do it later.'

I didn't give him a chance to react.

I just made a break for Porthtreno.

Naughton

Now

Naughton got to the bottom of the sloping sea of sand.

Everyone was still gathered where she'd left them. The ocean was barely forty feet from where they were standing, but it was like they were walled in. That was the point. That was why he'd led them there.

They couldn't escape.

As Naughton edged further around, the gun up in front of her now, she could see over the paramedic's shoulder to Glass in the centre of the space, feet planted on a large patch of sand, gesturing to the ground, obviously telling them that deep beneath were the two other women.

Except Naughton doubted they were here at all.

The paramedic turned, noticing her first.

It took him a second to react, to fully contextualize the gun and the fact that it was being pointed at him, and Naughton used the delay to her advantage. She moved fast, grabbing his jacket, and forced him to his knees in front of her. Before he'd even hit the sand, she'd moved to the next person: the armed officer, Dover.

She put the gun to the back of his head.

Dover stiffened, made half a turn, and as he did she grabbed his neck with her spare hand and stopped him.

'Throw your gun down,' she said into his ear.

By now, everyone was looking in her direction.

'Rosa?'

Phillips was staring, his face a mirror of the paramedic's a split second before. He couldn't compute what was happening.

'Rosa, what are –'

'Throw your gun to the ground,' she said again to Dover.

He hesitated.

She shoved her gun in hard against the back of his head. She was so terrified, she could barely even hold the weapon up, but she did a good job of masking it. Dover raised one hand, slowly looped the strap for the rifle up and over his head and, slightly bending, dropped it on to the sand.

'Rosa, what the hell are you doing?' Phillips asked.

'He's got Frankie,' she said.

The minute her son's name passed her lips, her eyes filled with tears again. She blinked them away, glanced at Glass.

Glass stared back at her blankly.

'He's got my son. *He's got my baby.*' Her voice started to break up. 'Frankie's not in Spain.'

'What?' Phillips said.

'He's not with his dad. I lied to you all.'

The emotion consumed her, sobs vibrating through her chest, emerging from between her teeth, an agonized wail.

Phillips looked between Glass and Naughton.

She didn't know if he was confused or in shock.

Naughton held an image of Raker trying to tell Phillips that they were being led into a trap, and then of Phillips shutting him down.

'You need to let Glass go,' she said through her tears, her words muffled, her hands gripping her weapon harder than ever. '*Please.* I just need my baby to be safe.'

'Rosa,' Phillips said, 'whatever he's told you is a lie.'

She glanced at Glass.

He stared back.

Phillips took a step towards her. 'He's lying to you.'

'No,' she said. 'Frankie wasn't in his bed.'

As she spoke the words, she was suddenly back in the moments after she got home that night; in the hours after she'd found a masked man in the back of her car and had a knife at her throat. That was when Vessler had told her they had Frankie.

That was when she'd been told she'd have to do this to get him back.

As soon as she'd returned to the house, she'd rushed through the front door of her home. Her partner, Todd, was away with work and the babysitter had been asleep on the sofa in the living room. She'd sprinted upstairs to Frankie's bedroom.

His bed had been empty.

His window had been ajar.

Naughton had broken down, the pain so immense it was like every bone in her body had fractured simultaneously. And then, as she'd heard the babysitter stirring downstairs – as Naughton listened to her calling up to ask if everything was all right – she'd had to gather herself, wipe away her tears and pretend Frankie was fine. She'd seen the babysitter out, closed the door and collapsed to the floor.

'Just put the gun down.'

Naughton pinged back into focus.

Phillips was talking to her again.

'Rosa, please. Just put the gun dow—'

'Where's my baby?' she shouted at Glass.

'Rosa,' Phillips replied, holding up a hand.

'Where's my *baby*?'

'He's safe.'

Two words, utterly devoid of emotion. Phillips looked at Glass, who was to his right now, and then his gaze snared on something else. It was fixed to the wall of the house, just beyond where Glass was standing. Naughton risked a look too and saw what had caught Phillips's attention: a box, high up, with an antenna on it.

Phillips went to his dead radio, to his dead phone.

It's a signal jammer.

'Pull the trigger,' Glass said. A ripple passed through the space they were in. 'Pull the trigger, Rosa, and kill Officer Dover.'

'*Rosa*,' Phillips said, trying to sound calm, 'don't listen to him.'

Naughton glanced around, at the horror in the faces of the others as they saw what she'd become.

'Pull the trigger,' Glass said again, 'or your son dies.'

Naughton started sobbing again. '*No.*'

'You don't have to do this,' Dover replied from in front of her. His voice was trembling.

'Rosa, put the gun down.' Phillips again.

'Pull the trigger and I will tell you where Frankie is,' Glass said. He'd taken a half-step forward and only Naughton seemed to have noticed. 'I'm the only one who knows where he is, Rosa. Vessler's dead, Pockman's dead. It's just you and me left.'

Naughton didn't know if that was true or not, and in this moment she didn't care. She just noticed Glass take another subtle half-step.

'If you don't pull the trigger,' he said, 'Frankie dies.'

In front of her, Dover started trying to reason with her. 'You don't have to do this, Rosa.' He was using her first name as if they were old friends and not people who'd only met for the first time a few hours ago. 'You don't have to do –'

'Frankie has no food,' Glass said.

'No,' Naughton cried. 'No, no, *no.*'

'Rosa,' Phillips said, hand still up. 'Rosa, think about –'

'Frankie has no water.'

'*No.*'

'If I go back to prison, Frankie will starve to death. He will die in pain. Is that what you want, Rosa? Do you want your six-year-old son to waste away and –'

Naughton pulled the trigger.

The gun clicked.

It was empty.

It took her a second to hear the click, a second to realize it was unloaded, and – through her tears – a second to take in everyone else's reaction: some of them had stepped back from her, some had frozen, Dover had flinched and bent over.

And no one was watching Glass.

By the time everything pulled back into focus, he'd already reached down and had his cuffed hands on Dover's weapon, thrown to the ground thirty seconds before and lying in the space between Glass and Naughton.

Glass fired at Dover.

The bullets hit the armed officer high up, somewhere on his front, the impact so hard, the shots taken from so close in, he was launched into Naughton, the immense dead weight of his body landing against her and cleaning her out. She fell back hard and then Dover fell on top of her, the rear of his head smashing into her nose, instantly stunning her.

Dazed, she heard more gunshots.

And then, finally, she blacked out.

63

. . . 4 minutes to go . . .

I sprinted across the walkway on to the island.

As I hit the sand, I heard gunfire.

I upped my pace, following the path between the dunes, reaching the V-shaped fork in the trail quickly, and then headed right, along the shoreline.

As I ran, the sun emerged for the first time, breaking out above the line of the horizon ahead of me. Its light bled across the swollen mounds of the Atlantic and then across the dunes, the sand suddenly a fiery orange.

I arrived at the bottom of the slope.

The last house was on my left, up a slight incline. I looked from there, up the slope to the rest of the broken houses, their shells silhouettes against the gathering daylight, their walls submerged like sinking ships.

Close to the top was one of the body recovery team.

'Help!' they were screaming, shouting the word across the water, towards the car park. 'Help!' They waved their arms above their head, their hood, their mask.

Their white forensic suit was covered in blood.

My stomach tightened.

I turned, looking into a darkened area behind the back wall of the last house. It seemed to be full of beachgrass, masonry and weeds, a sheltered space between the shell of the final home in St Petroc and the thin fringe of beach that ringed the island.

I heard the cries for help again from the top of the slope, but I didn't take my eyes off the scene behind the house.

As I got closer, I could see blood.

Closer, and I saw an arm.

Closer still and now all I could see were bodies.

They were lying in the half-light. It was difficult to see how many to start with, but then I realized it was the rest of the group who'd come over here.

A paramedic was furthest out, as if he'd been about to make a run for it. He'd been struck in the back of the head with something – blood leaking from his hairline, on to his neck and collar – and he seemed to be unconscious but alive.

Naughton was close to him, on her side. I thought she was dead to start with, but a few steps nearer, and I could see that she was still breathing. Her belly was gently rising and falling and she was moaning softly.

I edged forward again, even as every instinct begged me not to.

An armed officer was next to Naughton, his face and the front of his body riddled with bullets. Further in, the prison officer was slumped against some gorse, clutching his belly, blood seeping through his fingers. The second body-recovery specialist was on her knees, hands up, sobbing softly. She appeared unharmed, but – keeping her eyes fixed on the ground – tearfully began begging for her life.

'It's okay,' I said to her. 'It's okay.'

Except it wasn't okay.

Nothing about this was okay.

The Alsatian came out from behind her, barking. Its fur was specked with blood but it appeared to be unhurt.

I looked at Phillips and Dougan.

Dougan was on his back, face up, his nose busted, his face already swelling up. I couldn't see any bullet wounds, but he was unconscious.

Next to him, Phillips was on his front, arms splayed out, head turned my way, eyes staring off. He'd been shot twice in the face, at least once in the neck.

I'd barely had time to process that when my gaze landed on the person at the very back, half-concealed in the shadows, as if deliberately placed there.

It was the male member of the body-recovery team.

My watch started buzzing, telling me that it was 8 a.m. and the twenty-four-hour countdown had just hit zero.

Now I knew what it had been counting down to.

I looked at the male tech again. Just like his colleague, he'd been left alive. But this time he'd been undressed.

He was in his boxer shorts and a T-shirt.

His forensic suit was missing.

And so was Glass.

THE DAYS AFTER
Part One

64

As I opened the front door, the smell of bacon and coffee hit me. I stood there for a long time, looking along the hallway to the kitchen at the back of the house, watching Rebekah. She had the radio on, music playing loudly, one hand dealing with a frying pan, the other with the controls of my microwave.

She hadn't heard me yet.

I felt a tremble in my fingers, in my chest, felt it travel like an electrical surge to my shoulders, and my arms, and my throat. It was relief at finally being home, at returning to somewhere familiar and structured, and seeing someone who felt like a sanctuary. But it was for another reason too: I was exhausted and I was anxious, and it felt like I'd failed. My job, my purpose, my life, was finding the way to unanswered questions. But two days after the island, I hadn't been able to speak to Preston once – or Ellie – Glass hadn't been found, and I was no closer to finding out why Marco had been killed, nor what had happened to Sydney, Anna and Zauna.

I'd asked the police if I could just sit down with Preston and have a conversation, but had repeatedly been told no and – when I'd tried calling Ellie – all I got was her voicemail. As far as I knew, two days on, Preston was still being questioned by the cops, but the man I'd set out to find, who I'd finally discovered in the lifeboat station, felt as distant to me here at the end of the search as he had been at the start. It was disconcerting, an aggravation of a worry I'd had about this case from the second Healy and I had got into the office in Paddington and found the clock ticking down. The hunt for Preston had been spiralling by that point – I could see that now – but it had definitely escaped from my grasp after that. I'd had to work the entirety of day two in the shadow of the Met, taking orders from a police officer who loathed me, and I'd never fully got back the reins. And in the end, that intensity of feeling, the animosity that Phillips had felt for me and Healy, had corroded his judgement to such an extent that he'd allowed himself to be walked right into the teeth of Glass's trap.

Glass knew that, like us, Phillips had never forgotten the Dead Tracks and the fallout that had followed. So Glass had edged himself into the light – the promise of Marco Roy and the Lost Women as bait at the end of a line that Phillips would never swim away from – and he'd let the fractured, hostile nature of our history do the rest. I suspected, deep down and unspoken to anyone else, Phillips had been hoping to find some rope to hang us with somewhere; an infraction in my search for Preston that might allow him to charge me and Healy with a crime and finally exact some measure of revenge for perceived injustices fourteen years ago. Instead, his wife was now a widow and his children fatherless.

Marco Roy's remains had been exhumed from the grave in Hillgrove Woods and examined by a forensic anthropologist. The detectives who'd interviewed me in Cornwall had told me almost nothing, but I was able to piece together enough and fill in the rest through the ravenous TV and newspaper coverage. The media reporting used Ellie's star status as a ballast to hang everything from and it was soon confirmed, through various sources, that DNA analysis had identified the body as definitely belonging to Marco. I wondered if his elderly father, robbed of both of his children, would ever find any closure in finally being able to lay his son to rest.

The families of the Lost Women weren't as lucky.

There was nothing under the sand, despite Glass's assurances. What the radar and the Alsatian had picked up under the village was just another deception: the remains weren't human, they were animal, and they must have been placed there by Vessler, Pockman or someone else – along with the signal jammer, the gun, and Preston himself – in the hours or days beforehand.

In total, two police officers had been killed in the explosion at the lifeboat station, Phillips and Dover had been killed in the shoot-out behind the last house in the village, and thirteen others had been injured, some critically. Rosa Naughton was alive, but I had no idea what was happening with her. Her son had been found and – physically, at least – was unharmed. In newspaper reports, police sources said Frankie had described a man matching Oliver Vessler's description coming into his bedroom, through his window. Before the boy could shout for his babysitter, he was being hauled into Naughton's attic. It turned out Frankie had been in the house the whole time, wrists and ankles duct-taped, a gag in his mouth. Police found him after obtaining a search warrant for the property.

And somewhere in the shadows of winter, forty-eight hours on, hid the architect of it all.

From the very beginning, Glass's mission had been one of revenge and then escape, a carefully constructed piece of payback that deliberately played on two things: the tragedy, grief and horror of what he'd done fourteen years ago, and the strength of feeling it still awakened in Healy, Phillips and me. He'd played on what made us different from him – our empathy, our desire for answers and justice – and while his goal had been escape from the very beginning, he'd needed other people to get him there. He'd corrupted and blackmailed weaker men like Vessler, Pockman and Matthew Higgs in the same way he'd preyed on nine women before his arrest.

We just had to hope he made a mistake now.

'Hey.' Rebekah broke out into a smile and, turning down the stove, came along the hallway. 'Welcome home.'

'Something smells good.'

She eyed me. 'Are you okay?'

I was about to tell her I was, that everything was fine, but then I realized that would have been a lie. I didn't want to lie to her.

'Honestly?' I shrugged. 'No, not really.'

In the hours after Glass had vanished, I'd called my daughter, Annabel, and then Rebekah from the beach. In a bin under one of the awnings, a police officer had found the bloodied forensic suit that Glass had stripped off the male member of the recovery team. Everything had been chaotic: cars were arriving all the time, cops and paramedics flooding the scene, and Glass had utilized every second of that turmoil, vanishing among the crowds and the noise.

Rebekah took a step closer to me.

'I'm sorry,' she said, and slowly slid her arms around my waist, drawing me in to her. I felt the side of her face press against my chest, let my chin rest at the top of her head, and I put my arms across her back and brought her in even closer. I drew in the smell of her shampoo, the sweetness of her perfume, felt her heft and warmth, and – as I closed my eyes – allowed myself to become lost.

I felt the trembling stop.

I felt the anxiety fade.

Just for a moment, I was safe.

65

After breakfast, I showered and changed and then took the Tube with Rebekah to King's Cross. She had to return to Cambridge to sign the last of the forms for her mother's estate. As we found a bench and waited for her train to board, she reached over and threaded her fingers through mine. She didn't say anything, just squeezed.

'Thank you,' I said.

'For what?'

'I don't know. Just . . .' I trailed off. 'I know you could have done all of this over Zoom, but you didn't. You were exactly the person I needed at exactly the right time.'

'So are you saying you're going to discard me for the next person now?'

'No, that's definitely not what I meant.'

She smiled. 'I know it isn't. I'm glad I came too.' She squeezed my hand again, then paused, looking at me. 'Damn, Raker.'

'What?'

'I don't understand why they're not queuing around the block for you.'

I laughed.

'I'm serious,' she said. 'I don't think I've ever met a man who feels as much as you do. Whenever we chat, whenever we're together, it's just there the whole time. You carry it. It's a part of you. Whatever you do, don't ever let that go.'

She edged in closer and put her head to my shoulder, then I put my head to hers. And for a minute it didn't matter that she lived so far away. It didn't matter that her life was in New York. Suddenly, those things could be fixed.

Suddenly, nothing seemed impossible.

*

When I got back home to Kew, I tried calling Ellie again.

It rang out and went to voicemail.

I'd only heard from her once in two days, when she'd replied in response to a WhatsApp I'd sent her the morning after the events at the beach. I'd asked her if she was all right, if the police had called her, and whether she wanted to talk.

The message had been five words long.

On my way to Truro

I'd left it for a while, unsure what to read into the brevity of her response, and then tried her a second time. She didn't pick up. I'd tried her a third time after hiring a car to drive me and Healy back to London, but it had gone straight to voicemail.

'So she's gone AWOL on you?' Healy had said. We'd stopped at a service station on the M4 and were queuing for coffee. It had been an early start, both of us keen to get home, and for most of the journey we'd been quiet, trapped in our memories of what had happened at the island. 'Don't you think that's weird?'

'It's frustrating.'

'It's weird, Raker. She's ghosting you.'

'She's doing what she thinks is best.'

He frowned. 'She was the one that hired you to find Preston. And now you *have* found him, she doesn't want to hear from you? It makes no sense.'

We took our coffees back into the freezing cold of early morning, across the car park to the car. I fired it up and nosed it on to the motorway.

'If Preston was one of the two men who killed Marco Roy,' I said, 'he's never leaving that police station, so Ellie's circling the wagons. Her not picking up is damage limitation. The less she shows people of herself, the less she talks, the less there is to print. Ellie doesn't trust the media, doesn't trust the cops, maybe she didn't ever fully trust me. I was a means to an end, an option that was handed to her by a man she *did* allow herself to get close to, who then took that trust and completely destroyed it.'

'Matt.'

'Yeah. She let him all the way in, in a way she rarely does outside a tight circle of friends and family, and look how that ended up for her.'

'Still,' Healy said, 'it's pretty cold cutting you off.'

'It's how she survives in the world she inhabits.'

Healy shrugged, accepting my explanation, but in truth I was more conflicted than I was letting on. If Ellie really *was* just circling the wagons, then I understood it and didn't hold any ill will towards her. I felt disappointed that I wouldn't get a chance to help her see things more clearly – perhaps to understand how at least some of the pieces fitted together – but, in the end, it was her life to live and her choices to make.

Yet, even if all of that made sense, her silence had still left me disconcerted. At this point, what harm could come from hearing my side of the story? Why wouldn't she want to know as much as possible about what had happened and what I'd found out? Alone in my thoughts, as I retraced a path back through the case, I began finding myself agreeing with Healy's assessment: it was weird.

And not only weird.

It was suspicious.

A little while later, Healy said, 'Where do you think he's gone?'

It was the question everyone had been asking since we'd left Porthtreno in handcuffs, and the one that came up most frequently as I'd been pulled in and out of interviews at a police station in Truro. It was one of the first questions Rebekah had asked when I was finally released on bail, pending further investigation into my part in the explosion at the lifeboat station.

'I think he'll lie low for a few weeks,' I said, 'then he'll try to flee the country.'

'The cops will have the ports on high alert.'

'I'm sure they will.'

But Healy could hear the subtext clear enough. Prepping the Border Force for Glass was one thing. Stopping him was another. He was smart, resourceful and inventive, and had spent years before his arrest moving between identities. That was why I believed he'd wait a week or two before making his final escape. He'd let the focus on him drop just a fraction – because a fraction was all he'd need to disappear.

'Are *you* okay?' I asked Healy.

The man who killed his daughter, the man who destroyed his life, the worst man either of us had ever known, wasn't even going to rot in a cell without windows.

But, to my surprise, Healy just said, 'I'm okay.'

Later, as we finally reached the outskirts of London, I asked him if he'd spoken to Alice. My instinct was that she wasn't in any danger from Glass, even with him on the run. Glass felt nothing for her. She was just another pawn he'd used, drawing her into the orbit of his plan because he knew it would confuse us, play on fears that Healy would be holding about her, and drive a wedge between him and his family. Police had been stationed at Alice and Liam's house anyway, where Gemma was staying as well, just in case Glass resurfaced with the intention of using them to get at Healy.

'I spoke to Alice and Liam late last night,' Healy replied. He paused, looking down into his lap. He'd been playing with a pack of cigarettes almost constantly but hadn't smoked a single one of them. 'She's a good kid,' he said softly. 'She'll be fine.'

It might not have seemed much to someone who didn't know him as well as I did, but those last three words were huge. His daughter had been ripped from him in the most unspeakable way possible, and while she could never be replaced, with those three words – and with a pack full of unsmoked cigarettes – he was saying so much.

I'm going to try harder.
I want to try harder.
I want Alice and Leanne to be a part of my life.

66

Early the next morning, the doorbell woke me.

I rolled over, checking the time.

It was 8 a.m.

Peeling back the duvet, I moved quietly out of bed, Rebekah still asleep beside me, grabbed a T-shirt and some tracksuit trousers and headed downstairs. Behind the frosted glass of the front door were two distorted faces I recognized instantly.

Dougan and Bodie.

I opened up. Dougan's nose was covered in dressing and surgical tape, dark purple bruising leeching out from under both eyes. Next to him, Bodie's injuries didn't look as dramatic because most were hidden under his clothes, but his face was dotted with minor cuts and through the gap in his coat I could see bandaging under his white shirt.

'David,' Dougan said. 'Sorry about the early start.'

I looked between them. 'Have you found him?'

'No. Not yet.'

I tried to think why else they would be here.

'We wondered if you wanted to come for a drive.'

'To where?'

'Holland Park,' Dougan said. 'Ellie Snyder's place.'

I frowned. 'Will Ellie be there?'

'Yes.'

'She wants to talk now?'

'We're hoping so.'

I showered, changed and said goodbye to Rebekah, and then we headed out. As the city passed, frost sparkling on windowsills, winter sun winking in and out of existence beyond the rooftops, I asked, 'Why are you letting me tag along like this?'

Dougan turned fully in his seat. 'I thought maybe you and I could help each other.'

'Why would you help me?'

'Because you helped us.'

He genuinely seemed to mean it, the stoicism I'd seen in the days before – the blankness of his expression – gone. He appeared different, and not simply because his nose was busted and covered in bandaging.

Dougan looked at Bodie.

Bodie, at the wheel, glanced at me in the rear-view mirror. 'I didn't get a chance to thank you at the island,' he said. 'You saved my life.'

'I'm not sure I –'

'You did. That piece of metal in my hip – it severed a vein. You kept me alive long enough for the paramedic to get to me. If you hadn't done that . . .' He faded out again. 'I don't know what to say, really, other than thank you.'

Dougan was still turned in his seat, looking at me. 'Some of the decisions that were made on this case . . . Let's just say, I didn't agree with them.'

'So why didn't you say anything to Phillips?'

'I did in private, when it was just me and him. But I'm a DI, he was DSU, and when you're given a direct order by a superior, you don't go to war with them.'

'If you'd gone to war with him, Glass might not be in the wind now.'

'He'd still be in the wind, I just would have been clearing my desk when I got back to Guildford. Phillips was two ranks above me. He tells you to do something, makes a decision, you fall into line. That's how it works in an organization like ours. From what I know about you, from what I've seen myself, you're smart, intuitive, and I genuinely believe you're a good man. But you're out of touch. It's been a long time since you worked within any kind of structure, and when the only person you ever have to be accountable to is yourself, you forget what it's like in the real world.'

I heard clearly what he was saying, and could even see the sense in it, but the structure that Phillips and Dougan had been part of had catastrophically failed. If you knew what was right in your head and in your gut, but you still didn't stop decisions taken to the contrary, people were going to get hurt, they were going to get killed – and left behind in the smoking rubble would be a scene like Porthtreno.

Dougan leaned forward and for the first time, in the footwell, I noticed there was a folder at his feet. He brought it up and unclipped one of the pages, handing it to me. As he did, Bodie said, 'It didn't go down how you think.'

I took the sheet of paper from Dougan. It was a photocopy of a forensic report on the explosion at the lifeboat station.

'Do your bosses know you're showing me this?'

'No,' Dougan said. 'And we'd appreciate your discretion.' He stopped again, as if trying to articulate his thoughts. 'You want to know the truth? Everything you said to Phillips, every time you had a problem with something, every decision you made at that island, I kept finding myself agreeing with you.'

I studied what I could see of his face, searching it for something defective, a movement of the eyes that told me this was a game.

But it wasn't there.

'It wasn't Preston that set that timer going,' Bodie said. 'Those things taped to his hands weren't even detonators. They were just empty boxes. The wires were never connected to anything.'

'The whole thing was just a prop?'

I tried to skim-read the conclusions from the forensic tech, but there was too much of it, and I couldn't read it fast enough.

'You're not going to get charged,' Dougan replied. 'I mean, there's nothing to charge you *with*. Nothing you or Preston did in that lifeboat station set those explosives off. They were set off by someone else, using a second phone.'

My eyes went to a long list of mobile numbers in the bottom half of the page. I recognized mine. I recognized Healy's. But it was one in the middle that my eye was drawn towards. It had been circled in biro.

Dougan pointed to the report. 'Someone *outside* the lifeboat station set off those explosives – not you, not Preston.'

Something heavy hung in the air.

'And?'

'And whoever it was, it looks like they were in the car park at the time.'

I glanced at the report again.

'That's why forensics have compiled a list of every phone number of every person that was there that night.' Dougan pointed to the number that was circled. 'And that's the one that forensics believe sent a signal to the timer on that bomb.'

I looked at it; didn't recognize it.

'So who does this number belong to?'

They glanced at each other.

And then Bodie said, 'It belongs to me.'

67

I stared at Bodie in the rear-view mirror, unsure if I'd heard him correctly.

'This is *your* number?'

'Yes,' he said, glancing at me. 'Apparently I made a call to the phone in the lifeboat station and that set the timer going.'

'"Apparently"?'

'I only had my police radio on me – the Motorola. My personal phone was in the glovebox of the van the whole time. I never took it out from the moment we got to Porthtreno.'

'So what are you saying? Forensics have got it wrong?'

'No,' Dougan said. 'They didn't get it wrong.'

He shifted again, removing a second page from the folder and handing it back across his shoulder to me. It was another print-out full of data, difficult to take in and put into any sort of context rapidly. But one word stood out on repeat.

Malware.

'Someone mirrored your phone,' I said.

'Yes,' Bodie responded. 'Forensics found malware on it. The call appeared as if it was coming from me but it wasn't.'

'So who *was* it coming from?'

'We don't know yet. Forensics are still digging. But it looks like a similar sort of set-up to when Matthew Higgs was being blackmailed and was getting those emails and texts from "Noah Klein". We just keep running into proxy servers.'

I looked at Bodie's number, circled in biro.

'My suspicion,' Dougan said, 'is that, just like with the Noah Klein emails to Matthew Higgs, searching for the person who mirrored Bodie's phone will be a dead end. I never like to write the forensics guys off, but . . .' He shrugged.

'So how is driving out to Ellie going to help?'

'Well, we want answers. All of us here need the truth about what happened to Marco – why he was killed, who did it – and where the Lost Women are.'

'Yeah, but Ellie's not going to get us there.'

Dougan didn't say anything.

'She heard her husband drunkenly confess to a murder,' I said, 'and then deny it the next morning. That's the sum total of her knowledge.'

'Correct.'

'So what am I missing here?'

'Nothing,' Dougan replied. 'You're right, Ellie won't get us there.'

'Then what's the point of driving out to see her?'

'Preston has given his version of events to the cops down in Cornwall and now they have to go away and make sense of it all.' He turned again, glancing across his shoulder at me. 'While they do that, he's been electronically tagged.'

I looked between them. 'He's been released?'

'On bail, yes.'

So it wasn't just Ellie we were going to see.

It was Preston.

'The only thing we're officially allowed to talk to him about is the shooting of Matthew Higgs, because that happened on our patch,' Dougan said. 'But you aren't a police officer, you have no jurisdiction – so you can ask him anything you want.'

68

Photographers, journalists and TV crews swarmed the gates as we pulled into Ellie's house in Holland Park. There were so many of them, it took Bodie a full five minutes to get on to the driveway. None of us exited the car until the gates had closed.

Once they did, Ellie came to the door.

'David,' she said quietly.

'Hi, Ellie.'

'I'm sorry I haven't replied to you, or been in touch. This whole thing is . . .' She stopped. 'It's such a mess. I just needed to press pause and take some time to think.'

I watched her for any sense she wasn't being entirely honest with me — but if she was lying, whatever her reasons for doing so, it was well concealed.

'I understand.'

'Thank you,' she said, and led us into the same foyer I'd been in only five days before. As I looked in at the living room, I could see Preston sitting on one of the sofas. He was leaning forward, elbows on his knees, his body curving from ribs to crown, apparently deep in thought. Much of his face had been re-dressed in fresh bandaging, but what I could see of the bruising around the edges looked raw and unpleasant.

'Please,' Ellie said to me. 'Go on in.'

I headed through.

As Preston saw me, he got to his feet and, below the hem of his trousers, the tag on his ankle blinked.

'David,' he said, holding out a hand. 'I didn't really get the chance to speak to you at the beach. It was just so chaotic, wasn't it?'

'That's one way of putting it.'

'Oh, I didn't mean to sound flippant, I just . . .' He paused, a shimmer of emotion. 'I spent the first day after it happened believing I was responsible for all of it.' *All of the bodies. All of the suffering.* 'It's hard thinking you're a murderer.'

I noted his choice of words but didn't get a chance to follow up as Dougan and Bodie entered, Dougan doing the introductions. He sold Preston a story about how I'd been folded into the investigation and was best placed to ask him questions about his abduction because I'd been the one that Ellie had hired.

As I listened, I again tried to work out what the motivation was for bringing me all the way out here. Bodie's reasons for involving me felt less mysterious — I'd saved his life — but I couldn't decide on why Dougan was taking the risk. Maybe this really was just a reaction to him being sidelined by the other police forces. Maybe it was an apology for ignoring his gut at Porthtreno and not supporting me in front of Phillips. Or maybe all of this was more a cynical career move: with all the information at his fingertips, he could make himself indispensable. Whatever it was, I'd spent so many years fighting the police, it was disorientating to find them willingly involving me. My instinct was to take Dougan at his word — but I was still worried about a sucker punch.

Ellie asked what we'd like to drink and then disappeared into the kitchen.

'It's hard for her,' Preston said quietly. 'Our marriage wasn't supposed to come out to the public like this. It was supposed to be on her terms.'

I nodded, getting out my notebook, indicating I was ready to start.

The question I really wanted to open with was whether he'd been involved in the murder of Marco Roy, as he'd confessed to Ellie. But I held off for now. I wanted him comfortable, maybe even for his guard to be down a little, because I only had one chance to ask the question and that meant one chance to see the reaction in his face. The eyes were always where lies collapsed first.

I started with the day he disappeared.

Using photographs that Dougan had brought, Preston identified Vessler, and then went through how the abduction had happened. It was exactly how I'd guessed: they exited through the window of Preston's room, on to the roof, and Christopher Pockman had helped. Preston said he only recalled brief snatches of that day because the anaesthetic was still working its way through his system, which meant he was in and out the whole time – but he recognized Vessler straight away.

'The second he entered, I could see it was Oliver,' he said quietly. 'It was him, there, this guy I went to university with. Not that I got the chance to tell anyone.' He winced a little, lightly touching the stitches worming their way in towards his eye socket. 'After that, it's just snatches of memory. Oliver and the other guy getting me out through the window; being walked out of that alley – dragged, really – and down the high street to a side road. I don't remember anyone saying anything on the way. You know, questioning what was going on. I must have just looked like I was drunk.'

'What was in the side street?' I asked.

'Their car. The next thing I knew, I was tied up on its back seat and we were driving down to Cornwall.'

'To the lifeboat station?'

'Yes.'

'Were you there the whole time?'

'Yes.'

'So you were never taken to the flat in Camberwell?'

'No.'

'And Vessler? What happened to him?'

'After tying me up, he just left.'

'You didn't see him planting the charges around the doors?'

'No. I think they must have been there already.'

'And I was the next person you saw after that?'

'Yes.' Preston shifted in his seat. 'There was a hole in the wall beside where I'd been placed. I could see out, but no one could see in. It was too dark. I tried shouting at the police when they checked the station, but the gag meant no one could hear me – plus, there was all the noise from the sea. That was when I thought about Morse code. I learned it back in my teens when I was an army cadet. I've forgotten a lot of it, but I remembered how to say *Help me.*'

'Did Vessler ever communicate to you what the plan was?'

'No, he never said anything.'

'This guy you went to university with appearing out of the blue at the hospital and abducting you like he did – that must have come as a shock.'

'Yes, of course.'

'Had you seen him at all in the period between you and him attending Bristol University and him abducting you from your room at The Crest?'

'No.'

'So you hadn't seen this man for almost thirty years, then suddenly he turns up out of the blue and drives you to Cornwall. What did you think was going on?'

'I had no idea. All I knew was that I was terrified.'

The working assumption had always been that Vessler and Preston had killed Marco Roy together – whatever their motive might be for doing so – and then come back for Sydney, Anna and Zauna when the three of them dug too deep into Marco's case. So Preston was either lying about not having seen Vessler since university, or he was telling us he had no involvement in the disappearance of the Lost Women.

As Ellie returned with our drinks, I inched forward on the sofa.

Preston's guard had come down enough.

Now it was time to ask the question.

'Given you say you hadn't spoken to or seen Oliver Vessler in almost three decades before he kidnapped you, didn't you ever think to make the obvious leap?'

He frowned. 'Leap?'

'Didn't you think your abduction could be related to something in your past?'

He stopped, realizing where I'd led him.

'Preston,' I said. 'What happened to Marco Roy?'

Zauna and Marco

Marco

Marco crosses to the mainland and follows Emma back in the direction of the beach house, the two of them silent. In the shadows of the coastal path, they can see Oliver up ahead. Fran is a little way in front of him, walk-running, a ghost in the darkness.

He thinks back to the feeling he'd had as Oliver had stopped next to him — the tremor of fear, the fact that he'd been unable to look Oliver in the eye — and Marco suspects it's part of the reason he feels so angry. It's not just that he should have said something, should have called Oliver out on whatever had made Fran so upset; it's the fact that Oliver made him cower.

'Does he hurt her?' Marco asks.

Emma pretends not to hear him.

'Emma, does he *hurt* her?'

Emma stops.

Marco almost walks into her, and when he does, he can hear shouting coming from ahead of them. Oliver has caught up with Fran. She shrugs him off and breaks into a run. The wind carries the last of his words towards them — 'Come on, baby, why are you being like this?' — and that's when Oliver becomes aware that he's being watched. His head whips around and despite his eyes being hidden by the shadows, his face contoured by the darkness into an ashen, almost skeletal mask, Marco withers again. *I hate him looking at me. I hate how he makes me feel.*

Oliver moves again, disappearing into the black.

'He's just a prick,' Emma says, her eyes shining, even in the night.

'Does he hurt her?' Marco asks again.

'Physically?' A shake of the head. 'Not that I've ever seen.'
'So he's emotionally abusive?'
'He's never said one bad word to her in front of me. But I know he's not good for her. It's the little things I see: the way her mood darkens, the way she's always so tearful around him, the way . . .' She looks at Marco. 'The way he makes me feel.'

She must have been able to see that Marco felt the same way about Oliver.

'I didn't even invite him to this,' Emma says. 'I never invite him to anything – but he turns up because Fran does. I don't even know if they're actually still together or not. Fran doesn't ever want to talk about it. She just shuts me down when I try.' She stops, wipes her eyes. 'He can be so charming, you know? He can be really funny, even sweet sometimes. You can get seduced by it. And whenever he's like that, I think that's when Fran lets him in again because she's got her own history. Her own trauma. Both her parents died when she was young, and you don't need to be a psychologist to know she's been looking for a home ever since. Somewhere or someone to belong to.'

Some of the others are coming now, talking, laughing.

Marco recognizes Preston among them.

'Why don't we report him?' he says to Emma.

'For what?'

'I don't know, but the police could dig into it and –'

'No.'

'We can call them anonymously.'

'It won't make any difference.'

Marco frowns. 'Of *course* it'll make a difference if he's actually hurting her. We can't just do nothing if he's abusing h—'

'No.' Emma shakes her head.

The other group are almost upon them now.

'It won't make any difference, Marco.'

'Why not?'

She glances at him. 'Because Oliver knows people.'

Zauna

The three women look up the slope of sand, past the broken houses, to the silhouetted man at the top. They still can't see him properly from where they are because, as the sun is going down, it's passing over his right shoulder. But whoever he is, he knows them. He's just reeled off their names. And as Sydney shouts up to him again, 'You seem to know us, so why don't you tell us who *you* are?' Zauna can hear the first note of concern in her voice. It's like a vibration that passes through the sand. Anna looks at Zauna, and Zauna looks at her, and their expressions echo each other.

Something here feels wrong.

Sydney wades across, out into the middle of the slope, a solitary figure in an ocean of sand. It flows past her, towards Zauna and Anna further down.

'We're filming something,' she shouts to the man, moving even further up the incline, 'and you're not allowed to be here. So, with the greatest of respect, either let us know who you are and what you want, or piss off.'

'That's Oliver.'

A voice from behind them.

All three of them turn.

There's someone else here now. It's another man. He's come in along the shoreline, the path that traces the outside edge of Porthtreno, and none of the women even noticed. He's standing at the bottom of the flow of sand, forty feet from them, where it finally flattens out and merges with the frill of beach that rings the island.

Zauna stares at the second man.

He studies her – as if he's seen her before in a photo but never in the flesh – and then his attention switches to the one he called Oliver, the silhouette at the top.

Oliver is moving now.

He's wading down through the sand, getting deeper, dropping below the crest of the island, and as he does, he finally becomes something more than a silhouette: five-ten, dark hair, dark eyes. He gets to the halfway point when something suddenly sparks at the back of Zauna's head: a flash of recognition. She thinks about the research she's looked through – the names that Anna has dug into and tried to find out more about – and, as she does, she makes the connection.

Oliver Vessler.

He's one of the men who was in the pub the night Marco disappeared. He was a witness. Police interviewed him and dismissed him. And according to the other students Anna had talked to, he was at the beach house a week beforehand too.

As Zauna glances at Anna and Sydney, she can see they've also made the same leap, that they've also tethered the name *Oliver* to Oliver Vessler.

And now, as he gets closer, Zauna starts to feel scared.

There's something about him, she thinks.

As Vessler continues to descend, as he gets closer to where Sydney is, the three women turn and look back down the slope to the second man.

He's different from Vessler.

He's looking at the island, the broken houses, the river of sand, like he's been here before and had hoped never to return.

'What's going on?' Zauna says to him.

His eyes come back to hers. 'I'm sorry it has to come to this, Zauna.'

Marco

When Marco gets back to the beach house, there's no sign of Oliver or Fran.

Emma peels off into a group of girls who didn't go to the

island. As she sits down among them, Marco can see the relief in her face. Her eyes brighten. She pours some vodka into a plastic cup, a smile playing lightly at her lips as she joins the conversation. He can see what she's thinking and he understands why she's thinking it.

Being among women feels like a safe haven.

Marco goes through to the kitchen and fills a glass full of water. Out the back, Derek – Emma's boyfriend – is playing touch rugby in the dark of the garden. It breaks up after a few minutes and turns into a drinking game, Derek leading it, the six guys he's with taking it in turns to see how many beer cans they can empty.

Marco feels so alone here.

These aren't his people.

He looks at his watch, sees it's after midnight, and thinks of Zauna. He pictures his sister in bed, cocooned in her blankets, the toy sloth he gave her somewhere close by. He wants to be home now. He wants to be in his own bed. He wants –

A thump from above him.

He listens for a moment, looks up at the ceiling. Floorboards creak. A long period of silence. Then more creaking.

Something shatters.

Marco moves through to the hallway at the front of the beach house and looks up the stairs. He can't see much. To his right, on this floor, he has a view all the way through to the conservatory, where Emma and the other girls are. They're laughing so much that none of them has heard the noises from upstairs.

A toilet flushes, drawing Marco's attention back to the landing, and he can hear the bathroom door opening. Someone comes out.

Marco can see their shadow on the wall.

Whoever it is says, 'Ollie. Mate.'

It takes Marco a couple of seconds to match the voice to the name, but then he realizes who it is.

Preston.

Marco goes up to the first step.

'Ollie,' Preston repeats. 'Come on, mate, don't do that.'

Preston sounds scared.

No, not scared.

Terrified.

Marco goes up to the next step.

'Ollie, please,' Preston says again. 'Just stop.'

'Fuck off,' Oliver spits back.

At the top of the stairs, Preston finally comes into view. He's retreated, his gaze still fixed on something Marco can't see.

He hasn't noticed Marco below him.

Preston takes another step back, unable to tear his eyes away from whatever's going on, and then he wipes his mouth, and he swallows, and he tries to make himself look bigger and stronger.

And finally, tentatively, Preston says, 'Ollie, that's enough. You're hurting her.'

69

For a moment, the room was absolutely silent.

Eventually, Preston said, 'I know I should have stopped it.' He looked brittle, the memory of that night like a frost on his skin. 'I should have gone in there and grabbed Fran off the floor and pulled her out.' He glanced to Ellie, seated away from us in the corner of the room. She didn't look back. It was as if she couldn't even bear to make eye contact with her husband. 'I'm sorry,' he said, although it was hard to say who his apology was for.

'What happened to Fran?' I asked.

'Ollie calmed down, picked her up and then took her to the bathroom – cleaned the wound on her face, her bruises, spoke softly to her, told her he loved her. He treated her like this china doll ten minutes after throwing her across the room, and all I did was stand there, doing nothing. It was like I was paralysed. After cleaning her up, he sneaked her out of the back of the house and, because he had his own car, they left and none of the others had any idea what had happened. What I should have done then was report him. I *know* I should have reported him. But Oliver, he was just this . . .'

'Was just this what?' I said.

'He was a beast.' A blink, as if trying to extinguish the last image of Oliver Vessler from his head. 'But he was careful. The people close to Fran knew something wasn't right, but until that night he never showed that side of himself so openly. He didn't realize I was in the bathroom; he didn't realize anyone was upstairs. It was only when I came out of the toilet that I . . .' He stopped again. A long pause. 'He didn't even *want* Fran, that's the irony of it. But he didn't want anyone else to have her either. And no one would ever pull him up on it.'

'You could have,' I said.

'No.'

'You could have picked up the phone to the police.'

He didn't reply. I wasn't sure if he was so entrenched in his memories that he didn't hear, or if he'd deliberately avoided giving me a response because he knew I was right.

'I didn't even know Marco was there,' Preston said. 'When I finally went downstairs, he wasn't on the staircase. And when I got up the next morning, he was gone. He'd got a taxi to the train station. I had no idea he'd seen me there, had no idea he'd watched some of it happen – not until a week later.'

'So what happened then?'

'I heard Matt was shot and killed.'

The change of direction took me a moment to react to.

By the time I did, he was talking again: 'Matt started asking me about my uni days a few months back. I didn't think much about it at the time, but now it seems so obvious there was an ulterior motive. I mean, he was professional, courteous, and he looked after Ellie – and that was what mattered – but he would never get personal. There was always a distance with him.'

Dougan looked at me. *Are you going to get him back on track?*

But I held off.

Something was coming.

'I trusted him,' Preston went on, 'so I didn't think anything of it. I talked. Not about everything, but enough. And the more I talked, the more it all came back to me, the more it started to infect everything. I'd wake up in the middle of the night thinking about Marco. I'd be working, actually *in* surgery, and what happened back then would pop into my head. And when I was drunk, that was when it was the worst. I couldn't get rid of the voices, the images. It was why I started reading about the Lost Women again, watching the documentary. I mean, I guess Matt, and Vessler, this Glass person – they must have known I would.'

I didn't say anything.

I kept waiting, watching him.

'I played that documentary and I read that book because I wanted to see if it was as bad as the version in my head was.' He shrank a little. 'And it was. I'd listen to that archive footage over and over – the interviews that were recorded with Zauna. It was all the women ever got to make of their own film. And when she talked about her brother . . .' His voice began to break up. 'That was all you needed to see. I'd listen to Zauna just to punish myself. I'd want her pain to become mine.'

He was trying to stop himself from crying.

'Why would you want to do that?' I asked gently, edging closer to him, the rest of the room fading from my peripheral vision. I felt light-headed, the prize I'd sought, the answers, almost in reach. 'Do you know how Marco was killed?'

'Yes.'

'Do you know because you helped Vessler kill him?'

The slightest movement of his head.

'Is that a yes, Preston?'

He blinked.

'Preston?' Nothing. 'Preston, is one of the reasons you never called the police about Vessler back then because you helped him bury Marco's body in Hillgrove Woods?'

He glanced at Dougan.

Why's he looking at Dougan?

I logged it, kept my focus on him.

'Preston?'

I studied him, trying to get a read on him, but he'd tilted his head slightly and it was hard to see his face now. Across the room, Ellie looked at me and her lip started to tremble.

Something's changed.

I could feel it like a charge in the air.

I inched further forward – but then a sudden, overpowering wave of nausea hit me. I'd barely had the chance to register it when I started to feel light-headed again.

My vision softened.

My body started feeling sluggish and unresponsive.

And then, next to me, Dougan fell forward, plunging off the sofa like a dead weight and crashing into the coffee table. The table shattered and flipped.

Beyond him, Bodie was already slumped.

His arms were at his side, the notebook he'd been holding on the floor, and his eyes were starting to close.

I looked at Preston, and then at the half-finished cups of coffee that Dougan, Bodie and I had been drinking from.

And then I looked at the woman who'd brought them to us.

'Ellie?'

She was crying.

'Ellie, what have you done?'

Zauna and Marco

Marco

Emma calls Marco a week later to say they're all at the pub.

'Is Oliver there?'

'No,' she says. 'No, don't worry.'

'What about Fran?'

'I haven't seen her since the beach. She said she had some kind of accident on the treadmill and is still feeling a bit shaky.' Emma stops, and Marco wonders if she genuinely believes that.

'Is Preston there?' he asks.

'Yes.' Emma seems confused. 'Why, did you guys get on?'

Marco avoids an answer and just tells her he'll come. He takes the cordless phone back downstairs, where his mum is helping Zauna with some spelling homework.

When Zauna sees him, she says, 'Marco, Marco, listen.'

Marco's mind is elsewhere, but he pushes out a smile for his sister. She starts spelling *doubt* for him, and then *solemn*, and then *knight*, and she explains that she's been learning about words with silent letters. Marco reacts, tells her she's so smart, and then feels another little surge of love for her when he sees that she's brought the toy sloth he gave her to the table.

'I'm meeting some of the guys at the pub,' he tells his mum.

'Okay, love. That's wonderful.'

His mum seems happy that his social life is taking off, and then Zauna says, 'Don't get drunk,' and starts giggling.

Marco just nods, because his mind has skipped ahead again to the pub and to what he's going to say to Preston Stewart. He pictures him at the top of the staircase in the beach house. He hears him saying *Ollie* on repeat, a worthless, tremoring cry for

Vessler to stop what he was doing to Fran, and then – as Marco took another step up – he himself finally saw the damage that had been done in a mirror on the landing.

He hasn't been able to shake the image for a week.

He grabs a jacket from the peg in the kitchen.

'I'll see you later,' he says to his mum and sister and then moves through the house, to the front door. He doesn't realize this will be the last time he ever walks the passageways of the home he grew up in. As he heads out into the night, he happens to glance across his shoulder and sees Zauna at one of the windows, waving at him. He doesn't realize it'll be the last time he'll ever see his family either.

But the image of Zauna in the window will stay with him.

Her face as she waves goodbye.

The toy sloth in her hands.

When he gets to the pub, he toughs out the first hour, only vaguely listening to the conversation around him. He glances at Preston at the other end of the group, laughing with some of the others about a TV show they've all watched.

But Marco can tell something is on Preston's mind.

The laughter isn't as hard as it might be. The smile doesn't stretch as wide as it should. He's drinking faster than anyone else.

Eventually, Preston heads to the toilets.

Marco gives it a minute and then follows him. He's at one of the urinals. Marco pushes the door to the bathroom shut and Preston glances across his shoulder.

'Oh hey, mate,' he says, and when Marco doesn't respond, he frowns, shakes himself off and says, 'What's up?'

'I saw what Vessler did to Fran.'

Preston's face drops. 'What?'

'You heard.'

Preston's eyes go to the door, as if he's weighing up whether to head back to the table and just ignore Marco entirely. He's bigger than Marco, so he could do it; could easily push Marco aside. But what Marco has worked out by now is that, while Preston is tall and broad, he doesn't use it; maybe doesn't know how to.

'We're going to the police,' Marco says.

'What?' Preston shakes his head. 'No.'

'Yes. Vessler is an abuser.'

'Listen to me –'

'No, you listen to me. I've waited a week to see whether you would do anything about what you saw. I thought maybe you might report it. But I guess you don't care enough. Well, I do. You and me are leaving this pub now and we're going to the police. We're going to walk in there and you're going to tell them what you saw.'

'I didn't see –'

'Don't give me that shit, okay? I was there on the stairs. It happened right in front of your eyes.' He takes a step closer. 'You and I both know why Fran isn't here tonight and it's got nothing to do with an accident on a treadmill.'

Preston swallows. 'Listen, mate –'

'We're not mates.'

'All right.' He holds up a hand. 'All right.'

Marco takes another step. 'Vessler is a fucking animal. He shouldn't be learning how to be a doctor. He should be in prison.' Preston doesn't say anything. Marco angles his head, unsure exactly what to make of Preston's expression. 'You can't seriously think what he's doing is all right?'

'No. *No.* Of course I don't.'

'Then you need to do something about it.'

'Yeah. Yeah, I know I do.' Preston is quiet, his face inexpressive. 'Okay,' he says finally. 'Okay, follow me.'

Zauna

Oliver Vessler stops about five feet short of Sydney.

A blanket of sand sloughs off the surface, and it moves like a wave down the slope. It reaches Zauna and Anna about ten seconds later. By then, Vessler has taken something from his pocket.

A knife.

Sydney holds up a hand. 'Wait a minute –'

'Shut up,' Vessler says, and then looks at the knife in his hand, eyeing it like this is the first time he's noticed how fierce it is, how ugly. 'You three are going to fall apart like wet paper.'

To her left, Zauna sees the other man moving.

He's coming around, looking between the three women.

'Did you know it was me?' Vessler asks Sydney.

'Did I know *what* was you?' she responds, and Zauna can hear that she's trying to keep her voice even, trying to stop the fear from tearing down her words.

'Don't play games,' Vessler says. 'Did you know it was me?'

Sydney glances over her shoulder at Anna, who looks back at her. They're both terrified, just like Zauna, but a message passes between them: some understanding of what's going on and who Vessler is that they haven't shared with Zauna yet. But Zauna is clever. She knows what that look means.

They were just waiting for the right time to tell me.

'You were the one that killed my brother,' Zauna says to Vessler.

He looks over Sydney's shoulder, his hand moving, the knife catching the sun and casting a jagged flash of silver across the walls of St Petroc's broken homes.

And then she glances at the second man.

And she sees it all over his face too.

'Both of you,' she says. 'Both of you killed him.'

Marco

Marco and Preston leave through the back, pausing in the door of the pub, rain spitting out of the sky, as Preston says, 'I don't want him to get wind of this from anyone, so I'll go to the station with you, but we're not going together.'

Marco looks up and down the street. It's late and it's empty. 'How's he going to get wind of anything?' he says.

'I'm just not risking it.' Preston tenses. 'Do you know anything about him?'

'Other than he's a piece of shit?'

'He knows people.'

Marco stares at Preston like he might be joking. 'What?'

Preston takes a step closer to Marco. 'Everyone else inside only met him for the first time three months ago. Freshers' Week, halls, whatever. He's charmed most of them in there, but a few, like Emma, can already feel there's something wrong with him . . .' He drops his voice even more. 'But none of them knows him like I do, because I knew him before all of this. We went to school together in Bath.'

Marco shrugs. 'So?'

'So, after we finished our A levels, we were at this summer party in this farmhouse up by the motorway and . . .' He pauses, looking both ways. 'There was this girl and he . . .' Another, even longer pause. 'He took her out the back . . .'

A car passes. Rain swirls and eddies in the breeze.

'He raped her?'

Preston nods.

'Did anyone report it?'

'The girl did,' Preston says.

'And what happened?'

'Nothing.'

'*Nothing?* What do you mean, *nothing?*'

'Oliver called someone.'

'Who?'

'His older brother.'

'So?' Marco says. 'So what?'

'His older brother is the one that can make things go away.'

Zauna

The second man steps closer to Zauna.

'You killed Marco,' she says to him again.

'No,' the man replies, 'I just cleaned up my brother's mess.'

Marco

Preston tells Marco he will meet him at a park close to the police station. It's a fifteen-minute walk along Whiteladies Road.

'I'll meet you at the park,' he says, 'and then we can get our stories straight.'

Marco understands Preston's reasons for not wanting to leave the pub together, but a part of him is still wary. Marco reminds himself that he doesn't know this person at all. 'If you don't turn up, I'll tell the police you stood there and did nothing while he hurt her.'

Preston nods.

Marco hurries off into the night, the rain getting heavier. He doesn't know that fifty feet along Whiteladies Road he's recorded by a CCTV camera, and it will be the last time anyone sees him alive. He doesn't know that Preston goes back into the pub and says his goodbyes and then, on his way out of the door – with every intention of following through on his promise to Marco – bumps into Oliver.

Vessler wasn't supposed to be coming.

No one told him about the meet-up.

But somehow he's heard about it.

Preston panics. He greets Oliver as if everything is normal, trying his hardest not to show he's scared, heads back into the pub, and then says he needs another piss. But the panic is all over his face, and Oliver has seen it. As Preston stands there, Emma asks him if he knows where Marco is.

'I don't know,' Preston says quickly.

'Oh,' Emma responds. 'I thought he followed you into the toilets earlier.'

Preston pleads ignorance and hurries off to the bathroom. Marco, half a mile away, waiting at the park near the police station, has no idea that, less than a minute later, Oliver enters the toilets as well and finds Preston at one of the washbasins, splashing cold water on his face. Oliver grabs him, shoving him into one of the cubicles, and then starts choking him until he finally spills the truth.

'He's going to tell the cops about Fran,' Preston splutters. 'About what you did to her at the beach house last week.'

'You told him?'

'No. *No.* He saw.'

Oliver stares at him, teeth gritted.

'I didn't tell him, Ollie, I swear.'

'Where is he?'

Preston folds instantly. 'He's in the park by Clifton Cathedral.'

Oliver throws Preston aside and heads out, and Preston starts to cry. He knows Marco is going to get hurt. He knows this will end badly. And as Preston sobs alone – just as he will sob for months after – it feels like he's the one who's killed Marco.

But he's not the one who wields the knife.

Vessler finds Marco in the park. He approaches him from behind, using the same blade he will take to Porthtreno thirteen years later.

Marco doesn't hear a thing.

The knife is halfway inside him before he even realizes Oliver is there, and he's on the floor before he ever gets the chance to defend himself. He dies on his back, looking up at the stars as he chokes on his blood and his lungs collapse. And as his life escapes his body, the image of Zauna at the window comes back to him. He sees her, blinking behind his fluttering eyelids, her face so clear, her one hand waving, her other clutching the toy sloth he gave her.

She's saying goodbye to her brother.

And now, as he closes his eyes for good, Marco says goodbye to her.

I love you, Zauny.

Zauna

The second man looks from one woman to the next, and then his eyes come to rest on Zauna again. 'If it makes any difference, your brother seemed like a good person.'

'Bee!' Vessler shouts down the slope.

The second man doesn't react.

He's still looking at Zauna.

'Bee, are we doing this?'

'Your brother was a better person than mine will ever be,' he says to Zauna, ignoring Vessler again, the man's voice so quiet now – hidden by the wind, disguised by the sea – that no one else but he and Zauna are able to hear.

Tears fill Zauna's eyes as, for the briefest of moments, she pictures Marco. She sees him laughing with her, and waving to her, and telling her he loves her.

She hears him calling her *Zauny*.

And then the man pushes up through the sand towards her, and there's a knife in his hand now too. 'I'm sorry,' he says quietly. 'I'm sorry my brother is a monster.'

The man glances up the slope.

And that's when Vessler shouts, '*Bodie!* Are we doing this or what?'

70

Bodie peeled himself up off the sofa.

I tried to move, tried to do the same, tried to haul myself up, but it felt too far and too hard. My arms wouldn't shift. My muscles were lifeless. It felt like I was locked inside my body.

Adjusting himself, his shirt, his tie, he stood. 'Shit,' he said, looking at me. 'Why's he still awake?'

If there was a response, I didn't hear one. Preston was right at the edge of my vision and Ellie was on the other side of the room, where she'd always been, next to the door. She was staring at me in horror, the tears streaming down her face.

Bodie's attention was still on me, and because everything was moving so slowly, because my brain felt as listless as my body, it was only now that it clicked.

He hasn't been drugged like me and Dougan.
It had all been an act.
And I wasn't supposed to be awake to see it.

Bodie took a step closer, feet bumping into Dougan's chest. I managed to turn my head enough, force it downwards, to see that Dougan was still on the floor, eyes closed, cuts on his face from landing on the coffee table and shattering it.

'Did you give Raker the full dose?' Bodie said, looking at Ellie. She nodded. 'Yes.'

Bodie stepped over Dougan and dropped to his haunches in front of me. 'You've got a lot of fight, David.' He sounded different, looked different, was more confident, more measured, and for the first time I realized all of us had been wrong. He wasn't a subordinate. He wasn't a nodding dog. That had just been another act; a way for him to exist at the frontline without ever being looked at too closely. I could see his brain ticking over, his intelligence plain as he worked out what to do next. But there really wasn't much of a choice to make. He wasn't going to wait around for me to shake the drug off and risk whatever happened after.

'What a fucking mess,' he muttered.

He reached for one of my arms and picked it up. When he let it go, it dropped like a stone, back to my side. He pressed fingers into my ribs, digging into them hard and repeatedly. But I couldn't feel it and he got no reaction from my body.

I glanced at Ellie again, every movement an effort.

Bodie followed my eyeline. 'Don't blame her. She and Preston were just doing what they were told to do. When you're scared, you bend.'

There was so much in those last five words, so much history, but he didn't let me see it in his face for long. He got to his feet and walked across the living room to the front windows, to the view of the driveway. He was doing all of this with the full glare of the media only feet away from us.

'I know all about bending,' he said, almost to himself. 'I know all about being scared.' He drew in a long, protracted breath. 'The things we do for love, right?' He peeled one of the curtains back a little. 'I can't even tell you how many times I bailed Oliver out. Most of what he did I managed to fix. A report on him gets lost, or gets filled with information that isn't quite right. A piece of evidence ends up contaminated. I've done them all. Marco called Ollie an *animal*.' A beat. 'He was right about that.'

'He wasn't even your brother,' Preston said quietly.

Bodie looked at me, not Preston. 'That's true. We're not brothers. Well, not biologically. That's why no one's ever managed to connect us. I mean, you can dig down into the archives and we'll be there, but you'd have to go pretty deep.' A distant, long-dormant pain flickered in his eyes. 'St Gideon's. It was this fucking awful children's home on the outskirts of Bath, staffed by the kind of people that should never have been let within a million miles of young kids. You survived that place, nothing more.' He glanced at Preston. 'It made us brothers in all the ways that mattered.'

He stepped away from the windows, letting the curtains fall back into place, and then seemed to get lost in his memories. 'He was almost exactly four years younger than me, but we just instantly clicked. Everyone used to call me *Bodie* in that place, but he called me *Bee*. Neither of us remembered our real families – they were gone before we'd even learned to walk – but the sole memory I had of my parents was of my mum working in a flower garden, with all these bumblebees in it. I remembered her showing them to me on the flowers, buzzing around, doing their thing. So when he started calling me *Bee*, it felt like a sign. We bonded. I guess it also helped that we were both so angry, both hurting, both feeling like we'd been abandoned. We wanted to hit out at the shitty hand we'd got dealt. The difference was, I channelled all of that and put it into the police – something half-decent. I thought he had too. I mean, medical school. Wow. The idea of my little brother out there, doing good, saving lives, it was amazing. At that point, it felt like we were indestructible.'

He broke eye contact with me and, for a moment, I thought he was done; that he'd realized how openly he was talking, how easily this long-hidden confession was pouring out of him, and how dangerous it might be for him.

But then I saw the truth.

He knew that, whatever he chose to tell me, whatever he needed to get off his chest, there wouldn't be any fallout.

I couldn't move.

I couldn't respond.

I was just a vessel he could use until he'd cleared his conscience.

'I've done a lot of bad shit,' he said, eyeing me as if he could see exactly where my thoughts were, 'but denial, that was the worst of it. He was fourteen, fifteen, when I first saw the fractures in him. This broken bird. He told me years later that one of the staff at St Gideon's used to take him into their office at night. It went on for seven or eight years, from when he first got there to the time that place closed. Ollie was – what? – three when we arrived at that home?' Bodie glanced at Preston, at me. 'I'm not excusing what he became, but that destroyed something in him. I really believe that. What was done to him was so cruel.' He rubbed at his face. 'And now I'm fifty-three and it feels like I've spent my entire life dealing with the impact.'

'He was a monster,' Preston said softly. 'You both are.'

Bodie just nodded.

Finally, his eyes snapped back to me. 'Marco was the first person he killed, but Fran wasn't the first girl he hurt.' He glanced at Preston. *The girl at the summer party just outside Bath.* 'He made stupid fucking decisions, one after the other. In my head, I knew I couldn't keep making things go away. It would cost me my career and my freedom. My heart was different, though. When he called me in this mad panic and told me he'd killed Marco, I just dropped everything. We used my car, and Hillgrove Woods was my idea. He told me it was a mistake, an accident, an argument that got out of hand. He never told me what happened at the beach house a week before that. I only found out about that years later, when he said some documentary researcher had phoned him about Marco's disappearance.' He perched on the arm of the sofa, a few feet from Preston. 'That's when I should have let him rot. He lied to me about Marco. It wasn't an accident. It was deliberate. He knew exactly what he was doing. But then I thought to myself, "If I let him rot, he might roll over on me." So I told him to leave it with me, and I started looking into the production company that Sydney Roder ran and what they were up to.'

He seemed to become aware of Ellie then, still in exactly the same position at the door. She hadn't moved since bringing us the coffees. He frowned at her, as if something about her, or the way she was behaving, was concerning him.

'Sit over here,' he said to her.

She didn't move.

'*Sit.*'

Ellie flinched. He pointed to the seat next to me, and Ellie hurried over. She glanced at me, a tremor in her expression, but Bodie didn't notice it this time. Instead, his eyes moved fractionally as something old shuddered to the surface.

'What Preston was telling you earlier on,' he said, 'about the footage of Zauna discussing Marco – he was right. I watched some of the footage when I broke in to the production office, and you could just *feel* her pain.' He looked at Preston. 'That was hard to watch. I agree with you.'

A twitch in my fingers.

Bodie clocked the movement and turned to me. But I could see that he wasn't sure whether it had been me or Ellie that had moved.

He got up and came around the shattered coffee table, to where Dougan's body was still prone on the floor. Dragging a chair over from the living-room table, he placed it down in front of me. As he sat, the legs crunched on the chipped glass.

'I've watched you with Colm Healy,' he said. 'You and he have the same thing we had. I can see it. I recognize it. You don't even like each other sometimes, but in all the ways that count you're like brothers. You were there when he found his girl – the absolute worst moment of his life. That sort of thing, it fortifies you. Good or bad, it's those moments that bind you to one another forever.' He came forward, elbows on his knees now. 'When Ollie graduated from medical school and moved to London, I got a job with Surrey Police. He asked me to be close by, but I probably would have done it anyway, without him asking. He was my brother before he killed Marco – but he was my accomplice afterwards. I had to keep an eye on him. But when I looked at what the women had on him in their office, when I saw they'd tracked down some of the kids that Ollie had been at uni with,

I realized just how boxed in I was. The women had these transcripts, these interviews they'd done, and in at least two of them people talked about the beach house a week beforehand, and the fact that – when they all woke up there on the Sunday – Marco, Ollie and Fran were gone. The cops in Bristol hadn't seemed to think it was important, especially as they interviewed Ollie and Fran and nothing seemed off. But when the women started to dig around all those years later, Fran was older, braver, and more willing to talk about Ollie. If we didn't do something about the women, they were going to put what they knew on TV for the world to see. It would be over for Ollie, and it would be over for me. I'd be going to prison – and coppers don't last long inside.'

Quiet.

Ellie had started sobbing. Preston was silent. Bodie was looking down at the floor – at Dougan, at the remains of the coffee table, at this chaotic and broken plan.

Another twitch in my fingers.

This time, I couldn't disguise it from him. As Bodie looked up, I could feel my nerves firing, and – as they did – my arm shifted against the sofa again.

He looked at Ellie. 'You didn't give him the whole dose, did you?'

'I did.'

'You *didn't*,' he spat.

Ellie froze, her eyes filled with tears, the terror stark and awful in her face. I tried to move again, managed to alter my position slightly.

And then, tightening my throat, straining every sinew, I pushed out a word: 'Where?'

He frowned. 'What?'

'Where?' I repeated.

His confusion lasted a beat longer as he searched my face and then he found the answer. 'Oh,' he said. 'You want to know where the Lost Women are . . .'

71

'We hired a boat,' he said, his voice hushed, every single letter of every single word weighted with his guilt. 'I anchored it just off Porthtreno. It wasn't big, so I could get really close to the shore, but it was big enough for . . .'

He couldn't say it.

What happened at the island was different from when he'd helped Vessler bury Marco. His brother hadn't called him in a panic this time.

With the women, everything had been premeditated.

'We forced them to wade out to the boat,' he said, and then paused. 'I can still see their faces.' He blinked, trying to rid himself of whatever image he held. 'We sailed four or five miles out, just further and further into the night. It took forever. The whole time, they were begging for their lives.' He wasn't tearful, but he was close. 'It was fucking awful. But Ollie? It didn't even seem to affect him. When it came to the time, he just took care of them all like it was nothing.' The room seemed to list.

All of us knew what Oliver Vessler was capable of.

All of us could imagine it.

'When it was all over, we wrapped them in black bags, and we weighed them down, and we threw their bodies overboard. That was the moment when I realized all the bullshit I'd told myself down the years, all the lies I'd tried to convince myself of – that I was better than my brother, that I knew where the line was – it was all fiction. I wasn't better than him. I was the *same*. I *was* a monster.' For a long time, he was quiet and then he said to Preston, 'Why did you tell Ellie you killed Marco? I mean, you weren't even there.'

'I was drunk,' Preston replied softly.

'You were drunk, but you still confessed to a murder you didn't commit.'

'It felt . . .' Preston's voice wavered. 'It felt like I did. We were supposed to go to the police, but I handed Marco to Ollie. I'm the reason Marco died.'

I shifted against the sofa, able to move my whole body now. Maybe only an inch from left to right – maybe less – but every second I could feel sensation coming back. I could feel the strength returning to my throat, my voice, my breathing. And that was why he wasn't going to leave it much longer. This confession – this need to exorcize the ghosts of his past – was only going to last a few more minutes.

He reached into his jacket, holding his hand in there.

Then he took out a knife.

I heard Ellie suck in a sharp breath; across from me, Preston recoiled. It was big inside Bodie's hands, the blade disguised within a black-grey handle. But then he pushed a button and it sprang out.

I was right.

My time was almost up.

I looked around, trying to think of something, some plan, some way to delay what was coming, but then he started talking again. 'You're a good man, David.' His gaze dropped to Dougan on the floor. 'So is he. You might not have believed him, but he really did go into battle with Phillips about Glass. He became quite a fan of yours. That's why it was so simple to persuade him to bring you along today. I could see he felt he owed you. That's what happens with decent men. You float the possibility of doing the right thing, and it's pretty easy to control them. It's why it was easy to get you here too. You wanted answers. The truth. It's what you've spent your whole life chasing. When this is over, when people look back on your life, they will see that.'

He minutely adjusted the knife in his hand.

'Why here?' I was trying to keep him talking. 'Why do it here?' I glanced at Ellie, at Preston.

'You mean why involve them?' He shrugged. 'You're all loose ends and it's easier if you're together. This is the final thing I need to do before I collect.'

Loose ends.

Horror formed in Preston's and Ellie's faces.

But I'd zeroed in on his use of *collect*.

This is about money.

'Glass is paying you?'

'Yes. I've got to do this one last job and then I can get the rest of my money wired to me from whatever fucking country he's calling home now. And, after that, I never have to think about this shit again.'

His fingers moved against the knife. This was his last job, but he knew that he was fooling himself.

He was never going to be able to forget.

'Glass and Ollie didn't really give me a choice.' He was still moving the knife – one way, the other, as if hypnotized by it. 'What you have to understand is that Ollie was different after he did that stint inside. It was like Glass changed Ollie's DNA. He got released and he was so calm, so controlled. It feels ridiculous saying it now, but in those first few months I thought, "Maybe prison has changed him for the better."' He finally glanced at me, the naivety of that idea hard for him to even vocalize. 'It definitely changed him. *Glass* changed him. But not for the better. Glass just made it harder for me – for anyone – to see the real Ollie. My brother went into prison as this powder keg, and he came out like a precisely wired bomb. He was in so deep, Glass had such a command of him, he was almost unrecognizable. Ollie was infatuated. All his anger, all his violence, all his flaws – for the first time, Glass had found a way to control them and direct them.'

Ellie shifted right back into the sofa, her eyes on the weapon.

Preston tilted away in his seat, trying to get as much distance as he could between him and Bodie.

I tried to move.

I tried to force myself up.

But I got nowhere.

'Ollie came to me one day and he told me about Glass. He said, "If you don't help us, he's going to tell the world what we did." Marco. The Lost Women. All the times I bailed my brother out when he was busy ruining people's lives. Ollie had told Glass everything inside. *Everything*. I'd read about Glass, what he did – he was even worse than my brother. But Ollie said, "He'll pay you. He has shit-tons of money hidden away from when he used to work with the Russians." I still said no. I said, "This is wrong, I'm not doing it" – but then I turned up to work at the station a few days later and this envelope had been left on my desk. It was a print-out of an article you'd written' – he glanced at me – 'about the Lost Women. The message was clear.' A long, drawn-out silence. 'So I took the money and I was given a list of what he wanted me to do, and I did it.'

I shifted an arm.

Then the other.

With effort, I forced myself forward, up into a half-propped position, an elbow on the arm of the sofa, my body leaning sideways. I could feel my skin tingling.

Bodie watched it all blankly, distantly, uninterested in every movement I made towards him, because he knew I couldn't bridge the gap between us as fast as he could use the knife.

He got up, out of the chair. 'They told me to be in the area when Matt was shot, because a call would go out and I needed to be there first. I needed to see the investigation unfolding from the inside. And once Glass met Rosa Naughton in prison, they told me she would be involved too. They identified her as someone to get at.'

He picked up the chair.

'I was the one who made that phone call to Robert Lewellyn at The Crest. I told him what to do for the CCTV camera. I told him when to fit the voice changer to his face. Ollie basically handed me a script.'

He tossed the chair across the room. It landed against a wall, the sudden burst of movement forcing a gasp from Ellie. She brought her legs up to her chest.

'Please,' she sobbed. 'Please don't hurt us.'

But it was like Bodie couldn't hear her now.

'I helped Ollie take all those photographs in that office,' he said, taking a step towards me, the knife in his fist, the blade facing out. 'He thought Glass would like it, would thank him for it. He was just so blinded. And, yeah, my private phone *was* in the glovebox of that van at Porthtreno, just like I said it was – except I had a second phone on me that no one ever knew about. I'd mirrored my own phone.'

I'm going to die. I tried to move, tried to shift again, but everything was in slow motion. *He's going to put that knife in me and I'm not going to be able to stop him.*

'Ollie told me the explosion would take out you and Preston.' His blank expression dissolved a little. 'He said it would go inwards, *into* the lifeboat station.' He searched the space between us for a truth that wouldn't come. 'I don't know if he just fucked up when he laid that explosive, or whether he lied to me. I didn't know who he was, how he thought, or what part of him was still my brother . . .'

Another step.

He was only four feet from me now.

'When I heard Glass selling him out in that interview with you, when I knew an armed response team was being sent to his flat in Camberwell, as soon as I got a chance I rushed to the toilet and tried to warn Ollie. I tried to tell him to get out. Can you imagine what it felt like when I had to watch that bodycam footage afterwards? The plan was that Lewellyn would make that call to Ollie's burner phone, using the voice changer, and the phone would be the only thing left in the flat. Not Ollie. Ollie would be long gone. He and Glass, they just wanted the phone call to Lewellyn – and Lewellyn himself – to be another layer of confusion. Something to delay and throw off the cops. *Us*,' he corrected himself, as if he were still trying to convince himself he was fighting for the right side. 'But Ollie didn't leave the flat even when I called him. He just stayed there. He swallowed that pill because Glass had told him to, same as when Pockman took that poison in the woods rather than get arrested. They were so far gone, the both of them. They would have done anything he asked. Glass's plan – his escape – it was almost over by then, and Ollie just became another loose end he was getting rid of.'

'Like us,' I said, hoarsely.

His gaze pinged back to me.

But there were no words from him this time. Just a single nod of the head. He was trying to differentiate between the monster Glass was and the trapped figure that he himself had become. But he wasn't a victim.

As he'd said himself, he was a monster.

He was just another, different kind.

Bodie took a final step closer, legs sliding either side of mine, forcing my knees together with the inside of his thighs, trapping me in place on the sofa.

'Wait,' I whispered.

He shook his head.

'*Wait.*'

'I'm sorry, David,' he said.

'You don't have to do thi—' My voice caught.

I started coughing.

'I really *am* sorry. You saved my life.' When I looked at him, he was towering over me, his face a harrowing echo of every heinous act, every time he'd been silent about a crime he'd covered up, every body he'd buried in the earth and in the ocean. 'You saved my life,' he said again, his voice vibrating as he placed a hand on my chest, holding me down. 'But you should have let me die.'

He raised the knife above his head.

I closed my eyes, waiting for the end.

But the end never came.

72

'*Jason.*' A voice from the edge of the room. 'That's enough.'

Bodie stopped, the knife poised mid-air above me, its blade pointing at my chest. I opened my eyes, my heart pounding, my blood thumping in my ears. Ellie was sobbing, balled into the smallest possible version of herself; Preston had pushed back so hard on his chair, his reaction to Bodie so visceral, he'd almost tipped it over.

'That isn't necessary.'

Bodie turned, following the voice.

As he leaned away, I saw a figure enter – but, by then, I already knew who it was. I'd recognized the voice instantly – the timbre, the supernaturally calm delivery.

My heart sank.

It was Glass.

'What the fuck are you doing here?' Bodie responded, taking a couple of steps back. Ellie moved again, protecting herself even more, but not before I saw something in her face; that same expression I'd seen earlier and the reason she'd stayed in the corner of the room – almost cowering there – before Bodie had ordered her over.

Glass.

I thought of how the dose of the sedative she'd given me hadn't hit anywhere near as hard as Dougan's. So was it Glass who had told her how much to give me? Was he waiting for her in the kitchen when she went through to make the drinks? Preston was staring at Glass in a way that immediately told me he had had no idea that the man who had murdered nine women – the serial killer who'd escaped custody at Porthtreno – was here, in his house. In contrast, Ellie wasn't shocked by his being here, she was just terrified of him.

'You told me you were in Europe,' Bodie said to him.

'I *am* in Europe,' Glass responded, his eyes on me, not on Bodie. 'Now put the knife down, Jason. Calm down a little.'

'Calm down?' Bodie almost laughed. '*You* were the one who told me to do this. *You* were the one who told me they were loose ends.'

'They *are* loose ends.'

Glass had black jeans on, a long black coat, a black beanie. In the three days since the island, he hadn't shaved, and now his face was lined with stubble.

But he looked better, healthier.

Bodie frowned. 'Where's my money?'

Glass glanced at him for the first time – 'So it *is* about the money now?' – then back to me. Another step. 'I listened to your little speech from the kitchen,' he said, still talking to Bodie even as his attention was on me. 'I thought it would be a useful education for me. I guess it's true what they say, isn't it?' Another step. He was level with Bodie, facing me, everything else in the room irrelevant to him. 'When you kill, it changes you. Most people can't carry the weight of it. That's why they need to get it out, to confess it all, to cleanse whatever tiny part of their soul is left.'

Bodie shook his head. 'Where's my money?'

I moved a little, shifting further forward, right to the edge of the sofa – but it took so much effort, I had to stop and get my breath back.

Glass tilted his head, still studying me.

'I did what you asked,' Bodie said. 'Where's my fucking money?'

The tail end of his sentence wobbled, the nervousness affecting his delivery. Glass picked up on it immediately. I could see it; it was like a vulture scenting carrion on the wind. Bodie looked down at his feet, at the minimal gap that existed between them, and took a half-step back, as if he didn't want to be too close.

'No,' I tried to say.

I could see what was coming.

But I couldn't stop it.

'It's okay,' Glass said, 'It's okay, Jason, I've got your money.' But even before he'd finished speaking, he'd reached into his coat and had something in his hands.

A gun.

A snub-nosed pistol barely larger than his hand – and on the end of it was a silencer. Bodie glimpsed it, tried to get the knife up from his side, but by the time he had, Glass had already fired once into Bodie's temple.

Pfft.

The bullet exited Bodie's head and tore through a painting on the wall, his body lurching sideways and falling hard at Preston's feet.

Preston gasped.

Jumped out of his chair.

But then Glass fired once into his chest.

Pfft.

It went straight through the heart, Preston staggering back into the chair he'd just occupied. This time, he kept gasping repeatedly, drawing air in but unable to push any back out. His face blanched and he tried to say something, but his chest was filling with blood.

'Help!' Ellie screamed. 'Hel—'

Pfft.

He fired a third time, into Ellie's stomach, stopping her voice instantly. This time I managed to move, to go forward, but then I fell on to my knees, my hands, and – out of the corner of my eye, facing down at the floor – I saw Ellie slide off the sofa.

Her eyes stared at me.

Tears still in them; the light fading.

I'm sorry, I tried to say to her, *I'm sorry, Ellie, I'm so sorr—*

'This is what it feels like to be caged, David.'

From my hands and knees, I looked up at him. I couldn't move fast enough. I couldn't save anyone.

Pfft.

Glass fired a fourth shot into the back of Dougan's head.

I stared at the blood leaking from his hairline, at the sea of broken glass he was lying on, and then – in among the blood and the death and the horror – I thought of my daughter. I tried to find the courage in something better.

In someone I loved.

I pictured Annabel the last time I saw her, near her home in south Devon, laughing as we'd queued for ice creams. I saw Derryn before she got sick, when I'd taken her back to the farm I'd grown up on. I'd shown her the fields I used to run through as a boy, the trees I climbed, the rock pools and shingle beaches. And, in the spaces beyond them, less formed, newer, but still there, I glimpsed Rebekah, the woman I'd hoped to spend the second half of my life with, but who I now knew I would never see again.

Glass dropped to his haunches beside me.

'Do you know why I left Preston alive in that lifeboat station?' he said. 'Why we faked those detonators in his hands? It's because if he was dead, he was no use to me. I knew you'd come back to him. I knew you'd follow Bodie here, because it's how you're built. You're hard-wired to want answers. You live and *breathe* clarity and order.'

I closed my eyes.

Annabel.

Derryn.

Rebekah.

I thought of what was written across my wife's headstone.

In the end, all that matters is love.

'I didn't want you to get the full dose of that sedative because I wanted you to see. I wanted you to be in *exactly* this position, on your hands and knees in front of me, completely and utterly alone. I've been locked in that cage for fourteen years and you're the one that put me there. But today . . .' He placed the gun against the back of my head. 'Today I finally get my revenge.'

THE DAYS AFTER
Part Two

Healy

One Day Later

Healy spent the morning at Liam and Alice's house.

Alice had a work Zoom meeting and Liam had gone to an interview for an assistant manager's job at a gym in Camden Town, so he'd asked Healy if he could come and sit with Leanne while Alice was on the call.

Healy's first instinct had been to make an excuse.

He didn't know anything about babysitting. It wasn't something he'd mastered with his own kids, so how would he cope with someone else's?

'Wouldn't you rather get your mum to do it?' he'd said to Liam.

'Mum's got meetings all day.'

There was an edge to his son's voice – the familiar combination of anger and disappointment that came with the inevitability of Healy letting him down.

'I'd love to, son.'

'Yeah?'

'Yeah, of course,' Healy had said, worrying that he sounded false. 'What time shall I be there?'

The answer was 8.30 a.m., and although Healy was on the Tube by seven thirty, thanks to a signal failure on the Jubilee line he only arrived at the house in Wembley with a couple of minutes to spare. But when Alice answered the door, it was with a huge smile. 'Thank you for doing this,' she said. 'It's so kind.'

The gratitude was so plain in Alice's face that Healy felt guilty for having hesitated on the phone that morning.

For the next hour, he kept Leanne busy with toys, filling a

small paddling pool full of coloured balls, and watching TV programmes Alice said she liked, which – to Healy's mind – seemed to be unintelligible shite.

Leanne didn't cry once.

When Alice was done with her call, the two of them had coffee together. Leanne was in her highchair next to them, mashing an already mashed banana into a bright pink plate.

'Are you doing okay?' Healy asked Alice.

'The police say he'll probably go abroad,' she replied. 'So that's something, I guess.' A pause. 'Do you think that's what he'll do?'

'I don't know,' Healy said. 'That's the honest truth. He's unpredictable. But I can't imagine he escaped just so he could spend his life having to hide.'

Alice looked at Healy, her eyes saying everything.

That's what you did once.

He nodded. 'That's why I don't think he'll do it. It's miserable. You can make it work for a while but not forever.' He glanced at Leanne, and then – just for a moment – thought of his own Leanne; the way she'd come to him, living and breathing inside his head, when he'd been at the prison. *I still can't remember your voice*, he said to her now.

And then, in the shadows, he saw her again.

She smiled at him.

It's okay, Dad, the smile said. *You remember enough.*

Just before midday, he left and then headed back across London to his flat in Lewisham. The first thing he saw as he unlocked the front door was the empty bottle of Jack Daniel's he'd been drinking from a few days back. It was sitting on the edge of the kitchen cabinet, at the other end of the hallway.

He pushed the door shut, padded along the hallway and grabbed the empty bottle. Opening the bin, he dumped it inside. It rattled to the bottom. He went to the cupboard under the sink.

There were three more bottles inside.

He took them all out, unscrewed the lids on each and poured

them down the drain, one by one. Once he was done, he binned the other bottles.

The flat fell silent.

He could smell the booze.

He looked at the dregs of it in the sink, the knots of amber liquid on the steel, and then he stepped back, as if he needed to distance himself from it. In the living room now, he could see the pictures he'd put up on the wall. Liam. Ciaran. Leanne.

You need to stop drinking.

You need to stop spinning out.

You need to be better.

In his pocket, his phone started buzzing.

He didn't answer it for a moment, his thoughts still snared by a daisy chain of photos of Leanne – as a baby, as a toddler, as a little girl, as a young woman.

Then he took out his phone and looked at the number.

It was Raker's landline.

He pushed Answer. 'Raker?'

A minor hesitation and then a female voice: 'Is that Colm?'

'Yeah.' He felt thrown. 'Who's this?'

'It's Rebekah.'

Healy blanked on the name for a moment.

'Rebekah Murphy,' she said. 'David's friend.'

'Oh. Right. Hi.' He frowned. 'Is everything okay?'

'No,' she said. 'No, not really.'

She sounded emotional.

'What's the matter?'

A sniff. Was she crying?

'Rebekah, what's going on?'

'It's David,' she said quietly. 'He's missing.'

Author's Note

Not wanting to break with recent tradition, this is now the page where I do two things.

One is to admit that I've been flexible with police procedure for the purposes of the story. I always try to remain true to real-world practices where I can, but sometimes, in order to keep you inside the story, I've described things that, in reality, police forces would not, or could not, do. My hope is that it's done with a light enough touch for you not to have realized until now. I have also been told (by my family no less, who work in health care) that I have played fast and loose with general hospital policy. Again, my intention is not to cause offence but simply to keep you moving through those pages as rapidly as possible.

The second tradition is to remind you that all my books can be read as standalones (and if this is your first one, welcome aboard!), and that no prior knowledge of the David Raker series is required. However, if you're interested in finding out more about the history of the 'Dr Glass' case, and how Raker and Healy first met and became involved in it, then *The Dead Tracks* is your starting point. The book that follows that one, *Vanished*, also delves into the fallout from the Glass murders and covers Healy's last months as a detective at the Met.

For the full background on Healy and Rosa Naughton's history, seek out my novella collection, *The Shadow at the Door*, of which the story of the 'Red Woman' is a part. And, finally, my standalone novel, *Missing Pieces*, will fill in any blanks you have about Rebekah Murphy, her past, and how she and David Raker first came into contact with each other, and *The Last Goodbye* will reveal the full story behind Raker's search for Rebekah's missing mother.

Acknowledgements

I'm writing this halfway through 2025, but when *The Lost Women* is published it will be almost exactly sixteen years to the day that readers first got to meet David Raker. The time has gone so quickly (and I'm now, unfortunately, sixteen years older) but I still love writing these books and am so grateful to my publishing team at Michael Joseph (and across Penguin as a whole) who have been by my side since the very beginning.

A great big, extra special shout-out to my wonderful editor Maxine Hitchcock, who I'm so lucky to work with, and also to Clare Bowron and Stella Newing for reading early drafts of this novel and improving it immeasurably. Thank you also to Beatrix McIntyre, Mubarak Elmubarak, Jack Hallam, Jess Parker, Frankie Banks, Rachel Myers, Christina Ellicott, Laura Garrod, Kelly Mason, Hannah Padgham, Lottie Chesterman and Jon Kennedy. And, of course, a massive thank you, as always, to my wonderful copy-editor Caroline Pretty and her life-saving Raker Bible.

Michael Joseph were the only publisher who were ever interested in David Raker, and – with seven billion rejection letters as evidence! – Camilla Bolton was the only agent who ever saw the potential in him. Thank you so much to her, as always, for everything she does for me, and to the whole team at Darley Anderson: Jade Kavanagh, Georgia Schindler, Georgia Fuller, Ilaria Albani, Francesca Edwards, Rosanna Bellingham, Helen Dudley and Sarah Brooks. Thank you also to Sheila David at Catapult for all her hard work on the film and TV side.

Thank you to Chris Ewan, Claire Douglas and Gilly Macmillan for sharing the pain over lunches and texts, and to Elizabeth Kesses for her hard work on a long-in-the-making project which

I'm hoping I might be able to talk about around the time this book is published. (If not, let's just pretend I never said anything.)

A huge thank you to the Weavers, Ryders, Linscotts and Adamses, but especially to Mum and Dad, who bought me my very first typewriter, and to Sharlé and Erin who always make things better after a day of tearing my hair out about plotlines.

Finally, the biggest thank you of all to you, my amazing readers, without whom neither myself nor David Raker would ever get the chance to tell you stories.